About the Author

After spending three ... **Kate Hewitt** now live ... Lake District with he ... a golden retriever. In ... to writing intensely emotional stories, she loves reading, baking and playing chess with her son – she has yet to win against him, but she continues to try. Learn more about Kate at www.kate-hewitt.com.

Kat Cantrell read her first Mills & Boon novel in third grade and has been scribbling in notebooks since then. She writes smart, sexy books with a side of sass. She's a former Harlequin So You Think You Can Write winner and a former RWA Golden Heart finalist. Kat, her husband and their two boys live in north Texas.

At the age of eight **Michelle Douglas** was asked what she wanted to be when she grew up. She answered, 'A writer.' Years later she read an article about romance-writing and thought, Ooh, that'll be fun. She was right. When she's not writing she can usually be found with her nose buried in a book. She is currently enrolled in an English Masters programme for the sole purpose of indulging her reading and writing habits further. She lives in a leafy suburb of Newcastle, on Australia's east coast, with her own romantic hero – husband Greg, who is the inspiration behind all her happy endings.

Ruthless Revenge
COLLECTION

July 2018

August 2018

September 2018

October 2018

November 2018

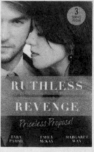

December 2018

Ruthless Revenge: Delicious Demand

KATE HEWITT

KAT CANTRELL

MICHELLE DOUGLAS

MILLS & BOON

Published in Great Britain 2018
by Mills & Boon, an imprint of HarperCollins*Publishers*
1 London Bridge Street, London, SE1 9GF

Ruthless Revenge: Delicious Demand © 2018 Harlequin Books S.A.

Moretti's Marriage Command © 2016 Kate Hewitt
The CEO's Little Surprise © 2016 Kate Cantrell
Snowbound Surprise for the Billionaire © 2014 Michelle Douglas

ISBN: 978-0-263-26827-0

09-1018

MIX
Paper from
responsible sources
FSC™ C007454

This book is produced from independently certified FSC™ paper to ensure responsible forest management.

For more information visit: www.harpercollins.co.uk/green

Printed and bound in Spain
by CPI, Barcelona

MORETTI'S MARRIAGE COMMAND

KATE HEWITT

To all my readers,
Thank you for your encouragement and support.
It's always a privilege to write stories for you.

CHAPTER ONE

LUCA MORETTI NEEDED a wife. Not a real one—heaven forbid he'd ever need *that*. No, he needed a temporary wife-to-be who was efficient, biddable, and discreet. A wife for the weekend.

'Mr Moretti?' His PA, Hannah Stewart, knocked once on the door before opening it and stepping inside his penthouse office overlooking a rain-washed Lombard Street in London's City. 'I have the letters for you to sign.'

Luca watched his PA walk towards him holding the sheaf of letters, her light brown hair neatly pulled back, her face set in calm lines. She wore a black pencil skirt, low heels, and a simple blouse of white silk. He'd never really bothered to notice his PA before, except at how quickly she could type and how discreet she could be when it came to unfortunate personal calls that occasionally came through to his office. Now he eyed her plain brown hair, and lightly freckled face that was pretty without being in any way remarkable. As for her figure…?

Luca let his gaze wander down his PA's slender form. No breathtaking or bodacious curves, but it was passable. *Could he…?*

She placed the letters in front of him and took a step back, but not before he caught a waft of her understated floral perfume. He reached for his fountain pen and began to scrawl his signature on each letter.

'Will that be all, Mr Moretti?' she asked when he'd finished the last one.

'Yes.' He handed her the letters and Hannah turned towards the door, her skirt whispering against her legs as she walked. Luca watched her, eyes narrowed, certainty settling in his gut. 'Wait.'

Obedient as ever, Hannah pivoted back to face him, her pale eyebrows raised expectantly. She'd been a good PA these last three years, working hard and not making a fuss about it. He sensed ambition and willpower beneath her 'aiming to please' persona, and the weekend would require both qualities, as long as she agreed to the deception. Which he would make sure she did.

'Mr Moretti?'

Luca lounged back in his chair as he drummed his fingers on his desk. He didn't like lying. He'd been honest his whole life, proud of who he was even though so many had knocked him back, tried to keep him down. But this weekend was different. This weekend was everything to him, and Hannah Stewart was no more than a cog in his plans. A very important cog.

'I have an important meeting this weekend.'

'Yes, on Santa Nicola,' Hannah replied. 'Your ticket is in your passport wallet, and the limo is set to pick you up tomorrow morning at nine, from your flat. The flight leaves from Heathrow at noon.'

'Right.' He hadn't known any of those details, but he'd expected Hannah to inform him. She really was quite marvellously efficient. 'It turns out I'm going to need some assistance,' he said.

Hannah's eyebrows went a fraction higher, but her face remained calm. 'Administrative assistance, you mean?'

Luca hesitated. He didn't have time to explain his intentions now, and he suspected that his PA would balk at what he was about to ask. 'Yes, that's right.' He could tell Hannah was surprised although she hid it well.

'What exactly do you require?'

A wife. A temporary, compliant woman. 'I require you to accompany me to Santa Nicola for the weekend.' Luca hadn't asked Hannah to accompany him on any business trips before; he preferred to travel and work alone, having been a solitary person from childhood. When you were alone you didn't have to be on your guard, waiting for someone to trip you up. There were no expectations save the ones you put on yourself.

Luca knew that Hannah's contract stipulated 'extra hours or engagements as required', and in the past she'd been willing to work long evenings, the occasional Saturday. He smiled, his eyebrows raised expectantly. 'I trust that won't be a problem?' He would inform her later just what extra duties would be required.

Hannah hesitated, but only briefly, and then gave one graceful nod of her head. 'Not at all, Mr Moretti.'

Hannah's mind raced as she tried to figure out how to handle this unexpected request from her boss. In her three years of working for Luca Moretti, she'd never gone on a business trip with him. There had been the odd, or not so odd, late night; the occasional all-nighter where she supplied him with black coffee and popped caffeine pills to keep sharp as she took notes. But she'd never *travelled* with him. Never gone somewhere as exotic as a Mediterranean island for the weekend. The possibility gave her a surprising frisson of excitement; she'd thought she'd put her would-be travelling days behind her long ago.

'Shall I book an extra ticket?' she asked, trying to sound as efficient and capable as she always was.

'Yes.'

She nodded, her mind still spinning. She needed to call her mother as soon as possible, make arrangements… 'I'll book an economy ticket—'

'Why on earth would you do that?' Luca demanded. He sounded irritated, and Hannah blinked in surprise.

'I hardly think, as your PA, I'd need to travel first class, and the expense—'

'Forget the expense.' He cut her off, waving a hand in dismissal. 'I'll need you seated with me. I'll work on the flight.'

'Very well.' She held the letters to her chest, wondering what else she'd need to do to prepare for such a trip. And wondering why Luca Moretti needed her on this trip when he hadn't needed her on any other. She studied him covertly, lounging as he was in his office chair, his midnight-dark hair rumpled, his thick, straight brows drawn into frowning lines, one hand still drumming the top of his ebony desk.

He was an incredibly handsome man, a compelling, charismatic, driven man; one business magazine had called him 'an elegant steamroller'. Hannah thought the nickname apt; Luca Moretti could turn on the charm, but it was only to get what he wanted. She'd observed him from the sidelines for three years and learned how to be the most efficient PA possible, and invisible when necessary. She liked her job; she liked Luca's force of personality, his boundless energy for his work. She'd always admired his determined work ethic, his drive for success. She might only be a PA, but she shared that drive, if not quite to the same degree.

'Very well,' she said now. 'I'll make the arrangements.' Luca nodded her dismissal and Hannah left his office, expelling her breath in a rush as she sat down at her desk. She and Luca were the only occupants of the top floor of his office building, and she appreciated the quiet to organise her thoughts.

First things first. She called the airline and booked an additional first-class ticket for herself, wincing at the expense even though Luca Moretti could well afford it. As CEO of his own real-estate development empire, he could have afforded his own jet.

That done, she quickly emailed her mother. She would have called, but Luca forbade personal calls from the office, and Hannah had always obeyed the rules. This job meant too much to her to flaunt them. She'd just hit Send when Luca emerged from his office, shrugging on his suit jacket and checking his watch.

'Mr Moretti?'

'You'll need suitable clothes for this weekend.'

Hannah blinked. 'Of course.'

'I don't mean that.' Luca gestured to her clothes, and Hannah was unable to keep from looking down at her professional yet understated outfit. She took pride in how she dressed, and she made sure to buy as high quality clothes as she could afford.

'I'm sorry...?'

'This weekend is as much a social occasion as a business one,' he explained tersely. 'You'll need appropriate clothing—evening gowns and the like.'

Evening gowns? She certainly didn't have any of those in her wardrobe, and couldn't imagine the need for them. 'As your PA—'

'As my PA you need to be dressed appropriately. This isn't going to be a board meeting.'

'What is it, exactly? Because I'm not sure—'

'Think of it more as a weekend house party with a little business thrown in.'

Which made it even more mystifying as to why he needed her along.

'I'm afraid I don't own any evening gowns—' Hannah began, and Luca shrugged her words aside.

'That's easy enough to take care of.' He slid his smart-phone out of his pocket and thumbed a few buttons before speaking rapidly in Italian. Although she heard the occasional familiar word, Hannah had no idea what he'd said or who he'd called.

A few minutes later he disconnected the call and nodded towards Hannah. 'Sorted. You'll accompany me to Diavola after work.'

'Diavola…?'

'You know the boutique?'

She'd heard of it. It was an incredibly high-end fashion boutique in Mayfair. She might have walked past the elegant sashed windows once, seen a single dress hanging there in an elegant fall of shimmery silk, no price tag visible.

She swallowed hard, striving to seem calm, as if this whole, unexpected venture hadn't completely thrown her. 'That might be a bit out of my price range—'

'I will pay, of course.' His brows snapped together as he frowned at her. 'It's all part of the business expense. I'd hardly expect you to buy a gown you'll only be wearing because of your work.'

'Very well.' She tried not to squirm under his fierce gaze. She felt as if he was examining her and she was not meeting his expectations, which was disconcerting, as she always had before. She took pride in how well she performed her job. Luca Moretti had never had any cause to criticise her. 'Thank you.'

'We'll leave in an hour,' Luca said, and strode back into his office.

Hannah spent a frantic hour finishing up her work and making arrangements for the trip, ensuring that each part of the journey could accommodate an extra passenger. She knew Luca was staying with his client, hotelier Andrew Tyson, and she hesitated to contact the man directly to make sure there was an extra bedroom. It seemed a bit cheeky, asking for a room for herself in the tycoon's luxurious villa, but what else could she do?

She was just composing an email to Andrew Tyson's PA when Luca came out of his office, shrugging into his suit jacket, his face settling into a frown as he caught sight of her.

'Aren't you ready?'

'I'm sorry, I'm just emailing Mr Tyson's PA—'

His frown deepened. 'What for?'

'To arrange for an extra bedroom—'

'That won't be necessary,' Luca said swiftly, and then leaned over and closed her laptop with a snap.

Hannah stared at him, too surprised to mask the emotion. 'But if I don't email—'

'It's taken care of.'

'It is?'

'Don't question me, Hannah. And in future please leave all communications with Mr Tyson to me.'

Stung, she recoiled a bit at his tone. 'I've always—'

'This negotiation is delicate. I'll explain the particulars later. Now let's go. I have a lot of things to do tonight besides buy you some clothes.'

Her cheeks burned at his dismissive tone. Her boss was often restless and impatient, but he wasn't *rude*. Was it her fault that her wardrobe wasn't that of a socialite? Wordlessly she rose from her desk and took her laptop, about to slide it into her messenger bag.

'Leave that.'

'My laptop?' She stared at him, flummoxed. 'But I'll need it if we're to work on the plane—'

'It won't be necessary.'

A finger of unease crept along her spine. Something felt very off about this weekend, and yet she could not imagine what it was. 'Mr Moretti, I don't understand...'

'What is there to understand? You're accompanying me on a weekend that is as much a social occasion as it is a business one. I'm asking you to use some sensitivity and discretion, as the situation is delicate. Is that beyond your capabilities, Miss Stewart?'

Her face burned at being given such a dressing-down. 'No, of course not.'

'Good.' He nodded towards the lift doors. 'Now let's go.'

Stiff with affront, Hannah took her coat and followed Luca to the lift. She waited, staring straight ahead, trying to master her irritation, until the doors pinged open and Luca gestured for her to go in first. She did so, and as he followed her she was conscious in an entirely new way of how he filled the space of the lift. Surely they'd ridden in the lift together before, many times. Yet now, as Luca stabbed the button for the ground floor, she felt how big he was. How male. His shoulders strained the seams of his suit jacket, and his rangy, restless energy made the very air seem as if it were charged. She snuck a glance at his profile, the square jaw shadowed with stubble, the straight nose and angular cheekbones. Long, surprisingly lush lashes, and hard, dark eyes.

Hannah knew women flocked to Luca Moretti. They were attracted to his air of restless remoteness as much as his blatant sexuality and effortless charisma. Perhaps they fooled themselves into thinking they could tame or trap him; no one ever could. Hannah had kept more than one tearful beauty from her boss's door. He never thanked her for that little service; he acted as if the women who practically threw themselves at him didn't exist, at least not outside the bedroom. Or so Hannah assumed—she had no idea how Luca Moretti acted in the bedroom.

Just the thought sent a blush heating her cheeks now, even though she was still annoyed with his uncharacteristically terse attitude. High-handed she could take, when it was tempered with wry charm and grace. But Luca Moretti merely barking out orders was hard to stomach.

Thankfully the doors opened and they left the confined space of the lift, Luca ushering her out into the impressive marble foyer of Moretti Enterprises. A receptionist bid them good day and then they were out in the rain-washed streets, the damp air cooling her face, the twilight hiding her blush.

A limo pulled to the kerb the moment they stepped out, and Luca's driver jumped out to open the door.

'After you,' Luca said, and Hannah slid inside the luxurious interior. Luca followed, his thigh nudging hers before he shifted closer to the window.

Hannah couldn't resist stroking the buttery soft leather of the seat. 'I've never been in a limo before,' she admitted, and Luca cocked an eyebrow at her.

'Never?'

'No.' Why would she? He might travel in this sort of style all over the world, but she stayed firmly on the top floor of Moretti Enterprises. Of course, she'd seen plenty of luxury from a distance. She'd ordered champagne to celebrate his business deals, heard the pop of the cork in the meeting room down from his office. She'd booked dozens of first-class tickets and five-star hotel rooms, had instructed concierges around the world on Luca Moretti's preferences: no lilies in any flower arrangements in his suite and sheets with a five hundred thread count. She'd just never experienced any of that expense or luxury herself. 'I haven't stayed in a five-star hotel or flown first class either,' she informed him a bit tartly. Not everyone was as privileged as he was. 'I haven't even tasted champagne.'

'Well, you can enjoy some of that this weekend,' Luca said, and turned to stare out of the window, the lights from the traffic casting his face in a yellow wash. 'I'm sorry,' he said abruptly. 'I know I must seem…tense.'

Hannah eyed him warily. 'Ye—es…'

He turned to her with a small, rueful smile. 'I think that was an inward "you've been an absolute rotter".' His expression softened, his gaze sweeping over her, lashes lowering in a way that made Hannah feel the need to shift in her seat. 'I am sorry.'

'Why are you so tense?'

'As I said before, this weekend is delicate.' He turned back to the window, one long-fingered hand rubbing his jaw. 'Very delicate.'

Hannah knew better than to press. She had no idea why this business deal was so delicate; as far as she could tell, the chain of family resort hotels Luca was planning to take over was a relatively small addition to his real-estate portfolio.

The limo pulled up to Diavola, the windows lit although it was nearly seven o'clock at night. Hannah suppressed a shiver of apprehension. How was this supposed to *work*? Would she choose the dress, or would her boss? She'd done many things for Luca Moretti, but she hadn't bought herself an evening gown for him. She didn't relish the idea of parading clothes in front of him, but maybe he'd just let her choose a gown and get on with it.

Of course he would. He was already impatient, wanting to get onto the next thing; Luca Moretti wasn't going to entertain himself watching his PA try on different dresses. Comforted by this thought, Hannah slid out of the limo.

Luca followed her quickly, placing one hand on her elbow. The touch shocked her; Luca *never* touched her. Not so much as a hug or a pat on the back in three years of working for him. Hannah had always got the sense that he was a solitary man, despite the parade of women through his life, and she hadn't minded because she appreciated the focus on work. She didn't have room in her life for much else.

Now Luca kept his hand on her elbow as he guided her into the boutique, and then slid it to the small of her back as a shop assistant came forward. Hannah felt as if he were branding her back, his palm warm through the thin material of her skirt, his fingers splayed so she could feel the light yet firm pressure of each one. His pinkie finger reached the curve of her bottom, and her whole body stiffened in response as a treacherous flash of heat jolted through her.

'I would like a complete wardrobe for the weekend for my companion,' he said to the woman, who batted over-mascaraed lashes at him. 'Evening gowns, day wear, a swimming costume, nightgown, underthings.' He glanced at the gold and silver watch on one wrist. 'In under an hour.'

'Very good, Mr Moretti.'

Underthings? Hannah felt she had to object. 'Mr Moretti, I don't need all those things,' she protested in a low voice. She certainly didn't need her boss to buy her a bra. She felt the pressure on the small of her back increase, so she could feel the joints of each of his fingers.

'Humour me. And why don't you call me Luca?' Her jaw nearly dropped at this suggestion. He'd never invited such intimacy before. 'You've been working for me for what, three years?' he murmured so only she could hear, his head close enough to hers that she breathed in the cedarwood-scented aftershave he wore. When she turned her head she could see the hint of stubble on his jaw. 'Perhaps we should progress to first names... Hannah.'

For some reason her name on his lips made her want to shiver. She stepped away from his hand, her body bizarrely missing the warmth and pressure of it as soon as it had gone.

'Very well.' Yet she couldn't quite make herself call

him Luca. It seemed so odd, so intimate, after three years of starchy formality and respectable distance. Why was Luca shaking everything up now?

The sales assistant was collecting various garments from around the boutique, and another had come forward to usher them both to a U-shaped divan in cream velvet. A third was bringing flutes of champagne and caviar-topped crackers.

Luca sat down, clearly accustomed to all this luxury, and the sales assistant beckoned to Hannah.

'If the *signorina* will come this way…?'

Numbly Hannah followed the woman into a dressing room that was larger than the entire upstairs of her house.

'First this?' the woman suggested, holding up an evening gown in pale blue chiffon and satin. It was the most exquisite thing Hannah had ever seen.

'Okay,' she said, and, feeling as if she were in a surreal dream, she started to unbutton her blouse.

CHAPTER TWO

LUCA WAITED FOR Hannah to emerge from the dressing room as he sipped champagne and tried to relax. He was way too wound up about this whole endeavour, and his too-clever PA had noticed. He didn't want her guessing his game before they'd arrived on Santa Nicola. He couldn't risk the possibility of her refusal. Although Hannah Stewart had proved to be biddable enough, he suspected she had more backbone than he'd initially realised. And he didn't want her to use it against him.

Moodily Luca took a sip of champagne and stared out at the rainy streets of Mayfair. In less than twenty-four hours he'd be on Santa Nicola, facing Andrew Tyson. Would the man recognise him? It had been such a long time. Would there be so much as a flicker of awareness in those cold eyes? If there was it would completely ruin Luca's plan, and yet he couldn't keep from hoping that he would garner some reaction. Something to justify the emotion that had burned in his chest for far too long.

'Well?' he called to Hannah. She'd been in the dressing room for nearly ten minutes. 'Have you tried something on?'

'Yes, but this one's a bit...' She trailed off, and Luca snapped his gaze to the heavy velvet curtain drawn across the dressing room's doorway.

'Come out and let me see it.'

'It's fine.' She sounded a little panicked but also quite firm. 'I'll try something else on—'

'*Hannah.*' Luca tried to curb his impatience. 'I would like to see the dress, please.' What woman didn't enjoy showing off haute couture for a man? And he needed to make sure Hannah looked the part.

'I'm already changing,' she called, and in one fluid movement Luca rose from the divan and crossed to the dressing room, pulling aside the heavy curtain.

He didn't know who gasped—Hannah, in shock that he'd intruded, or himself, for the sudden dart of lust that had arrowed through his body at the sight of his PA.

She stood with her back to him, the dress pooling about her waist in gauzy blue folds as she held the front up to her chest, her face in profile, every inch the outraged maiden.

'Mr Moretti—' she muttered and he watched a blush crawl up her back and neck to her face.

'Luca,' he reminded her, and sent an iron glare of warning to the assistant, who was waiting discreetly in the corner. He did not want anyone gossiping about the oddity of the occasion.

'Luca,' Hannah acquiesced, but she sounded annoyed. Luca felt a surprising flicker of amusement. His little sparrow of a secretary sometimes pretended she was a hawk. 'Please leave. I am *changing.*'

'I wanted to see the gown. I'm paying for it, after all.' He folded his arms, feeling no more than a flash of remorse for pulling that particular trump card. Hannah, however, did not look particularly impressed. 'How much is this gown?' he asked the sales assistant.

The woman hesitated, but only for a millisecond. 'Nine thousand pounds, Signor Moretti.'

'Nine thousand—' Hannah whirled around, the dress nearly slipping from her hands. Luca caught a glimpse of pale, lightly freckled fresh, the hint of a small, perfectly round breast. Then she hauled the gown up to her chin, her face now bright red with mortification.

'Careful,' he advised. 'That material looks delicate.'

'As delicate as this weekend?' she retorted, and he smiled.

'I never knew you had a temper.'

'I never knew you could spend nine thousand pounds on a *dress.*'

He raised his eyebrows, genuinely surprised. 'Most women of my acquaintance enjoy spending my money.'

'Your acquaintance is quite limited, then,' Hannah snapped. 'Plenty of women aren't interested only in shopping and money.'

'Point taken.'

'Anyway,' Hannah muttered, 'it's wrong.' She turned around so her back was once more to him.

'Wrong? But how can you object if it's my money?'

'Do you know what could be done with nine thousand pounds?' she demanded, her back straight and quivering with tension.

'Oh, no, tell me you're not one of those bleeding hearts,' Luca drawled. 'I expected more of you, Hannah.'

'I'm not,' she said stiffly. 'I've never objected to you spending money on yourself. But when it's for me—'

'It's still my choice.' He cut her off. 'Now zip up that dress and let me see it on you.'

Taking her cue, the sales assistant stepped forward and zipped up the back, although in truth there wasn't much to zip up. The dress was almost entirely backless, with a halter top and a gauzy chiffon overlay that lent some respectability to the plunging neckline, as Luca saw when Hannah reluctantly turned around.

He schooled his face into an expression of businesslike interest, as if he were assessing the gown simply as an appropriate garment for the occasion rather than for the effect it had on his libido. Why on earth he was reacting to his PA's unexceptional body this way he had no idea. He supposed that was what you paid for with Diavola. The dresses worked.

'Very good,' he told the assistant. 'We'll take it. Now we need something casual to wear for the day, and a semi-formal dress for the first night.'

'I have some of these things at home,' Hannah protested.

Luca held up a hand. 'Please cease this pointless arguing, Hannah. This is a business expense, I told you.'

She went silent, tight-lipped, her brown eyes flashing suppressed fury. Unable to resist baiting her just a little bit, or maybe just wanting to touch her, Luca reached over and pulled the tie of the halter top of her dress.

'There,' he said as she caught the folds of the dress, her eyes wide with shock. 'Now hurry up. I want to be out of here in forty-five minutes.'

Hannah's hands trembled as she stripped off the evening gown and flung it at the assistant, too unsettled and overwhelmed to care how she treated the delicate material.

What was going on? Why was Luca treating her this way? And why had she reacted to the sight of him in the dressing room, her body tightening, heat flaring deep inside when she'd turned around and seen his gaze dip to her unimpressive cleavage?

Perhaps, she thought resentfully, she'd simply never seen this side of her boss before. Outside the office, Luca Moretti might well be the kind of man who flirted and teased and stormed into women's dressing rooms and undid their gowns...

She suppressed a shiver at the memory of his fingers skimming her back as he'd tugged on the tie. Stupid, to react to the man that way. At this moment she wasn't even sure she liked him. And yet it had been a long, long time since she'd been touched like that.

Not, of course, that Luca had had any intention other than discomfiting her when he'd undone her dress. Hannah was savvy enough to realise that.

And as for the cost… Maybe it was irrational to protest when a millionaire spent what was essentially pocket change, but it was a lot of money to her. With nine thousand pounds she could have redone her kitchen or afforded a better life insurance policy…

'*Signorina?* Would you like to try on the next ensemble?'

Letting out a long, low breath, Hannah nodded. 'Yes, please.' This whole evening had entered into the realm of the utterly surreal, including her own reactions. When had she ever dared to talk back to her boss? Yet he didn't feel like her boss when she was in a dressing room, her back bare, her breasts practically on display. And yet at the same time he felt more like her boss than ever, demanding and autocratic, expecting instant compliance. It was all so incredibly bizarre.

The assistant handed her a shift dress in pale pink linen that fitted perfectly. Would Luca want to see this dress as well? And what about her swimming costume, or the lacy, frothy underthings she could see waiting on a chair? A blaze of heat went through her at the thought, leaving her more disconcerted than ever.

'It's fine,' she told the assistant, and then took it off as fast as she could. Maybe if she worked quickly enough Luca wouldn't bother striding into her dressing room, acting as if he owned the world, acting as if he owned *her*.

Forty-two minutes later all the clothes Hannah had tried on, including the most modest bikini she'd been able to find and two sets of lingerie in beige silk and cream lace, were wrapped in tissue paper and put in expensive-looking bags with satin ribbons for handles. She hadn't even seen Luca hand over a credit card, and she dreaded to think what the bill was. Why on earth was he spending a fortune on her clothes, and for such a negligible business deal? She didn't like feeling beholden to him in such a way. She worked hard and earned everything she got, and she preferred it like that.

'I think you've spent more on me tonight than you'll make taking over these resorts,' she remarked as they stepped out into the street. The rain had cleared and a pale sickle moon rose above the elegant town houses of Mayfair. 'Andrew Tyson only owns about half a dozen resorts, doesn't he?'

'The land alone makes it worth it,' Luca replied, buttoning his jacket. Seconds later the limo appeared at the kerb, and the sales assistant loaded the bags into the boot.

'I should get home,' Hannah said. She felt relieved at the thought of being away from Luca's unsettling presence, and yet reluctant to end the bizarre magic of the evening. But it was a forty-five-minute Tube ride to her small terraced house on the end of the Northern Line, and she'd be late enough as it was.

'I'll drive you,' Luca answered. 'Get in.'

'I live rather far away…'

'I know where you live.'

His calm assertion discomfited her. Of course her boss knew where she lived; it was on her employment record. And yet the thought of Luca invading her home, seeing even just a glimpse her private life, made her resist.

'I don't…'

'Hannah, get in. It's nearly eight and we're leaving at nine tomorrow morning. Why spend nearly an hour on the Tube when you don't have to?'

He had a point. As it was she'd be getting back later than she liked. 'All right, thank you.' She climbed into the limo, sitting well away from Luca. She could still remember the feel of his fingers on her back. *Stupid, stupid, stupid.* He'd probably been amused at how embarrassed she'd been. He probably undressed women in his sleep. The only reason she'd responded to him like that was because he was attractive and she hadn't been touched by a man in over five years. Her mother had told her it was more than time to jump back in the dating pool, but Hannah hadn't had time even to think about dipping a toe in.

The limo pulled into the street and Hannah sat back, suddenly overwhelmed with fatigue. The last few hours had taken an emotional toll.

'Here.' Luca pressed a glass into her hands, and her fingers closed around the fragile stem automatically. She looked in surprise at the flute of champagne. The driver must have had it ready. 'You didn't have any in the boutique,' Luca explained, 'and you said you had never tasted it before.'

'Oh.' She was touched by his thoughtfulness, and yet she felt weirdly exposed too. When had her boss ever considered what she wanted in such a way? 'Thank you.'

'Drink,' Luca said, and Hannah took a cautious sip, wrinkling her nose as the bubbles fizzed their way upward. Luca smiled at her faintly, no doubt amused by her inexperience.

'It's a bit more tickly than I thought,' she said. She felt incredibly gauche. Luca had most likely first imbibed Dom Perignon from a baby's bottle. He kept a bottle in his limo, after all. And here she was, saying how the bubbles tickled her nose.

She handed back the champagne with an awkward smile, and Luca took it, one dark eyebrow arched. 'Is it not to your liking?'

'It's just…I haven't eaten anything. And you know, alcohol on an empty stomach, never a good idea…' She was babbling, out of her element in so many ways. She, the calm, capable, unflappable PA, had been reduced to stammering and blushing by her boss, who was acting more like a man than an employer. She couldn't understand him or herself, and it was incredibly annoying.

'I'm sorry,' Luca murmured. 'I should have thought.' He pressed the intercom button and issued some directions in Italian. Hannah eyed him askance.

'What are you doing...?'

'I asked him to stop so we can eat. You don't have plans?'

Surprised alarm had her lurching upright. 'No, but really, it's not necessary—'

'Hannah, you're hungry. When you work late at the office, I provide dinner. Consider this the same thing.'

Except this didn't *feel* like the same thing. And when the limo stopped in front of an elegant bistro with red velvet curtains in the windows and curling gold script on the door, Hannah knew their meal would be a far cry from the sandwiches and coffee Luca usually had her order in when they were both working late.

She swallowed audibly, and then forced back the feelings of uncertainty and inadequacy. She'd been working as PA to one of the most powerful men in real estate for three years. She could handle dinner at a restaurant.

Straightening her spine, she got out of the car. Luca opened the door to the restaurant for her and then followed her in. The muted, understated elegance of the place fell over her like a soothing blanket.

'A table for two, Monsieur Moretti?' The French waiter asked, menus already in hand. Was her boss known *everywhere*?

Luca nodded and within seconds they were escorted to a private table in the corner, tucked away from the few other diners in the restaurant.

Hannah scanned the menu; it provided a temporary escape from Luca's penetrating gaze. *Foie gras. Roasted quail. Braised fillet of brill.* Okay, she could do this.

'Do you see something you like?' Luca asked.

'Yes.' She closed the menu and gave him a perfunctory smile. 'Thank you.'

The waiter came with the wine list, and Luca barely glanced at it before ordering a bottle. He turned to Hannah the moment the man had gone, his gaze resting on her. Again she had the sense of coming up short, of not being quite what he wanted, and she didn't understand it.

'It occurs to me that I know very little about you.'

'I didn't realise you wanted to,' Hannah answered. Luca had never asked her a single personal question in her three years of employment.

'Information is always valuable,' he answered with a negligent shrug. 'Where did you grow up?'

'A village outside Birmingham.' She eyed him warily. Where was this coming from? And why?

'Brothers? Sisters?'

'No.' Deciding this could go both ways, Hannah raised her eyebrows. 'What about you?'

Luca looked slightly taken aback, his eyes flaring, mouth compressing. In the dim lighting of the restaurant he looked darker and more alluring than usual, the candlelight from the table throwing his face into stark contrast from the snowy whiteness of his shirt, his whole being exuding restless power, barely leashed energy. 'What about me?'

'Do you have brothers or sisters?'

His mouth flattened into a hard line and he looked away briefly. 'No.'

So apparently he didn't like answering personal questions, just asking them. Hannah couldn't say she was surprised. The waiter came to take their order, and she chose a simple salad and the roasted quail, which she hoped would taste like chicken. Luca ordered steak and then the sommelier was proffering an expensive-looking bottle. Hannah watched as Luca expertly swilled a mouthful and then nodded in acceptance. The sommelier poured them both full glasses.

'I really shouldn't...' Hannah began. She didn't drink alcohol very often and she wanted to be fresh for tomorrow. And she didn't relish getting a bit of a buzz in Luca's presence. The last thing she needed was to feel even sillier in front of her boss.

'It won't be on an empty stomach,' Luca replied. 'And I think you need to relax.'

'Do you?' Hannah returned tartly. 'I must confess, this is all a bit out of the ordinary, Mr—'

'Luca.'

'Why?' she burst out. 'Why now?'

His dark gaze rested on her for a moment, and she had the sense he was weighing his words, choosing them with care. 'Why not?' he finally replied, and reached for his wine glass. Hannah deflated, frustrated but also a tiny bit relieved by his non-answer. She didn't know if she could handle some sort of weird revelation.

Fortunately Luca stopped with the personal questions after that, and they ate their meal mainly in silence, which was far more comfortable than being the subject of her boss's scrutiny, but even so she felt on edge, brittle and restless.

Which was too bad, she realised as Luca was paying the bill, because, really, she'd just had the most amazing evening—being bought a designer wardrobe and then treated to a fantastic meal by an undeniably sexy and charismatic man. Too bad it didn't feel like that. It felt...weird. Like something she could enjoy if she let herself, but she didn't think she should. Luca Moretti might have dozens of women at his beck and call, at his feet, but Hannah didn't intend to be one of them. Not if she wanted to keep her job, not to mention her sanity.

They drove in silence to her little house; by the time they'd arrived it was nearly ten o'clock. Her mother, Hannah thought with a flash of guilt, would be both tired and worried.

'I'll see you here tomorrow at nine,' Luca said, and Hannah turned to him in surprise.

'I thought I would be making my own way to the airport.'

'By Tube? And what if you're later? It's better this way. Here, let me get your bags.'

Hannah groped for her keys while Luca took the bags from the boutique to her doorstep. 'Thank you,' she muttered. 'You can go—'

But he was waiting for her to open her front door. She fumbled with the key, breathing a sigh of relief when the door finally swung open.

'Hannah?' her mother called. 'I've been wondering where you were—'

'I'm fine—' Hannah turned to Luca, practically grabbing the bags from him. 'Thank you very much. I'll see you tomorrow at nine.'

He was frowning, his gaze moving from her to the narrow hallway behind her, her mother coming around the corner. Clearly he was wondering about her living situation.

'Goodnight,' Hannah said, and closed the door.

Her mother, Diane, stopped short, her eyes widening as she saw all the expensive-looking bags by Hannah's feet. 'What on earth…?'

'It's a long story,' Hannah said. 'Sorry I'm so late. Did Jamie…?'

'Went to bed without a whimper, bless him,' Diane said. Her gaze moved to the bags. 'Goodness, that's a lot of shopping.'

'Yes, it is,' Hannah agreed rather grimly. 'Let me go see Jamie and then I'll tell you all about it.' Or at least some of it. She'd probably omit a few details, like Luca undoing her dress. The memory alone was enough to make a shiver go through her. Again.

'I'll make you a cup of tea,' Diane said. Hannah was already heading up the narrow stairway and then down the darkened hall to the small second bedroom. She tiptoed inside, her heart lifting at the familiar and beloved sight: her son. He slept on his back, arms and legs flung out like a starfish, his breathing deep and even.

Gently Hannah reached down and brushed the sandy hair from his forehead, her fingers skimming his plump, baby-soft cheek. He was five years old and the light of her life. And she wouldn't see him for a whole weekend.

Guilt niggled at her at the thought. Hannah knew her job was demanding and she wasn't able to spend as much time with Jamie as she would like. She also knew, all too well, the importance of financial independence and freedom. Working for Luca Moretti had given her both. She would never regret making that choice.

With a soft sigh Hannah leaned down and kissed her son's forehead, and then quietly left the room. She needed to get ready for her weekend with her boss.

CHAPTER THREE

LUCA DRUMMED HIS fingers against his thigh as the limo pulled up in front of Hannah's house. He'd been there less than twelve hours ago, dropping her off after their shopping and meal. He'd been strangely disquieted to have a tiny glimpse into her life—the narrow hall with its clutter of coats and boots, the sound of a woman's voice. Her mother? Why did he care?

Perhaps because since he'd met her he'd viewed Hannah Stewart as nothing more than a means to his own end. First as his PA, efficient and capable, and now as his stand-in wife-to-be. Last night he'd realised that if this ridiculous charade was going to work, he needed to know more about Hannah. And he hadn't learned much, but what he had discovered was that getting to know Hannah even a little bit made him feel guilty for using her.

Sighing impatiently at his own pointless thoughts, Luca opened the door to the limo and stepped out into the street. It wasn't as if he was making Hannah's life difficult. She was getting a luxurious weekend on a Mediterranean island, all expenses paid. And if she had to play-act a bit, what was the big deal? He'd make it worth her while.

He pressed the doorbell, and Hannah answered the door almost immediately. She wore her usual work outfit of a dark pencil skirt and a pale silk blouse, this time grey and pink. Pearls at her throat and ears and low black heels complemented the outfit. There was nothing wrong with it, but it wasn't what his fiancée would be wearing to accompany him on a weekend house party. She looked like a PA, not a woman in love on a holiday.

'What happened to the outfits I bought you yesterday?' Luca demanded.

'Hello to you too,' Hannah answered. 'I'm saving them for when I'm actually on Santa Nicola.' She arched an eyebrow. 'Being on the aeroplane isn't part of the social occasion, is it?'

'Of course not.' Luca knew he couldn't actually fault Hannah. She was acting in accordance to the brief he had given her. He'd tell her the truth soon enough...when there was no chance of anything going wrong. Nothing could risk his plan for this weekend. 'Are you packed?'

'Of course.' She reached for her suitcase but Luca took it first. 'I'll put it in the boot.'

'Hello, Mr Moretti.' An older woman with faded eyes and grey, bobbed hair emerged from behind Hannah to give him a tentative smile.

'Good morning.' Belatedly Luca realised how snappish he must have sounded when talking to Hannah. This whole experience was making him lose his cool, his control. He forced as charming a smile as he could and extended his hand to the woman who took it.

'I'm Diane Stewart, Hannah's mother—'

'Lovely to meet you.'

'I should go, Mum,' Hannah said. She slipped on a black wool coat, lifting her neat ponytail away from the collar. Luca had a sudden, unsettling glimpse of the nape of her neck, the skin pale, the tiny hairs golden and curling.

'I'll say goodbye to Jamie for you,' Diane promised and Luca looked sharply at Hannah, who flushed.

Jamie—a boyfriend? Clearly someone close to her.

Although maybe Jamie was a girl's name. A friend? A sister?

'Thanks, Mum,' she muttered, and quickly hugged her mother before walking towards the limo.

Luca handed the suitcase to his driver before getting in the back with Hannah. She was sitting close to the window, her face turned towards the glass.

'Do you live with your mother?' he asked.

'No, she just stayed the night because I was so late getting home.'

'Why was she there at all?'

She gave him a quick, quelling look. 'She's visiting.'

Hannah Stewart seemed as private as he was. Luca settled back in the seat. 'I'm sorry if I've cut your visit short.' He paused. 'You could have told me she was visiting. I would have made allowances.'

Hannah's look of disbelief was rather eloquent. Luca felt a dart of annoyance, which was unreasonable since he knew he wouldn't have made allowances. He needed Hannah's attendance this weekend too much. Still he defended himself. 'I'm not that unreasonable an employer.'

'I never said you were.'

Which was true. But he felt nettled anyway, as if he'd done something wrong. It was that damned guilt, for tricking her into this. He didn't like lying. He'd always played a straight bat, prided himself on his plain dealing. He'd lived with too many lies to act otherwise. But this was different, this was decades-deep, right down to his soul, and his revenge on Andrew Tyson was far more important than his PA's tender feelings. Feeling better for that reminder, Luca reached for his smartphone and started scrolling through messages.

Hannah sat back in her seat, glad to have that awkward goodbye scene over with. Luca had been surprisingly curious about her life, and she'd thankfully managed to deflect his questions. She'd never told her boss about her son, and she wanted to keep it that way. She knew instinctively that Luca Moretti would not take kindly to his PA having such an obligation of responsibility, no matter what he said about allowances. She was fortunate that her mother lived nearby and had always been happy to help out. Without Diane's help, Hannah never would have been able to take the job as Luca Moretti's PA. She certainly wouldn't have been able to perform it with the same level of capability.

Now she tried to banish all the thoughts and worries that had kept her up last night as she'd wondered what she was getting into, and if she was doing the right thing in leaving her son for two days. She wanted to stop wondering if she was coming across as gauche as she felt, or why her normally taciturn boss was suddenly turning his narrow-eyed attention to her.

No, today she'd told herself she was going to simply enjoy everything that came her way, whether it was champagne and caviar or a first-class plane ticket. This was an adventure, and she'd got out of the habit of enjoying or even looking for adventures. Since she'd had Jamie her life had become predictable and safe, which wasn't a bad thing but sometimes it was boring. She realised she was actually looking forward to a little bit of a shake-up.

'You're smiling,' Luca observed and, startled, Hannah refocused her gaze on her boss. He'd been watching her, she realised with a lurch of alarm. Or maybe it was simply awareness that she felt. A tingling spread through her body as his gaze remained resting on her, his mahogany-brown eyes crinkled at the corners, a faint smile tugging at his own mobile mouth. He wore a navy blue suit she'd probably seen before, with a crisp white shirt and silver-grey tie. Standard business wear, elegant and expensive, the suit cut perfectly to his broad shoulders and trim hips. Why was she noticing it today? Why was she feeling so *aware*?

'I was just thinking about flying first class,' she said.

'Ah yes. Something else you haven't done before.'

'No, and I'm looking forward to it.' She smiled wryly. 'I'm sure it's same old, same old for you.'

'It's refreshing to see someone experience something for the first time.' His mouth curved in a deeper smile, the look in his eyes disconcertingly warm. 'Tickly or not.'

She lifted her chin, fighting a flush. 'I admit, I'm not very experienced in the ways of the world.'

'Why aren't you?'

'Maybe because I'm not a millionaire?' Hannah returned dryly. 'Most people don't travel first class, you know.'

'I'm well aware. But plenty of people have tasted champagne.' He cocked his head, his warm gaze turning thoughtful. 'You seem to have missed out a bit on life, Hannah.'

Which was all too perceptive of him. And even though she knew it was true, it still stung. 'I've been working,' she replied with a shrug. 'And I have responsibilities...' She left it at that but Luca's eyes had narrowed.

'What kind of responsibilities?'

'Family,' she hedged. 'Nothing that interferes with my work,' she defended and he nodded, hands spread palm upward.

'As well I know. I do appreciate you coming for the weekend.'

'I didn't think I really had much choice,' Hannah returned, then drew an even breath. 'Why don't you tell me more about this weekend? You said it was a social occasion? How so?'

The warmth left Luca's eyes and Hannah felt tension steal into his body even though he'd barely moved.

'Andrew Tyson is a family man,' he stated. 'Wife, two children, resorts dedicated to providing people with the ultimate family experience.'

'Yes, I did some research on them when I was booking your travel,' Hannah recalled. '"A Tyson Holiday is a memory for ever,"' she quoted and Luca grimaced.

'Right.'

'You don't like the idea?'

'Not particularly.'

She shouldn't have been surprised. Luca Moretti had never struck her as the wife-and-kids type, which was why she'd kept her own son secret from him. He was never short of female company, though, and none of them lasted very long. A week at the most. 'Why are you going after these resorts if you don't really like the idea behind them?'

'I don't make business decisions based on personal preferences,' Luca answered shortly. One hand closed in a fist on his powerful thigh and he straightened it out slowly, deliberately, his palm flat on his leg, his fingers, long and tapered, stretching towards his knee. 'I make business decisions based on what is financially sound and potentially profitable.'

'But Andrew Tyson only has a handful of resorts, doesn't he? The Santa Nicola resort, one on Tenerife, one on Kos, one on—'

'Sicily, and then a couple in the Caribbean. Yes.'

'It's small potatoes to a man like you,' Hannah pointed out. Luca had orchestrated multibillion-dollar deals all around the world. A couple of family resorts, especially ones that looked as if they needed a bit of updating, hardly seemed his sort of thing.

Luca shifted in his seat. 'As I told you before, the land alone makes this a lucrative deal.'

'Okay, but you still haven't told me why this is a social occasion.'

'Because Tyson wants it to be one. He's always espoused family values, and so he wants each potential owner to socialise with him and his family.'

'So chatting up little kids?' Hannah couldn't quite keep the note of amusement from her voice. 'It sounds like your worst nightmare.'

'His children are grown up,' Luca answered. 'The son is only a year younger than I am.'

'Do his children have children?'

'I have no idea.' Luca sounded eminently bored. 'Probably. The son is married.'

Hannah considered the implications of everything he'd just said. So she'd be socialising with Andrew Tyson and his family, chatting up his children and generally being friendly? She was starting to realise why Luca had wanted her to come along.

'So you want me to be your front man,' she said slowly.

Luca swivelled to face her. 'Excuse me?'

'To do the talking,' Hannah explained. 'Chatting to his wife and children while you get on with the business side of things. Right?'

He gave one terse nod. 'Right.'

She settled back in her seat. 'All right. I can do that.'

'Good,' Luca answered, and he turned back to his phone.

The VIP lounge at the airport fully lived up to Hannah's expectations. She enjoyed the plush seats, the complimentary mimosas and breakfast buffet, and when Luca suggested she take advantage of the adjoining spa and get a manicure and pedicure, she decided to go for it. Why not enjoy all the opportunities that were on offer? It wasn't as if she had many chances to relax in a spa.

By the time they boarded the plane she was feeling pleasantly relaxed; one of the spa attendants had given her a head and neck massage while her feet had been soaking.

It had felt lovely, as had Luca's look of blatant male appreciation when she'd emerged from the spa—the attendant had insisted on doing her hair and make-up as well.

'You look good,' he said in approval, and, while Hannah knew she shouldn't care what Luca thought of her looks, his masculine admiration spoke to the feminine heart of her.

'I think,' she told him as they took their seats in the plane's first-class section, 'I could get used to this.'

Luca's mouth quirked up at one corner. 'I'm sure you could.' He accepted two flutes of champagne from the airline steward and handed one to Hannah. 'And now you should get used to this.'

'Why are you so determined to have me become used to champagne?' Hannah asked as she took a sip. Second time round the bubbles didn't tickle her nose quite so much.

'Why not? You should enjoy all of these new experiences.'

'True,' Hannah answered. 'And since you said this was a social occasion, I might as well.' She took another sip of champagne. '*Are* we meant to be working during the flight?'

'No.'

'So why did you put me up in first class?'

'I wanted to watch you enjoy the experience.'

Hannah felt her stomach dip at this implication of his words, the intimacy of them. She was suddenly conscious of how this all seemed: the champagne flute dangling from her fingers, the cosy enclave of their first-class seats, and Luca Moretti lounging next to her, not taking his warm gaze from hers. She swallowed hard.

'Well, I am enjoying it,' she said, striving for normality. 'Thank you.' The last thing she needed was to start crushing on her boss. He'd probably find that amusing—or maybe offensive, and fire her. She handed her half-drunk champagne to the steward and buckled her seat belt. Time to get things back to the way they'd always been.

Luca must have been thinking along the same lines because he reached for the in-flight magazine as the plane took off, and then spent the rest of the four-hour flight looking over some paperwork. Hannah asked him once if he needed her to do anything, and he snapped at her that he didn't.

In fact, with each passing hour of the flight, he seemed to get more and more tense, his muscles taut, his eyes shadowed, his face grim. Hannah wondered what was going on, but she didn't dare ask.

She tried to watch a movie but her mind was pinging all over the place, and so she ended up simply staring out of the window at the azure sky, waiting for the minutes and hours to pass.

And then they did, and they landed on Santa Nicola, the Mediterranean glittering like a bright blue promise in the distance.

'Is someone meeting us at the airport?'

'Yes, one of Tyson's staff is picking us up.' Luca rose from his seat and shrugged into his suit jacket. 'Let me do the talking.'

Okay... 'I thought you wanted me to socialise.'

'I do. But not with the staff.'

Bewildered, Hannah stared at him, but Luca's deliberately bland expression gave nothing away. He held a hand out to her to help her from her seat, and after a second's hesitation she took it.

The feel of his warm, dry palm sliding across and then enfolding hers was a jolt to her system, like missing the last step in a staircase. Instinctively she started to withdraw her hand but Luca tightened his hands over hers and pulled her forward.

'Come on,' he murmured. 'People are waiting.'

With his hand still encasing hers she followed him out of the plane, blinking in the bright sunlight as she navigated the narrow steps down to the tarmac. She was just thinking that she wished she'd packed her sunglasses in her carry-on rather than her suitcase when she heard someone call a greeting to Luca and then felt his arm snake around her waist.

Hannah went rigid in shock at the feel of his fingers splayed on one hip, her other hip pressed against his thigh.

'Signor Moretti! We are so pleased to welcome you to Santa Nicola.' A tanned, friendly-looking man in khaki shorts and a red polo shirt with the Tyson logo on the breast pocket came striding towards them. 'And this is...?' he asked, glancing at Hannah with a smile.

'Hannah Stewart,' Luca filled in smoothly, his arm still firmly about her waist. 'My fiancée.'

CHAPTER FOUR

HANNAH STOOD BLINKING stupidly at the man who had come forward. He reached for her hand and numbly she gave it to him.

'Signorina Stewart. So pleased to meet you! Signor Moretti mentioned he was bringing his fiancée, and we look forward to getting to know you. I am Stefano, one of the members of Mr Tyson's staff.'

Hannah could only stare at Stefano, trying to find the brain cells to string two words together. The only word she could think of was the one Luca had used with such confident precision. *Fiancée.*

What on earth...?

'Hannah,' Luca murmured, and she felt the pressure of his hand on her waist, the warmth of his palm seeping through her skirt.

Still reeling, she forced a smile onto her face. 'Pleased to meet you, I'm sure.'

As soon as she said the words she wished she hadn't. Now she was complicit in this...whatever *this* was. A lie, obviously. A ruthless deception—and for what purpose? Why on earth would Luca pretend she was something she wasn't?

Because he was pretending he was something he wasn't.

The answer was so blindingly obvious Hannah couldn't

believe she hadn't twigged earlier. Andrew Tyson was a family man, and this weekend was meant to be a social occasion. *Of course.* Luca Moretti, the famous womaniser, needed a woman. A fiancée to show he was the kind of family man Tyson must want him to be. What other reason could he have possibly had for introducing her that way? For *lying*?

'Come this way,' Stefano said, beckoning towards the waiting open-topped Jeep emblazoned with the Tyson logo, a dolphin jumping in front of a sun. 'Mr Tyson's villa is only a few minutes away.'

Hannah walked like an automaton towards the Jeep, Luca next to her, his arm still around her. She wanted to shrug it off but she didn't think she'd be able to; his grip was like a vice. She tried to catch his eye but he was staring blandly ahead. Damn the man. What on earth was she supposed to do now?

They got in the back of the Jeep and Stefano hopped in the front. Hannah was barely aware of the gorgeous surroundings: mountains provided a stunning, jagged backdrop to lush greenery that framed both sides of the paved single-track road. She'd read that Santa Nicola was virtually unspoilt, save for the resort, and she could see it now in the jungle of bright flowers that gave way to superbly landscaped gardens and high walls of pink sandstone.

'*Luca,*' she muttered meaningfully, although she hardly knew where to begin, how to protest. 'You can't—'

'I already have,' he murmured as the Jeep came to a stop in front of a sprawling villa, its pale stone walls climbing with ivy and bougainvillea.

'I know,' Hannah snapped. 'And you shouldn't have—' She was prevented from saying anything more by Stefano coming around to open the door on her side and help her out onto the cobbled pavement.

'Mr Tyson looks forward to welcoming you properly

this evening, during the cocktail hour. In the meantime you can both rest and refresh yourselves.'

'Thank you,' Hannah muttered, although everything in her cried out to end this absurd charade. She was so angry and shocked she could barely manage to speak civilly to Stefano, who of course had no idea what was going on. *Yet*.

And Hannah wondered how on earth she could tell him, or anyone here, the truth. Luca had made it virtually impossible, and yet still she fantasised about coming clean and watching Luca Moretti get the send-up he undoubtedly deserved. How dare he put her in this position?

Stefano led them into the gracious entryway of the villa, a soaring foyer that made the most of the house's unparalleled view of the sea. Down a long terracotta-tiled corridor, and then through double louvred doors into a spacious and elegant bedroom, a massive king-sized bed its impressive centrepiece, the French windows opened to a private terrace that led to the beach, gauzy curtains blowing in the sea breeze.

'This is marvellous, thank you,' Luca said, shaking Stefano's hand, and with a murmured farewell Stefano closed the doors behind them, finally, thankfully, leaving them alone.

Hannah whirled around to face Luca, who stood in the centre of the bedroom, hands in the pockets of his trousers, a faint frown on his face as he surveyed the room with its elegant furnishings in cream and light green.

'How could you?' she gasped out. 'How *dare* you?'

Luca moved his gaze to her. He seemed utterly unmoved, without a shred of remorse or embarrassment. 'If you are referring to the way I introduced you—'

'Of *course* I'm referring to that!'

'It was necessary.' And he strolled over to the windows as if that was actually the end of the discussion.

Hannah stared at his broad back, watching as he closed

and fastened the windows. Finally she managed to say in what she hoped was a level, reasonable voice, 'Do you actually think this can work?'

Luca turned around to face her, eyebrows arrogantly raised. 'I don't embark on ventures that are doomed to failure.'

'I think you may be in for a new experience, then,' Hannah snapped.

'Why? Why shouldn't Andrew Tyson believe you're my fiancée?'

'Because I'm *not*—'

'Are you not suitable?' Luca steamrolled over her, his voice silky and yet underlaid with iron. 'Are you not pretty or smart or sophisticated enough?'

A hot flush broke out over Hannah's body as she glared at him. 'No, I'm not,' she answered flatly. 'As you well know. I hadn't even flown first class before today—or drunk champagne—' Suddenly the memory of him pressing the flute into her hands, smiling at her with such gentle amusement, was enough to make her burst into tears. She swallowed hard before continuing furiously, realisation ripping away any illusions she'd had left. 'So everything you've done has been to maintain this…this ridiculous facade.' She glanced down at her varnished nails, her hands curling instinctively into fists. 'The manicure and pedicure?' she spat. 'The hair and make-up…' She remembered the look of approval in his eyes. *You look good.* And she'd inwardly preened at his praise. 'You just wanted me to look the part.'

'Is that so objectionable?'

'This whole farce is objectionable! You *tricked* me.'

Luca sighed, as if she were being so very tedious by objecting. 'I'm asking for very little, Hannah.'

'Very little? You're asking me to lie to strangers. To pretend to—to be in love with you!' The words rang out, making her wince. She hadn't meant it quite like *that*, and yet…that was what he was asking. Wasn't it?

'I'm not asking anything of the kind,' Luca returned evenly. 'Although surely it wouldn't be too hard?'

Hannah recoiled, horrified at the implication. Did he think he was so desirable—or simply that she was so desperate? 'Yes, it would,' she said stiffly. 'Since in actuality I barely know you. Which was the point of the little "getting to know you" spiel last night at dinner, wasn't it?' She shook her head, disgusted with both him and herself. She'd known something was off, but how on earth could she have suspected this? 'Well, at least now you know I'm an only child. That's something, I suppose. Make sure to mention it during the cocktail hour.'

'You know me well enough,' Luca answered, his tone deliberately unruffled. 'You've worked for me for three years. In fact,' he continued, strolling towards her, 'you probably know me better than anyone else does.'

'I do?' She blinked at him, surprised and a little saddened by this admission. She'd known Luca was a solitary man, but surely he had closer people in his life than his PA. 'What about your family?'

'Not around.'

'Where—?'

'You're the only person who sees me every day, Hannah. Who knows my preferences, my foibles and quirks. Yes, I think you know me very well.'

'Yes, but you don't know *me*.' And she didn't care whether she knew him or not. She wouldn't want to play-act as his fiancée even if they'd been best friends. Which they were most decidedly not.

'I think I know you a little bit,' Luca said, a smile curving the sensuous mouth Hannah suddenly couldn't look away from.

'What? How?' He didn't know anything. 'You've never asked me anything about my life until last night.'

'Maybe I don't need to ask.'

'What are you saying?' He'd taken a step closer to her and her stomach writhed and leapt in response, as if she'd swallowed snakes. She pressed one hand to her middle, knowing the gesture to be revealing, and stood her ground even though she desperately wanted to take a step away from him.

Instead he took a step closer. 'Let's see,' he murmured, his voice a low hum that seemed to reverberate right through her bones. He was close enough so that she could inhale the cedarwood scent of his aftershave, see the muscles corded in his neck. Some time since entering the room he'd loosened his silver silk tie and undone the top two buttons of his shirt, so she could see the strong brown column of his throat, the dark hairs sprinkling his chest below. She jerked her gaze away from the sight.

'You don't know me,' she stated firmly. 'At all. Because if you did, you'd know I'd never agree to something like this.'

'Which is why I didn't ask you, so perhaps I do know you after all.'

'You don't,' she insisted. He was close enough to breathe in, to feel his heat. If she reached one hand out she could place a palm on his chest, feel the crisp cotton of his shirt, the steady thud of his heart, the flex of his powerful muscles...

Hannah drew her breath in sharply, horrified by the nature of her thoughts. What kind of sorcerer was Luca Moretti, to weave this spell over her so easily?

'I think I do,' Luca murmured. He stood right in front of her, his gaze roving over her, searching, finding, feeling as intimate as a caress. 'I know you drink your coffee with milk and two sugars, although you pretend you have it black.'

'What…?' Her breath came out in a rush. It was such a little thing, but he was right. She added the sugar when she was alone because she was self-conscious about taking it. Every working woman in London seemed to drink their coffee black and eat lettuce leaves for lunch.

Somehow she managed to rally. 'That's not very much,' she scoffed.

'I'm only beginning,' Luca answered. 'I know you look at travel blogs on your lunch break. I know you have an incredible work ethic but you seem embarrassed by it sometimes. I know you're determined to be cheerful but sometimes, when you think no one is looking, you seem sad.'

Hannah drew a deep breath, too shocked to respond or even to blush. How had he seen all these things? How did he *know*?

'And,' Luca finished softly as he turned away, 'I know there is someone in your life named Jamie whom you care about very much.'

She stiffened. 'Well done, Sherlock,' she managed. 'You're obviously very perceptive, but it doesn't change what I think—that this is wrong, and you never should have forced me into this position.'

Luca turned back to her, the warmth she'd just seen in his eyes evaporated, leaving only chilly darkness. 'How exactly,' he asked, his voice dangerously soft, 'did I force you?'

'It's not as if you gave me a choice,' Hannah exclaimed. 'Introducing me as your fiancée! What was I supposed to do, tell them you were a liar?'

He shrugged, the movement elegant, muscles rippling underneath his shirt. 'You could have done.' He lifted his gaze to hers, those dark, cold eyes so penetrating. 'Why didn't you?'

'Because…'

'Because?' Luca prompted softly.

'It would have been very awkward,' Hannah said. 'For both of us.'

'What's a little awkwardness?'

'You might have fired me—'

He arched an eyebrow. 'And be sued for sexual harassment?'

'I could already sue you for that,' Hannah dared to suggest. Luca's eyes narrowed.

'And then you really would lose your job, just as I would lose mine.'

She swallowed. 'You could have paid me off.'

The smile he gave her was cynical and hard. 'Is that what you're suggesting?'

'No.' Appalled, Hannah wondered how on earth they'd pursued this line of conversation. She wasn't going to sue him, even if part of her inwardly railed that she should, that Luca Moretti deserved everything he had coming to him, including a whole lot of *awkwardness.*

'I don't want money,' she informed him stiffly. 'I simply don't want to be in this position, and I resent that you put me in it. Why didn't you tell me before?'

'Because you would have refused.'

She stared at his calm expression, his hard eyes. He stood before her, arrogant and assured, utterly unrepentant. 'You don't have a shred of remorse, do you?' she asked wonderingly.

'No,' Luca agreed, 'I don't. Because if you let go of your huffy indignation for a moment, Hannah, you'll realise I'm not asking very much of you.'

'You're asking me to lie.'

'And you've never lied before?'

She bit her lip. 'Of course, everyone's lied, but this is different—'

'Andrew Tyson is putting unreasonable expectations on the real-estate developer who buys his precious resorts,' Luca cut across her flatly. 'I *know* I'm the best man for the job, and I shouldn't have to be married to be selected. The injustice is his, not mine.'

'How many other developers are bidding on it?'

'Two, and they're both married.'

Somehow she found the temerity to joke. 'You weren't tempted to say I was your wife?'

'I was tempted,' Luca admitted. 'But I figured that would be too hard to pull off.'

'How pragmatic of you,' Hannah murmured. Her mind was still spinning but some of her self-righteous fury had deflated. She didn't know whether it was simply the awesome force of Luca's personality or because she actually sympathised with him a little. Or maybe it was because she was just too tired to keep it up.

Slowly she walked to a cream divan positioned in an alcove and sank onto its soft seat. 'So how do you propose—no pun intended—to make this work? Not,' she informed him with swift asperity, 'that I'm actually thinking of going along with this idea.'

'Of course not,' Luca murmured. Hannah watched, mesmerised, as he tugged off his tie and then began to unbutton his shirt.

'What are you doing?' she squeaked.

'Changing. We're due for cocktails in less than an hour.'

'Can't you use the bathroom?' She nodded towards the door that led to what looked like a sumptuous en suite.

'Why should I?' Luca's smile was wicked. 'We're engaged to be married, after all.'

'You're impossible.' Hannah closed her eyes against the sight of Luca shrugging off his shirt. Even so she'd had a glimpse of bronzed, burnished skin, rippling muscles, and crisp, dark hair that veed down to the waistband of his trousers.

'You're not the first person to say so,' Luca answered. She could hear him undressing and even with her eyes closed she could imagine it, picture him kicking off his trousers, revealing long, muscular legs, wearing nothing but a pair of boxer shorts, perhaps in navy satin...

Good grief, but she needed to get a grip. Hannah took a deep breath. 'So you still haven't told me how this is going to work.'

'We're going to act like we're engaged. Simple.'

'Simple?' She opened her eyes to glare at Luca; he stood across the room, buckling the belt on a pair of grey trousers. His chest was still gloriously bare. 'It's not simple, Luca. We're not engaged. We barely know each other. If someone asks either one of us anything about our relationship or how we met, we'll have no idea what to say.'

'It's best to keep as close to the truth as possible,' Luca advised as he reached for a light blue shirt and shrugged into it. 'You're still my PA.'

'And we just happen to be engaged. Convenient.'

He shot her a quick, hard smile. 'It is, isn't it? Now you should get ready. We're due to meet Tyson for cocktails shortly.'

CHAPTER FIVE

LUCA STARED OUT at the setting sun turning the placid sea to gold and waited for Hannah to emerge from the bathroom. He tried to ignore the guilt that flickered through him, an unpleasant ripple of sensation. All right, so he'd tricked her. He shouldn't have. But he hadn't had any choice. Not that Hannah would be able to understand that, and he had no intention of explaining it to her. She didn't seem to be quite so angry now, although she had shut the door rather firmly after flouncing in there to get changed.

Sighing restlessly, Luca turned away from the spectacular view. Every nerve ending tingled with anticipation at coming face to face with Andrew Tyson. In the three months since Tyson had announced he was selling his chain of family resorts, Luca hadn't actually spoken to the man, not even on the telephone. Everything had been done through intermediaries, until this weekend. Until now, when he would finally look upon the man he'd hated for so long. He *had* to close this deal. And he'd do whatever it took to accomplish that.

'Are you ready?' he called to Hannah. They were due on the terrace for drinks in five minutes.

'Yes.' She unlocked and opened the door, emerging from the bathroom with her head held high even as uncertainty flickered in her eyes. Luca felt the breath rush from his lungs as he took in her appearance.

She wore a cocktail dress in plum-coloured silk; the pure, clean line of the material across her collarbone drew his attention to the elegance of her shoulders and neck as well as the slight, enticing curve of her breasts. The dress fitted perfectly to her tiny waist and then flared out around her thighs, ending at her knees. Her long, shapely legs were encased in sheer stockings and she'd worn her hair not in its usual neat ponytail, but in loose waves about her face. She looked clean and fresh and utterly alluring.

Luca finally found his voice. 'You look…good.'

'I meet with your approval?' Hannah surmised tartly. 'Well, I need to look the part, don't I?' She went over to her suitcase and riffled through her belongings. 'I don't feel at all guilty for letting you buy me a fortune in clothes, by the way.'

'And so you shouldn't.' The rays of the setting sun caught the golden glints in her hair. Luca watched as she moved her hair over to one shoulder in order to put on her earrings. He found something almost unbearably erotic about watching her do this, her neck exposed, her slender hands fitting the earring into her ear. Her feet, he saw, were bare.

'I suppose I'll have to give them back when this charade is over?' she asked as she reached for a pearl necklace.

'No, not at all. You may keep them. They're yours.'

She fiddled with the necklace, unable to do the clasp, and Luca walked towards her. 'Here, let me.' His fingers brushed her nape as he did the clasp and he felt a shudder go through her. Felt it go through himself. He couldn't resist brushing his fingers against that tender, silky skin one more time before he stepped away.

'Thank you,' she murmured, not looking at him. He could see a rosy flush spreading across the creamy skin of her throat and face.

'I should have bought you some appropriate jewellery.'

'I think that would be going above and beyond,' she answered lightly. 'Pearls surely suffice.'

'Yes…but I'd like to see you with diamonds. And sapphires. They'd look lovely against your pale skin.'

She dipped her head, hiding her expression. 'Thank you.'

Luca watched her, wishing he had a reason to touch her again. 'You don't seem as angry as you were before.'

She glanced quickly at him before lowering her lashes. 'I suppose I'm not. The truth is, I actually do like you, Mr—'

'Surely now is the time to call me Luca.'

'Luca. Sorry, old habits die hard, I suppose.' She sighed and then straightened before moving away from him. 'I'd better not slip up with that one, huh? Anyway.' She reached for a wrap in matching plum-coloured lace; it looked as fragile and delicate as cobwebs. 'I like working for you, even if I resent having to participate in this farce of an engagement. I don't want you to lose face or your job, and I certainly don't want to lose mine. So.' She turned to him, a determined smile on her face. 'Here we are.'

'Here we are.' He gazed at her and she gazed back, and the moment stretched and spun out while the sun continued to set and the room became dark with shadows.

Eventually, Luca didn't know how long it took, he roused himself and reached for her hand. 'We should go.'

'All right.'

And with her fingers loosely threaded through his, he led her out of the room.

The terrace was bathed with the last rays of the setting sun as Luca led her through the open French windows and out onto the smooth paving stones. Torches flickered in the deepening twilight and couples milled around along with several staff members proffering trays of champagne and frothy-looking cocktails.

Smiling wryly to herself, Hannah took a flute of champagne with murmured thanks. She took a sip, enjoying the crisp bubbles bursting on her tongue, and gazed around at the assortment of people. There were two other couples, an urbane, blond man with a tall, bony-looking woman who Hannah vaguely recognised, and a middle-aged man with greying hair and a smiling wife who had squeezed herself into a dress of green satin. Their host, as far as she could tell, was nowhere to be seen.

Next to her Luca looked relaxed and faintly amused, but Hannah could feel the tension emanating from him. The fingers that clasped his flute of champagne were white-knuckled. She wondered again why he cared so much, and knew he would never tell her. And she would probably never work up the courage to ask.

'Greetings!' A jovial-looking man in his seventies appeared in the French windows, rubbing his hands and smiling in expectation. Hannah recognised Andrew Tyson from the photograph she'd seen on the Tyson Resorts website. Genial, running slightly to fat, with sandy silvery hair and deep-set brown eyes. In his youth he must have been quite handsome. He still possessed a vigorous charisma now.

'I'm so pleased to have you here at last,' he said as he strolled onto the terrace. 'Luca, James, and Simon. You all know each other?'

The men exchanged quick glances and terse nods. 'Excellent, excellent. And you all have drinks?' His gaze moved over the crowd to rest on Luca.

'Luca Moretti,' he said as if accessing a mental Rolodex. 'We've never actually met, but I have, of course, heard of your many accomplishments in the world of real estate.'

Hannah glanced at Luca and saw his expression was bland. 'Thank you,' he murmured.

'And you are recently engaged?' Andrew's gaze sharpened, his smile turning almost sly. 'For I've heard of your accomplishments elsewhere.'

Luca drew Hannah forward, as if displaying a trophy. She tried to smile even though she didn't like being pushed forward as if for inspection. 'Indeed. Please meet my wife-to-be, Hannah Stewart.'

'Hannah.' Tyson glanced at her appraisingly, and for one horrible second Hannah wondered if he would see through this whole ridiculous charade. And she realised she didn't want to be exposed in such a way, and she didn't want Luca to be exposed. He might have lied and tricked her terribly, but now that she was embroiled in this ploy she wanted it to succeed.

'I'm very pleased to meet you,' she told Tyson, and stuck out her hand for him to shake. He kissed it instead, his lips a little damp, and next to her Luca shifted restlessly.

'Likewise, of course,' Tyson said. 'Now how did the two of you meet?'

'Hannah is my PA,' Luca intervened swiftly. 'We met at work. I'm not one to advocate mixing business with pleasure, but in this instance it was impossible not to.' He sent Hannah a lingering, loving glance that didn't quite meet his eyes. Still she felt herself tingle. Her body was reacting to Luca's, or maybe it was her mind reacting to his words. She knew them to be lies but they affected her anyway. It had been a long time since she'd been complimented by a man in any shape or form.

'I can see why,' Andrew said with a charmingly flirtatious smile for her. 'How did he propose, Hannah? If you don't mind me asking?'

Uh-oh. Her mind blanked for one awful second before she thought *screw it* and gave a light, teasing laugh. 'Oh, it was so romantic, wasn't it, Luca?' she practically purred, sliding an arm around her intended's waist. His body tensed under her hand and she enjoyed the feel of bunched muscle and taut abs before she continued with her story. 'He surprised me with a trip to Paris for the weekend—on a private jet.' She slid Luca what she hoped was an adoring look from under her lashes, enjoying the way his wary expression changed to one of cautious interest. He wanted to know where she was going with this. 'And then one magical evening he took me to the top of the Eiffel Tower—he'd rented the whole thing out so it was completely private.'

'I didn't think you could rent the Eiffel Tower,' Andrew said and Hannah continued without missing a beat.

'Oh, you can, if you know the right people.' She dared to wink. 'Isn't that right, Luca?'

He smiled blandly. 'It is.'

'And then what happened?' The woman in green satin had asked. Everyone was listening to her story now, clearly intrigued by the over-the-top romanticism. Hannah knew she shouldn't lay it on too thick; this was Luca Moretti, after all, and his reputation had clearly preceded him. And yet…if Luca was going to do a thing, she knew he'd do it properly, proposing marriage included.

'And then he told me how madly in love he was with me,' she finished blithely, 'and he proposed. Down on one knee.' She ended this utter fabrication with a happy sigh.

Andrew Tyson smiled faintly as he nodded towards her hand. 'But you don't have a ring, my dear.'

'Oh, but I do,' Hannah assured him. 'Luca presented me with the most magnificent ring—a family heirloom, actually, hundreds of years old, although he changed the design for me. Sapphires and diamonds,' she added, remembering what Luca had said earlier. 'Gorgeous.' She paused for a moment, picturing the fictitious ring, while everyone remained silent and spellbound.

'What happened to it, then?' asked the lanky woman rather sulkily.

'Oh, it was too big. Silly Luca.' She patted him playfully on the cheek and ignored the glimmer of warning in his mahogany eyes. 'It's at the jeweller's being resized.' She turned a twinkling smile onto Andrew Tyson. 'But I assure you, the next time I see you, you'll be suitably blinded.' Now *why* had she said that? She didn't want to see Andrew Tyson again. She certainly didn't want to keep up this pretence. She'd just got carried away.

'I'm sure,' Andrew murmured. 'Charmed, my dear, charmed.' He turned to another guest and Hannah only just kept from sagging with relief, now that the adrenaline was leaving her in a cold rush. She could feel the watchful gazes of the other businessmen and their wives, no doubt wondering what a man like Luca Moretti saw in her.

'You're a natural,' Luca murmured in her ear. 'You should be on the stage.'

'Shh,' Hannah chided. They eased away from the group as they both gazed out at the sea, now swathed in darkness. The moon was just rising, sending a sheen of silver over the water. 'Actually, I quite enjoyed myself.'

'I could tell.' He shot her an amused look, although Hannah could still feel how tense he was. 'You almost had me believing I gave you an heirloom ring.'

'Well, that's the point, isn't it?' Hannah replied. Actually, she had enjoyed believing in the fantasy for a few moments. Wearing the dress, drinking the champagne, acting as if a gorgeous, powerful man adored her. It could get addictive, enjoying all this attention and luxury, and she needed to remember none of this was real.

'If I'd known how much you'd get into the spirit of the thing,' Luca remarked, 'I would have let you in on the secret earlier.'

'I think it's more of a case of needs must,' Hannah returned. She glanced back at the assembled group. 'We should mingle, I suppose.'

'I suppose.'

'Tyson's wife isn't here? Or his children?'

The traces of amusement on Luca's face disappeared. 'They're joining him tomorrow. Tomorrow's dinner will be the big black-tie event.'

'When will he announce who has won the bid?'

Luca shrugged. 'Who knows? I think he's toying with all of us.'

Hannah glanced at Andrew, who was working his way through the crowd, talking to everyone individually. 'He seems a nice man.'

'Appearances can be deceiving.'

She turned back to Luca, surprised by the hardness in his voice. 'You don't like him.'

'I don't know the man,' Luca answered as he tossed back the rest of his drink. 'But I don't like being forced into play-acting. His demands are unreasonable and irrelevant.'

'And yet you still chose to go after his resorts.'

'I told you twice now, the land is valuable. Now let's go.' He took her arm and moved back to the crowd, and Hannah had no choice but to follow his lead. The Luca Moretti she knew wouldn't kowtow to anyone's demands, especially if he thought they were unreasonable. So why was he in this case?

She had no time to ponder the question as they were plunged back into the complicated social dynamics of three men who clearly respected if not liked each other, and were all bidding for the same job, while Andrew Tyson presided over them all.

At dinner Hannah sat next to Daniela, the sulky, beautiful woman who was partner to James, the CEO of a slick development company in the City. 'So how long have you been working for Luca?' she asked Hannah as the first course was served.

Luca, was it? Hannah covertly studied Daniela's tall,

lithe build, the long blond hair she kept tossing over her shoulder in an artful, deliberate way. 'Three years.'

'And you have been engaged for how long?'

A couple of hours. 'A few weeks.' Hannah took a sip of the cold cucumber soup to keep from having to say anything else.

'I never thought a man like Luca would marry,' Daniela said with a burning stare for the man in question, who was chatting with Simon, the third developer, across the table. 'He always seemed like the type to love and leave.'

'Until he found someone he wanted to stay with,' Hannah returned.

Daniela arched an eyebrow, the scepticism evident on her face. 'You're quite different from the women Luca is usually seen with. Not quite as...polished.'

Stung by this unsubtle put-down, Hannah lifted her chin. 'I didn't realise you knew him.'

'Oh, I know him,' Daniela said darkly and Hannah inwardly seethed. Luca could have warned her that a former paramour would be here, unsheathing her claws and trying to draw blood. And what if she gave something away to this elegant harpy? Daniela might know more about Luca than she did. Judging by her smouldering looks, it seemed almost a certainty. The idea made her feel unsettled in a way she didn't like. She wasn't *jealous*, just annoyed and angry all over again at Luca putting her in this position.

By the time the dessert plates had been cleared and coffee served, Hannah was having trouble keeping up her sparkly pretence. The excitement of pretending to be someone she wasn't had worn thin, and she longed only to return to their room and go to sleep. Actually, what she really wanted to do was go back to London and snuggle with her son. When she'd been in the bathroom changing she'd managed to speak to Jamie on the phone for a few minutes, listening to him chatter about his day, but it wasn't enough. It was never enough.

Luca must have seen the slump of her shoulders or the fatigue on her face for in one graceful movement he rose from the table. 'It's been a lovely evening, but I fear I've tired my fiancée out. Do you mind if we excuse ourselves?'

'Not at all, not at all,' Andrew replied as he also rose. 'We'll see you both in the morning.'

Luca and Hannah made their farewells to the rest of the group and then they walked in silence to their bedroom; with each step Hannah was remembering that big bed and how small it now actually seemed. They surely wouldn't share it. Luca would be a gentleman and make up a bed on the divan. Or so she hoped.

And yet even the thought of sharing the same room with Luca made her head go light and her palms turn damp. He was so *male*, so potently virile and sexual. She'd been immune—mostly—in their usual office environment, but she felt it keenly here, when they were sharing a bedroom and the moonlight and the gentle whooshing of the sea conspired to make everything seem romantic.

Luca opened the door to their bedroom, stepping aside so Hannah could go in first. He shrugged off his jacket while Hannah kicked off her heels with a groan. 'Wretched things.'

'You're not a fan of high heels?'

'I like taking them off.' The room was bathed in moonlight, the windows open to the sea breeze, the light from the lamps on the bedside tables giving out a cosy glow. Hannah glanced at the bed, which had been turned down, the cream duvet folded back to reveal the silky sheet beneath. A heart-shaped chocolate in gold foil nestled on each pillow. 'How is that going to work?' she asked, deciding to tackle the problem head-on.

Luca barely glanced at the bed. 'How is what going

to work?' His fingers had already gone to the buttons of his shirt, and, heaven help her, he was going to take it off again. And this time she might let herself watch.

'Sleeping arrangements,' Hannah said, dragging her gaze away from the tantalising glimpse of Luca's chest. 'We can't both sleep in the bed.'

'Oh?' He sounded amused. 'Why can't we?'

'Because!' Startled, she turned back to him and watched as he shrugged out of his shirt and then went for his belt buckle. '*Luca.* Can't you change in the bathroom?'

'What are you, a nun? If it makes you feel better, I won't sleep in the nude as I usually do.'

'What a prince,' Hannah gritted through her teeth. 'Seriously, Luca—'

'Seriously,' he said as he reached for a pair of drawstring pyjama pants that were going to leave very little to the imagination. 'It's a bed. It's huge. We can both sleep in it. I need my sleep, and I don't want anyone suspecting that we're not sleeping together. And, in case you're worried, I'm perfectly capable of sharing a bed without ravishing the other occupant.'

Hannah swung away as Luca dropped his trousers to change into his pyjamas. 'I'm not afraid of that,' she said, staring hard at the curtains drawn against the French windows. She could hear the whisper of fabric over Luca's legs, imagined his powerful thighs, muscles flexing…

Stop. Hannah pressed one hand to her flaming cheek. She really had to get a grip on her imagination. *And* her hormones.

'I'm dressed,' he said mildly. 'You can turn around.'

Taking a deep breath, Hannah did so. And dropped her gaze to his bare chest, his perfectly sculpted pectoral muscles lightly dusted with dark hair. The pyjama bottoms were slung low on his hips, so she could see the taut muscles of his abdomen, tapering down to… Quickly she jerked her gaze back up.

'If you're not worried that I'm going to ravish you, what are you afraid of?' Luca asked.

Why did he have to sound so reasonable? And make her feel so ridiculous? 'It just doesn't seem appropriate,' Hannah muttered.

'Hannah, we passed "appropriate" a while ago.' He took a step towards her, his hands outstretched. 'Look, you were magnificent back there. The whole thing about the Eiffel tower and the ring? I was practically believing it myself. And you seemed like you were having fun.' Hannah looked away, biting her lip. 'Well?' Luca pressed. 'Were you?'

'Sort of,' she admitted. What woman wouldn't like to step into a fairy tale for an evening, even if it was fake?

'So maybe you should let go of what's appropriate in this situation,' Luca suggested, his voice dropping to a beguiling murmur, standing only a step away from her.

She had the insane urge to reach out and *stroke* his chest.

'Let yourself enter into the spirit of the thing,' Luca continued, his voice all honeyed persuasion. 'Like you did tonight.'

'And share your bed.'

'In the literal sense only.'

'Oh, you know I didn't mean *that*,' Hannah protested, her face flaming once more. She shook her head. 'Honestly, you're incorrigible.'

'You've only just realised that?' He turned to the huge bed and plucked the chocolate from the pillow. 'So what are you waiting for?' he asked as he unwrapped the chocolate and popped it into his mouth. 'Come to bed.'

CHAPTER SIX

LUCA LAY IN BED, his arms braced behind his head, as he waited for Hannah to emerge from the bathroom. She'd been in there for quite a while, no doubt summoning her nerve to come out.

He didn't feel bad about sharing the bed with her. He'd even suggested, before she'd huffed into the bathroom clutching her pyjamas, that she was free to construct a barrier of pillows between them if she really did fear for her virtue.

She'd rolled her eyes. 'I can handle it,' she'd retorted, which amused him because she'd been the one to get all worked up about the issue in the first place.

She'd been incredible tonight, though. Sparkling and funny and charming, and he'd seen how Andrew Tyson had come under her spell. *He* almost had. Luca had found his gaze continually moving towards her, ensnared by her tinkling laugh, her teasing smile, the way the light caught the honeyed highlights in her hair.

Several times he'd leaned forward to try to catch what she was saying, needing to know and not because of the pretence. Because he really wanted to hear.

Then he'd reminded himself that she was playing a part and so was he, and Andrew Tyson was falling for it. That was all that mattered. He had no sympathy for the man, no pity whatsoever. Watching Tyson, Luca had barely been able to sit across from him and keep a smile on his face. Hannah had at least provided a distraction from the rage that simmered beneath the surface, threatening to bubble over.

The door to the bathroom opened and Hannah stepped out. Her hair was loose about her face and she wore...

'What the hell is that?'

Hannah glanced down at her roomy, faded T-shirt and shapeless boxer shorts. 'My pyjamas.'

'Didn't you get pyjamas at the boutique?'

'If you mean the scrap of lace that barely passes for a negligee, then yes. But I am not wearing that.' She glowered at him, a flush firing her face. 'There are limits, Luca.'

'You can't wear those. The staff come in to serve us breakfast in bed in the morning.'

Hannah didn't look at him as she crossed the room and climbed into bed, dragging the duvet up to her chin. 'So?'

'So,' Luca answered, 'I want them thinking that we spent the night ravishing each other as any newly engaged couple on holiday would.'

The minute he said the words images emblazoned themselves on his brain. Heat flared inside him. And he felt Hannah stiffen next to him.

'And they won't think of that if I'm dressed like this?' Hannah said after a moment. Her voice sounded suffocated. 'Too bad.'

She turned away from him, her body radiating tension. Luca sighed and snapped off the lights. He'd pushed it far enough, he supposed, although in truth he wanted to see Hannah in a sexy nightgown for his own sake, never mind the staff who would come in the next morning.

'You could have warned me about your friend,' Hannah said after a tense silence when Luca had been willing the desire coursing through his body to fade.

'My friend?' he asked, nonplussed.

'Daniela. She obviously knows you.'

'We've met.'

'You mean you've slept with her.'

Luca was silent, considering the assumption. He hadn't slept with Daniela, although the Russian model had made it clear she'd wanted to. And considering what he was asking Hannah to do, he supposed she deserved to know the truth. 'We went on a date,' he said. 'About a year ago. But nothing happened.'

'I suppose she wished something did.' Her voice was slightly muffled.

'Maybe,' Luca allowed.

'Judging by the burning looks she was giving you over dinner, I'd say definitely. And she wasn't impressed with me either. Not like that's too surprising, though.'

Hannah's words ended on a sigh and surprise flickered through him. 'Why do you say that?' he asked quietly.

Hannah didn't answer for a moment. In the darkness he couldn't see her features, only the taut shape of her body under the duvet. He heard the soft draw of her breath and it felt weirdly intimate. He realised he'd never actually slept in the same bed with a woman before. His assignations—he couldn't even call them relationships—had always ended with a definitive post-coital farewell.

'Well,' Hannah said at last, 'it's obvious, isn't it? A Plain Jane PA is hardly your type.'

'You're not a Plain Jane, Hannah.'

She laughed, a snort of genuine amusement that made him smile. 'Come on, Luca. Your normal type is supermodels and socialites, right? I'm neither.'

'That doesn't mean you're plain.'

'I'm not glamorous or gorgeous,' she returned. 'I don't

mind.' She shifted where she lay, so he felt the mattress dip beneath them. 'Why do you date socialites and super-models? I mean, why not a normal woman?'

'Well.' Luca cleared his throat, caught between amusement and a surprising embarrassment. 'I'm not really interested in their personalities.'

Hannah was silent for a moment. 'Well, that's blunt,' she said at last.

'I try to be honest.'

'Except when you're duping a houseful of people into believing you're about to be married.' She rolled over so she was turned towards him, although Luca couldn't actually see her face in the darkness. He had the alarming impulse to reach out to her, curve a hand around her neck and draw her closer. Kiss those lush lips he'd found himself sneaking looks at all evening. 'Why do you go for shallow?' she asked. 'Why is it just sex for you? Because that's what you're saying, isn't it?'

Luca was silent for a long moment, struggling to form an answer that was honest without being too revealing. 'Because it isn't worth it,' he finally said. 'To have more.'

He waited for Hannah's response, his body tensing against the possible onslaught of questions. Her voice came out in a soft, sorrowful sigh.

'Maybe it isn't,' she agreed quietly.

Luca waited for her to say more but she didn't. He closed his eyes, telling himself it was better that way, because he didn't want to explain his answer even if part of him wanted to know why Hannah agreed with him.

With his eyes closed, his other senses were heightened, so he could breathe in her light floral scent, feel the warmth of her body so close to his, hear the gentle draw and sigh of her breathing.

Desire flared through him again and more intensely this time, and ruefully Luca acknowledged that he might be the one in need of a pillow barrier. He rolled onto his other side, away from Hannah, and tried to will himself to sleep.

If this were a romcom, Hannah thought wryly, she and Luca would fall asleep and then somehow, in the night, they would wake tangled up in each other's arms. They'd gaze into each other's eyes, still caught in the throes of sleep, and then Luca would brush a kiss across her lips, slide his hand down her body, everything fogged with sleep...

Hannah realised her rueful imagination was fast turning into fantasy, and heat flooded her belly at just the thought of Luca looking at her that way. Touching her that way.

She squeezed her eyes shut, trying to banish the images. Maybe her mother was right, and she needed to start dating again. Diane was always worried that Hannah worked too much, that she didn't have a social life of her own. Hannah replied that she didn't have the time for a social life, but the truth was relationships were too much risk. Maybe that was something she and Luca had in common.

She sighed, the sound loud in the stillness of the room.

'Problem?' Luca asked, his voice sounding strained.

'This is a bit awkward,' Hannah said into the darkness.

'Just go to sleep, Hannah.' Luca sounded annoyed now, and, chastised, Hannah rolled away from him. She could do this. She was exhausted, for heaven's sake. She needed her sleep. Yet all she could think about, all she could focus on, was Luca's body a few feet from hers. Maybe only a foot. And his chest was bare. She imagined resting her cheek against it, her arms around his waist, their legs tangled together.

She stifled a groan. It was going to be a very long night.

Hannah woke to a light knock on the door and she blinked blearily as she raised her head from the pillow.

'Just a moment,' Luca called, and then his arm snaked out, hooking around her waist, and drawing her towards the hard wall of the chest. The feel of his body coming into full, intimate contact with hers stole the breath from her lungs and she froze in shock. Then she felt his obvious arousal nudging her thighs and she gasped aloud.

'It's morning,' Luca muttered. 'That's all it is.'

All right, fine. She was a grown-up; she understood basic biological functions. But *honestly*. This was way, way past the call of duty. And yet it felt so very nice.

As the door opened, Hannah adjusted to the feel of Luca's body against her own. This was what she had fantasised about last night, and the reality felt even better than she had imagined. His chest was warm and solid and the smell of him was intoxicating, overwhelming. The press of his hand on her lower back made her rock helplessly into his hips, his erection settling between her thighs, making heat flare sharply inside her. Luca's breath hissed between his teeth as his body instinctively pushed back before he stilled.

'Hannah.'

Mortified, she tried to move away, but Luca's arms were like steel bands around her. 'Stay still,' he commanded in a low voice that was as hard as iron.

Two staff members wheeled in a cart laden with two breakfast trays, and Luca eased up in bed, taking Hannah with him so they were both reclining against the pillows, the duvet pulled demurely across their laps. Hannah wished, bizarrely perhaps, that she were wearing the gorgeous lace negligee, revealing as it was. She felt ridiculous in her oversized T-shirt that had faded to an unappealing grey colour from too many washes. And her hair... She lifted her hands to the tangle around her face and Luca smiled at her, tucking a stray strand behind her ear.

'Nothing like a little bedhead in the morning,' he said

with a teasing smile, and Hannah blinked, discomfited, until she realised he was putting on a show for the staff.

'I'm glad you love me no matter what I look like,' she replied sweetly. 'Or what I wear.'

The staff handed them their trays and with murmured thanks Hannah sat up straighter, taking in the freshly squeezed orange juice, the carafe of coffee, toast and fresh fruit and the most delicious-looking omelette. She could definitely get used to this.

The members of staff left quietly and Hannah reached for a piece of toast. She was not going to look at Luca, and remember how it had felt to have his arms around her, to arch into him... *What* had possessed her to do that?

'So what's the plan for today?' she asked, deciding that ignoring that whole brief interlude was the best way to go. Luca, it seemed, did not agree.

'Just to be clear,' he said flatly, 'we're going to keep this as play-acting, and nothing more.'

Hannah eyed him resentfully, trying to keep the hot tide of embarrassment at bay. 'You're the one who insisted we share a bed.'

'You're the one who rocked against me like a wanton,' Luca snapped.

'A wanton?' Hannah pushed aside the breakfast tray, her appetite having vanished, and scrambled out of the bed. 'What century do you live in?'

'I mean it, Hannah—'

'Trust me, I take the warning. And just like you, Luca Moretti, I am perfectly able to sleep in the same bed as someone without ravishing them!' Caught between fury, mortification, and tears, she grabbed her clothes and slammed into the bathroom.

Luca sighed and closed his eyes as the slam of the bathroom door echoed through the room. He'd handled that about as badly as possible. Calling Hannah Stewart a wanton was like calling Andrew Tyson a saint. Absurd. Laughable, except there was nothing remotely funny about either situation.

He opened his eyes and raked a hand through his hair, wondering how best to do damage control. Honesty? The truth was, he'd been far more aroused and tempted by Hannah's slender body than he'd any right to be. When she'd rocked into him he'd felt his precious control starting to disintegrate, and it had taken its last shreds to keep from shouting at the staff to leave them alone so he could bury himself deep in her willing body. *He* was the wanton, not Hannah.

He had no idea why his pretty enough PA affected him this way; perhaps it was simply the strangeness of the situation, or that his senses and emotions felt raw from facing Tyson again after so many years. He couldn't deny it, though; he'd been fighting an unreasonable and most inconvenient attraction to her since this whole charade had begun.

He drank his coffee, musing on the unwelcome distraction of his surprisingly delectable PA. He needed to focus on the real reason he'd come to Santa Nicola. He couldn't let anything distract him from his purpose. Having Hannah upset or embarrassed was just as difficult and distracting as having them both fighting—and flirting with—a sexual attraction he didn't think either of them had expected. It was time to nip this in the bud.

Fifteen minutes later Hannah emerged from the bathroom, her hair damp, her face composed. She wore a pretty pink linen sundress that skimmed her breasts and hugged her slim waist. She didn't so much as look at Luca.

'I'm sorry,' Luca said as he pushed his breakfast tray away. 'I shouldn't have said that.'

'You do have a tendency towards bluntness,' Hannah

replied as she struggled to put on her pearl necklace. This time Luca didn't offer to help.

'I wasn't being blunt,' he said. 'I was dissembling.'

She glanced at him and then quickly away again. 'How so?'

'I'm attracted to you,' he stated flatly. 'To my own surprise.'

'I thought it was just the morning,' she returned tartly, but he could see her cheeks pinken.

'It was more than the morning,' Luca admitted gruffly. 'I was angry at myself, and my body's reaction, rather than at you.'

'It must be terribly irritating to be attracted to someone like me,' Hannah agreed. Luca realised that underneath her embarrassment, she was blisteringly angry. 'Someone with feelings and a normal bra size.'

'Hannah,' he warned through gritted teeth. The last thing he needed this morning was a big, messy row with the woman who was supposed to be his compliant, biddable faux fiancée.

'*Luca,*' Hannah returned mockingly. She whirled around, her colour high, her golden-brown eyes blazing. 'How about you listen to me for a change? I didn't ask to come to this island. I didn't ask to pretend to be your fiancée. I didn't ask to share your bed! In fact, at every step, I've asked for the opposite. I've wanted more space, not less. And then you have the audacity, the wretched nerve, to call me a wanton!'

'I told you why—'

'And you think that makes it better? You said it like you couldn't even understand why you were attracted to someone like me. *To my surprise.* Well, thanks for that, Luca. Thanks very much.' She turned away again, her hands shaking as she reached for her pearl earrings.

All right, he could see how what he'd said might have sounded insulting, but... 'I didn't mean it that way.'

'Actually, I think you did. But never mind. I don't really care.' She put her earrings in, shaking her hair over her shoulders. 'Let's just get this day over with, shall we?'

Luca hesitated, wanting to defuse her anger, but sensing that she wasn't in the mood to be placated. Wordlessly he headed into the bathroom to shower.

As soon as the door closed Hannah released a shaky breath and slumped onto the divan. She couldn't take much more of this ping-ponging from one emotion to the next, from overwhelming desire to incredible rage. *What was happening to her?*

She knew the answer to that one. Luca Moretti was. She took a steadying breath, and then, taking advantage of Luca being in the shower, reached for her phone.

Diane answered on the first ring. 'Hey, Mum,' Hannah said, her voice sounding weary and just a little bit wobbly. 'It's me.'

'Hannah. Are you all right?'

'Why— Do I sound that bad?' She tried for a laugh, pressing a hand to her forehead. It didn't help her seesawing emotions that she'd got very little sleep last night.

'You sound tired,' Diane admitted cautiously. 'Is everything okay?'

'Fine. Just an intense work weekend.' Work being the word she could drop from that sentence. 'Is Jamie awake yet?'

'Yes, he's just having his breakfast. I'll put him on for you.'

Hannah closed her eyes, listening to the familiar sound of her mother's murmur, her son's excited answer. The squeak of a chair, and then the sound of him scrabbling for the phone.

'Mummy?'

A tidal wave of homesickness crashed over her, threatening to pull her under. 'Hello, sweetheart. I miss you.'

'I miss you, too. Nana says you're on an island.'

'Yes, it's very pretty. I'll try to bring you back a present. Maybe some shells or rocks for your collection?'

'Ooh, yes,' Jamie crowed. 'Can you bring back a big one? A conch?'

'I don't know about that,' Hannah said with a little laugh. 'I think they might be protected. But I'll bring you back something, Jamie, I promise. Be good for Nana now.'

'I will.'

'He always is,' Diane assured her when Hannah had said goodbye to her son. 'Don't work too hard.'

'I always work hard,' Hannah answered, and heard how grim she sounded. Maybe she did work too hard. Maybe the sacrifices weren't worth it, no matter what she believed about being financially independent and free. 'I love you, Mum,' she said.

'Hannah, are you sure you're all right...?'

'I'm fine,' Hannah said, and then, hearing the bathroom door open, she quickly said goodbye and disconnected the call.

She was just putting the phone away when Luca emerged from the bathroom, freshly shaven, his hair damp, a towel slung low on his hips. 'Were you on the phone?'

Hannah turned away from the alluring sight of his nearly naked body. 'Is that a crime?'

Luca sighed. 'No, of course not. I just wondered.'

'Then the answer is yes, I was.'

'Hannah, look, I said I was sorry.'

'In about the worst way possible.'

'Can we please call a truce?'

Hannah took a deep breath, knowing she was being childish and emotional. She was a professional, for heaven's sake, and Luca was her boss. She could handle this. 'I'm sorry,' she said evenly. 'Let's forget it. Clean slate today, all right?' She turned to him with a bright, determined smile just as Luca dropped his towel.

CHAPTER SEVEN

HANNAH WHIRLED AWAY from the sight of Luca's naked body, one hand clapped to her eyes.

She let out a trembling laugh. 'You are so not making this easier.'

'I'm sorry. I don't like dressing in the bathroom.'

'That message has been received, trust me.'

'I'm dressed now,' Luca told her dryly, and Hannah lowered her hand.

'Wearing a pair of boxer briefs does not, in my opinion, constitute dressed.'

'The important bits are covered,' he answered and reached for a shirt.

'I don't understand you,' Hannah said slowly. 'You flirt and drop your clothes and act like it's ridiculous for me to be outraged, and then you get angry with me and basically accuse me of being a slut for responding when you're practically naked next to me.' She tried for a wry smile but felt too confused and weary to manage it. 'I thought it was women who usually sent mixed messages.'

Luca stilled, his hands on the buttons of his shirt, his gaze lowered. 'This is a new situation for me,' he admitted gruffly. 'And a tense one. I know I'm acting out of character.'

'Considering you're acting as my fiancé, you certainly

are.' She sighed and reached for the strappy sandals that went with her sundress. 'So what is the schedule for today, anyway?'

'You spend the day with the other wives, touring the island, and I give my presentation.'

'Wow, that's not sexist or anything.'

Luca arched an eyebrow and resumed buttoning his shirt. 'You're not here as my PA.'

'Well I know. So you spend your day in the boardroom while I fend off Daniela's digs?'

'She's harmless. I barely know her.'

'She might disagree.' Hannah hesitated, noticing the lines of strain from Luca's nose to mouth, the fatigue she could see in his eyes and the weary set of his shoulders. She felt a surprising dart of sympathy and even compassion for him. For whatever reason, this weekend was difficult for him. 'So what is your presentation about?'

He stilled for a second and then reached for a pair of charcoal-grey trousers. 'How I'm going to rehabilitate the Tyson brand.'

'The resorts did look a bit shabby on the website.'

'They're tired,' Luca affirmed with a terse nod. 'They haven't been updated in over twenty years.'

'Why is Tyson selling them, anyway? Don't his children want to take over his business?'

A grim smile curved Luca's mouth. 'No, they're not interested.'

'That's sad, considering what a family man he is.'

'Heartbreaking,' Luca agreed dryly. He selected a cobalt-blue tie and began to knot it. There was, Hannah reflected, something quite sexy about a man putting on a tie, long, lean fingers manipulating the bright silk. Especially a man who looked like Luca.

'So what are your plans for the resorts?' she asked as she forced her gaze away from the mesmerising sight of

Luca getting dressed. 'How are you going to rehabilitate them? I never printed any documents out about it.'

'No, I did it myself.' He slid her a quick smile. 'I am capable of working a printer, despite how often I ask you to do it.'

'May I see them?' Hannah asked, and surprise flashed across Luca's face. 'I'm curious.'

His fingers slowed as he finished knotting his tie, his forehead furrowed. 'All right,' he said at last, and he went to his briefcase and took out a manila folder of documents.

Hannah joined him on the divan, their thighs nudging, while Luca opened the folder and took out the presentation he'd put together. The colourful image on the front page was an architect's visualisation of what the resort could look like, with villas in different pastel colours, cascading pools with water slides and whirlpools, and lots of colourful flowers and shrubbery. It looked inviting and fresh and friendly.

Hannah reached over to turn a page, scanning the paragraphs that described Luca's plans in detail. She knew Luca's real-estate projects always focused on sustainable energy and recyclable materials, and this was no different. But this proposal went a step further, and sought to incorporate the local culture and economy of each of the islands where there was a Tyson resort, instead of making it an exclusive enclave behind high stone walls, separate from the local residents.

She saw how family-friendly it was too, with hotel rooms and changing areas to accommodate both children and adults. Jamie would love the cascading pools and water slides outlined in one of the resorts' plans. She glanced up at Luca, who was frowning down at the images.

'For someone who doesn't have children, this is very astute.'

He shrugged one powerful shoulder. 'I did the research.'

'I like it,' she said and handed the folder back to him. 'I really like it.' Luca might have done the research, but there had been a passion and commitment to his ideas that spoke of more than just having a finger on the marketing pulse. It surprised and touched her, and it felt as if his plans for the resort had revealed something about him, something he didn't even seem to realise. He *cared*.

The last of her reservation about performing in this fake engagement fell away. She was here, and she'd agreed to help Luca. She was going to do the job properly, and maybe she'd even have fun while she was at it.

'Okay,' she said as she stood up with a bright smile. 'It's time to face the fearsome Daniela.'

A smile tugged at Luca's mouth. 'She's not that bad.'

'Why didn't it work out between you two, anyway?' Hannah asked lightly, ignoring the sting of jealousy her question caused.

'She was too clingy.'

'What, she wanted to stay the night?' Hannah quipped.

'I told you. It never got that far. Anyway, last night you agreed with me that relationships weren't worth it,' Luca reminded her.

Hannah stilled. How had they got onto this? 'I said "maybe",' she corrected him. 'The verdict is still out.'

'But you're not in a relationship?' Luca pressed, his gaze narrowed.

Hannah cocked her head. 'Is that really any of your business?'

Luca's gaze flicked to the bed, reminding him all too well of what had just happened there. 'Considering the nature of this weekend,' he answered, 'yes.'

'Fine. No, I'm not.' And hadn't been in anything close to one for over five years. 'Work keeps me busy,' she added before turning away.

They left the bedroom to join the other guests for coffee and pastries in the spacious front hall. A marble table held a huge centrepiece of lilies, and Hannah saw Luca's mouth compress as he turned away from the ostentatious display. She knew he disliked lilies, but now she wondered at the nature of that particular quirk. She was curious about Luca in a lot of new and unsettling ways, thanks to the nature of this weekend.

After about half an hour of chit-chat, Andrew Tyson called the men away to his private office for a day of presentations. Meanwhile one of his staff ushered the three women towards a waiting car, where they would be given a tour of Santa Nicola.

Hannah was looking forward to seeing some of the island, but she didn't relish Daniela's hostile company. Fortunately the third woman of their trio, Rose, plopped herself next to Hannah and chatted to her about her three young children for the drive into the island's one town, Petra. Daniela sat in the back, sulking and staring out of the window.

Hannah spent a surprisingly enjoyable morning, strolling through Petra's cobbled streets, admiring the white-washed buildings with their colourfully painted shutters and terracotta roof tiles.

At an open-air market she bought a wooden toy boat with a sail made of shells for Jamie, smiling to think of him receiving the present. It was even better than a conch shell.

'And who is that for?' Daniela asked, coming up next to her at the stall of toys in the market square. Hannah accepted the paper-wrapped boat from the vendor with a smile of thanks. She'd managed to avoid Daniela for most of the day, but she supposed a confrontation was inevitable. Daniela dripped with the venom of a woman scorned.

'It's a boat,' she said pleasantly. 'For my nephew.' She didn't like lying about her son, but Daniela was the last person she'd trust with any confidence, and her having a child Luca didn't know about would shatter any illusions that their engagement was real.

Daniela raised perfectly plucked eyebrows. 'Have you met Luca's parents yet?' she asked, and Hannah tensed.

The question might seem innocent enough, but she knew Daniela well enough to know it was loaded. She tucked the present for Jamie in the straw bag she'd brought, stalling for time. Luca had told her to stick as close to the truth as she could, so she supposed that was what she'd have to do.

'No, I haven't,' she said as she looked into Daniela's pinched face, trying for a pleasant tone and smile. 'Not yet.'

'Not yet?' Daniela repeated, a sneer entering her voice and twisting her pretty features. 'Then you don't know he's an orphan? His parents died when he was young.' She smirked in triumph and Hannah tried to school her features into an acceptably bland expression although inwardly she cursed herself. She knew Daniela had been setting her up somehow. She'd seemed to suspect her from the start. *Because you're not the kind of woman Luca Moretti is normally seen with. Certainly not the kind of woman he'd fall in love with.*

'We had a whirlwind courtship,' she dismissed as best she could. 'We're still learning all sorts of things about each other.'

'We went on one date and he told me,' Daniela returned.

'One date?' Hannah couldn't keep from matching the woman's cattiness. 'Then perhaps it's time you got over him.'

The conversation dogged her for the rest of the day, and she breathed a sigh of relief when they headed back to the resort. Luca wasn't in the bedroom when she arrived, and she put her purchases away before running a deep bubble bath. Before dropping them off, the member of staff had informed the three women of the evening's itinerary: cocktails on the terrace with Tyson and his family, followed by a formal dinner and dancing.

Hours and hours of pretending, a prospect that made Hannah feel both tense and exhausted, even as she tingled with anticipation at spending an evening with Luca. Would he dance with her? The thought of swaying silently with him, breathing in his heat and scent, his arms strong about her, was enough to make her stomach flip-flop.

Which was *fine*, Hannah assured herself. So she was attracted to Luca. What woman wouldn't be? Why shouldn't she enjoy dancing with him? It wasn't as if it were going anywhere. She wasn't looking for a relationship or even a one-night stand. Both were too risky. All she wanted was a few moments of enjoyment and pleasure.

Except Luca had admitted he was attracted to her. Reluctantly, yes, and to his surprise, but *still*. Over the course of the day she'd got over the sting of his obvious bemusement at being attracted to her, and accepted the compliment that it was.

The door to the bedroom opened just as Hannah was stepping out of the bathroom, swathed in an enormous terrycloth bathrobe.

'How did it go?' she asked and then watched in dismay as Luca jerked his tie from his collar and strode over to the minibar, pouring himself two fingers' worth of whisky and downing it in one hard gulp.

'Fine.'

Hannah knotted the sash on her robe and pulled her damp hair out from under its thick collar. 'You're not acting like it's fine,' she observed cautiously.

'I said it was fine, it's fine,' Luca snapped, and poured another drink.

Hannah watched him, wondering what demon was riding his back. Because that was what Luca looked like: a man who was haunted. Tormented. And she didn't understand why.

'Daniela asked me about your parents,' she said, knowing she needed to tell him what had happened that afternoon. Luca stiffened, his glass halfway raised to his lips.

'Why would she do that?'

'Because she was trying to trip me up. I think she suspects something.'

'Daniela?' He shook his head, the movement curtly dismissive. 'I barely know the woman. I haven't seen her in over a year. She's been married to James Garrison for nearly six months.'

'Well, I think she still holds a candle for you. And she asked me about your parents and I told her I hadn't met them. Yet.' She waited, but Luca's face was blank.

'And?' he said after a pause.

'And she informed you were an orphan. I didn't know that, Luca, and clearly I should have. *She* knew it.'

Hannah couldn't tell anything from his expression; his eyes looked pitilessly blank. 'I'm sorry,' she said inadequately. 'For your loss.'

'It was a long time ago.'

'Still, it's a big thing.' She knew that all too well. 'And now Daniela knows I didn't know it.'

Luca pressed his lips together and tossed his empty glass on top of the bar, where it clattered and then rolled onto its side. 'There's nothing we can do about it now.'

'All right.' Hannah didn't know how to handle him in this mood; his usual energy had been transformed into a disturbing restlessness, a latent anger. 'I just thought you should know.'

'Fine. I know.'

Stung, Hannah did not reply. The tentative enjoyment she'd been nurturing for this evening was draining away like her cold bathwater. If Luca stayed in this foul mood, the night was going to be interminable.

'I'll go get ready," she said stiffly, and went to gather her clothes. She was definitely changing in the bathroom.

Luca stared at the closed bathroom door and swore under his breath. The afternoon with Tyson had been nearly unbearable, the latent fury he'd felt for so long bubbling far too close to the surface, threatening to spill over. Maintaining a professional manner had been the acting job of the century; all he'd wanted to do was haul Tyson out of his chair by his lapels and slap the smug smile off his face.

He hadn't expected to be this angry, this raw. He'd thought he'd mastered his emotions far better than that, and it only exacerbated his fury to know that he hadn't. But he shouldn't have taken it out on Hannah.

As for Daniela's suspicions... Raking a hand through his hair, Luca swore again. If his fake engagement was exposed, the humiliation he'd face in front of the man who had flayed him once already would be unendurable. He could not even contemplate it.

Luca's mouth twisted grimly as he considered the options. If Daniela or anyone suspected something, then he and Hannah would have to make doubly sure that they were convincing. Striding towards the wardrobe, he reached for his tux.

He was just straightening his bow tie when Hannah emerged from the bathroom, her chin held high, her eyes veiled. Luca's gaze dropped to her dress and his throat went dry. It was the one she'd modelled at the boutique, ice-blue with a plunging neckline only partially obscured by the gauzy overlay. She'd styled her hair in an elegant chignon, exposing the delicate, swanlike curve of her neck.

'It's all right, isn't it?' Hannah asked, nervousness making her voice wobble a bit.

'Yes...' Luca's voice came out gruff and hoarse.

Hannah tugged at the material self-consciously. 'It's just you're looking at me strangely.'

'It's only...' He cleared his throat. 'You look beautiful, Hannah.'

Colour flared in her face. 'So why are you glaring, then?' She turned away, fidgeting with her earrings, her necklace, clearly uncomfortable in the sexy, diaphanous gown.

'Hannah.' Luca crossed the room to put a hand on her shoulder, her skin cool and soft beneath his palm. 'I'm sorry I've been in such a foul mood. It's not fair to you.' He paused and then admitted with more honesty than he'd been planning to give, 'Nothing about this weekend has been fair to you.'

Hannah bowed her head, a tendril of soft brown hair falling against her cheek, making Luca want to tuck it behind her ear, trail his fingers along her skin. 'I was actually looking forward to this evening, you know,' she admitted. 'Until...'

'Until I returned to our room?' Luca finished with a wry wince, and then sighed. 'I am sorry. You don't deserve to bear the brunt of my bad mood.'

'So many apologies.' She turned around, a teasing smile curving her lips. 'I should record this conversation, otherwise I might never believe it actually happened.'

'I'll deny it, of course,' he teased back. He'd dropped his hand from her shoulder when she'd turned around but he itched to touch her again. Her waist looked so tiny he thought he could span it with his hands. The gauzy overlay of the dress made him want to peel it away and touch the pale, creamy flesh beneath. He remembered untying the halter top of the dress back when she'd first tried it on and he wanted to do it again. He wanted her...and he could tell she wanted him.

He saw it in the way she swallowed convulsively, her eyes huge and dark in her pale face. She bit her lip and Luca nearly groaned aloud. The attraction he felt for his PA was both overwhelming and inconvenient, but in that moment he couldn't even think about the consequences, the difficulties, the dangers. He just wanted to touch her.

And so he did.

He reached out with one finger and stroked her cheek; her skin was just as soft as he'd imagined, silky and cool. She shuddered under his touch, her whole body quivering in response, and that made Luca ache all the more.

'Hannah…' he began, although he didn't even know what he would say. How much he would admit.

Hannah didn't let him finish. She took a halting step away, nearly tripping on the trailing hem of her gown. 'It's—it's getting late,' she stammered. 'We should go.'

And Luca told himself he felt relieved and not crushingly disappointed that he'd had such a narrow escape.

CHAPTER EIGHT

HANNAH SIPPED THE frothy cocktail Andrew Tyson had insisted she try, an island speciality involving fruit and strong liquor, and tried to soothe the ferment inside her. Now more than ever she felt confused and disturbed, and, more alarmingly, *tempted* by Luca Moretti.

She couldn't understand how one moment he could be so aggravating and arrogant and the next so sweet and sincere. She'd gone from wanting to slug him to wanting to purr under that single, seductive stroke of his finger. The tiniest touch had created a blaze of want inside her that was still making her hot and bothered. She imagined what he could do with his whole hand, his whole body, and felt another sizzling dart of heat arrow through her.

She could not start thinking about Luca Moretti that way. All right, yes, his sex appeal had started affecting her ever since they'd left their normal employer–employee relationship behind at the office, but she hadn't taken it *seriously.* She hadn't actually entertained the possibility of something happening between them.

Now her mind skirted around that intriguing thought, flirted with the possibility of—what? A fling? A one-night stand? Hannah was sensible enough to know Luca Moretti wasn't interested in anything more, and she wasn't interested in any relationship, much less one with a man who had sworn off marriage and children, and was a notorious womaniser. But she wasn't the type to have casual sex; she never had before. And to contemplate it with her *boss*…

And yet desire was a powerful thing. The sight of him in his tuxedo was enough to make her head spin and her mouth dry. The crisp white shirt emphasised his bronzed skin, and the tuxedo jacket fit his broad shoulders and narrow hips perfectly. He was incredible, darkly magnificent, so next to him James Garrison looked like a weedy fop, Simon Tucker a corpulent would-be Santa Claus. Luca was literally head and shoulders above the other men, a gorgeous, arrogant Colossus who looked as if he could straddle the world. The only man who nearly matched his height was Andrew Tyson, and his shoulders were stooped with age, his face lined and eyes faded.

Luca had spent the first part of the evening by her side, charming and solicitous to everyone, clearly working the room. When Tyson had entered the opulent sitting room, Luca had slid an arm around Hannah's waist, practically gluing her to his side. The bump of his hip against hers was enough to make sensation sizzle through her. She could feel the heat of his thigh through the thin material of her dress, and her insides tightened to an exquisite, aching point of desire.

She'd never responded so physically, so overwhelmingly, to a man before. Not, Hannah acknowledged, that she had a lot of experience. Ben, Jamie's father, had been her only lover, and while she'd enjoyed being with him she hadn't felt this desperate, craving physical touch like water in a parched desert.

Sliding sideways glances at Luca, she felt an overwhelming urge to touch him, to feel the rough stubble on his jaw, to discover if his lips felt soft or hard against hers. To feel his body against hers as she had that morning, and rock against him again, and then deeper still.

Heat flashed through her at the thought and Luca must have felt it, must have sensed her response, because he gave her a single, burning look before turning back to address Simon Tucker.

He knew how he affected her, maybe even how much. The thought would have been mortifying except that she knew she affected him too. He'd told her he'd been attracted to her that morning, and surely she couldn't feel this kind of chemistry if it were merely one-sided.

So the question was, could she do anything about it? Did she dare? She wasn't looking for a relationship, wouldn't put herself or Jamie at risk of being hurt. She knew what happened when you loved people. You risked losing them. She'd lost too many times already to try again.

'Hannah?' Luca prompted, and she realised she had no idea what anyone had been saying for the last few minutes.

'Sorry?' She tried for a conciliatory yet loving smile. 'I'm afraid I was a million miles away.'

'No doubt planning your wedding,' Simon joked goodnaturedly. 'Have you set a date?'

'As soon as possible, as far as I'm concerned,' Luca answered swiftly, with a squeeze of Hannah's waist. 'But Hannah wants more of a do.'

Hannah lifted her shoulders in a helpless shrug. 'You only get married once.'

'Hopefully,' James joked, an edge to his voice that made a frozen silence descend on the little group for a few seconds.

'What's your secret to a happy marriage, then, James?' Simon asked, trying for jocular.

'A limit-free credit card and no questions asked,' James replied with a pointed look at his wife. Daniela pressed her lips together and said nothing.

Hardly a response of a family man, Hannah thought.

James Garrison was a slick study, and looked to share Luca's view on relationships.

'I'll take that on board,' Luca answered in a tone that suggested he would do no such thing.

'Falling for your PA isn't like you, is it, Luca?' James said, malice entering his ice-blue eyes. 'I thought you made sure never to mix business and pleasure.'

'As I said last night, this time it was impossible to resist.' He glanced down at Hannah, who tilted her head up to look at him so their mouths were only a few inches apart. She felt her insides shudder even though she knew Luca was only play-acting. That simmering heat in his eyes might not have been real, but the response Hannah's body gave certainly was. Her lips parted in helpless expectation, her whole being trained on Luca's sleepy, hooded gaze.

'Irresistible,' he murmured, and then closed those scant inches separating them.

The feel of his mouth on hers was a complete surprise and yet also a sigh of relief and wonder. *At last.* Her mouth opened underneath his and Hannah clutched at his lapels, barely aware of what she was doing. Luca's tongue swept into her mouth with sure possession, turning her insides weak and liquid. Her fingers tightened on his jacket.

'No doubt that you two are heading for the altar,' Simon joked, and Luca finally broke the kiss. Hannah sagged against him, her heart thudding, her mind spinning, her whole body feeling as if she'd been lit up inside like a firework.

'Like I said,' Luca said with a wry smile. 'Irresistible. I didn't stand a chance.'

And neither did she.

Her lips were still buzzing from his kiss when they headed out to the terrace where tables had been set up for dinner, laden with crystal and silver that glinted under the moonlight. Torches flickered, casting warm shadows across the terrace, and the sea was no more than a gleam of blackness in the distance, the tide a gentle shooshing sound as the waves lapped the shore.

They were just about to take their seats when Andrew Tyson turned expectantly to the open French windows. 'Ah,' he said, his voice filled with pleasure. 'My family has finally arrived from New York. Please let me introduce you all to my wife and children.'

Luca froze before slowly turning to face the French windows, where Andrew Tyson's wife, Mirabella, and their two children stood, framed by the gauzy white curtains.

He'd been waiting for this moment, both expecting and bracing himself for it, and yet now that it was finally here he found every thought had emptied from his head, the smile wiped from his face. Even the electric, intoxicating buzz of Hannah's kiss was forgotten in that horrendous, endless moment.

Distantly, as if he were down a long tunnel, he heard people exchanging pleasantries. Words were said, but it was as if everyone had started speaking another language. Tyson's two children, Stephen and Laura, came forward, smiling and shaking hands. Stephen had the dark hair of his mother and Tyson's brown eyes. Laura was the opposite, with her father's sandy hair and her mother's blue eyes. They were both relaxed, friendly, completely in their element, and in a few seconds he was going to have to shake their hands. Say hello. Act normal.

He acknowledged this even as he didn't move. Had no idea what the expression on his face was. Felt nothing but the relentless, painful thud of his heart. He'd been waiting for this moment for years, decades, and yet he hadn't been prepared for it, not remotely.

Then he felt a soft, slender hand slide into his, fingers squeezing tightly, imbuing warmth and strength. He glanced down at Hannah's face, the worry and concern in her eyes, the compassion in her smile, and he felt as if he'd fallen out of that tunnel with a thud, as if he'd rejoined reality, and was strong enough to deal with it—thanks to the woman next to him.

'Stephen. Laura.' His voice came out on a croak that he quickly covered, extending his hand for them both to shake. 'Luca Moretti and my fiancée, Hannah Stewart.'

Hannah stepped forward to greet them both and Luca forced himself to breathe normally, to school the expression on his face into one of friendly interest. To will his heart rate to slow.

He felt the delayed reaction of shock kick in, an icy wave that swept over him and left his knees weak, his whole body near to trembling. He had to get out of there.

'If you'll excuse me,' he murmured, and went in search of the bathroom.

Once inside, safely away from all the prying eyes, he splashed his face with cold water and then stared hard into the mirror, willing himself to get a grip. He'd climbed his way out of appalling poverty, negotiated dozens of million-and billion-dollar deals, was a man of power and authority and wealth. He'd conquered all these old fears and insecurities. He didn't need to feel this way now. He *wouldn't*.

Except he did.

He released a shuddering breath and rubbed a hand over his face. He needed to get back to the dinner. James Garrison was chomping at the bit to take this deal out from under him, simply out of spite. Garrison had always been jealous of Luca's success, of the huge deals he brokered that James hadn't a chance in hell of managing. Luca knew he couldn't afford to throw himself a damned pity party in the bathroom.

Taking a deep breath, he straightened his tux and then

opened the door to the hall, stopping short when he saw Hannah there waiting for him.

'What are you—?'

'I was worried about you.' She put a hand on his sleeve, and he glanced down at her fingers, long and slender, the nails buffed and glistening with clear varnish. Every part of her was simple and yet so elegant. 'Luca, what's going on? Can't you tell me?'

'It's nothing.'

'That's not true.' Concern threaded her voice. 'Please, Luca. Do you know how hard it is to act the part when I have no idea what you're going through?'

'You're doing fine, Hannah.' He shrugged off her hand. 'You certainly acted the part when I kissed you.'

Colour surged into her face but her gaze was steady, her voice calm. 'Don't take out your frustrations on me, Luca. All I'm asking for is the truth.'

He raked a hand through his hair, knowing she had a right to understand at least a little of what was going on. 'Tyson and I have a history,' he said in a low voice. 'Not a pleasant one. I didn't expect it, but seeing him again brings it all back.'

'And his family?' Hannah asked. Luca tensed.

'What about his family?'

'You obviously didn't like their arrival. You went white—'

'I did not,' he denied shortly, even though it was point-less. Hannah was gazing at him in a cringing mixture of pity and disbelief.

'Luca—'

'We need to get back in there.' He cut her off, and then reached for her hand. Tonight he'd show Andrew Tyson and his damned family just how much he had, how happy he was.

By the time they arrived back on the terrace, everyone

was seated and the first course had been served. Luca and Hannah took their places with murmured apologies. Luca saw he was seated next to Stephen Tyson, and he braced himself to talk to the man.

Stephen, he knew, had chosen not to take on the family's business but was a doctor in New York instead. Now he gave Luca a friendly smile.

'I'm sorry, but have we met before?'

A hollow laugh echoed through the emptiness inside him and he swallowed it down. 'No, I'm quite sure we haven't.'

Luca could feel Hannah's concern, the tension tautening her slender body. It was strange how attuned they'd become to each other and their moods, but perhaps that was simply an effect of the parts they had to play.

'Really?' Stephen shrugged, still smiling. 'Strange, but you look familiar.'

'Perhaps you've seen his photograph in one of the industry magazines?' Hannah suggested with a smile of her own. 'Luca is quite famous in his own right.' She placed a hand over his, squeezing his fingers, and Luca felt his heart twist inside him. He'd never had someone fight his corner before, even in the smallest way. He'd always been alone, had gone through childhood with his fists up and his nose bloody. Seeing Tyson made him feel like that battered boy again, and yet having Hannah hold his hand reminded him that he wasn't.

'Of course you are,' Stephen acknowledged. 'I know you developed the cancer centre in Ohio. It was really a masterwork of art and functionality. Utterly brilliant.'

'Thank you,' Luca said gruffly. He hadn't expected Stephen Tyson to be so friendly and sincere. It made it hard to hate him.

Somehow he managed to get through three courses, making small talk, smiling when necessary. He'd brought

Hannah's hand underneath the table after the first course to rest on his thigh and he wrapped his fingers around hers, clinging to her, craving her warmth. She didn't let go.

As the coffee and petits fours were being served, Andrew Tyson rose to make a toast.

'It's such a pleasure to have three dedicated family men here,' he began with a genial smile for all of them. 'As someone who has always determined to put family first, it is of course important to me that the man who takes on Tyson Resorts share my values.' He paused, his smiling gaze moving to his wife and then to his children. 'While I am saddened that my own children have not chosen this task, I understand completely why they've decided to pursue their own dreams—as I of course wish them to. My children are my pride and my joy, the touchstone of my life, along with my wife. The happiness I've experienced with my family is what I wish for each of you, and for every family who visits a Tyson resort.'

Luca couldn't bear to hear any more. He shifted in his seat, and Hannah squeezed his hand in warning. He couldn't leave now, but he could at least tune out Tyson's words.

Finally Tyson raised his glass and everyone else did as well, murmuring 'Hear, hear...' dutifully. Luca drained his glass of wine and then pulled away from Hannah.

'Luca,' she began, but he just shook his head.

'Later,' he managed, and then strode down the terrace steps, out into the darkness.

Hannah dabbed her mouth with her napkin, trying to cover the worry that she was sure was visible on her face. What kind of terrible history could Luca possibly have with Andrew Tyson? She glanced at the man who was now chatting with Simon and Rose Tucker, and decided she would make her excuses as well. If Luca left without her, it might look as if they were having a lovers' tiff. If they both left, people might assume it was a romantic tryst instead.

She made her farewells to the Tysons, telling them that Luca had wanted to steal her away for a moonlit walk on the beach.

'Ah, young love,' Andrew answered with a genial smile. 'There's nothing like it.'

No indeed, Hannah thought grimly as she held handfuls of her dress to keep from tripping down the stone steps that led directly to the beach.

Away from the candlelit terrace, the beach was awash in darkness, the white sand lit only by a pale sickle of moon. Hannah couldn't see Luca anywhere. Impatiently she kicked off the silver stiletto heels that made walking in sand impossible, and gathered a big handful of gauzy dress around her knees so she could walk unimpeded. Then she set off in search of her erstwhile fiancé.

CHAPTER NINE

HANNAH FOUND LUCA about half a mile down the beach, away from the villa, with nothing but a few palm trees for company. He sat with his elbows resting on his knees, his head cradled in his hands. Hannah had never seen such an abject pose; every powerful line of Luca's body seemed to radiate despair.

She hesitated, not wanting to intrude on his moment of sorrowful solitude, but not wanting to leave him alone either. He looked too lonely.

'I'm not going to bite your head off,' Luca said, his voice low and so very weary. 'Although you have good reason to think I would.'

She came closer, her dress trailing on the sand that was cool and silky under her bare feet.

'I wasn't thinking that,' she said quietly, and came to sit beside him, drawing her knees up as his were. He didn't lift his head. She thought about asking him yet again what pain and secrets he was hiding, but she didn't think there was much point. Luca didn't want to tell her and, truthfully, she didn't blame him. She had pain and secrets of her own she didn't want spilling out. Still, she felt she had to say something.

'The petits fours weren't actually that good,' she ventured after a moment. 'So you really didn't miss much.'

Luca let out a soft huff of laughter, and somehow that sounded sad too.

'I know what it's like to grieve, Luca,' Hannah said quietly.

'Is that what you think I'm doing?'

'I don't know, and I won't ask because I know you don't want to tell me. But...' she let out her breath slowly '...I know what it's like to feel angry and cheated and in despair.'

'Do you?' Luca lifted his head to gaze at her speculatively; she could only just make out the strong lines and angles of his face in the moonlit darkness. 'Who do you grieve, Hannah?'

It was such a personal question, and one whose answer she didn't talk about much. Yet she was the one who had started this conversation, and if Luca wasn't able to talk about his pain, perhaps she should talk about hers.

'My father, for one,' Hannah answered. 'He died when I was fifteen.'

'I'm sorry.' Luca stared straight ahead, his arms braced against his knees. 'How did it happen?'

'A heart attack out of the blue. He went to work and dropped dead at his desk. It was a complete shock to everyone.'

'Which must have made it even harder.'

'Yes, in a way. My mother wasn't prepared emotionally, obviously, or financially.'

Luca glanced at her. 'Your father didn't leave her provided for?'

'No, not really. He'd always meant to take out a life insurance policy, but he never got around to it. He was only forty-two years old. And savings were slim... He wasn't irresponsible,' she hastened to add. 'Just not planning for the disaster that happened.' And she'd decided long ago not to be bitter about that. She'd simply chosen to make different choices.

'So what did your mother do?'

'Got a job. She'd been a housewife for sixteen years, since before I was born, and she'd been a part-time preschool teacher before that. It was tough to find work that earned more than a pittance.'

'And what about you?'

'I worked too, after school. We sold our house and rented a small flat. That helped with expenses.' But it had been hard, so hard, to go from the simple, smiling suburban life she'd had as a child to working all hours and living in a small, shabby flat.

'I'm sorry,' Luca said again. 'I never knew.'

'I never told you.' She paused, waiting for him to volunteer something of his own situation, but he didn't. 'What about you?' she asked at last. 'What happened to your parents?'

Luca was silent for a long moment. 'My mother died when I was fourteen.'

'I'm sorry.'

His cynical smile gleamed in the darkness. 'We're both so sorry, aren't we? But it doesn't change anything.'

'No, but sometimes it can make you feel less alone.'

'How do you know I feel alone?'

She took a deep breath. 'Because I do, sometimes.' Another breath. 'Do you?'

Luca didn't answer for a long moment. 'Yes,' he said finally. 'Yes, all the time.' He let out a hollow laugh. 'And no more so than when I was looking at Andrew Tyson and his damn kids.' His voice broke on the words and he averted his head from her, hiding his face, shielding his emotion.

'Oh, Luca.' Hannah's voice broke too, for her heart ached to see this proud, powerful man brought to such sadness.

'Don't.' His voice was muffled, his head still turned away from her. 'Don't pity me, Hannah. I couldn't bear it.'

'I don't—'

'I'd rather someone attacked me than pitied me. It's the worst kind of violence, cloaked as something kind or virtuous.' He spoke scathingly, the words spat out, making her wonder.

'Who pitied you, Luca?' she asked quietly. 'Because you seem the least likely person for anyone ever to feel sorry for.'

'I wasn't always.'

'When you were a child? When you lost your mother?'

He nodded tersely. 'Yes. Then.'

But she felt he wasn't telling her the whole truth. 'What happened to you after your mother's death? Did you live with your father?'

'No, he wasn't around.' Luca expelled a low breath. 'I went into foster care, and managed to secure a scholarship to a boarding school in Rome. It saved me, lifted me up from the gutter, but not everyone liked that fact. I stayed on my own.'

It sounded like a terribly lonely childhood. Even though she'd lost her father, Hannah was grateful for the fifteen years of happy memories that he'd given her. 'How did your mother die?' she asked.

He let out a long, weary sigh and tilted his head towards the sky. 'She killed herself.'

Startled, Hannah stared at him in horror. 'Oh, but that's terrible—'

'Yes, but I could understand why she did it. Life had become unendurable.'

'But you were only fourteen—'

'I think,' Luca said slowly, still staring at the starlit sky, 'when you feel that trapped and desperate and sad, you stop thinking about anything else. You can't reason your way out of it. You can only try to end the sadness.'

Tears stung Hannah's eyes at the thought. 'You have great compassion and understanding, to be able to think that.'

'I've never been angry with her,' Luca answered flatly. He lowered his head to gaze out at the sea, washed in darkness. 'She was a victim.'

'And were you a victim?' Hannah asked. She felt as if she were feeling her way through the dark, groping with her words, trying to shape an understanding out of his reluctant half-answers.

'No, I've never wanted to think of myself as victim. That ends only in defeat.'

'I suppose I felt the same,' Hannah offered cautiously. 'My father's death left my mother in a difficult situation, and I wanted to make sure I never ended up that way as an adult.'

He gave her a swift, searching glance. 'Is that why you agreed with me that relationships aren't worth it?'

'I only said maybe,' Hannah reminded him. 'But yes, that has something to do with it.' She thought of Jamie's father and felt a lump form in her throat. She'd moved on from her grief years ago, but opening those old wounds still hurt, still made her wonder and regret. If she'd done something differently...if she'd handled their last argument better... 'When you lose someone,' she said, 'you don't feel like taking the chance again.'

'But he was your father, not a boyfriend or husband.'

'I lost one of those too,' Hannah admitted. 'A boyfriend, not a husband.' They'd never got that far. They'd never had the chance. And she had to believe that they would have, if Ben hadn't died. That he would have changed his mind, she would have had a second chance.

'When?'

'Almost six years ago.'

Luca turned to her, the moonlight washing half his face in lambent silver. 'You bear your sorrows so well. You don't look like someone haunted by grief.'

'I'm not,' Hannah answered staunchly. 'I choose not to be.' Even if it was hard, a choice she had to make every day not to wallow in grief and regret.

'That's a strong choice to make.'

'It hasn't always been easy,' Hannah allowed. 'And I can't say I haven't had my moments of self-pity or evenings alone with a tub of mint-chocolate-chip ice cream,' she added. 'But I try not to wallow.'

His mouth twisted wryly. 'Is that what you think I'm doing? Wallowing?'

Horrified, Hannah clapped a hand to her mouth. 'Luca, no—'

'No, it is.' He cut her off. 'And I despise myself for it. I thought I could come here and stare Andrew Tyson in the face. I thought I could smile and shake the man's hand and feel nothing, because I'd schooled myself to feel nothing for so long. But I can't. I *can't.*' His voice broke on a ragged gasp and he dropped his head in his hands. 'I don't want to feel this,' he muttered. 'I don't want to be enslaved by something that happened so long ago. I wanted this to be a clean slate, a second chance—' He drew in a ragged breath, his head in his hands, and Hannah did the only thing she could, the only thing she felt she could do in that moment. She hugged him.

She wrapped her arms around him, pressing her cheek into his back, trying to imbue him with her comfort. 'Oh, Luca,' she whispered. *'Luca.'*

He went rigid underneath her touch but she hung on anyway. Luca could be as strong and stoic as he liked, but he still needed comfort, and in that moment she was determined to give it to him.

He reached up to grip her wrists that were locked across his chest as if he'd force her away from him, but he didn't.

'Why are you so kind?' he demanded in a raw mutter.

'Why are you so afraid of kindness?' Hannah returned softly.

He turned, his hands still on her wrists, and for a second she thought he would reject her offer of comfort and push her away, but then his features twisted and with a muttered curse he reached for her instead.

Their mouths met and clashed and the fierce desire to comfort him turned into something far more primal and urgent. His hands were everywhere, clenching in her hair, stroking her back, cupping her breasts, and all the while his mouth didn't leave hers.

They fell back on the sand in a tangle of limbs, and when Luca's thumb brushed over the taut peak of her nipple Hannah arched into his hand, craving an even deeper caress.

She tore at his shirt, studs popping, desperate to feel his bare, glorious skin. She let out a gasp of pleasure and satisfaction when she finally parted the shirt and ran her palms along his hair-roughened chest, revelling in the feel of sculpted muscle and hot skin.

Luca's breath came out in a hiss and then he was pulling at her dress, the gauzy folds tearing under his urgent touch, and Hannah didn't even care.

'Luca,' she gasped, and it was both a demand and a plea. She needed to feel his hands on her body. She felt as if she'd explode if she didn't. He pulled the tattered dress down to her waist, leaving her completely bare on top as she hadn't worn a bra with the halter-style dress.

Then he bent his head to her breasts, his tongue now touching where his hands had been, and Hannah clutched his head to her, nearly sobbing in pleasure at the feel of him tasting her.

But even that wasn't enough. She needed more from him, of him, and when his hand slipped under her bunched dress, his fingers deftly finding and stroking her centre, she thought she almost had it. The pleasure was so acute it was akin to pain, a sharp ache that left her gasping. She skimmed the length of his erection, sucking her breath in at the way his body throbbed in insistent response to her touch. She pulled at his trousers, fumbling with the ties of his cummerbund, and with a muttered oath Luca ripped it away from him and tossed it on the sand. Hannah let out a gurgle of laughter that he swallowed with his mouth as he kissed her again and she gave herself to him, offering everything as her hands clutched at his shoulders and her hips rocked against his.

'Hannah,' Luca muttered against her mouth. 'Hannah, I need...'

'Yes,' she answered almost frantically. 'Yes, *please*, Luca, now.'

She parted her legs as he fumbled with the zip on his trousers. She didn't have a second to consider if this was a good idea, if she'd regret this afterwards. She couldn't think past the haze of overwhelming need that consumed her.

Then Luca was inside her, an invasion so sudden, so sweet, so *much*, that Hannah felt tears sting her eyes. It had been so long since she'd given her body to a man. So long since she'd felt completed, conquered. She wrapped her legs around him, enfolding herself around him as she accepted him into her body.

He stilled inside her as they both adjusted to the intense sensation. Luca's eyes were closed, his arms braced by her shoulders. Then Hannah flexed around him and with a groan of surrender he started to move.

It had been a while, and it took her a few exquisite thrusts before she managed to find the rhythm and match it, and then with each thrust she felt her body respond, opening up like a flower, everything in her spiralling upward, straining towards that glittering summit that was just out of her reach—

Until she found it, her body convulsing around Luca's as she cried out his name and the climax rushed over them both, their bodies shuddering in tandem, tears slipping down her face as she gave herself to the tidal wave of pleasure.

In the aftermath Hannah lay there, Luca's body on top of hers, the thud of his heart matching her own. She felt dazed and dizzy and yet utterly sated. She couldn't regret what had happened, not even for a second.

Then Luca rolled off her with a curse, lying on the sand on his back, one arm thrown over his eyes. Okay, maybe she could.

Hannah felt a whole bunch of things at once: the cold sand underneath her, the stickiness on her thighs, the grit in her hair, the torn dress about her waist. The pleasure that had overwhelmed her only moments before now felt like mere vapour, a ghost of a memory.

She pulled her torn dress down over herself, wincing at the shredded gauze. To think Luca had spent nine thousand pounds on this one gown. Not that she would have had a chance to wear it again, even if it hadn't been ruined.

Luca lifted his arm from his face and turned his head to rake her with one quick glance. Even in the moonlit darkness Hannah could see how indifferent he looked, and inwardly she quelled.

This had been a mistake. A wonderful, terrible mistake, and one she would most certainly regret no matter the pleasure she'd experienced. How could she work with Luca from now on? What if he fired her? But even worse than the fears for her job was the piercing loneliness of the thought that he might shut her out of his life. He already was, and she'd barely been in it to begin with.

She took a deep, calming breath and told herself not to jump to conclusions.

'Your dress,' Luca stated flatly.

Hannah glanced down at it. 'I'm afraid it's past repair.'

'I'm thinking of getting back to the room,' he clarified impatiently. 'I don't care about the dress.'

'Oh. Okay.' She bit her lip, trying not to feel hurt. This was a far cry from pillow talk, but then they hadn't even had a bed. They'd had a few moments of frenzied, mindless passion that Luca undoubtedly regretted, just as she was starting to.

Luca sat up, readjusting his trousers and then searching for the studs on his shirt. He found enough to keep the shirt mostly fastened, and he stuffed his tie and cummerbund in his pocket. Then he shrugged off his tuxedo jacket and draped it over her shoulders.

'There. You're mostly decent. Hopefully we can sneak into the room without anyone seeing us.'

'And if they do?' Hannah asked, thankful her voice didn't wobble. 'Wouldn't they just think we'd done exactly what they'd expect us to do, and made love under the stars?'

Luca's mouth compressed and he stood up, brushing the sand from his legs before he reached a hand down to her. She took it only because she knew she'd struggle getting up on her own. She was torn between an irrational anger—how had she expected Luca to act?—and a deep and disturbing hurt. She shouldn't care this much. She hadn't had *feelings* for Luca, not really.

Except somehow, in the last twenty-four hours, she had begun to develop them. She'd seen intriguing glimpses into a man whom she'd already respected and admired—glimpses of strength and emotion. She'd seen him determined and arrogant but also humble, concerned for her even while he was in the throes of his own emotional agony. Luca Moretti had depths she'd discovered this weekend that he hadn't even hinted at before.

And he was hiding them all from her now. He dropped her hand the moment she was upright and started walking back towards the villa, its lights glimmering in the distance. Hannah followed him, clutching his jacket around her shoulders, wincing at the sand she could feel in her hair and clothes.

They skirted around the terrace that was now empty to the other side of the house, where the bedrooms' French windows overlooked the beach.

'You'd better pick the right room,' Hannah muttered darkly. Hurt and anger were giving way to a weary resignation as she scrambled to think of a way to navigate this awful aftermath.

Luca didn't even reply, just stalked ahead and then flung open a pair of windows and ushered her into their bedroom. Hannah stepped inside, her glance taking in the turned-down bed, the chocolate hearts on the pillows. Had it been only twenty-four hours ago that she'd been in this same room, this same position, except now everything felt drastically different?

'Why don't you get cleaned up?' Luca said, nodding towards the bathroom without looking at her. 'And then we'll talk.'

CHAPTER TEN

LUCA SHRUGGED OFF his torn shirt as Hannah disappeared into the bathroom. What had he been *thinking*, slaking his lust with his PA? The trouble was, he hadn't been thinking. He'd been utterly in the grip of his own awful emotions, and Hannah's tentative comfort had been the balm he'd so desperately craved. It was only afterwards, after the most sexually and emotionally explosive encounter he'd ever experienced, that the regrets came rushing in. Regret to have slept with his PA at all, and, worse, shame that he'd allowed her to see him in such a vulnerable state. What must Hannah think of him? It had practically been a pity lay.

Except she had been just as gripped by the raw, urgent need that he'd felt consume him. She'd been just as desperate to have him inside her as he'd been to be there.

The knowledge didn't make him feel any better. The whole thing was an appalling mistake, made about a thousand times worse by the fact that they hadn't used any protection.

Hannah emerged from the bathroom, dressed in the same awful pyjamas she'd worn last night, but at least tonight Luca was grateful for the way they hid her body. The last thing he needed was to feel tempted again.

She didn't look at him as she came into the room, going

directly to the bed. Her body was stiff with affront and Luca watched in bemused disbelief as she reached for her book by the bedside table and then buried her nose in it.

He took a deep breath. 'Hannah.' She didn't so much as look up from her book. 'We need to talk.'

'Oh, *now* we need to talk?' Finally she looked up, and Luca saw anger firing her brown eyes, turning them to gold. Her hair was tousled about her shoulders, her face flushed, and, pyjamas aside, she looked utterly lovely.

But he had to stop thinking that way.

'Yes, now we need to talk.'

'Not right after?' Hannah filled in. 'No, you couldn't bother to say boo to me then.'

Luca's insides tightened with both irritation and remorse. He hadn't treated her very well, back on the beach, but she'd blindsided him, in so many ways. 'Clearly what happened took us both by surprise.' She took a deep breath and nodded, her hands folded across her abandoned book. 'So much so that I didn't think to use any protection.'

Hannah's lips parted on a soundless gasp as her eyes widened in shocked realisation. 'I didn't even think of that.' She nibbled her lip. 'But it's not...I mean, based on the time of the month, I don't think it's risky.'

'You'd let me know? I mean, if...?'

Her gaze locked with his and her breath came out in a rush. Luca felt the import of the moment, the enormous impact of what they'd shared together. More than he'd ever shared with any other woman, pregnancy or not. 'Yes, of course,' she answered. '*If*. But I really don't think there's going to be an if. So that's one less thing to worry about.' She tried for a smile but it wobbled and slid off her face, and she looked away, blinking rapidly.

'Hannah...' He expelled a shaky breath. He was finding this all a lot harder than he would have wished. He didn't like the realisation that he'd hurt her.

Hannah glanced down at her laced fingers. 'You don't need to worry about me, Luca,' she said quietly. 'I wasn't looking for some kind of fairy tale, and I certainly don't have any expectations because of…well, you know.'

And that proclamation, which should have only brought blessed relief, caused him the most absurd flicker of disappointment. His emotions were clearly all over the place. 'Good,' Luca said shortly. 'Then we can forget this ever happened and move on.'

With effort Hannah kept her face blank. *Forget this ever happened.* As if she could ever do that. Those passionate moments with Luca were emblazoned on her brain, his touch branded on her body. She swallowed and nodded.

'Yes,' she agreed, because what else could she say? Luca wasn't looking for a relationship, and neither was she—and certainly not with a man like him. If she ever dared to risk her heart—and her son's—it would be with someone who valued family, who wanted a child. *Her* child.

And yet Luca had put so much care into his plans for the family resort, and just a moment ago he'd almost looked disappointed that she was most likely not pregnant.

But she couldn't go chasing after rainbows where none existed. He'd made his intentions more than clear.

Luca nodded, seemingly satisfied with her agreement. 'You'll tell me if the situation changes?'

'If I'm pregnant?' she clarified wryly. 'Yes, Luca, I'll tell you. It's not as if it's something I could hide, working for you.'

'But you wouldn't try to hide it?'

'No, of course not.' She frowned at him. 'But let's cross that bridge when we come to it, shall we?'

A terse nod was all the response she got and he disappeared into the bathroom while she tossed her book on the bedside table, too unsettled to read.

Even though she'd just told Luca they didn't need to think about how to handle a pregnancy yet, she found herself doing just that—and her scattered thoughts soon morphed into the most absurd fantasy of Luca as a doting dad. This child could have what Jamie had missed out on. She pictured Luca cradling their newborn, his big, strong hands so tender with that tiny scrap of humanity. She thought of all the things that Jamie would experience without a dad—a lost tooth, riding a bike, Christmas and birthdays. This child wouldn't miss out at all.

Then Luca came out of the bathroom and got into bed, his movements brisk and businesslike, and Hannah forced her wayward thoughts to a screeching halt. What on earth was she thinking, casting Luca Moretti of all people, into the role of a devoted father? He was anything but—not to the imaginary child they most likely hadn't conceived, and certainly not to her son by another man. If she was pregnant, he'd probably pay her off and remain completely uninvolved. The antithesis of a happily-ever-after.

No, she had to clamp down on that kind of dangerous and foolish thinking right now. Luca wasn't interested in relationships, and neither was she. As he'd told her, it simply wasn't worth it.

The next morning Hannah woke to an empty bed; she'd been so exhausted from everything that had happened, she'd fallen asleep without any restless wondering of what Luca was thinking or feeling next to her.

Now, in the bright light of a Mediterranean morning, the events of last night took on a sordid and reproachable cast. What had seemed irresistible and exciting in the sultry darkness now felt shameful. She was glad Luca wasn't in the room because she didn't think she could look him in the eye. Just the memory of how she'd begged him to touch her made Hannah's face flame.

Half an hour later, after eating breakfast delivered by staff and dressed in another one of her ensembles from Diavola, her hair and make-up done, Hannah felt more in control of the situation, or at least as if a mask of calm respectability had been put in place.

Luca hadn't returned to the room and so she decided to go in search of him. She saw several suitcases in the foyer and realised Andrew Tyson's guests were starting to depart. She'd known she and Luca would be leaving some time today, and the thought of returning home to Jamie, to her mother, to normal life, brought a rush of relief. She couldn't handle any more of her seesawing emotions.

She wandered through a few more rooms before she found some of Tyson's guests along with his family in a breakfast room, enjoying coffee and pastries. Laura Tyson gave her a friendly smile as she came into the room.

'You're Luca Moretti's fiancée, isn't that right?'

'Yes…'

'I saw the two of you sneak out at the end of the dinner last night,' Laura said confidentially, her eyes sparkling. 'I don't blame you. Luca is certainly a handsome man, and he obviously adores you.'

That sincerely delivered statement nearly made Hannah choke. 'Thank you,' she murmured. She couldn't manage any more. This awful pretence was straining at its seams. Another lie and it would explode. *She* would.

Laura leaned closer to Hannah and lowered her voice. 'To tell you the truth, I think my father favours your fiancé to take over the resorts. He mentioned how impressed he was with his plans.'

'Oh…well, that's encouraging to hear.' Hannah smiled, genuinely glad for Luca even amidst the turmoil of all her feelings. Based on the proposal she'd seen, he deserved to win the commission.

'He'll make the announcement shortly, I'm sure.'

'Today…?'

Laura wrinkled her nose. 'Probably not for a week or two. This is a big decision for him.' Her smile fell as she admitted, 'I think he's still hoping one of us will show an interest, but Stephen and I had different dreams.'

'He's a doctor…'

'And I work in pharmaceutical research. Our little sister died of leukaemia when she was only four years old,' Laura explained quietly. 'It had a big impact on all of us… and I think we've chosen to honour her memory in different ways.'

'I'm sorry for your loss,' Hannah said, knowing the words were inadequate yet meaning them utterly. She knew what it was like to lose someone at a young age.

'I'm glad that someone is interested in taking the resorts on,' Laura said. 'I know they're a bit worn. Dad hasn't had as much energy as he used to, and he's never been good at delegating. But I hope with your Luca on board things will change for the better.'

Her Luca. As if. 'I hope so too,' Hannah said and Laura gave her one more smile before turning away.

Luca came in the room a short while later, his face and body both tense. Even grim-faced as he was he looked devastatingly attractive in a grey pinstriped suit matched with a crisp white shirt and dark blue tie. The elegantly cut suit showed off his muscular body to perfection, and he strode into the room as if he owned it, his gaze searching out Hannah.

As his deep brown eyes locked with hers Hannah felt a fiery heat start a blaze in her belly, much to her irritation. She'd worked for the man for three years and he'd never caused that reaction in her in all that time. Yet right now she couldn't deny the magnetic pull of attraction that had her unable to break away from his penetrating stare. She could only pretend it didn't exist.

'Hannah.' He nodded towards the door. 'Are you ready to leave?'

No lovey-dovey play-acting this morning, she noted. He must have known that he'd sealed the deal.

'I didn't realise we were leaving so soon,' Hannah answered. 'I'll pack right away.'

Luca followed her down the hall and into their bedroom. The huge, airy room felt claustrophobic as she got out her suitcase and started neatly folding her clothes into it. Her hands trembled and she hid them in the folds of a dress.

'I spoke to Laura just now,' she said, her voice an octave higher than normal. She cleared her throat and tried again. 'She seems quite sure that you've secured the bid.'

'Tyson is keeping us on leading strings,' Luca answered. He prowled around the room, his hands shoved into his pockets, every stride predatory and restless.

'Laura said it was a big decision for him to make.'

'I think he just likes toying with us,' Luca answered dismissively. 'That's the kind of man he is.'

'If there really is bad blood between you,' Hannah said slowly, amazed that she hadn't thought of this earlier, 'why would he sell the resorts to you?'

Luca stilled, his back to her as he gazed out at the sparkling sea. 'Because he doesn't know it was me.'

'What do you mean?'

'It's complicated,' he answered on a shrug, his voice gruff. 'Suffice it to say, Tyson doesn't realise there is any history between us. Only I do.'

Hannah frowned, Luca's admission making her uneasy. How was what he'd said even possible? And yet Luca clearly meant it. He also very clearly wasn't going to tell her anything else, and she didn't want to ask. She'd got in too deep with Luca Moretti already.

'I just need to get my wash bag from the bathroom,' she said. 'And then I'll be ready to go.'

Fifteen minutes later they'd made their farewells and were bumping down the road to the airport in the same Jeep they'd arrived in only forty-eight hours ago, which seemed unbelievable. Hannah felt as if she'd lived an entire lifetime in the space of a few short and incredible days. And that lifetime, she reminded herself, was over.

An hour later they were settled in first class in the aeroplane to London. Luca waved away the offers of champagne and Hannah looked out of the window, stupidly stung. A few days ago he'd said he'd enjoyed watching her taste champagne. But she'd had quite a bit of champagne since then, and she had a feeling it would taste flat now anyway. So much for tickly.

As soon as they'd taken off Luca got some papers out of his briefcase and spent the entire flight immersed in work. Hannah told herself she was grateful not to have to make awkward small talk, but silence gave her the unwelcome space to remember every second of last night's encounter.

Just thinking about the way Luca had kissed her, with such overwhelming intensity and passion and *desperation*, made her inner muscles clench and she shifted restlessly in her seat. She *had* to get over this. Her job and her sanity were both at stake. She couldn't work with Luca every day and remember how he'd felt. How he'd tasted.

And she'd forget in time, Hannah assured herself. Of course she was still thinking about his kiss. It hadn't even been twenty-four hours. But the memory would fade in time, and who knew? Maybe in a week or month or ten years, she and Luca would laugh about the one bizarre interlude they'd had on a Mediterranean island.

Hannah settled back into her seat and started to flick through the films available on her entertainment console. Yes. That was exactly how it was going to be.

CHAPTER ELEVEN

THE NEXT MORNING Hannah dressed for work in her smartest pencil skirt and silk blouse, slipped on her highest, sharpest stiletto heels. She needed armour.

On the Tube on the way into the Moretti Enterprises office, she worried if she was making too much effort. Maybe Luca would think she was trying to impress him. But she'd nip that prospect right in the bud the second she arrived. She'd make it quite clear to Luca that she was as interested and invested as he was in getting their relationship back on a firm, professional footing.

She needed to get her life back to normal, both for Jamie's sake as well as her own. She'd had a happy reunion with her son last night, reading stories and cuddling before bed.

Once Jamie had been tucked in bed, Diane had regaled Hannah with stories of their weekend together: a trip to the zoo, baking fairy cakes on a rainy afternoon. Then her mother had cocked her head and swept her with a knowing yet inquisitive gaze.

'I didn't realise Luca Moretti was so handsome.'

'Haven't you seen his picture in the tabloids?' Hannah had answered a touch too sharply. 'He's often photographed with some socialite or other.'

'You know I don't read the tabloids.' Her mother had

sat back, arms folded. 'But going on a business trip with him was a departure from the way things usually are, wasn't it?'

That, Hannah had reflected sourly, was a complete understatement. 'Yes, it was,' she'd answered.

'Do you think you'll go on another trip with him?'

'No,' Hannah had answered firmly, and thankfully her mother hadn't asked her any more questions.

That morning as dawn light had filtered through the curtains Jamie had crept into her bedroom, teddy bear dangling from one chubby fist, and climbed into bed with her. Hannah had snuggled his warm little body against her, savouring the precious moment. It had reminded her of her priorities, and put the events of the weekend firmly into their place—a moment out of reality, nothing more.

Luca had not yet arrived when she reached the penthouse office, and Hannah breathed a sigh of relief that she had a few moments to compose herself and begin work without worrying about her boss.

She was well into her in-tray when he arrived, striding through the lift doors, looking devastatingly sexy in a navy blue suit, his close-cropped dark hair bristly and damp from the rain.

Hannah looked up as he entered, and the breath bottled in her lungs, every thought emptying from her head as her gaze locked on his body and her mind played a reel of X-rated memories. With effort she yanked her gaze away, staring down at the spreadsheet she'd been working on, the numbers blurring before her distracted gaze.

'Good morning.' Luca's voice was brisk and business-like, giving nothing away. 'I'll be in my office if you need anything.' And he strode past her desk, closing the door behind him with a decisive click.

Hannah ignored the pinpricks of hurt and disappointment she felt at his obvious dismissal and refocused on her work.

Luca didn't emerge from his office all morning, and Hannah managed to plough through paperwork until just before lunch, when she needed Luca's signature on some letters.

She approached his door with trepidation, bracing herself for his hostility.

'Come in,' Luca barked after she knocked on the door, and she pushed it open, the letters in her hand.

'I just need you to sign these,' she murmured, and Luca beckoned her forward. It was no more than he would have done a week ago, but now the command seemed autocratic and unfeeling. Her problem, she told herself. She had to get over her unreasonable reaction to this man.

She placed the letters on the desk, taking a careful step away as he signed them so she wouldn't breathe in his cedarwood scent or feel the heat emanating from his powerful body.

'Here.' Luca handed her the letters, and his hand brushed hers as she took them. Hannah felt as if she'd been scorched. A tremor went through her body, followed by a wave of helpless longing that she knew she couldn't disguise. Everything in her yearned to have him touch her again, and this time with intent.

Luca cursed under his breath and heat surged into Hannah's face. 'I'm… I'm sorry,' she muttered, embarrassed beyond belief that her reaction was so cringingly obvious to him. 'I thought I'd go to lunch if you don't need me.' *Wrong* choice of words. 'I mean, if there's nothing you need me to do…in the office…' Could she make this any worse?

'I know what you meant,' Luca answered tersely. 'Yes, you can go.'

With relief Hannah fled from the room.

* * *

Luca watched Hannah leave his office as if she had the fires of hell on her heels, and let out a weary groan. This was all much more difficult than he'd thought it would be. Much more tempting. The merest brush of Hannah's hand against his own had made his body pulse with desire, hardly the distraction he needed during the working day.

They'd both settle down, he told himself. Their attraction, without anything to nurture it, would surely fade. Perhaps he'd take a business trip to the US, check on some of his properties in development there. Give them both a chance to cool off. An opportunity to forget.

Except Luca didn't think he'd ever forget the feel of Hannah's slender body yielding to his, or, more worryingly, the way she'd held him when he'd been so angry and defeated, the sweet, heartfelt way she'd comforted him. That was something he definitely needed to forget.

Abruptly Luca rose from his desk to stare out at the bustling city streets. He wasn't used to craving another person's company or comfort. He'd lived his life alone, ever since his mother had died, battling his way through boarding school and foster care, and even before then, when she'd been too busy or despairing to care for him.

He'd chosen to lift his chin and ignore the taunts and scorn that had been heaped upon him as a bastard growing up fatherless in a remote Sicilian village. He'd pretended the snubs and jibes of the entitled boys at school had bounced off him. He'd always acted as if he didn't care and he'd almost convinced himself he didn't...until he'd come face to face with Andrew Tyson, the man who had rejected him once already. His father.

Letting out a shuddering breath, Luca turned from the window. In a week or so Tyson would seal the property deal, and he'd be the owner of the resorts his father's legitimate children had refused to take on. He'd have control of the inheritance that would have been his, as firstborn son, if Tyson, the alleged family man, had deigned to marry the woman he'd impregnated.

Then he would finally have his revenge.

In the meantime, he needed to get hold of his rampaging libido and shut Hannah Stewart firmly back in the box where she belonged: as his PA, an employee like any other.

Hannah took an unaccustomed full hour for lunch, walking the streets of the City, trying to talk herself out of this ridiculous reaction to Luca Moretti. She reminded herself of how she used to be with the man, calm and cool and professional. That was how she needed to be again.

She felt more herself when she'd returned to the office, and thankfully Luca was closeted behind a closed door, taking a conference call. Hannah got on with her day and had just about convinced herself that she had this thing under control.

Then Luca opened the door to his office and heat and memory and longing all surged through her body, an unstoppable force.

'I'm going home for the day, to pack,' Luca announced. Hannah kept her gaze glued to her computer screen and willed her hands not to tremble.

'Pack...?'

'I'm going to America for a week, to check on some of my properties there.'

'Would you like me to make travel arrangements?' Hannah asked.

'No, I've taken care of it myself.' He paused, and Hannah forced herself to meet his iron gaze. 'This thing between us, Hannah. It will fade.'

Hannah didn't know whether to be gratified or embarrassed that he was acknowledging it. Was he actually saying that he felt it too, as much as she did? 'Of course,' she managed. 'I'm sorry, I don't mean things to be awkward.'

Luca shrugged. 'It never should have happened. I'm sorry it did.'

Ouch. 'Of course,' Hannah said stiffly, trying to keep the hurt from her voice. She shouldn't care. She really shouldn't.

'But,' he continued, his voice and expression both inflexible, 'you will tell me if there is a result?'

A result? It took Hannah a second to realise he meant a pregnancy. 'I told you I would. But I don't think—'

'Good.' For a second she thought she saw regret in his eyes, longing in his face. But no, she was imagining it; he looked as hard and unyielding as ever as he nodded once in farewell and then walked out of the office.

Hannah spent the week trying to get on with her life. She spring-cleaned her house and bought several new outfits and had her hair and nails done, not for Luca Moretti's sake, but her own. She took Jamie to the cinema and the park on the weekend, and told herself she was blessed in so many ways, and she didn't need anything more in her life. Certainly not a man who would only break her heart—again.

At least, she discovered a few days after Luca had left, she wasn't pregnant. The realisation brought relief that was tinged by a little impractical disappointment. Honestly, what on earth would she have done with another baby? It was hard enough being a single mum to one child.

The day Luca arrived back at work she'd dressed carefully in one of her new outfits, a slim-fitting dress in silvery grey silk with a tailored black blazer. She had her hair in a more glamorous chignon rather than her usual practical ponytail, and she felt polished and confident and strong.

Then Luca walked through the lift doors. Hannah's

heart seemed to stop as her gaze swept over him and she noticed the weariness in his eyes, the lines of strain from nose to mouth. She had a nearly irresistible urge to go to him, offer him comfort as she had once before.

And look where that had ended.

'Hello,' she said stiffly, turning back to her computer. 'Welcome back.'

'Thank you.' Luca paused by her desk, and Hannah breathed in the spicy male scent of him. 'Has anything of note happened while I've been away?'

'No, not particularly.' She'd kept him abreast by email, and even that had felt like too much contact. 'The post is on your desk.'

'Thank you.' Still he didn't move away, and Hannah tore her gaze away from her computer to look up at him. His gaze locked on and burned into hers, and she felt as if she could lose herself in the deep brown of his eyes.

'Luca,' she whispered, her voice breathy and soft. Luca's expression hardened.

'I'll be in my office.'

A week away hadn't changed anything. Luca swivelled in his chair, restless and angry with himself for still responding to Hannah in such a basic and yet overwhelming way. The mere sight of her looking so poised and elegant had made him yearn to sweep her into his arms, pluck the pins from her hair and lose himself in the glories of her mouth.

While in New York he'd tried to distance himself from the memory of her touch by going out with a model he'd once been friendly with, but the elegant, gorgeous woman had left him completely cold. He hadn't been able to summon the interest even to kiss her, and she'd been quite put out as a result.

Maybe, he mused, he was going about this the wrong way. Maybe instead of forgetting Hannah he needed to get her out of his system. He'd been able to tell, simply from that one small exchange, that she still reacted to him just as powerfully as he did to her. Why not have a fling? They'd work out this inconvenient attraction and then resume their professional relationship. He didn't want to lose his PA, and he knew Hannah didn't want to lose her job. Surely they could be sensible about this. Businesslike, even. They'd both agreed that neither of them wanted the risk of a real relationship, so Hannah should surely be amenable to the kind of arrangement he was thinking about. All he had to do was offer.

CHAPTER TWELVE

HANNAH HAD JUST put Jamie to bed and changed into comfy yoga pants and a fleece hoodie when the doorbell rang. She was exhausted, emotionally spent from having been on high alert with Luca in the office, and she wanted to do nothing more than kick back with a glass of wine and maybe some ice cream and watch several hours of soothingly mindless reality TV.

Suspecting her elderly neighbour needed help opening a jar or reaching something on a high shelf—Hannah was called on for these kinds of services several times a week—she opened her front door with a sunny smile pasted onto her face and felt it slide right off when her stunned gaze took in the sight of the powerful form filling her doorway.

'Luca…what are you doing here?'

'I want to talk.' He bent his head so as not to hit the low stone lintel. 'May I come in?'

Hannah had a kneejerk reaction to refuse. She didn't want him in her house, overwhelming her life with his presence, his power. She glanced behind her, as if looking for assistance but none was forthcoming. 'All right.'

She led Luca to the small sitting room, which, after a quick post-tea tidy-up, was free of any evidence of her son. 'Is something wrong?'

'Not exactly.' Luca's perceptive gaze took in the little

room with its worn sofa and coffee table, the small TV in the corner. With framed prints on the walls and bookcases overflowing with paperbacks, it was homey and cosy but a far cry from the luxury Hannah knew he was accustomed to.

'I'm not pregnant,' she blurted. 'If that's why you came. It's certain.'

'Oh.' Luca looked surprised, and then discomfited. 'No, that's not why I'm here.'

'Oh. Okay.' Flummoxed, she gestured to a chair. 'Would you like to sit down?' It felt surreal to have Luca in her little house, taking up all the space and air. She sat on the sofa and he sat in a chair opposite, his hands resting on his muscular thighs.

'This isn't working, Hannah.'

Her stomach lurched unpleasantly. She couldn't pretend not to understand what he was talking about. 'I'll get over it,' she said a bit desperately. 'It *can* work—'

'It's not just you,' he interjected. 'I feel it too.'

Her heart somersaulted at that admission but she still felt wary. She *couldn't* lose her job. 'So what are you suggesting? I need my job—'

Luca grimaced in distaste. 'Do you actually think I'd fire you over this?'

'You might think of a convenient reason to let me go or at least shift me to another position in the company.' The latter wouldn't necessarily be a bad thing, even if she'd miss the status and salary, not to mention the challenge, of being the CEO's executive assistant. And, she admitted painfully, she'd miss Luca.

'That's not the kind of man I am,' he answered stonily, and Hannah thought she detected hurt underneath his hard manner.

'I'm sorry, I'm just paranoid, I suppose.' She spread her hands. 'You hold all the cards, Luca.'

'Then let me play one now. I want you, Hannah. I want you in my bed. Properly, and not just for a few mindless minutes.'

Hannah stared at him in shock, the blood draining from her head, making her dizzy. She could not think to string two words together.

'I don't see any reason why we shouldn't have an affair,' Luca stated. 'We're obviously attracted to one another, and those feelings are not going away. I think it would be far better to explore this mutual attraction to our satisfaction, and then part on good terms.' His eyes glittered as he pinned her with his stare. 'I'm a very considerate and generous lover, Hannah.'

'I know you are,' she answered numbly. The shock was dissipating, replaced by anger, and, far worse, hurt. 'I've arranged the courier from Tiffany & Co. enough times to realise,' she added tartly.

Luca didn't look remotely abashed at this statement. 'Then you agree?'

'To what, exactly? Being your mistress?' Her voice rang out, making him blink in surprise. Hannah held on to her rage. Better to be angry than to break down into tears, bitterly disappointed that *this* was what he was offering her. No-strings sex. How could she even be surprised?

'"Mistress" is an outdated term,' Luca observed. 'And not one I'm entirely comfortable with.'

'But isn't that what you have? Mistresses?'

'Lovers,' he corrected swiftly. 'And one at a time. You're an independent woman, Hannah. I'm not suggesting I take that away from you.'

'But what are you suggesting? Because I've seen you with other women enough to know what you want.'

Ire flashed briefly in his eyes. 'I had no idea you were so knowledgeable of my desires,' he remarked. 'What is it that you think I want?'

'Availability,' Hannah answered. 'You like your women to drop everything when you crook your little finger. Yet at the same time you like them not to fuss when you don't reciprocate.'

'I'm a busy man.'

'And I'm a busy woman,' Hannah snapped.

Luca raised his eyebrows in eloquent disbelief. 'Is that your only reservation? Because I feel quite confident that we can work something out.'

'I bet you do.'

'Why are you so offended?'

'Because I don't want to be your bit on the side,' Hannah cried, rising from the sofa and pacing the confines of the room in her agitation. 'I don't want to be *anyone's* bit on the side.'

'You wouldn't be. To say that is to suggest I'd be entertaining other women at the same time, and I assure you I am always faithful to my current partner.'

'Oh, well, then.' Hannah rolled her eyes. '*That's* a relief.'

Luca pressed his lips together. 'What, exactly, is your objection?'

Hannah stared at him, knowing she was being emotional and unreasonable. This offer was *exactly* the sort of thing she should have expected from Luca. It was what she'd been contemplating herself over that fateful weekend. So why was she acting all outraged now?

With a sigh Hannah ceased her pacing and sat back down on the sofa. 'I'm sorry, Luca, but I find everything about your offer objectionable. It's tempting, of course it is, because you're right. I am attracted to you, very much so, and it's hard to ignore that.'

Luca's eyes glittered starkly in his set expression. 'Then don't.'

'But I don't want an affair,' Hannah explained, even

though at the moment she was questioning her own sanity at turning down the most desirable and compelling man she'd ever known. 'At least, I don't want *just* an affair.'

'Ah.' Comprehension dawned on Luca's features and his lips gave a cynical twist. 'So that really was a "maybe".'

Hannah laughed sadly. 'I suppose it was.' She took a deep breath, needing to explain herself further. 'I know what it's like when a man wants you to simply slot into his life, and that's not what a relationship is about.'

'The boyfriend of six years ago?'

'Yes.'

'But you miss him.'

'Yes, although it isn't as simple as that. But a relationship, for me, is give and take. Wanting to be with a person no matter what comes your way, not only in a set of circumstances arranged to your liking. And frankly, Luca, I don't want to be dropped when you've burned through this thing between us.'

Luca's mouth quirked upwards even as his eyes remained hard. 'Maybe I'd be the one to be dropped.'

'Considering how quickly you've worked through women, I think that's unlikely,' Hannah answered. 'You're only the second man I've ever been with. Perhaps I'm responding more emotionally because of that. But the answer has to be no, Luca.' Her heart twisted in protest but Hannah remained firm. 'I want more from a relationship, if I ever choose to have one. I'm not even sure I would. It *is* risky. We both know that. You clearly don't want to take the risk and I'm not sure I do, either.'

'So you want more than I'm offering, except you're not even sure you'd be willing to risk it?' Luca surmised tersely. 'You can't have it both ways, Hannah.'

'I'm not having it any way,' Hannah answered with wry sorrow. 'But I'm definitely not interested in the kind of arrangement you're suggesting.' She took a deep breath and squared her shoulders. 'It's not for me.' Even though it hurt, more than she'd ever admit, to turn him, and her only offer of happiness and companionship, down.

It wouldn't end well, she knew that. She'd start to care too much and Luca would get bored with her. He'd treat her like any of his other women and that would shatter her confidence and break her heart. It was better this way, to end it before it began, even if it felt as if she were being torn in two.

Luca stared at her for a long moment. 'If you're sure,' he said quietly.

'I'm not sure,' Hannah admitted on a despondent laugh. She couldn't keep the yearning from her voice or the desire from pooling inside her. 'All you'd have to do is touch me, Luca,' she admitted, and she knew she wasn't warning him; she was asking him.

Knew Luca realised it as well as heat flared in his eyes, turning them nearly black, as he eased off his chair, coming to kneel before her. She could see the light glinting on the blue-black strands of his hair and wonderingly she reached out and touched the rough-smooth stubble on his jaw. She shouldn't do this. She really shouldn't do this, and yet she *had* to.

'Hannah, do you *know* what you do to me?' he breathed.

'Tell me,' Hannah answered. She felt transfixed, almost drugged, by the desire that stole through her veins at the mere thought of Luca touching her. Wanting her.

'You drive me crazy,' Luca muttered as his hands slid under her hair, cradling her face and tilting her towards him so their lips were a whisper apart. 'You make me lose my mind. All I've been thinking about for the last week is this.' And then he kissed hers, his lips slanting across hers in blatant, primal possession.

Hannah opened herself up to his kiss, yielding everything under the delicious onslaught of his mouth and hands, her body arching towards his as her hands tangled in his hair.

'How can you say no to this?' Luca demanded as he slid his hands under her hoodie, his bare palms cupping her breasts, the friction of skin on skin making her shudder with longing.

'I'm not saying no, am I?' she muttered thickly as Luca tugged the zipper down her hoodie.

'Don't ever say no,' Luca commanded as he pulled her hoodie off. 'I can't bear it. Don't ever say no to me, Hannah.'

Hannah knew she was powerless to say anything at that moment. Her hands roved greedily over his chest, tugging his shirt out of his trousers, for she longed to feel his skin against hers. With a groan Luca tore at his shirt and Hannah was about to tug her own shirt over her head when some distant, desire-fogged part of her brain registered the creak on the stair.

Her hands stilled and Luca glanced at her, his breathing ragged, a question in his eyes.

No, Hannah thought. *No, please...*

The door creaked open. 'Mummy...?'

CHAPTER THIRTEEN

LUCA FROZE AT the same moment that Hannah frantically pushed her T-shirt down and scrambled up from the sofa. He turned, his whole being numb with shock, as she went to the sleepy little boy standing in the doorway. *Her son.*

'Hello, sweetheart.' Hannah scooped up the boy in her arm, nuzzling her cheek against his hair even as she shot Luca a nervous look. 'You're meant to be asleep.'

'I had a bad dream.'

'Let me tuck you back up in bed, Jamie.'

Jamie. So this was the man in her life. He realised he'd stopped wondering who Jamie was, mainly because he'd been so consumed by his desire for Hannah. Now the realisation slammed into him with the force of a sledgehammer, leaving him winded and reeling.

Jamie's eyes rounded as he looked directly at Luca. 'Who's that, Mummy?'

'The man I work for, Jamie. He…he was just here for a meeting.' She shot Luca another look, almost as if she were angry with him. And shouldn't he be the one to be angry? He was the one who had been duped, deceived…

A *son.* Why had Hannah never told him she had a child?

With Jamie cuddled in her arms, Hannah turned towards Luca. 'You can see yourself out…?'

Luca gazed at her for a tense moment. 'I'll wait here,' he answered coolly.

He was questioning that decision when Hannah disappeared upstairs to settle her son, and he was left alone with the ferment of his own thoughts. Hannah had a child. In light of this new information his suggestion of an affair seemed sordid and distasteful.

A *mother* wasn't going to drop everything to parade about in sexy lingerie in the penthouse suite of the next up-and-coming five-star hotel. He might not have outlined his proposal in such vivid detail, but Hannah knew him well enough to understand what he'd had in mind. Sex, uncomplicated and available, without questions, demands, or prevarications. That was how he'd conducted all his affairs. It was what he'd been aiming for with Hannah.

No wonder she'd rejected him.

With a groan of frustration Luca sank onto the sofa. His mind was spinning with this new information. He had no idea what to do with it, but he knew he was angry that Hannah had kept it from him.

He heard the creak of the stairs and then the door opened. He looked up and saw Hannah looking calm and determined, her face pale.

'Why didn't you tell me?' he demanded in a low voice.

'You have no right to know anything about my personal life.'

He jerked back, stung by this biting assessment. 'Didn't this last weekend give me some right?'

Her chin lifted a fraction and she remained by the door, her arms folded, her look haughty. 'Honestly? No.'

Luca suppressed the angry retort he wanted to make. If he calmed down for a second, he could acknowledge that she had a point. He'd dismissed their encounter out of hand last weekend. The fact that she wasn't falling in with his plans now was a source of frustration and disappointment, but it didn't mean she'd been duplicitous or unreasonable. Betrayal couldn't be involved when there had been no relationship to begin with.

He just *felt* betrayed.

'Tell me about him,' he said.

Hannah's eyebrows rose. 'Why, Luca? There's nothing between us. I think it's better if we try to—'

'Humour me.' He cut her off, his teeth gritted.

She stared at him for a long moment, and then finally, thankfully, she unbent. She dropped her haughty stance and came to sit across from him. 'What do you want to know?'

'How old is he?'

'Five.'

'His father?'

'The man I told you about.'

'Your boyfriend? You weren't married?' He heard the prudish censure in his voice and inwardly winced.

'No, we weren't married,' Hannah answered evenly, 'although I think we would have got married if he hadn't died.'

'How did he die?'

'A motorcycle accident.' She pressed her lips together. 'Why do you want to know all this now?'

'I don't know,' he admitted. 'This blindsided me, Hannah. Everything about you has blindsided me, since we first landed on Santa Nicola.'

'Are you regretting ever introducing me as your fiancée?' Hannah asked with a weary laugh. She looked sad, and that made him feel sad. His earlier determination to make her his mistress—and, yes, he would use that word—felt as if it had happened to a different man. Been intended for a different woman.

In truth, though, he didn't regret anything about the

weekend on Santa Nicola. He didn't regret getting to know Hannah, or experiencing the wonder of her body. He just wanted more.

But not that much more.

'So why didn't you ever mention you had a child?' he asked after a moment. 'It's kind of a big thing. Most employers know such details about their employees.'

'You're not most employers, Luca. You never asked.'

'I assumed you were single.'

'I *am* single.'

'And childless,' he clarified. 'If you'd had a child, I would have expected you to mention it.'

She folded her arms, her stance turning defensive again. 'Well, I didn't. I like to keep my personal life private. And frankly, I suspected you wouldn't be thrilled to know I had such a demand on my time. Executive assistants are expected to drop everything for work.'

'And you did drop everything, on many occasions,' Luca observed. 'Who had Jamie?' It felt strange to say the boy's name.

Hannah's mouth tightened. 'My mother.'

'So she lives nearby?'

'Yes.'

Which was why she'd been here the night he'd dropped her off after their shopping and dinner. He sat back, still absorbing all the implications of what he'd discovered.

'Are you asking all these questions as my employer,' Hannah asked slowly, 'or something else?'

Surprised, Luca jerked his gaze to Hannah's. And realised he didn't know the answer to that question. 'I'm just surprised,' he said gruffly, knowing that was no answer at all.

'Well, now you know the truth. And I can assure you, it won't affect my work. It never has.'

Luca thought of the all-nighters and weekends they'd

worked together, suppressing a stab of angry guilt at the realisation. She should have told him she had a child at home who needed her care. He would have made provisions.

Maybe. Or maybe he would have informed her that she really wasn't suited to the demands of the role.

'I should go,' he said, rising from his chair. Hannah watched him, a look of sadness on her face that he didn't understand. *She* was the one who had rejected him. Not that he'd have made that offer if he'd *known*…

'I'll see you tomorrow,' he said and with a brusque nod of farewell he stalked out of the room.

Hannah spent a sleepless night wondering if she should have done things differently. Maybe if she'd been upfront about Jamie from the beginning, or at least from last weekend, Luca wouldn't have made his offer of an arrangement. Maybe he would have tried for something more.

Or maybe he would have run a million miles in the opposite direction. She'd known all along that Luca wasn't dad material. She'd known full well he wasn't interested in a relationship. Her stupid, stubborn heart had insisted on feeling differently, but it didn't change facts.

Rejecting Luca's proposal of an affair made her realise just how much more she wanted—if she dared. Not just with anyone, but with him. With Luca, a man whose heart was clearly off limits.

At least, Hannah reflected, the knowledge of her son would probably put Luca right off her. And, God willing, her attraction to him would fade when it wasn't reciprocated. That was a relief, even if it didn't feel like one.

Her heart couldn't be that broken, considering how quickly things had progressed between them. A little dented maybe, but she'd survived much worse before, and she would again. It really was better this way.

She was still giving herself this pep talk when she dropped Jamie off at school, mentally kicking herself when she saw that his class was having a bake sale and she was the only mother who hadn't brought in a home-made tray bake.

'Didn't you read the letter we sent home?' the teacher asked, her concerned tone still managing to hold a note of reproach.

'I must have forgotten,' Hannah said. She turned to Jamie, who was watching the parade of parents with their offerings of baked goods with a stoic expression that strangely reminded her of Luca. 'Sorry, sweetheart.'

Her little man squared his shoulders. 'It's okay.'

But it wasn't. She tried not to drop the ball like this, but occasionally it happened. Hannah supposed she could excuse herself considering all the distractions she'd had, but she still felt guilty for not putting Jamie first even in such a small matter.

She rang her mother on the way to work, hating to call in yet another favour but also wanting to please her son, asking if Diane could run something in that morning.

'Oh, Hannah, I'm sorry,' her mother said. 'I'm volunteering at the day centre today. I would otherwise…'

'Of course.' Her mother volunteered several times a week with a centre for elderly people and Hannah knew she enjoyed the work. It wasn't fair of her to call her mother away from her own life. 'Don't worry, it's not a big deal,' she said as brightly as she could. And then spent half an hour on the Tube battling a crushing sense of guilt.

She supposed she could blame Luca for this, for questioning her choices, but Hannah was honest enough to admit, at least to herself, that she'd always struggled with working mother's remorse. It might not have been fair or reasonable, but she felt it all the same.

Luca was shut away in his office when Hannah arrived,

and so she got right down to work, trying to push away all the distracting thoughts and worries that circled her mind.

Luca came to discuss some travel arrangements about an hour later, and she instinctively tensed as he approached her desk. She felt both weary and wired, but at least it kept her from shaming herself with an obvious physical response to his presence.

'What's wrong?' he asked after she'd taken down some dates for a trip he was planning to Asia next month.

'What do you mean?' she asked, startled. 'Nothing's wrong.'

'You look worried.' His whisky-brown gaze swept over her as he cocked his head. 'Is it Jamie?'

Hannah stared at him, dumbfounded. 'You've never asked me that before.'

'I never knew you had a child before.'

'Yes, but...' She shook her head, more confused than ever. 'If you had known, you would have been annoyed that I seemed worried and distracted while at work. Not...'

'Not what?' Luca prompted, his gaze locked on hers.

'Not concerned.'

'Perhaps you don't know me as well as you thought you did.'

'Perhaps I don't.' She had thought she knew what kind of man he was. But that had been a week ago, and everything had changed since then.

'So is it your son?' Luca asked. 'That's worrying you?'

Still surprised by his perception as well as his interest, Hannah relented. 'Yes, but it's only a small thing.'

'What?'

'I forgot his class had a bake sale today. Everyone brought in biscuits and cakes, lovely home-made ones, except for me.' She shook her head, almost wanting to laugh at the bemused look on Luca's face. This was so outside his zones of both familiarity and comfort. 'I told you it was a small thing.'

Luca didn't answer for a moment. Hannah sighed and turned back to the notes she'd been making. Clearly she hadn't advanced the cause of working mothers through this exchange.

'So,' Luca said slowly, 'Jamie is the only child in the class without cakes or biscuits?'

'Yes, but it doesn't really matter—'

'It does matter,' Luca stated definitively. 'Let me make a few calls.'

Hannah stared at him in stunned disbelief as he went back into his office. Not knowing what else to do, she got on with making his travel arrangements. Fifteen minutes later, Luca reappeared.

'Come on,' he said. 'My limo is waiting downstairs.'

'Your limo—where are we going?'

'To your son's school.'

'What—?'

'He can't be the only one without cakes,' Luca stated, and stabbed the button for the lift.

Hannah had no choice but to grab her handbag and coat and follow him into the lift. 'Luca, what are you doing? He can manage—'

'But why should he, when I can do something about it?'

'I could have done something,' Hannah muttered. 'Couriered a cake to the school—' Now she felt even more guilt.

'We'll do better than that,' Luca announced. 'We'll deliver them in person.'

The cakes turned out to be forty-eight of the most glorious creations from a nearby exclusive patisserie. Hannah peeked into the white cake box and her jaw dropped at the berries glistening like jewels in folds of perfectly whipped cream.

'These are amazing,' she told Luca. 'And they must have cost—'

'It was no trouble.'

Hannah closed the cake box. 'I'll pay.'

'You will not,' Luca returned swiftly. 'This is my gift. Do not presume to take it from me, Hannah.'

She shook her head slowly, overwhelmed but also befuddled by his generosity. 'I really don't understand you. Last night you seemed angry…'

'I was surprised,' he corrected. 'And I don't deal well with surprises.'

'And now?'

'Now I want to help.'

'But you don't even like children,' Hannah burst out.

Luca glanced at her, affronted. 'Why would you think that?'

'Maybe because you had to make me masquerade as your fiancée to impress a self-proclaimed family man?' Hannah returned dryly. 'Just a thought.'

'Just because I don't want children myself it doesn't mean I don't like them.'

'But why don't you want them, if you like them? Most people do.'

Luca was silent for a long moment, his gaze hooded, his jaw bunched tight. Hannah held her breath as she waited; she realised she really wanted to know the answer.

'I told you it wasn't worth it,' he finally said.

'But what does that even mean—?'

'Since you partially agreed with me, what do you think it meant?' he shot back, his eyes glittering.

Hannah considered the question for a moment. 'It means that you're scared of getting hurt,' she said quietly. 'Afraid of someone leaving you, or stopping to love you. Of loving someone causing you pain rather than joy.'

She held Luca's gaze, willing him to answer, to admit

the truth. 'Well, then,' he said, breaking their locked gazes as he looked out of the window. 'Then you know why.'

Hannah was silent, struggling with her own emotions as well as Luca's. 'It sounds very lonely,' she said finally.

Luca shrugged, his gaze still averted. 'I'm used to being alone.'

She remembered what he'd said on the beach, how he'd felt alone all the time. 'You don't even want to try?' she asked, her voice squeezed from her throat. She didn't know when the conversation had gone from the abstract to the personal, but she knew she was asking him more—and revealing more herself—than just what he thought about relationships in general. She was asking him what he thought about her.

'I don't know if I can,' Luca said in a voice so low Hannah had to strain to hear it.

'You'll never find out if you don't,' Hannah answered and he turned to look at her, his eyes like burning black holes in his tense face.

'That's a very pat answer, and the reality is more complex when there are people involved,' he said. 'Children involved.'

Hannah's breath hitched. She wasn't the only one who had made this conversation intensely personal. 'Luca...'

'If you want to know why I want to help Jamie, it's because I know how he feels,' Luca continued, and her world, which had tilted on its axis for one glorious moment, righted itself with a thud. 'As a child. My mother wasn't often capable of being there for me. Not,' he cut across any protest she'd been going to make, 'that I'm equating you to her. I'm not. I'm quite sure you're a very good mother to your son.'

'Thank you,' Hannah said uncertainly.

'But it doesn't feel good, being the only kid in your class who doesn't have the right kit for PE, or who can't pay for the school dinner. Not that those things happened to Jamie—'

'They happened to you,' Hannah said softly.

'Yes.' Luca's gaze shuttered. 'After my mother died, I had a scholarship to an exclusive boarding school, but it didn't cover everything. I might as well have had "charity orphan" tattooed on my forehead.' He sighed, rolling his shoulders to excise the tension. 'I can relate to feeling left out.'

And the fact that he was doing something about it, trying to make it better for her son, made Hannah's heart feel as if it could burst. Luca was making it very difficult to stop caring about him. One more little act of kindness and she'd be halfway to falling in love with him. More than halfway; she was almost there.

She gave the driver directions to Jamie's school, and the limo pulled up outside the gates while the children were at playtime. They all ran up to the fence, eyes rounded at the sight of the stretch limo. When she and Luca got out, Hannah could hear the whispers running through the huddle of children.

'Isn't that Jamie's mummy—?'

'What is she doing in that fancy car—?'

'That man is so *big*.'

'He's got cakes!'

The whispers turned into excited jabbers as Luca proffered the huge white cake box. 'These are for Jamie Stewart,' he announced in a voice that managed to be both commanding and friendly. 'I heard he needed some cakes for the school bake sale.'

And as the children clambered excitedly around him, Hannah realised that Luca had needed to do this for his sake as much as Jamie's. The knowledge was enough to bring tears to her eyes. After a childhood that had been far too sad and neglected, and an adolescence that hadn't been much better, Luca was finally able to be the boy who had the cakes. Who could make things better.

Jamie beamed at both of them as Luca handed the box into Reception. 'Thank you, Mummy,' he whispered, and threw his arms around her waist, squeezing tight.

Hannah ruffled his baby-soft hair. 'Thank Mr Moretti,' she answered with a smile. 'He was the one who insisted we bring the cakes.'

Jamie turned the full wattage of his smile onto Luca. 'Thank you, Mr Moretti!'

Luca looked startled, and then moved. He nodded once. 'It was my pleasure,' he said gruffly.

They didn't speak as they got back into the limo. Luca looked lost in thought, and Hannah felt as if she might burst into tears. Finally she managed, 'You're a good man, Luca Moretti.'

He turned his startled gaze on her, his expression ironing out to a familiar and heart-sinking blandness. 'You might not think that in a moment.'

'Why not?' Hannah asked, her heart now nearing her toes.

'Because Andrew Tyson emailed me this morning. He wants to have dinner with us tomorrow night.'

CHAPTER FOURTEEN

HANNAH GAZED AT herself in the mirror, frowning at her pale cheeks and sparkling eyes. She felt both terrified and elated at the thought of the evening ahead, posing once again as Luca's loving fiancée, and it showed in her face. She had no idea what to expect of this evening, of Luca. Her hopes careened wildly, and it was impossible to keep a leash on them.

Her mother's eyebrows rose as Hannah appeared in the sitting room. 'This is a business dinner?' she asked sceptically, because the emerald-green satin dress hugged her slender curves lovingly and was a far cry from her usual pencil skirt and silk blouse ensemble. She'd bought it on her lunch break, spending far more on a single garment than she ever had before, and she couldn't make herself regret it.

'It's more of a social occasion,' Hannah hedged.

Her mother's eyebrows rose higher. 'A date?'

'Maybe,' Hannah admitted, and then added hastily, before her mother got completely carried away, 'But probably not.'

Almost certainly not, she reminded herself sternly. No matter how much her stubborn heart couldn't help hoping since she'd seen a softer side of Luca yesterday, Hannah knew tonight was about donning the pretence once more. If

Luca acted lovingly towards her, it was because he needed to convince Andrew Tyson, not because he actually felt something for her. And if he did feel something for her... was she even willing to try? To risk her heart again, to lose someone she loved again?

Because Luca Moretti was a dangerous proposition.

The burden of pretending felt heavier that night than it had over the weekend in Santa Nicola. How was she supposed to pretend to love a man she was afraid she already had those feelings for? She didn't know what part of herself to hide, and what part to reveal. And she didn't like the thought of deceiving Andrew Tyson again, no matter what kind of history existed between him and Luca. The man was kind, with a genuine desire to see a family man take over his resorts. No matter that Luca had a good plan for the resort, lying was still lying.

Despite these concerns, Hannah's insides lit up with excitement when Luca's limo pulled up in front of her house. Jamie was still awake, his face pressed to the glass as he inspected the limo.

'That is a *cool* car.'

'Yes, well.' Hannah kissed her son's cheek. 'Be good for Nana.'

'I will.' His gaze was glued on the limo, and Luca's powerful form as he exited the vehicle and started towards their front door. Hannah's heart flipped over at the sight of him in a grey business suit with a crimson tie. *Why* did she react this way to him, when she'd seen him in such a suit dozens, hundreds of times? Her body didn't care. Everything had changed.

Luca knocked on the door and Jamie raced to open it.

'Jamie—' Hannah began half-heartedly, because she hated to dampen her son's excitement.

'Did you bring me any cakes?' Jamie demanded of Luca, and Hannah put a restraining hand on her son's shoulder.

'Jamie, don't be rude.'

'But of course I did,' Luca answered with an easy smile, and took a perfectly wrapped mini chocolate cake from behind his back. Jamie crowed in delight. 'Share with your grandmother,' Luca advised while Hannah simply stared, dumbfounded.

'What?' he asked as he caught her stunned look. 'Why are you so surprised?'

'I'm just…' Hannah shrugged helplessly. 'I didn't expect you to be so thoughtful.' Towards her son. He was turning all her preconceived notions on their head, and that was dangerous. Her head was counselling her heart to hold back, stop hoping. Meanwhile her heart was doing cartwheels.

'That's quite a backhanded compliment,' Luca remarked. 'But I'll take it.' His heated gaze scorched her for one breathtaking second. 'You look amazing.'

'Thank you.' Hannah's breath dried in her throat. He looked amazing too, his eyes burning almost gold in his bronzed face, his lithe, muscular body encased in a superbly cut suit, every atom of him radiating both beauty and power.

'Enjoy yourself,' Diane said, a knowing twinkle in her eye, and Hannah decided it was time to get themselves out of there, before her mother said—or she did—something revealing.

'Thank you,' she said belatedly, once they were settled in the car. 'For giving Jamie the cake. You're practically spoiling him.'

'I don't mind.' He sat back against the sumptuous leather seat, and Hannah eased away from him a little bit, because the temptation was to snuggle closer.

'So why does Andrew Tyson want to meet us again?' she asked, determined to keep focused on why they were there together.

'I don't know. He simply said he wanted to have dinner with us, to discuss the plans and get to know us better.'

'Get to know us better?' Hannah repeated as alarm bells started clanging. 'But what if he suspects something? We could get tripped up easily enough.'

'Could we?' Luca asked softly. His eyes glittered in the darkness of the car. 'I think we know each other rather well by now.'

Hannah was glad the darkness hid her blush. 'That may be so, but there are still questions he could ask us, about how you proposed—'

'On top of the Eiffel Tower.'

'*Luca.*' Hannah's breath came out in a rush. 'You know what I mean.'

'Yes, I know you're tired of the pretence, just as I am. But tonight will be the last, Hannah. I'm hoping Tyson will announce his intentions for the resorts tonight.' He glanced out of the window. 'I need him to,' he said in a low voice.

Hannah gazed at his tense profile for a few seconds before asking quietly, 'What is the source of the bad blood between you and Tyson, Luca? What happened, that he doesn't even know about it?'

'It was a long time ago.'

'That's not an answer.'

'It's all the answer I'm going to give.' Luca hesitated. 'I'm sorry, Hannah. That part of my life is not up for discussion.'

Luca saw Hannah's expression close up and knew she was hurt that he'd put her off. But how could he admit the truth? He'd already revealed enough about his childhood. He didn't want to invite more pity—or condemnation, for his plans for Tyson. That part of his life wasn't up for discussion, and neither was it negotiable.

And while his plans for revenge remained crystalline

clear, his feelings for Hannah were more confused than ever. He'd surprised himself by going to Jamie's school yesterday, and then buying the boy a cake tonight. Even more unsettling was the excitement he'd felt at seeing Hannah; she looked amazing in the emerald-green dress that clung to her like a second skin and brought out the golden glints in her hair and eyes. His palms itched to smooth over her curves, to tug down the zip and watch the bright, satiny material fall away.

Nothing had dampened his desire for her, not the discovery that she had a son, not the flat refusal of his offer. In fact, both things made him want her more, which was contrary and frustrating. He'd enjoyed seeing her cuddle her son, and witnessing her obvious love for her child made a powerful ache reside inside him, for what he'd missed as a child himself, but also for what he hadn't attempted to have as a man. The fact that she'd refused his sex-only offer made him respect her—more than he respected himself. She wanted more from a relationship. She wasn't afraid to try for it.

But he was.

It was fear, pure and simple, that was keeping him from asking Hannah to have a real relationship. The knowledge was shaming. When had fear ever held him back? He'd brokered huge deals, taking massive business risks. He'd started virtually empty-handed, a twenty-two-year-old fresh out of university with nothing to recommend him but a degree. How could he be afraid now? And not just now, but all along?

He'd thought staying solitary was being strong, but since coming to know Hannah, since witnessing her own particular brand of courage, he wondered if it was actually weakness.

And that thought was the most terrifying of all. Because if he did try just as Hannah had asked him to, if he risked

himself, heart and soul, what then? What happened if—
when—Hannah walked away from him?

The limo pulled up in front of the upscale restaurant
Tyson had suggested for their meeting. Luca glanced at
Hannah, the lights from the streets washing over her pale,
strained features. She wasn't looking forward to pretending again, and, God knew, he wasn't either.

'Hannah.' He rested a hand over hers, savouring the
warmth of her skin, the comfort of the contact. 'I promise this is the last time. We won't have to pretend again,
ever, no matter what.'

She turned to face him, her eyes huge in her face. 'Do
you really mean that?'

'Yes.'

'What if Tyson asks for another meeting? What if he
wants us to come to the opening of the resorts?'

'He won't,' Luca stated flatly and Hannah shook her
head, her expression turning wild.

'But don't you see, Luca? The pretence never ends. He
might be expecting an invitation to our wedding—'

'He won't. And in a few weeks or months, we can quietly announce our broken engagement.'

'Oh.' She sat back against the seat as if she'd been
winded. 'I see. So I'm thrown over for the next supermodel?'

'I never suggested such a thing,' Luca returned sharply.
'We can make it a mutual decision, or you can be the one to
throw me over. I deserve it, after all I've put you through.'
And yet the thought made everything inside him clench in
denial. They were talking about a fake engagement and yet
he still felt rejected. Because he didn't want to end things
with Hannah. Not yet. Not until…when?

He knew he was being ridiculous. It was better to be
safe than sorry. Better to be alone and strong than broken-
hearted and weak. He'd *lived* by that. He'd built his life on
that knowledge. He couldn't change now.

Could he?

'We should go in,' Hannah said tiredly as she reached for the door handle. She turned her face from him, and Luca felt the loss.

The excitement Hannah had felt at spending the evening with Luca had fizzled out. She felt tired and sad and strangely empty, and the prospect of pretending for several hours filled her with despair. She didn't want this. She wanted Luca to love her for real. She wanted to be honest about her feelings, not play this wretched game—and for what? A business deal that was practically pocket change to a man like Luca?

He hadn't wanted to tell her about his history with Tyson, and his flat, final tone had made her afraid to push. Luca had made it clear she had no rights in his life, even if she wanted them.

The restaurant was quiet and elegant, with each table afforded maximum privacy. Waiters moved discreetly around the room with its frescoed walls and plush carpeting, and the only sound was the tinkle of expensive crystal and silver, the low murmur of conversation.

The understated ambiance reminded Hannah poignantly of that first dinner she'd had with Luca, when he'd bought her clothes and she'd felt gauche and unsure and yet also excited. Before everything had begun. It hadn't even been two weeks ago, and yet it felt like a lifetime. She felt like a different person, one who had lived and loved and lost.

Hannah told herself she was being melodramatic. Two weeks. You couldn't fall in love with someone in two weeks, especially when you hadn't even been looking for love in the first place.

But you've known him for three years.

'Luca, Hannah.' Andrew Tyson's melodious voice floated out to them as he stood up at the private table he'd reserved for them in a corner of the restaurant. 'So nice to see you again.'

Luca's arm snaked around her waist and he drew her close enough so their hips nudged. Heat stroked along Hannah's veins at the contact. The attraction she felt for Luca was as potent as ever.

Tyson stuck out his hand for Luca to shake and after the tiniest pause Luca shook it. 'Andrew.' His voice was even, businesslike without being friendly.

Tyson kissed Hannah's cheek and then they all sat down while he had the waiter bring them a bottle of the restaurant's best champagne.

'To celebrate your engagement,' he said with a smile. 'Among other things. Have you set a date?'

Hannah snuck a glance at Luca, waiting for his cue, and watched as he smiled easily. 'In the summer. You always hear talk of June weddings.'

June? That was only two months away. Hannah schooled her face into a smile as Tyson turned to her. 'Will that give you enough time to plan, Hannah?'

'Oh, I think so.' Her smile felt as if it were stretching like a rubber band across her face, ready to snap. 'With Luca's contacts, things can happen quite quickly.'

'Oh, I'm sure.' Andrew gazed at them both speculatively, and Hannah tensed, wondering if he suspected. What if Daniela had whispered something into his ear? Then his face relaxed and the waiter popped the cork on the champagne, and then Andrew raised his glass of bubbly in a toast.

'To marriage,' he said. 'And family. And true love, of course.'

'To all three,' Hannah said as gamely as she could, and they clinked glasses.

'Are you planning on having a family?' Andrew asked. 'I know that's a personal question, but—'

'We both want children,' Luca cut in swiftly. 'Two or three, at least. I prefer an even number.'

'Why not four, then?' Hannah suggested a bit tartly. This from the man who had told her less than an hour ago that he didn't want children at all.

Luca slid her a burning glance. 'Four it is, then.'

And just like that she imagined a dark-haired baby in her arms, a toddler on Luca's shoulders, which was idiotic. This was *pretend*.

'Good thing they come one at a time,' Andrew said with a laugh. 'Generally speaking.'

They ordered their food then, and Hannah tried to relax. Tried not to take every smiling glance or casual caress that Luca gave her like a dagger to the heart, but they hurt all the same. Because he was only acting for Andrew Tyson's sake, and yet no amount of reminders could keep her body from responding, her heart from yearning.

When he held her hand throughout the first course, and gave her a bite of his dessert as he smiled into her eyes, and referenced an in-joke she hadn't even known they'd had...all of it made her feel a potent, impossible mixture of hope and despair. This wasn't real, she knew that, and yet it *felt* real. She wanted it to be real.

By the end of the evening her nerves were well and truly frayed. Andrew had remained jovial, Luca loving. Hannah had been the only one who had seemed to feel the strain.

As they were settling the bill she excused herself to go to the ladies'. She needed a break from the play-acting. In the bathroom mirror her face looked pale, her eyes too dark. She touched up her make-up and tried to find a smile. Not much longer now, a thought that brought both relief and disappointment. As soon as they left the restaurant, would Luca revert to his normal, businesslike self?

Luca and Tyson were shaking hands as she came out of the bathroom. 'I'll be in touch soon,' Tyson promised.

'Has he not told you for certain yet?' Hannah asked as they left the restaurant for the waiting limo. Luca opened the door for her before sliding in beside her.

'Not yet, but I think it's almost certain.'

'Why did he want to see us?'

'To make sure he's making the right decision, I suppose.'

The limo pulled away from the kerb and in the wash of streetlights Hannah saw the lines of tension bracketing Luca's mouth and eyes.

'At least it's over,' she said quietly.

He glanced at her, a frown pulling his eyebrows together. 'You didn't enjoy it.'

It was a statement, and one Hannah couldn't contradict, at least not completely. 'I'm tired of pretending,' she said. 'You know that.' But that wasn't the whole truth, and the events of the evening, as well as the past couple of weeks, compelled her to continue. 'But it's not just that. I don't like pretending, Luca. With you.' She took a deep breath and turned away so he couldn't see the tears sparkling on her lashes. 'It hurts.'

Luca was silent for so long Hannah was afraid she'd appalled him with her honesty, and yet she felt too sad to be embarrassed. This hurt past mere humiliation.

'Hannah.' He cupped her cheek in his palm, turning her face so she was looking at him. He caught the tear trembling on her lash with his thumb. 'Don't cry. I can't stand it if you cry.' His other hand came up to cup her face, and his voice came out on a groan. 'I can't stand the thought of hurting you,' he said, and then he kissed her.

CHAPTER FIFTEEN

LUCA'S LIPS CRASHED down on Hannah's and it felt like coming home. Her mouth opened under his and her hands clutched his lapels. He heard her soft moan and it incited him further. He wanted her. He *needed* her.

'Luca…' she muttered and he pulled her to him, his hands sliding over the slippery satin, anchoring on her hips, wanting to keep her as close as possible.

She pressed against him, the softest part of her arching against him so he could barely restrain himself from peeling her dress away from her body and burying himself inside her warmth.

The limo began to slow to a stop and with a gasp Hannah pulled back, her face flushed, her lips swollen.

'I'm home…'

'This is home,' Luca growled, and pulled her towards him. She came willingly, melting into him, her lips finding his as she rubbed against him.

'I can't, Luca,' she mumbled but then let out a breathy sigh as his hand cupped her breast.

'You really can.'

She laughed shakily. 'Is this really a good idea?' She pulled back again, and even in the darkness of the limo he saw the unhappy confusion in her eyes.

Luca took a deep breath, willing the fire in his body to fade. 'It seems like a very good idea to me.'

'I still don't want a fling, Luca.'

He glanced away, feeling cornered and yet knowing it was unfair. Just because Hannah didn't want what he did…

And hell if he actually knew what he wanted.

'Couldn't we just take one day at a time?' he asked. 'And see what happens?'

Hannah stilled and he turned to face her. She looked delectable, half-sprawled on his lap, her hair falling down from its chignon, her eyes bright and luminous, rosy lips parted.

'What exactly are you saying?'

'That I don't want to lose you. But I don't know how much I have to give.'

She let out a trembling laugh. 'That's honest, I suppose.'

'Most people don't start a relationship promising for ever,' Luca said gruffly.

Hannah's gaze sharpened. 'Is that what you're suggesting? A relationship, rather than a fling?'

'Yes.' The word came reluctantly, and Hannah could tell. She laughed again, the sound one of both sorrow and hope.

'Well?' Luca asked. 'What about it?'

'One day at a time?' she said slowly, and Luca nodded, holding his breath, amazed at how much this meant to him. How much he needed her to say yes.

A slow, shy smile bloomed across her lovely face. 'Sounds pretty good to me.'

The next morning, as she headed into work, Hannah was fizzing with both anticipation and anxiety. She couldn't wait to see Luca, but she was afraid he might have changed his mind. Afraid that one day at a time might mean one day, full stop. Last night, in the darkness of the limo, after the intensity of their charade for Tyson and then that passionate, overwhelming kiss, maybe Luca had said things he regretted in the cold light of morning.

Her doubts were swept away when Luca strode into the office and, going right to her desk, pulled her towards him for a thorough kiss.

'Good thing no one else is on this floor,' Hannah exclaimed, her lips buzzing, when he'd finally released her. 'What if someone saw?'

'No one did,' he returned before heading into his office. Hannah sat down at her desk, her lips buzzing, her heart singing with joy.

She told herself to slow down, to take one day at a time just as Luca had said, because neither of them had any idea what tomorrow could bring. But her mind and heart both went leaping ahead anyway. Seemed as soon as she'd got over the anxiety of actually starting a relationship she went tumbling in, head-and-heart-first.

Luca asked her to spend Saturday with him—the day with Jamie and the night the two of them alone. Both prospects filled Hannah with both excitement and nervousness. Introducing her son properly to Luca was a big step—and as for the night…

She just felt excitement about that.

Luca had asked her what kinds of things Jamie liked to do, and she'd told him the usual five-year-old-boy pursuits: the park, the zoo, football. 'And he's mad about planes,' she'd confided. 'We always go outside to look at them heading for Heathrow.'

Luca had typed it all into his smartphone, looking as serious as he did when conducting a million-pound business deal. Hannah's heart had ached with love.

Yes, she was falling in love with this man, and it was happening so hard and fast it scared her. Luca might not be keeping up. In fact, she was quite sure he wasn't. Every interaction that didn't have his hands on her body and his mouth on hers was difficult for him, the words stilted but sincere. He was trying, but it was hard. And maybe one day, even one day soon, it would become too hard.

But in the meantime…

She would do as Luca said and enjoy each day as it came. She knew she couldn't stop herself from falling in love with Luca, even when her mother worried about her, even when she stared at her son's sleeping face and wondered if she was setting everyone up for a catastrophic fall. She knew what it was like to love and lose. She didn't want that to happen again, no matter what she'd told Luca about wanting to try.

Saturday dawned sunny and warm, a perfect spring day that felt like a promise. Luca picked them up not in his usual limo, but in a flashy sports convertible that Hannah had never seen before. Jamie leapt up and down with excitement at the prospect of travelling in such a vehicle; Luca had even gone to the trouble of installing an appropriate car seat.

'It's perfectly safe,' he told Hannah, even though she hadn't said anything. 'I can see the worry in your eyes. But this car has been crash-tested in all sorts of situations.'

'Is it yours?'

'Yes, although I don't drive it as often as I could. I usually prefer to be driven, and use the time to work.'

'You do have an admirable work ethic,' Hannah said with a smile. She buckled Jamie into his seat. 'So where are we going?'

Luca waggled his eyebrows. 'You'll see.'

She smiled, enjoying seeing this lighter side to the man she loved. 'It's a surprise?'

'Yep.'

The surprise turned out to be a visit to a private airfield, with Jamie being allowed to scramble in and out of planes, from private jets to a retired fighter plane, culminating in a helicopter ride over London. Jamie's eyes were huge as he pressed his face to the window and Luca pointed out the London Eye, Big Ben. Hannah's heart felt so full she couldn't keep from grinning. From squeezing Luca's hand the whole ride, simply because she needed to show him how much he meant to her.

They had a luxurious picnic lunch that Luca had arranged on a field overlooking the planes, and as Jamie cavorted around, running off his excess energy, Hannah turned to Luca and put her hand over his.

'Thank you. This day has been amazing. Jamie will remember it for ever.' She squeezed his hand. 'But, you know, the park or the zoo would have been fine, too.'

'I know not every day can be like this,' Luca admitted wryly. 'But I suppose I wanted to make a good first impression.'

'Trust me, you'd already done that with the cakes.' She paused, her hand still over his, longing to know more about this man her heart had already yielded to. 'How is it you grew up with so little and yet now you have so much?'

Luca shrugged. 'Hard work, a lot of determination, and a good dose of luck.'

'Where did you grow up?' Hannah asked. 'I'm ashamed to admit I don't even know.'

'A small village in Sicily.' Luca's expression closed, and Hannah knew this had to be hard for him. 'My mother was unwed when she had me, and in that kind of remote, traditional community we both suffered badly, albeit in different ways.'

'Oh, Luca, I'm sorry.' Now she understood why he'd asked if she'd been married when she'd had Jamie.

'It made me determined to escape.'

'And foster care? Was that hard?'

He shrugged, the negligent movement belying the deep emotion she saw fermenting in his eyes. 'It was what it was. A home for orphan boys in rural Sicily—what do you expect? But I had a good teacher and he encouraged me to apply for a scholarship. From there I went to university, and when I was twenty-two I bought my first property, a falling-down building in one of the worst districts in Naples.'

'And what did you do with it?' she asked, intrigued.

'I developed it into a halfway house for homeless teens and sold it to the government.'

'You've never forgotten your roots,' Hannah said slowly. She'd known that Luca had been committed to certain principles in all of his property deals. She just hadn't understood what had motivated him.

'I never have,' Luca agreed, his voice going a bit flat. 'And I never will.' His tone had turned ruthless, almost menacing, and it made Hannah afraid to ask any more questions. In any case, Luca asked one instead. 'Tell me about Jamie's father.'

Hannah tensed even though she knew he had a right to ask the question. 'What about him?'

'Did you love him?'

'Yes, but it feels a long time ago now.'

'You told me you knew what it felt like for someone to expect you to slot in his life.'

Hannah sighed. 'Yes, that was what Ben expected, and I didn't realise it until I stopped.'

'What do you mean?'

She hesitated, not wanting to access all these old memories yet accepting that Luca had a right to the truth. 'I met Ben while in college. He had dreams of travelling afterwards, seeing the world. When we'd started dating we planned this carefree life, traipsing around Europe and Asia, taking jobs as we could, living totally free.'

Luca studied her, his gaze both serious and intent. 'And then what happened?'

'And then I fell pregnant. Accidentally. And I realised

that I wanted to keep the baby, that Ben's dreams of travelling the world weren't really my dreams, even though I'd convinced myself they were. I'd never been anywhere, as you know, and I liked the idea of an adventure. I just liked the idea of a bigger adventure, of being a mother, better. I couldn't turn away from that.'

'And how did… Ben react?'

'He wasn't pleased, to say the least. He was furious with me, and he demanded I have an abortion.' She tucked her knees up to her chest, resting her chin on top as she recalled that last, awful confrontation, felt the ensuing, needling guilt. 'I could sympathise with him a little, because I'd done a complete about-face, and now wanted something we'd both agreed to *not* wanting, at least not for a long while.' She paused, her gaze unfocused as she recalled Ben's parting words. *I'll damn well go alone, then.*

'Hannah?' Luca's voice was gentle, breaking into her unhappy thoughts. He squeezed her fingers. 'What happened?'

'We had a huge row. He said he was going to travel anyway, and leave me behind. And then he stormed out and jumped onto his motorcycle, and twenty minutes later crashed into a lorry. He died instantly.' She raised her eyes, giving Luca a sorrowful smile. 'I've chosen to believe that he might have come round. He was shocked, and understandably so, and he always did have a temper. And I felt terribly guilty, still do really, for yelling right back at him. But he would have come round. He wouldn't have left me or our child, not if he had a choice.' Luca didn't answer and Hannah let out a wobbly laugh. 'You probably don't believe that. And maybe he wouldn't have, but I don't want Jamie to know that about his father. You're actually the only person I've told.'

'Not even your mother…?'

'I didn't want her to think badly of Jamie's father…and I

felt guilty for my part in the whole mess.' She sighed. 'But it did make me realise what I wanted a relationship to be, and it's not simply wanting to be with someone when they go along with your plans. It's wanting to be with someone *whatever* the plans. Because plans fall apart. People change. I've learned that lesson more than once.'

Luca turned her hand over, stroking her palm with his thumb. 'So have I.'

'I don't want to rush you,' Hannah blurted. 'I know this is new…for both of us. But with Jamie involved…'

'I understand.'

'It can't all be fancy cakes and helicopter rides.'

'I know.' Luca's expression turned distant. 'But I can't help but want to give Jamie some of the things I never had.' He gave her a quick, reassuring smile. 'I won't spoil him, I promise.'

'I know you won't. I can't believe we're even talking about this. You've exceeded my expectations in so many ways,' she admitted with a laugh. 'I should have told you I had a child ages ago.'

'I would have reacted differently,' Luca said sombrely. 'You've changed me, Hannah.'

Her heart lifted and she lifted his hand to her mouth to press a kiss to his palm. 'Not too much, though. Because I like you the way you are.'

'Just enough,' Luca assured her, and then leaned across to kiss her tenderly.

Jamie fell asleep on the way back home, and Luca carried him inside to a waiting Diane.

'Have fun,' Diane said, kissing her daughter on the cheek, and then Hannah was back in the sports car with Luca driving to his flat in Mayfair.

She'd never been to his home before, had no idea what to expect. She'd been touched that Luca had wanted to bring her there, and not to some anonymous luxury hotel. He was inviting her into his life in so many ways.

As excited as she was to be alone with Luca, she was also incredibly nervous. The last and only time they'd made love it had been hurried and desperate, a moment of passion neither of them had been expecting. Tonight would be completely different…a deliberate coming together and giving of themselves. Hannah didn't want to disappoint him.

'I feel a little nervous,' she admitted after Luca had parked the car in the underground garage and they were riding up the lift to his penthouse flat.

'Nervous? Why?'

'Because this is different. What if…what if I'm not good enough?'

Luca's eyebrows rose nearly to his hairline. 'Trust me, Hannah, you're more than good enough. I feel like I've been waiting for this night for most of my life.'

She smiled tremulously, pleased by his words but not quite sure if she could believe them. Luca had had dozens, hundreds of women, and was the most powerful, compelling, and attractive man she'd ever met.

And what was she? A single mum with stretchmarks and a B-cup bra size.

The doors of the lift opened directly onto his flat, a single open space with a soaring ceiling and panoramic views of the city. Hannah stepped out onto the marble parquet floor, her heart making its way up to her mouth.

Luca stepped behind her and rested his hands on her shoulders. 'Hannah. Trust me. I want to be with you more than I've wanted to be with anyone in my life.' Gently he brushed her hair aside to kiss the curve of her shoulder, his lips lingering on her skin so a shudder ran through her body.

'I feel the same way,' she whispered, because how could

she not? Luca was amazing. He'd blown her world clean apart.

'Good,' Luca said gruffly, and slid his arms around her waist, drawing her back to rest against the hard wall of his chest. She could already feel his arousal, felt an answering desire race through her veins, pool between her thighs.

'I brought lingerie,' she told him on a shaky breath. 'But I don't know if I want to wait long enough to put it on, just so you can take it off again.'

'I don't,' Luca answered in a growl. 'Save it for another night.' He spun her around, his hands delving into her hair as his mouth found purchase. Hannah returned the kiss, revelling in it, in him, in the freedom and luxury of the whole evening ahead of them.

Still kissing her, Luca backed her towards his bedroom, separated from the living area by linen-covered screens. The bedroom contained nothing but a massive bed, the navy silk duvet stretched invitingly across. With a little smile Luca pushed her back onto it, and then covered her body with his own.

They kissed and kissed, legs and limbs tangling, hands smoothing over every body part they could find. Laughing, both of them, breathless with anticipation and joy.

After a few frenzied moments Luca rolled away, his breath ragged. 'We don't need to rush.'

'I rather feel like rushing,' Hannah admitted. Every part of her ached with the need for Luca to touch her, and, more than that, to feel that glorious sense of completion and unity she'd felt before.

'Well,' Luca answered as he rolled back to rest lightly on top of her. 'You can't always have everything you want.' He popped the button on her jeans and ran his hand lightly over her belly. 'Sometimes you have to be patient.'

'Are you going to teach me, then?' Hannah asked, her

breath coming out in a shudder as Luca tugged down her zip.

'If I can,' he admitted and pressed a kiss to her belly. 'If I can be patient myself. I want you so very much, Hannah.'

His heartfelt words made her heart sing even as his hands made her body burn. He stripped off her clothes and then it was her turn to unbutton his shirt, tug down his jeans. She ran her hands over the sculpted muscles she'd only glimpsed in the dark.

'You really are the most beautiful man. It's most unfair,' she complained laughingly.

'Unfair? Do you really want to look like me?'

She curled a hand around his impressive biceps as his mouth dipped to her breasts. 'No,' she confessed breathlessly, 'but sometimes I feel like an ugly duckling to your swan.'

Luca lifted his head, his gaze locking on hers. 'Hannah, you're beautiful.'

'To you, maybe, but from a purely objective—'

'To me, yes. Completely to me.' He brushed the hair away from her face and pressed a gentle kiss to her lips before saying, 'I can't be objective when it comes to you. All I see is a woman who makes me burn. Who cares what anyone else thinks?'

'When you put it like that...' Hannah said, her laugh turning to a gasp as Luca's mouth moved lower.

She writhed underneath his sure and knowing touch as he used his mouth and hands on her most sensitive places. Arched her hips, inviting him to a deeper caress and then sighing with both satisfaction and need as he took her up on her blatant offer.

And she touched him, revelling in the hard planes of his chest, the sharp curve of his hip, and the pulsing strength of his arousal.

Luca groaned as she wrapped her hand around him. 'You're going to kill me.'

'But you'll die happy,' Hannah teased.

Then, finally, he was moving inside her, her body stretching to accommodate him, her eyes widening as she felt him in her deepest part. She wrapped her legs around his waist, her hands clutching his shoulders as he began to move and she matched his rhythm.

'Luca…'

She closed her eyes as she surrendered herself to the wave of pleasure they were both riding to the crest, until Luca touched her cheek and whispered raggedly, 'Look at me, Hannah. I want to see you as I make love to you. I want you to see me.'

Hannah opened her eyes to see Luca gazing at her with burning need, and that blazing look was what had her tumbling over the edge of that wave, until they were both lost in pleasure.

Afterwards they lay in a tangle of limbs and covers, their heart rates slowing as their breathing settled. Hannah stretched and then snuggled into Luca, his arm coming around her shoulders. She felt sated and happy, her body nearly boneless.

She smoothed her hand down Luca's chest, enjoying the liberty of touching him. Her hand drifted lower and he caught it in his.

'Give me a few minutes, at least,' he murmured, and she laughed softly. 'Vixen,' he teased, and pressed a kiss to her hair.

'I like taking one day at a time,' Hannah told him lazily. 'And one night at a time.'

'Glad to hear it.'

'It's funny to think that if you hadn't needed a fake fiancée we wouldn't be here like this.' She'd meant to tease but she felt Luca tense next to her. She rolled onto her side, her hair brushing his chest as she looked at him. His expression was bland, and she'd learned how he used that to hide his true, deeper feelings. 'Luca? What is the history between you and Tyson?'

'I told you before, it happened a long time ago.'

'But it matters,' Hannah said quietly. 'It certainly mattered to you during that weekend. And yet he doesn't even know...how can that be?'

'Leave it, Hannah.'

She recoiled at the taut note of warning in his voice. She'd thought they'd moved past that kind of thing. She'd thought they'd been opening up to each other. She'd certainly told Luca more about herself than she had anyone else.

'Why can't you tell me about it?' she asked, and Luca rolled off the bed so he was sitting on the edge, his back to her.

'Because it's not important.'

Hannah knew she shouldn't push. She might be risking everything they'd only just started to build, and yet...what *had* they built, if they couldn't talk about this?

She took a deep breath. 'It is important, but you obviously don't want to tell me.' She waited for something from Luca, but he didn't reply.

CHAPTER SIXTEEN

'ANDREW TYSON FOR you on line one.'

Hannah's deliberately neutral voice made Luca grimace. They'd managed to get beyond that awkward moment on Saturday night, when she'd asked about Tyson and he hadn't given her any answers, but only just.

Part of him had wanted to admit to her what Tyson was to him, but he'd held back out of instinct, not willing to part with that painful information yet. Not wanting to be so exposed. Now he wondered if he should have, because once the deal was signed Hannah would know his plans for the resorts. And what would she think then?

It didn't matter. This had nothing to do with Hannah. What they had together was sacred, and what had happened with Tyson had no part in that.

Realising he was keeping Tyson waiting, Luca picked up the phone.

'Moretti here.'

'Luca.' Tyson's voice oozed genial warmth, making Luca flinch. Tyson had turned away from him once before, utterly and without any remorse. The fact that he was friendly now, not knowing who Luca really was, made his kindness grate.

'Hello, Andrew.' He managed to keep his tone neutral. When he'd decided to go after Tyson's resorts, he hadn't considered the impact of dealing with the man himself. He'd told himself he didn't care, that he felt nothing for the man who'd fathered him, the man he'd seen only once. Even if the scent of lilies still made him retch. Every interaction with the man showed those assertions for the lies they were.

'I have good news for you, Luca,' Andrew said. 'And I'm sure you know what it is.'

'I believe I do.' Luca listened as Andrew outlined the deal he'd been waiting for: a takeover of the Tyson resorts.

'Because,' Andrew finished, 'if I can't have one of my own children running the place, I'd like to have you.' A sentiment that nearly made Luca choke.

They finished the conversation with plans to finalise the paperwork next week, when Tyson was in London. Luca put down the phone and stared vacantly out of the window at the busy streets far below, the sky cloudless and blue above.

Distantly he registered a tap at the door, and then the sound of it opening. 'Luca?' Hannah asked, her expression wary. 'That was Andrew Tyson, wasn't it? Did he give you an answer?'

'Yes.' Luca forced himself to face Hannah and smile. 'He's accepted my bid.'

Hannah's answering smile morphed into an uncertain frown. 'But…aren't you happy?'

Was he happy? He'd been happy this last week with Hannah. As for Tyson… He didn't feel the satisfaction, the triumph and the sense of retribution that he'd thought he'd feel upon owning his father's business. When it came to Tyson, he felt…empty.

'Luca?' Hannah asked softly. She walked towards him, laying a hand on his arm. 'I wish you'd tell me what was wrong.'

This was the time to tell her about Tyson. To tell her the truth. Luca gazed up into Hannah's voice, saw the concern and care shining in her eyes, and his throat closed.

'Nothing's wrong,' he said gruffly, the words squeezed out of his too-tight throat. The smile on his face felt plastic and he reached for her so she couldn't see how fake it was. 'Nothing's wrong at all.'

He didn't think he'd fooled her because she just frowned before kissing him gently on the lips, making Luca feel as if something inside him were breaking.

'I've got a good idea,' he said afterwards, his arms still around her. 'I have a boring black-tie dinner tonight that I was thinking of skipping. Why don't we go to it together instead?'

Hannah pulled away from him so she could study his face. 'You mean...as a couple?'

'Yes, that's exactly what I mean. I've become part of your world, but you haven't yet become part of mine.'

Tremulous hope lit her eyes even as she frowned uncertainly. 'I don't have anything to wear.'

'Hmm, your last evening gown didn't survive the trip, did it?' Luca teased. 'I think it's time for another visit to Diavola.' Hannah didn't light up at this prospect as he'd expected her to. 'What? You don't want to buy a new dress?'

'You'd be buying the dress,' Hannah replied. 'And I don't want to be treated like your mistress.'

Luca suppressed a sigh. 'So am I never allowed to buy you things? It's as much, if not more, of a pleasure for me, Hannah.'

She chewed her lip, clearly torn. 'I don't know,' she admitted. 'But I don't want to be treated like one of your women.'

'You aren't.' Luca's lips twisted in wry self-deprecation. 'I never even spent the entire night with a woman before you, Hannah. Not that I want to admit that, but you're different. I'm different when I'm with you.'

She studied him for a moment, a faint frown creasing her forehead, and Luca could practically read the thoughts

going through her mind. *How different are you, really?*
Why won't you tell me about Tyson?

She didn't say any of it though, just smiled and kissed
him. 'I suppose you can buy me a dress.'

Eight hours later Hannah stood next to Luca, sheathed
in an elegant Grecian-style gown of ivory silk. She'd had
her hair and make-up done at the boutique, and felt every
inch the regal princess as Luca introduced her to various
acquaintances.

'Ah, so this is your fiancée,' a paunchy man remarked
with a sweeping, appreciative gaze for Hannah. She stiffened, as did Luca. Clearly the rumour of their forthcoming nuptials had got around. Had they really thought it
wouldn't?

'When is the date, by the way?' the man asked.

'Soon,' Luca answered in a tone that brooked no more
questions. The man moved on.

'You must really be starting to regret the whole fake-
fiancée thing,' Hannah murmured.

Luca shot her a swift, searching look. 'I don't regret
anything, because it brought us together. But I'll be glad
to put it behind us.'

But would it ever be behind them? This was the danger
of taking one day at a time, Hannah acknowledged bleakly.
You never knew what was lurking just ahead.

She still felt worried that Luca might tire of her or of
the whole 'happy families' routine he'd entered into with
such surprising enthusiasm. Maybe she—and Jamie—were
nothing more than a novelty.

And maybe she needed to choose to believe what Luca
said, that he was different, that he did care. Maybe she
needed to believe in him. She'd made that choice with Ben
after he'd died, when it had been too late. She'd decided to

believe the best would have happened, even if they'd never got the chance to see it become a reality.

Now she needed to believe the best *could* happen, that Luca could be the man he wanted to be. That she could help him be that man. They just needed time.

They didn't leave the reception until after midnight, and Hannah's feet ached in the silver stilettos Luca had bought her to go with the dress.

'You were magnificent,' he said as he opened the door to the limo waiting at the kerb.

'I liked being by your side even if it all felt a bit grand for me,' Hannah admitted.

Once inside the limo Luca reached for her hand. 'Stay the night?'

Guilt and temptation warred within her. 'I can't,' she said regretfully. 'I've been away too much as it is.'

Luca didn't answer, just played with her fingers, his head lowered. Hannah resisted the impulse to apologise. Luca knew what he was taking on. Her responsibility for Jamie was part of the package, and she wouldn't say sorry for that.

'I don't want to be apart from you,' Luca said finally.

Hannah's heart lifted at this admission. 'You could stay with me,' she suggested tentatively.

Luca lifted his head. 'What about Jamie?'

'What about him?' She smiled teasingly. 'He has his own bedroom, you know.'

'You don't mind me being there? When he wakes up, I mean?'

'I don't think Jamie's old enough to realise exactly what it means,' Hannah returned. 'But even a five-year-old will get the message that you're an important part of our lives.' She hesitated, feeling as if she had one foot poised over a precipice. 'And you are, Luca.' He didn't respond and she couldn't keep herself from rushing in with caveats. 'I mean, I know it's happened so quickly and we're taking one day at a time…'

'Hannah.' Luca took her face in his hands and kissed her lips. 'You don't need to say things like that. You're an important part of my life.' He paused. 'The most important part.'

Relief rushed through her even as doubts niggled at her mind. If she was the most important part, why wasn't he being more open? Why didn't she feel as if she could totally trust him?

Time, she reminded herself. It would come with time.

'Let's go home,' Luca said, and leaned forward to tell his driver where to go.

Back at her house, Hannah tiptoed upstairs, Luca behind her. Her mother had left with a smile on her face, glad to see Hannah finally finding some happiness.

Her bedroom felt small and shabby compared to Luca's glorious open-plan penthouse, but he assured her he didn't mind as he framed her face with his hands.

'All I want is you. One day you will believe that.'

'Why don't you keep trying to convince me?' Hannah murmured, and Luca did just that.

They'd made love many times since that first unexpected encounter on the beach, and yet Hannah never tired of the feel of Luca's body against hers, inside her. Now, as he slid inside her and filled her up, he looked in her eyes, his body shuddering with the effort of holding back.

'I love you,' he said, his voice ragged with emotion, and Hannah blinked back tears.

'I love you too,' she whispered, wrapping her arms around him, and Luca began to move.

Afterwards they lay together, silent and happy, needing no words.

'You sign the contract for the Tyson resorts next week,'

Hannah said as she ran a hand down his chest, loving the play of his muscles under her palm.

Luca wrapped his hand around her own. 'Yes.'

'Maybe we could go there one day, the three of us,' Hannah said. 'I'd love to see how you implement all your ideas.'

Luca didn't answer and Hannah wondered if she'd presumed too much. Talking about anything to do with the resorts felt fraught. Then he rolled over and drew her tightly into his arms, his head buried in her shoulder as a shudder went through his body. Surprised and unsettled, she returned the embrace. Luca didn't say anything, and Hannah could only wonder what emotion gripped him. She decided not to ask; it was enough he was sharing this with her, and she knew some things went too deep for words.

A week later Luca shook hands with Tyson for the last time as the contracts were signed and witnessed. Tyson's resorts were officially his.

'I look forward to seeing you implement your plans,' Tyson told him as he closed his briefcase. 'I was deeply impressed by your ethos.'

Luca smiled tightly and said nothing. He told himself that he wouldn't feel so flat and empty once he'd put his plans in motion. Once he'd taken from Tyson what the older man had refused him all along, he'd finally sense that satisfaction that had eluded him. The justice that he had deserved for his whole life.

'Stephen mentioned that you looked familiar,' Tyson remarked as he shrugged on his coat. 'But we hadn't met before Santa Nicola, had we?'

Words bubbled in Luca's throat, thick with rage and remembrance. He remembered staring into Tyson's face, those faded brown eyes flat and hard. *You will leave here. Now.*

A push at the small of the back, the overpowering stench

of lilies from the vase in the foyer. Then a door closed in his face.

'No,' he said coolly. 'We haven't.'

After Tyson had left, Luca looked down at the contract with the signatures boldly scrawled. For a moment he imagined what Hannah had suggested last week: the Tyson resorts as he'd proposed them to be, a holiday with her and Jamie. The family life he'd never had, the *happiness* he'd never had. He had a diamond ring in his jacket pocket he was intending to give to Hannah that evening. A whole life about to unfold, a life he now realised he wanted desperately.

Then Luca's jaw hardened and his fist clenched. It couldn't be that simple, that easy for Tyson. He wouldn't let it be. He'd been waiting for this, working for this, his whole life. Justice would be had. How could he hold up his head otherwise? How could he let go of the one thing that had driven his ambition, his whole life?

Grimly focused, Luca reached for his phone. It was time to make a few calls.

Hannah was humming as she stepped onto the Tube. She'd been humming or smiling or practically prancing down the street for over two weeks now, ever since she and Luca had started a real relationship. Ever since it had felt as if her life had finally begun.

Already her mind was jumping ahead to scenarios she wouldn't have dreamt of a month ago. Images of frothy wedding dresses and newborn babies, a house in the country, a whole life unfolding that she knew she wanted desperately—with Luca.

Her mother had cautioned her to slow down, and Hannah had tried, but it was hard when she was so happy, and Luca seemed so happy as well. He was a changed man just as he'd told her, and she needed to believe in that. Trust in his love for her and not let the small things worry her. If Luca still harboured secrets, he would tell her in his own time. She simply needed to be patient.

Her unfocused gaze skimmed across the train car of commuters on smartphones or reading newspapers. Some distant part of her brain clanged in alarm and she tensed, her gaze moving back to a headline she'd only dimly registered in the newspaper across from her. It was the business section, and in big black letters it blared *Tyson Resorts to Close*.

She leaned forward, sure it must be misinformation, and made out the first words of the news story.

In a shock move by real-estate tycoon and property developer Luca Moretti, the newly acquired Tyson Resorts, a chain of six family-orientated vacation spots, are set to close—effective immediately. When contacted, Moretti gave no comment.

Hannah sat back, her mind a welter of confusion. It couldn't be right. The newspaper must have got it wrong, or was attempting to stir up trouble. Luca wasn't going to close the resorts. He was going to turn them into something wonderful. She'd seen the plans herself.

Despite these reassurances a sense of foreboding dogged Hannah as she made her way into the Moretti Enterprises building and up to the penthouse. She'd known Luca was hiding something, something that tormented him. Had seen how affected he'd been on Santa Nicola, having to leave the table after Tyson's toast. She'd tried to find out what was going on but she'd been afraid to press too hard. But maybe she should have. Maybe she should have seen this coming.

The reception area was empty as the lift doors opened onto the penthouse floor, but Hannah could see the lights in Luca's office were on. She dropped her bag and coat on her desk and went straight to his door.

'Come in,' he called at her knock.

Hannah opened the door, her heart starting to thud. Luca sat at his desk, his gaze on his computer screen. He glanced up at Hannah as she came in, a smile transforming his features even as the expression in his eyes remained guarded.

'Good morning.' His voice was low and honeyed and it made both heat and hope unfurl inside her. Here was the man she knew, the man she loved. He would explain everything to her now. He *had* to.

'I read the most ridiculous thing in the newspaper this morning,' she said, and Luca stilled.

'Oh?'

'Yes, in the business section. It said that you were going to close the Tyson resorts, effective immediately.' She waited for his disbelieving laugh. Willed him to rise from his desk and take her in his arms. She needed to believe this wasn't true, that Luca was the man she'd thought he was. He didn't move. 'Luca?' she asked, her voice starting to wobble. 'It's not true, is it? I mean…it can't be true.' Silence stretched and spun out, started to snap. *'Luca.'*

'It is true,' he said finally, his voice flat. 'I'm closing the resorts.'

'Why?' she cried. 'After all your plans…' She snagged at a fragile thread of hope and pulled. 'Is something wrong with them? Did you discover something—the buildings need to be condemned, or—?'

'No.' Luca snipped off that thread with a single word. 'Nothing's wrong with them besides being a bit shabby.' He took a deep breath and laid his hands flat on his desk, his gaze direct and cold and yet somehow also vulnerable. 'The truth is, Hannah, it was always my intention to close them.'

CHAPTER SEVENTEEN

LUCA STARED AT Hannah's shocked and lovely face and wondered at the wisdom in telling her this much truth. But how could he have avoided it? She would have found out about his plans at some point. He'd accepted that he needed to come clean, but he'd been delaying the revelation because he'd known instinctively that Hannah wouldn't like it.

'This decision has nothing to do with us,' he stated.

She shook her head slowly, her face pale, her eyes wide and dark. 'What does it have to do with, then?'

'With Tyson and me. That's it. Old history.'

'So this is revenge,' she said, realisation dawning in her face. Slowly she made her way to the chair in front of his desk and sat down with a thud. 'It was always about revenge.'

'Justice,' Luca corrected. His hands clenched into fists on top of his desk and he forced himself to flatten them out. 'This is about justice, Hannah. It always was.'

'Justice for whom? For what? What did Andrew Tyson ever do to you, Luca, that he doesn't even know about?'

Luca stared at her for a long moment, his jaw clenched so hard it ached. 'He fathered me,' he stated flatly.

Hannah jerked back with surprise. *'Fathered...'* She shook her head slowly. 'I don't understand.'

'My mother was a chambermaid at his resort in Sicily.

He seduced her and then, when she fell pregnant, he promised to marry her. She went back to her home village with her head held high, certain that he'd come for her like he said he would.'

Hannah's face looked pale and waxy with shock. 'And he never did...?'

'No. My mother waited for him for six years. Six *years*. All the while insisting he would come. At first she told me there were letters. Promises. And then nothing.' His throat worked and he swallowed down the lump that had formed there. 'Do you know what it's like to grow up in a place like that as a bastard? My mother was branded a whore, and I was no better. Everyone made our lives a misery, and we couldn't escape. My mother had no money and she was still waiting for Andrew Tyson to ride in like a white knight on his charger.' Bitterness surged through him, bile rising in his throat, and he rose from the desk and paced the room, unable to keep still.

'What happened after six years?' Hannah asked quietly.

Memories jangled and clanged in Luca's mind, an unholy cacophony of unhappiness. 'My mother decided to find him. She discovered when he was going to be back in Sicily, and she went to his house in Palermo. Took me with her.' He closed his eyes against the tidal rush of pain.

'So you saw him? You met him?'

'"Met" may be stretching things,' Luca returned, his voice sharp and hard, cutting. 'We stood in his doorway while he told us to get out. He didn't even let my mother tell him my name. He never looked me in the eye. Just pushed me right out the door and told us never to come back.'

'No...'

Luca's eyes snapped open. 'You think I'm lying?'

'No, of course not,' Hannah whispered. 'It's just so terrible to think a man like him would do that.'

'A man like him? Do you even know who he is? That

kindly-old-man shtick he's got going? It's a *lie*. I know who he is, Hannah. I've always known who he is.'

Hannah was silent for a moment, struggling with her own emotions just as Luca was struggling with his. He felt so angry, so raw and wounded, and he hated it. He wanted to lash out to cover his pain, and he only just kept himself from it.

'So all this time you've been waiting to get back at him? To take his resorts, his life's work, and ruin it all?'

Luca stared at her in disbelief, even as realisation crystal lised inside him. She was taking Tyson's side. Of course she was. His whole life he'd been the interloper, the unwanted. Nothing had ever changed that.

'Yes, that's exactly what I've been doing,' he said, his voice hard. 'That's exactly what I've wanted to do since I was five years old. There were lilies in his foyer, when my mother took me there.' He didn't know why he told her that; maybe he wanted her to understand how much that encounter had affected him. 'Even now the smell makes me retch.'

Her face started to crumple. 'Oh, Luca.'

Luca took a step away. 'Don't. Don't pity me. I just want you to understand.' He took a deep, jagged breath. 'This doesn't have to change anything between us, Hannah. I still love you.' He reached into his pocket, his hand closing over the little black velvet box, its presence reassuring him.

But Hannah was shaking her head, her eyes swimming with tears. Luca felt the bottom of his stomach drop out; it felt as if his empty insides had been suddenly filled with ice water. Hannah was looking at him as if she didn't love him, as if she didn't even know him.

'Hannah…'

'Do you know,' she asked quietly, a jagged edge to her voice, 'why Andrew Tyson built so much into these family resorts? Why his son is a doctor and his daughter a pharmaceutical researcher?'

Luca stared at her, his eyes narrowed. 'No, and I don't care.'

'Because his youngest child died of leukaemia when she was only four years old. And they all responded to her death in different ways.' Hannah gazed at him, her face full of pain, a tear splashing onto her cheek. 'Your half-sister, Luca.'

'Don't.'

'I made a choice a long time ago, when my father died,' she continued as she sniffed back her tears. 'I wasn't going to be angry with him for leaving my mother and me virtually destitute. I accepted that he had no idea he was going to have a heart attack at only forty-two, that he would have provided for us if he could have.'

'And you think Tyson is the same?' Luca surmised incredulously. 'You think he would have provided for my mother and me, if he could have? Because what I saw then was a choice, very clearly made, to get us the hell out of his life.'

'And when Ben didn't want our baby,' Hannah continued over him, 'when he screamed at me to get rid of it and walked out of my life, I made a choice to believe he would have come back when he'd cooled down. He would have married me.' Luca shook his head. He could see where she was going with this, and he didn't buy it. Not for Tyson. Not for him.

'Maybe you think I'm naïve,' Hannah stated with quiet dignity. 'Stupidly optimistic. And maybe my father wouldn't have provided for us. Maybe Ben really would have chucked me over for the carefree life he wanted. But I didn't believe otherwise for their sakes, Luca. I believed it for mine.' He stared at her, uncomprehending, a muscle ticing in his jaw. 'I didn't want to be consumed by bitterness and anger. I wanted to live my life free and forgiving. I wanted to make different choices, *right* choices, and not be bound and ensnared by the past. And I want the same for you.'

'It's different.' He could barely squeeze the words out from his constricted throat.

'It feels different,' Hannah allowed. 'It always does. But think about what you're doing, Luca. Those resorts employ hundreds and maybe even thousands of innocent people. They could revitalise the economy of so many deprived places—you know what it's like from your childhood, don't you, to live near luxury but never be a part of it? You wanted to change that. Those plans for the resort came from your heart, your soul. They showed me the man I fell in love with.'

Luca let out a hard, disbelieving laugh. 'You fell in love with me because of some real-estate plans?'

'Partly. I fell in love with a man who had vision and hope.' She took a deep breath. 'Not a man bent on revenge.'

Luca stared at her, feeling sick. 'So you're giving me an ultimatum.'

'I'm asking you not to do this,' Hannah cried, her hands stretched out to him. 'Not for Tyson's sake or all the employees' sake, but for your own. Don't let the past define you, Luca. Don't let revenge guide you.'

Luca was silent for a long moment, struggling with all the emotions he felt. Anger, that it had come to this, and fear, that he was losing her, and underneath all that a deep-seated certainty that Hannah would have left him at some point anyway. 'So what are you saying, Hannah? That if I go through this you'll leave me?' He took the velvet jewellery box out of his pocket and tossed it on the desk. 'I was planning to give you that tonight. I want to marry you, Hannah.'

Pain flashed across her features. As far as a proposal

went, Luca knew it was terrible, but he felt too cornered to care. Too hurt.

Hannah's expression smoothed out and she picked up the box, snapped it open. She stared at the ring nestled inside, a diamond with sapphires on either side, for a long moment. 'It's beautiful,' she said, and then she closed the box and put it back on the desk. Luca watched, saying nothing, not trusting himself to speak.

'I love you, Luca,' Hannah said. 'But I can't marry you. Not if you're going to be consumed by revenge and hatred and bitterness. I feel for you,' she continued, tears trickling down her face, making him ache to comfort her, even now. 'I grieve for you and the hard childhood you had. Part of me wants to punch Andrew Tyson in the face.' She gave him a wobbly, heartbreaking smile. 'But this level of revenge? This depth of hatred? I can't have that in my life. I can't have that in my son's life. And I don't want it in your life.' She took a deep breath, not bothering to swipe at the tears that trickled down her cheeks unchecked. 'You're a better man than this, Luca. You're a good man. A great one, and I love you so much it hurts. But I can't...' Her voice choked, the last of her composure slipping away. 'I can't,' she managed on a half sob, and turned quickly and ran from the room.

Hannah wiped the tears from her face as she grabbed her bag and coat. She couldn't stay here. She couldn't bear to be so close to Luca and yet feel so agonisingly far away from him.

How could she not have known?

She'd known something was off with the whole deal. She should have asked him more about the history between him and Tyson; she should have tried to make it better. If only she could have done something before they'd reached this awful point, with Luca bent on revenge and her heart breaking.

Even through her agony she knew she'd made the right decision. She couldn't be with someone who was so bent on revenge. It would twist their entire relationship, their whole future, out of shape. And yet right now the shape she was in was broken, shattered into a million desolate pieces.

Hannah stumbled into the lift and then out of the office building, at a loss as to where to go or what to do. Her whole life was in tatters. Her job, her love, all her hopes…

For a second she wondered if she'd been unfair to Luca. God knew she understood how hurting he had to be. And yet he'd been so angry and cold, so determined not to give up on his plan for revenge. How could she cope with that? How could she compete with it?

Tears starting afresh, Hannah walked numbly down the street, going nowhere.

Luca stood completely still for a good five minutes, the silence of the office and the emptiness of his own heart reverberating around him. Then the pain rushed in and he bent over, breathing hard, as if he'd just been punched in the gut. He felt as if he had. He felt as if he'd had a dagger directly to his heart.

Hannah had left him. Hadn't he been waiting for this, secretly? Hadn't he feared that she wouldn't stick around, because nobody ever had? He'd told her relationships weren't worth the risk. He'd told her he wanted to try. And he *had* tried, and he'd failed.

Fury bubbled through him, adding to the pain and grief. Hannah had no right to judge him, no call whatsoever to make demands. She had no idea what he'd been through, what it felt like to be pushed out of Tyson's house, cut out of his life. He wasn't motivated by revenge so much as by justice. Why couldn't Hannah have seen that? Why had she ruined everything, simply because of a business deal?

Frustrated, furious, Luca spun away from his desk, paced his office like the cage it had become. His office phone buzzed and he waited for Hannah to answer it before he remembered that she was gone. He thought about ignoring the call but then decided he shouldn't. He wasn't going to change one iota of his life, damn it, not for anyone or anything.

Grabbing the phone, he bit out a terse greeting.

The building's receptionist answered imperviously. 'Andrew Tyson is in the foyer, requesting to see you.'

'Tyson?' Luca demanded in disbelief. Had his father come to beg for his precious resorts? Now he could send him away, just as Tyson had once done to him. 'Send him…' he began, and then stopped. Why not see Tyson, acknowledge the defeat in the older man's eyes? Maybe this was the reckoning he needed. Maybe now he would finally find the satisfaction he craved. 'Send him up,' he ordered, and slammed the receiver back in its cradle.

When the lift doors opened and Andrew Tyson emerged, Luca recoiled at how much older the man looked, as if he'd aged ten or even twenty years. He walked slowly, almost shuffling, his shoulders stooped, his head bowed in defeat. And Luca felt no satisfaction.

Andrew lifted his head to gaze straight into Luca's eyes. 'I know who you are,' he said, and he sounded sad.

Luca didn't flinch or look away. 'Do you?' he asked, as if it were a matter of little interest.

'Yes.' Andrew drew a deep breath. 'You're my son.'

Something broke inside Luca at that simple admission, and he resisted it, the feeling that the shell he'd constructed about himself was starting to crack. 'No,' he said. 'I've never been that.'

'You're right.' Andrew moved slowly past him to Luca's private office. After a pause Luca followed him. He found Andrew standing by the floor-to-ceiling window, gazing out at the city streets. 'You've done well for yourself. But I already knew that.'

'No thanks to you.' As soon as he spoke the bitter, childish words he regretted them. 'Why are you here?' he asked. 'And how did you know?'

'I think some part of me suspected all along,' Andrew answered as he turned to face him. 'Some ashamed part of my subconscious.'

Luca's gaze narrowed, his lips compressed. 'Ashamed?'

'I've always been ashamed of the way I treated you, Luca,' Andrew said quietly.

Rage spiked so hard and fast Luca struggled to frame a response. 'You say that now? Thirty years later? You've been *ashamed*?' His voice rang out, angry and, worse, agonised. Andrew bowed his head, a supplicant.

'I know it doesn't do much good now.'

'It doesn't do *any* good.'

Andrew lifted his head, and with a cold ripple of shock Luca saw that his father's eyes were damp. 'I know. And I'm sorry, which I also know doesn't do any good.' Andrew drew a ragged breath. 'I'm the worst sort of hypocrite, Luca. You were right to close the resorts.'

Luca's jaw dropped. His father thought he was *right*? Where was the savage satisfaction of vengeance now? 'You can't mean that.'

'No?' Andrew lifted shaggy eyebrows, his mouth twisting in a sad parody of a smile. 'You don't think I regret treating you the way I did?'

'No,' Luca gritted. 'I don't. Considering you never once found me in thirty years, never sought out my mother... She killed herself,' he told him, the words raw with pain. 'Did you know? When I was fourteen.'

Andrew's face slackened, his colour turning grey. 'I didn't know that,' he said hoarsely.

'If you regretted turning us away,' Luca asked, 'why did you never come find us?'

'Because I was afraid to,' Andrew admitted starkly. 'When I told Angelina to wait for me, I meant it. I was going to come to her. But then my father was pressuring me to take over the resorts and marry a suitable woman—'

'And my mother wasn't.'

'No,' Andrew said. 'A Sicilian chambermaid? My father would have disowned me.'

'So you disowned us instead.'

'Yes.' Andrew lifted his chin, meeting Luca's gaze squarely. 'I was a coward, Luca. A dishonourable coward.'

'And it never occurred to you that going on to present yourself as a wonderful family man was just a little bit hypocritical?' Luca demanded.

'Yes, of course it did.' Andrew seemed to visibly diminish. 'It occurred to me all the time.'

'Not enough to do anything about it, though.'

'No.' Andrew was silent for a moment. 'I never even knew your name.'

'You never gave my mother the chance to tell you.' Luca could feel his throat thickening with emotion, a telltale sting at the backs of his eyes. 'It helped me, in the end,' he forced out. 'I knew you wouldn't recognise my name.'

Andrew smiled sadly. 'And you didn't think I'd remember you from back then? When you were…five?'

'No, I didn't. Considering you never even looked directly at me.'

'I was a coward, Luca. I admit it fully and freely. I'm sorry.' He paused. 'I know I don't deserve your forgiveness, but I will ask for it.'

The softly spoken words filled Luca with a fresh rage that possessed an intensity akin to sorrow or grief. Perhaps he felt all three. 'My forgiveness?' he repeated hoarsely. 'How do you even dare?'

'You're right,' Andrew said quietly. 'I don't have the right to dare. I shouldn't presume. But in the thirty years since I rejected you, Luca, I've realised how wrong I was. I've loved and lost…even my own child. Another child,' he clarified quickly. 'In addition to you.'

Luca remembered what Hannah had told him, about the daughter who had died of leukaemia. He could not quite frame the words of condolence that bubbled in his throat. Suddenly he felt confused, mired in sadness, the rage trickling away. He didn't understand himself.

'I'll go,' Andrew said, rising from the chair where he'd sat slumped. 'I only came to ask for your forgiveness, and to say I understand why you did what you did. I don't begrudge you anything, Luca.' And with one last tired smile, Andrew left.

Luca stood there for a moment, his mouth agape, his heart thudding and yet also strangely empty. After so many years planning his revenge, so long craving for a blazing moment of justice and vengeance, he got this? Sorrow and forgiveness and no satisfaction whatsoever?

Luca swore aloud. The sting at the backs of his eyes intensified and he closed them, willing it back. Willing it all back. And then he thought of Hannah.

'Where's Luca?'

Jamie's plaintive question was enough to make Hannah swallow back a sob.

'He's not coming tonight, sweetheart.'

In just a few short weeks Luca had become an important, integral part of her son's life. *And hers.* How was she supposed to go on without him?

All day, since leaving Luca's office in a state of numb grief, Hannah had wondered if she'd made a mistake.

Been too harsh. Why hadn't she tried to understand Luca's perspective more? Why hadn't she practised what she'd preached to him and been more forgiving of *him*? She'd told him she'd chosen not to be bitter, but that morning she'd acted bitterly towards him. She'd turned away from him when he might have needed her understanding most.

But he hadn't acted as if he needed her. He'd been iron-hard, refusing to change or even acknowledge that his decision might have been wrong. And to close all the resorts…

Laura Tyson had somehow managed to find Hannah's home number and had called her in tears, begging her to ask Luca to reconsider.

'Why would he do something like that?' she'd said, more sad than angry. 'I don't understand.'

Hannah did, but she couldn't explain it to Laura. That was Luca's prerogative.

'Mummy…?' Jamie took her face in his hands, his gaze serious. 'Are you sad?'

'No,' Hannah assured him, but her voice wobbled. She put her arms around her son and hugged him tightly. At least she had him. She'd always have him, and she'd always put him first. It was small comfort when her heart felt as if it were in pieces on the floor, but she clung to it all the same.

A little while later she put Jamie to bed and then drifted around the downstairs of her house, unable to do anything but wonder and mourn. After an hour of simply staring into space she broke down and called Luca. She'd do what Laura had asked and beg him to reconsider. She'd apologise for her own harshness, even as she recognised that Luca wasn't the kind of man to back down or unbend. But he'd changed… She'd changed him.

Except, to make the decision he had, had he really changed that much, or even at all?

In any case his mobile switched over to voicemail and Hannah disconnected the call without leaving a message, feeling lonelier and more desolate than ever.

A few minutes later a knock sounded on the door, a determined tap-tap that had her heart turning over. It couldn't be Luca, she told herself. She was thinking it might be simply because he was dominating her thoughts. Because she wanted it to be him so badly.

It was most likely her elderly neighbour, Veronica, asking her to open a pickle jar. Sighing, Hannah rose from the sofa. And opened the door to see Luca standing there, just as she'd been hoping he would.

It took her a few seconds for her mind to catch up to her sight. Her mouth gaped as she struggled to find words. Luca found them first.

'May I come in?'

'Yes—' She stepped aside even though she longed to throw herself into his arms. She reminded herself she didn't actually know why he was here.

Luca walked into the sitting room where they had already spent so many enjoyable evenings. It felt like a lifetime ago that he'd first walked into this room, that he'd asked her to be his mistress.

He turned around slowly. Hannah's heart quelled because he didn't look like a man who had made the right decision, who was buoyed by hope. He looked tired and defeated.

'Andrew Tyson came to see me,' he said.

Hannah pressed one hand against her chest, as if she could will her heart to slow. 'And?'

'And he asked for my forgiveness.' Luca let out a harsh laugh and Hannah recoiled. Maybe he hadn't changed, after all.

'And?' she asked softly.

'And I don't know what to do with that.' Luca shook his

head. 'I don't know what to do or how to feel.' His voice broke as he looked at her in genuine confusion and hurt. 'If I let go of my anger, what am I? If I stop seeking justice, what do I do?'

'Oh, Luca.' In that moment Hannah realised this was her second chance as much as it was Luca's. She could offer him the comfort now that she hadn't that morning. She could give him the encouragement to make the right choice instead of judging him for making the wrong one. 'I'm so sorry.'

'Why?' Luca asked, his handsome face filled with a new and unhappy bewilderment. 'What are you sorry for, Hannah? That I didn't get what I wanted? But you didn't want me to get that.'

'I'm sorry because you're hurting,' Hannah answered. 'And I love you and I don't want you to hurt.'

His face twisted. 'Even now, you love me?'

'Yes.' She spoke with such certainty that Luca took a step towards her, his hands outstretched.

'Do you mean that, Hannah? Even though I tried to destroy a man's life? Even though I put hundreds of people out of a job?'

'Even though,' Hannah said quietly. 'I should have been more understanding this morning, Luca, but I still mean what I said. Revenge is a road to self-destruction—'

'I know.' His mouth twisted wryly. 'I think I self-destructed this afternoon. Having Tyson admit everything... He knew I was his son, and he was sorry. He said I was justified in closing the resorts.' He let out a weary laugh. 'Talk about stealing your thunder.'

'And what's left?' Hannah asked softly. 'Without your thunder?'

'Regret. Sorrow.' He stared at her, his eyes burning. 'And love. Regret and sorrow will fade and heal with time, but the love never will. If you can still love me, Hannah...'

Hannah went to him then, arms outstretched, voice cracking. 'You know I do.'

His arms closed around, his face buried in her hair. 'I love you. So much. You gave me something else to live for. Something good.'

'You gave me that too, Luca.' She let out a shaky laugh, her voice ragged with tears. 'The last twelve hours have been the longest of my life.' Luca didn't answer, just held her more tightly. And Hannah rested there, content to live in that moment. She wasn't going to press Luca for promises he couldn't give. She wasn't going to ask—

'I'm not going to close the resorts,' Luca said quietly. Hannah eased back to look at his face.

'Is that what you want?'

'It is now. What you said...the way Tyson was...I realised you were right. I would only be hurting—even destroying—myself. And us. And that's the last thing I want, Hannah. I love you too much to throw away both our futures.'

'And I love you,' Hannah answered fiercely.

Luca tipped her head up so his lips could meet hers. 'Then that's all I need,' he said softly.

EPILOGUE

HANNAH OPENED THE French window of the villa and stepped out onto the silky sand. The waves were shooshing gently onto the beach; the sky was a brilliant blue above. Behind her she could hear Jamie scampering around, exclaiming over everything, and Luca's answering chuckle.

They'd arrived at the newly renovated Tyson resort on Tenerife that morning, and Jamie hadn't stopped for a second. Fortunately Luca had the energy to keep up with his newly adopted son.

This was their honeymoon, taken with Jamie after a wedding in London and a weekend just the two of them in Paris. It had been the wedding she'd always wanted, with family and friends and a gorgeous white dress from Diavola. Jamie had been the ring bearer and Andrew Tyson and his family had been among the guests. It had been another step onto the road to both healing and happiness.

The weekend in Paris had been glorious, too. Luca had surprised her by renting out the Eiffel Tower just as she'd dreamed up on Santa Nicola, and they'd danced alone on the terrace with the stars spangled above them, their hearts full to overflowing…just as they were now.

Hannah let out a sigh, the sound replete with both contentment and thankfulness.

'Now, that was quite a sigh, Signora Moretti.' Luca

stepped out onto the sand, standing behind her as he rested his hands on her shoulders.

Hannah leaned her head against the solid wall of his chest. 'It was a happy sound,' she assured him.

'I'm glad to hear it.' Luca slid his arms around her waist. 'Because I'm happy. Happier than I ever thought I had a right to be.'

The last year had been full of blessings and challenges as Luca had reopened the Tyson resorts and made steps to building a relationship with his father as well as being a father to Jamie. They'd become a family, a proper one, strong and loving, and Hannah had hopes that they would add a fourth person to their little tribe before too long.

She'd continued to work for Moretti Enterprises, and to enjoy the challenges of her job, although she'd reduced her hours to spend more time with Jamie. It hadn't always been easy, learning and loving and changing, but it had been wonderful.

Luca tilted her head up to brush her lips in a kiss. 'To think that just over a year ago we were on a beach like this one, but only pretending. Although perhaps not as much as I thought I was.'

Hannah laughed softly. 'Are you rewriting history?'

'No. I think I was taken with you from the moment I saw you try on that dress. It was as if a switch flipped inside me. I started seeing you differently. I started feeling different myself.'

'I did too,' Hannah admitted. 'I was quite annoyed by it, actually.'

Luca laughed at that. 'As long as you're not annoyed now.'

'Annoyed?' Hannah smiled and shook her head. 'No, I'm overwhelmingly happy and thankful that you love me as much as I love you.'

'More,' Luca assured her, and pulled her to him. 'I love you more.'

'I don't think that's possible,' Hannah murmured, her head tilting back as Luca kissed her.

'Then we'll call it even,' Luca murmured, and deepened the kiss.

* * * * *

THE CEO'S
LITTLE SURPRISE

KAT CANTRELL

One

By the time Gage Branson's tires hit the Dallas city limits, Arwen had started howling along with the radio. Not for the first time since leaving Austin, Gage questioned the wisdom of bringing his dog on a business trip.

Of course, it wasn't a normal business trip—unless showing up at your ex-girlfriend's office building unannounced and uninvited counted as customary. And Arwen wasn't a normal dog. She was his best buddy, and the one and only time he'd left her at one of those pet hotels, she'd refused to speak to him for a week.

Arwen shared Gage's love of the open road and honestly, he didn't mind the company as he drove to Dallas to collect a long overdue debt from the CEO of Fyra Cosmetics.

GB Skin for Men, the company he'd just pushed into the billion-dollar-a-year category, had enjoyed a good run as the top skin-care line of choice for the discerning guy who spends time in the elements: professional athletes, outdoorsmen, even the occasional lumberjack.

Gage had spent millions designing a new product to heal scars. The product's launch a month ago had outperformed his carefully executed publicity strategy. GB Skin instantly cornered the market. But now his former lover's company was poised to steal his success out from under him with a product of their own. That wasn't going to happen.

A Black Keys song blasted through the speakers and the howling grew unbearable.

"Arwen! Really. Shut up."

She cocked her ginger-colored head and eyed Gage.

"Yeah, never mind," Gage grumbled good-naturedly and flicked off the music.

The exit for Central Expressway loomed and Gage steered the Hummer north. He drove a few miles and before long, he rolled into the parking lot at the headquarters for Fyra Cosmetics.

Nice. Of course, he'd done an internet search for pictures before driving up from Austin. Just to check out the company Cassandra Claremont had built alongside her business partners–slash–friends after graduating from the University of Texas. But the internet hadn't done justice to the sharply modern, glass and steel, five-story building. Cass's multimillion-dollar cosmetics company lived and breathed inside these walls, and the deep purple Fyra logo dominated the landscape.

"Stay here and keep your paws off the gearshift," he muttered to Arwen and got the trademark vizsla smile for his trouble. It was a cool day, so he parked in the shade and left her in the car with the windows cracked.

Cass had done very well for herself thanks to him. Gage *had* been her mentor for eight months and turnabout was fair play. She owed him. And he'd help her see that by reminding her of how he'd guided her at a time when she had no idea how to navigate the shark-infested waters of the cosmetics industry.

With any luck, Cass would be curious enough to see him on short notice. Gage couldn't call ahead and lose the advantage of surprise. Not when he was here to get his hands on Cass's secret formula.

So secret, he shouldn't even know about it since it wasn't on the market yet. His sources had whispered in his ear about a miracle formula developed in Fyra's labs that worked with a body's natural healing properties to eliminate wrinkles and scars. His intel adamantly insisted it was better than his. And he wanted it.

You didn't spring that kind of request on anyone over the phone, not even a former girlfriend. They hadn't even spoken in eight or nine years. Nine. Maybe it was closer to ten.

"Gage Branson. To what do I owe the pleasure?"

The husky feminine voice raked over Gage from behind before he'd managed to get ten feet from the Hummer.

He spun to face the speaker and did a double take. "Cass?"

"Last time I checked." High-end sunglasses covered her eyes, but her tone conveyed a hint of cool amusement just fine. "Did I leave my face in my other purse again?"

"No, your face is right where I left it." Gorgeous and attached to a hell of a woman.

But *this* überchic version in five-inch heels and a sexy suit with cutaway panels at her hips did not resemble the Cassandra Claremont who lived in his memories. Her voice wasn't even the same. But something about the way she held herself was very familiar. Confidence and the ever-present "look but don't you dare touch" vibe had always been a huge part of her attractiveness.

Obviously *he* hadn't changed much since graduate school if she'd recognized him from behind.

"Moving into the dog transportation business, are you?" she asked blithely.

He glanced at the Hummer. "You mean Arwen? Nah. She's just company for the drive. I came up from Austin to see you, actually. Surprise."

"Do you have an appointment?"

The lack of question in that question said she already knew the answer. And wasn't planning to adjust her calendar one tiny bit, even for an old boyfriend. He'd change that soon enough.

"I was hoping you'd see me without one." He grinned, just to keep things friendly. "You know, for old times' sake."

His grin grew genuine as he recalled those old times. Lots of late-night discussions over coffee. Lots of inventive ploys to get Cass's clothes off. Lots of hot and truly spectacular sex when she finally gave in to the inevitable.

She pursed her lips. "What could we possibly have to say to each other?"

Plenty. And maybe a whole lot more than he'd originally come to say. Now that he was here and had an eyeful of the new, grown-up Cass, a late-night dinner and a few drinks with a former lover had suddenly appeared on his schedule for the evening.

Everyone here was an adult. No reason they couldn't separate business from pleasure.

"For one, I'd like to say congratulations. Long overdue, I realize," he threw in smoothly. "I've been following along from afar and what you've accomplished is remarkable."

Once her name had been dropped in his lap as a potential game changer, he'd searched the internet for details, first with an eye toward how well she was executing his advice and eventually because he couldn't stop. Strangely, he'd liked seeing her picture, liked remembering their relationship. She was one of a small handful of women from his past that he recalled fondly, and for a guy who held on to very little in his life, that was saying something.

"Thank you." She inclined her head graciously. "It was a group effort."

He waited for her to say she'd been following his entrepreneurial trajectory in kind. Maybe a congrats or two on the major retail distribution deals he'd scored in the past few years. An attaboy for Entrepreneurs of America naming him Entrepreneur of the Year. If nothing else, Fyra's CEO should be brushing up on her competition the way he had.

Nada. She hadn't been a *little* curious about what he'd been up to? Was their time together such a blip in her life that she'd truly not cared?

But then, their affair had been brief, by design. Once he'd escaped his restrictive childhood home and overprotective parents, he'd vowed to never again let his wings be clipped. He owed it to his brother, Nicolas, to live on the edge, no regrets. To experience all the things his brother never would thanks to a drunk driver. Sticking to one woman didn't go with that philosophy and Gage liked his freedom as much—or more—than he liked women, which meant he and Cass had parted ways sooner rather than later, no harm, no foul. He could hardly blame her for not looking back.

"Come on." He waved off her "group effort" comment. "You're the CEO. We both know that means you call the shots."

She crossed her arms over that sexy suit, drawing attention to her breasts. In spite of the cool breeze, the temperature inched up a few degrees.

"Yes. Because someone has to. But Trinity, Harper, Alex and I run this company together. We're all equal owners."

Yeah, he'd figured she'd say that. The four women had been inseparable in college and it wasn't hard to imagine they'd extended their tight circle into the company they'd created together. Fortunately, he'd always gotten along with the quartet of savvy females, but Cass was the one he had his sights set on. She'd make this deal happen.

"Can we take this inside?" Hoping she'd like the idea of getting behind closed doors as much as he did, he sidled closer. "I'd like to catch up."

"Gage."

Her husky voice wound through him as she moved closer in kind, tilting her head toward his in a way that shouldn't feel as intimate as it did. A hint of jasmine filtered through his senses and it was a powerful punch. "Yeah, Cass?"

"You can save the 'Kumbaya,'" she murmured. "You're here because you've heard about Fyra's breakthrough formula and you want it."

Back to business, then.

He grinned and reined in his thundering pulse. Going toe-to-toe with Cass was such a turn-on. Smart, sexy women who didn't take any crap had always floated his boat. "Am I that easy to read?"

Cass laughed in his ear, a throaty sound he instantly wanted to hear again. "I'm afraid so. Sorry you've wasted your time. The formula is not for sale."

All right, then. Cass needed persuasion to see how his

tutelage had launched her into the big leagues. He'd anticipated that.

"Of course it isn't. Not to the rest of the world. But I'm not one of the masses," he reminded her. "I'm not unreasonable. I'll pay fair market value."

He turned his head at just the right angle to almost bring their lips together. The pull between them was magnetic, and he nearly forgot for a second that he'd instigated this sensual tease to get him closer to his goal—the formula.

She didn't flinch, holding herself rock steady. "You think you have special rights because of our former relationship? Think again."

His element of surprise hadn't worked to catch her off guard and, for some reason, that made her twice as attractive. Or maybe the unexpected draw had come about because they were equals now. It was an interesting shift in their dynamic he hadn't expected, and it was throwing him off.

So he'd up his game. Gage had never met a woman he couldn't charm. When he wanted something, he got it. "That's no way to talk to an old friend."

If he moved an inch, they'd be touching. He almost did it, curious if she still felt the same—soft, exciting and warm. Except he had the distinct impression Cass was all business and little pleasure these days. And that she wasn't interested in mixing them up.

"Is that what we are?"

There came that sexy laugh again and it did a powerful number on his already-primed lower half. She really shouldn't be so intriguing, not with his agenda and the lost element of surprise. But all of that actually heightened his sense of awareness, and he had a sharp desire to get under her skin the same way she'd managed to get under his.

"Friends. Former lovers. At one time, mentor and student."

"Mmm. Yes." She cocked her head. "You've taught me a lot. So much that I'm running a successful company I need to get back to. You'll excuse my rudeness if I request you make an appointment. Like anyone else who wants to talk business."

All at once, her heat vanished as she pulled away and clacked toward the entrance to her building. Ouch. He'd been relegated to the ranks of "anyone else."

He let her go. For now.

There was no way a former pupil of his was going to take away even a single point of his market share, and he'd pay handsomely to ensure it. But one had to do these things with finesse.

Remind her of what you've done for her. Remind her how good it was.

The voice in his head was his own conscience. Probably. But sometimes he imagined it was Nicolas guiding him from beyond the veil. A big brother's advice in times of need, which usually led Gage down the path of living life to the fullest. Because Nicolas couldn't.

The philosophy had never steered Gage wrong before.

He wasn't about to stop listening to sound advice now, especially when it aligned with what he wanted. Cass clearly needed a good, solid reminder of how tight they'd been. So tight, he knew every inch of her body.

Your best strategy is to use pleasure to influence business.

Nicolas had spoken. And that pretty much solidified Gage's next steps because that genie wasn't going back in the bottle. He wanted her. And her formula. If he did it right, one would lead to the other.

He gave her a good five minutes and went after her.

Turnabout was fair play in love *and* cosmetics.

* * *

Hands shaking, Cass strode to her office and checked her strength before she slammed the door behind her. That would only invite questions and she had no answers for why her entire body still pumped with adrenaline and… other things she'd rather not examine.

Okay, that was a flat-out lie. Gage Branson was the answer, but why seeing him again so severely affected her after all of this time—*that* she couldn't explain.

God, that smile rocked her to the core, even all these years later. And his still-amazing body had been hidden underneath casual-Friday dress, when it should clearly be on display in a pinup calendar. He'd always had the messiest, most casually cut hair that somehow managed to look delicious on him. Still did. Oh, yes, he was just as sexy and charismatic as he'd always been and she hated that she noticed. Hated that he could still put a quiver in her abdomen. Especially after what he'd done.

Breathe. Gage was just a guy she used to know. Put that on repeat a thousand times and maybe she'd finally believe it. Except he wasn't just a guy from college; that was the problem.

Gage Branson had broken her.

Not just her heart, but *her*. Mind, body and soul. She'd fallen so hard for him that the splat hadn't even registered. Until he casually declared their relationship over, and did she want the clothes back that she'd left at his place?

Nine years later and she was still powerless to move on, unable to fall in love again, incapable of forgetting and far too scarred to forgive. And that's why her hands were still shaking. Pathetic.

The only positive was she felt certain Gage hadn't picked up on her consternation. God forbid *he* figure out how greatly he'd affected her. Emotions had no place here, not at work, not in her personal life. *No place.* That's the most important lesson she'd learned from her former mentor. Thankfully, he'd taken her advice to make an appointment without too much protest, giving her much-needed regroup time.

Her phone beeped, reminding her she had five minutes until the meeting she'd called would begin. Five minutes to put her thoughts together about how Fyra should handle the leak in the company. Someone reprehensible had publicized Harper's nanotechnology breakthrough before they'd even gotten FDA approval or a patent. Five minutes, when she should have had an hour, but didn't because of the car wreck on Central and the surprise appearance of the man who'd laced her nightmares for nearly a decade.

And maybe a few need-soaked dreams. But he didn't have to know about that.

Great. This was exactly what she needed, a come-to-Jesus meeting with Trinity, Harper and Alex so soon after locking horns with the offspring of Satan. Who was here strictly because of a leak that never should have happened.

Well, she'd have to get her wild swing of emotions under control. *Now.* It wasn't as though she didn't already know how she felt about the leak—sick, furious and determined to find the source. They'd not only lost a potential competitive advantage, until they figured out who had spilled, there was also no guarantee the same person wouldn't leak the secret formula—or steal it.

But five minutes was scarcely enough time to settle her racing heart before waltzing into a room with her best friends, who would see immediately that Something Had Happened. They'd probably also realize "Something" had a man's name all over it.

Working with people who'd held your hair when you drank too much and borrowed your clothes and sat with you in a tight huddle at your grandfather's funeral meant few secrets. Most of the time, Cass appreciated that. Maybe not so much today.

In the bathroom, she patted her face with a blotting cloth and fixed her makeup, which was equal parts wardrobe and armor.

No one saw through Cass when she had her face on—with the right makeup, no one had to know you were hurting. The philosophy born out of the brokenness Gage had left her with had grown into a multimillion-dollar company. Best Face Forward wasn't just the company tagline, it was Cass's personal motto.

No man would ever put a crack in her makeup again.

Fortified, Cass pasted on a cool smile and exited the bathroom. Only to run smack into Fyra's receptionist, Melinda. Her wide eyes spelled trouble as she blurted out, "There's an extremely persistent man at the front desk who seems to believe you have an appointment with him."

Gage. When she'd said make an appointment, she meant for later. Much later.

Her not-so-settled nerves began to hum. "I don't have an appointment with him. I have a meeting."

"I told him that. But he insisted that you'd scheduled time with him, and he drove all the way from Austin." Melinda lowered her voice. "He was very apologetic and sweet about it. Even asked if there was a possibility you accidentally double booked your appointments."

Did his audacity have no end?

The stars in Melinda's eyes were so bright, it was a wonder she could still see around Gage's charm. Well, Cass didn't suffer from the same affliction. "When have I ever done that?"

"Oh, I know. Never." Her shoulders ducked slightly.

"But I...well, he asked if I'd mind checking with you and he just seems so sincer—"

"Why is Gage Branson in our reception area?" Trinity Forrester, Fyra's chief marketing officer, snapped, her short, dark hair nearly bristling with outrage. Since Trinity possessed the main shoulder Cass had cried on back in college, the statement was laced with undercurrents of the "hold me back before I cut off his fingers with a dull blade" variety.

Cass stifled a sigh. Too late to have Melinda throw him out before anyone saw him. "He's here with a business proposition. I'll take care of it."

As the woman in charge, she should have taken care of it in the parking lot once she'd figured out he wanted her formula. But he'd been so... *Gage*, with his wicked smile. He fuzzled her mind and that was not okay.

This was strictly business and she would die before admitting she couldn't handle a competitor sniffing around her territory.

"That's right." Trinity crossed her arms with a smirk. "You take care of it. You toss him out on his well-toned butt. Shame such a prime specimen of a man is riddled with health problems."

Melinda's gaze bounced back and forth between her employers, clearly fascinated by the exchange. "Really? What's wrong with him?" she asked in a stage whisper.

"He's got terrible allergies to commitment and decency," Trinity explained. "And Cass is going to hand him his hat with class. Can I watch?"

Strangling over a groan, Cass shook her head. This was her battle, and there was no way she'd deal with Gage for a second time today in front of a bevy of onlookers. "It's better if I talk to him in my office. Trinity, can you tell Alex and Harper I'll be there in a few minutes?"

Trinity harrumphed but edged away as Cass stared her down. "Okay. But if you're robbing us of the show, you better come prepared to spill all the details."

With Melinda dogging her steps—because the receptionist likely didn't want to miss a thing at this point—Cass marched to the reception area.

Arms crossed and one hip leaning on the desk as if he owned it, Gage glanced toward her as she entered, his deep hazel eyes lighting up at the sight of her. His slow smile set off a tap dance in her abdomen. Which was not okay. It was even *less* okay than his ability to fuzzle her mind.

Steeling her spine against the onslaught of Gage's larger-than-life personality, she jerked her head toward the hallway. "Five minutes, Mr. Branson. I'm late for a board meeting."

"Mr. Branson. I like the sound of that," he mused, winking. "Respect where respect is due."

Flirting came so naturally to him, she wondered if he even realized when he was doing it. She rolled her eyes and turned her back on his smug face, taking off toward her office in hopes he'd get lost.

He drew abreast with little effort, glancing down at her because he still topped her by several inches no matter how high her heels were, dang it. His powerful masculinity dominated the small hallway that had always seemed quite large enough for every other person who'd accompanied her to her office.

"Trying to score the first one-minute mile? You can't outrun me barefoot, let alone while wearing icepick stilettos." He eyed them appreciatively, his too-long hair flopping over his forehead. "Which I like, by the way."

Her toes automatically curled inside her shoes as heat swept over her skin. "I didn't wear them for you."

Why had she thought taking care of this in her office

was a good idea? She should have gone to her board meeting and had Melinda tell Gage to take a hike.

But he would have just shown up over and over again until she agreed to an appointment.

So she'd get rid of him once and for all.

Two

When she halted by her open office door, Gage raised a brow as he read its deep purple placard. "Chief enhancement officer?"

His amused tone rankled but she just smiled and silently dared him to do his worst. "Branding. We put incredibly careful thought into every single aspect of this business. Seems like I had a mentor once who taught me a few things about that."

He grinned in return and didn't acknowledge her sarcasm. Nor did he say a word about her outstretched arm, choosing to humor her and enter first as she'd meant him to, but he didn't miss the opportunity to brush her, oh, so casually. She pretended the skin he'd just touched wasn't tingling.

"Yeah, we did have a few lively discussions about business strategies," he mused. "Branding is why I drive a green Hummer, by the way."

Cass had decorated her office with the same trademark Fyra deep purple hue, down to the glass-topped desk and expensive woven carpet under it. He took it all in with slightly widened eyes.

"Because you want everyone to see it and think GB Skin has zero environmental consciousness and its owner is obnoxious?" she asked sweetly before he could make a crack about her decor.

Sleek and modern, the offices had been decorated by an expensive, trendy uptown firm. It had cost a pretty penny, but the results had been worth it. This company was hers, from the baseboards to the ceiling and she loved it. They'd moved to this building three years ago, once Fyra posted its first annual revenue of fifty million dollars. That was when she knew they were going to make it.

She'd do whatever she needed to do in order to keep her company alive.

He laughed as he slid into a purple chair and then swept her with a pointed once-over. "You know the name of my company. I was starting to think you didn't care."

How did he manage to make understanding the competitive landscape sound so...*personal*? It was a skill he'd clearly bargained with the devil to obtain.

"I'm good at what I do. Of course I know the names of my competitors." Cass remained standing near the door. Which she pointedly left open. "You've got your appointment. And about three minutes to tell me why you didn't take the no I gave you earlier and run back to Austin."

Casually, he swiveled his chair to face her and waved a hand to the empty chair next to him. "Sit and let's talk."

She didn't move. There was no way she could be in close quarters with him, not on the heels of their earlier encounter when he'd barely breathed on her and still managed to get her hot and bothered. At least by the door, she had a shot at retaining the upper hand. "No, thanks. I'm okay."

"You can't keep standing. That tactic only works if you inflict it on someone other than the person who taught it to you," he said mildly.

The fact that he saw through her only made it worse.

"Really, Gage," she snapped. "Fyra's executives are waiting in a boardroom for the CEO to arrive. Cut the crap. Why are you here?"

His expression didn't change. "The rumors about your formula are true, right?"

She crossed her arms over the squiggle in her stomach. "Depends on what you've heard."

"*Revolutionary* is the word being thrown around," he said with a shrug. "I've heard the formula works with your natural stem cells to regenerate skin, thus healing scars and eliminating wrinkles. Nanotech at its finest."

She kept her expression schooled, but only just. "I can neither confirm nor deny that."

Her lungs hitched as she fought to draw a breath without alerting Gage to her distress. The leak was worse than they'd assumed. When Trinity had stormed into Cass's office yesterday to show Cass the offending blurb in an online trade magazine, she'd read the scant few lines mentioning Fyra's yet-to-be released product with horror. But it could have been so much worse, they'd assured each other. The trade magazine had few details, especially about the nanotechnology, and they'd hoped that had been the extent of the information that had traveled beyond their walls.

Apparently not.

It was a disaster. Full-blown, made even worse by Gage's arrival on the scene.

Gage watched her carefully, his sharp gaze missing

nothing. "But if my intel is correct, a formula like that might be worth about a hundred million or so. Which I'm prepared to pay."

Oh, no, he had *not* just dropped that sum on her. She shut her eyes for a blink. Money like that was serious business, and as the CEO, she had to take his offer to the others for due consideration.

But she knew her friends. They'd agree with her that the formula was priceless. "I told you, the formula isn't for sale."

He stood suddenly and advanced on her, clearly over the power play she'd instigated by standing by the door. The closer he got, the harder her pulse pounded, but she blinked coolly as if lethally sexy men faced her down on a daily basis.

"It's smart business to consider all opportunities," he said as he leaned against the doorjamb not two feet from her. "If you sell, you don't have to worry about little things like FDA approval and production costs and false-claim lawsuits. You just roll around in your millions and leave the hard work to someone else."

The scent of clean forest and man wafted in her direction.

"I'm not afraid of hard work," she stated firmly as she fought to keep from stepping back, out of the line of his masculine fire. It was a battle of wills, and if she fled, he'd figure out how much he truly affected her.

The man was a shaman, mystical and charismatic. One glance, and she'd follow him into his world of hedonistic pleasure. Or at least that had been true in college. She'd learned a few tricks of her own since then, along with developing a shield around her fragile interior.

His gaze held her captive as he reached out and tucked

a chunk of hair behind her ear, his fingers lingering far longer than they should have.

"What *are* you afraid of?" he asked softly, his expression morphing into something almost...warm.

You. She swallowed. Where had that come from? Gage didn't scare her. What scared her was how easily she forgot to control her emotions around him.

This cat-and-mouse game had veered into dangerous territory.

"Taxes," she muttered inanely and ignored the way her pulse raced.

When was the last time she'd been touched? Months and months. She'd developed a reputation among single men in Dallas as a man-eater and unfortunately, that just made her even more popular as men vied for her attention so they could claim victory. Mostly she just shut them down because the whole scene exhausted her.

And she couldn't lose sight of the fact that the reason she chewed up men and spit them out was staring her in the face. He was very dangerous indeed if she'd forgotten for a second the destruction he'd caused.

And that's when it hit her. She was handling Gage all wrong.

This wasn't college and Gage wasn't her mentor. They were equals. And he was on her turf. That meant she called the shots.

If he wanted to play, she'd play.

Once Gage had tucked the errant lock of hair behind her ear, he'd run out of legitimate excuses to have his hands on her. Which didn't keep him from silently running through a litany of illegitimate excuses.

"Gage," she murmured throatily and the base of his spine heated. "The formula's not for sale. I have a board meeting. Seems like we're done here…unless you've got a better offer?"

Her eyelids lowered to half-mast and she didn't move, but the sensual vibe emanating from her reached out and wrapped around him, drawing him in. Those cutaway panels at her waist would fit his palms perfectly and with any luck, the mesh inserts would allow him to feel her while fully clothed. The thought sent a rush of blood through his veins and the majority of it ended up in a good, solid erection that got very uncomfortable, very fast.

"I just might have something in mind," he said, his vocal chords scraping the low end of the register. God, she'd even affected his voice.

Down boy. Remind her why the formula is *for sale… but only to you.*

Yeah, he needed to get back on track, pronto, and stop letting her get into his head. He dropped his hand but leaned into her space to see about turning those tables on her. "You're doing amazing things here, Cass. I'm proud of what you've accomplished.'

Wariness sprang into her gaze as she processed his abrupt subject change. "Thank you. I'm proud of what the girls and I have built."

He crossed his arms before an errant finger could trail down the line of her throat. Because his lower half wasn't getting the message that the goal here was to get *her* hot and flustered. Not the other way around. "Remember that project I helped you with for Dr. Beck's class?"

That was before they'd started sleeping together. He didn't recall being so magnetically attracted to Cass back then. Sure he'd wanted to get her naked. But at twenty-four, he'd generally wanted women naked. These days, his taste was a bit more refined, but no woman he'd dated over the years had gotten him this hooked, this fast.

Of course, he never looked up his old girlfriends. Maybe any former lover would affect him the same. But he couldn't imagine that would be true.

Her eyes narrowed a touch. "The project where I created a new company on paper, complete with a marketing plan and logo and all of that?"

"That's the one," he said easily. "You got an A plus, if memory serves. Except you didn't do that alone. I was right there every step of the way. Guiding you. Teaching you. Infusing you with CEO superpowers."

In fact, he'd done such a good job, here he was smack in the middle of her corporation negotiating over a Fyra product that was better than his. He appreciated the irony.

An indulgent smile bloomed on her face and he didn't mistake it for a friendly one. "Nothing wrong with your memory. As much as I'm enjoying this trip down memory lane, if you have a point, now would be the time to make it."

"Your success here…" He waved a hand at her office without taking his eyes off her. "Is amazing. Your C-suite is unparalleled. But you didn't get here without me. I'm a big factor in your success."

"Yes, you are," she agreed readily. Too readily. "You taught me some of the most important lessons I've learned thus far in my life. Fyra's business philosophy grew 100 percent out of my experience with you."

She blinked and undercurrents flowed between them but hell if he could figure out what they were. Regardless, it was a great segue. Exactly what he'd hoped for.

"I'm glad you agree. That's why I'm here. To collect on that long-outstanding debt."

"Oh, really?" Her head tilted slightly as she contemplated him. "Do tell."

"You know what I'm talking about. Without me, Fyra

might never have existed. You might never have achieved your goals, particularly not to this degree. Don't you think turnabout is fair play?"

"Hmm." She touched a finger to her cheek. "Turnabout. Like I owe you for what you've done. That's an interesting concept. It's kind of like karma, in a way."

"Kind of."

But he didn't like the comparison, not the way she said it. Karma was rarely a word used in the context of reward. More like you were getting what you deserved.

"What I'm saying," he interjected smoothly before this conversation went in a direction he didn't like. "Is that I want to buy your formula. My role in your success should be a factor in your decision-making process. In all fairness, you do owe me. But I'm fair, too. I'm not asking you to *give* me the formula for old times' sake. One hundred million dollars is a lot of tit for tat."

He watched her as she filtered through his argument, but her expression remained maddeningly blank.

"Here's the thing, Gage." She leaned in, wafting a whole lot of woman in his direction. "You did teach me and I'm grateful. But you must have been sick the day they taught corporate structure, so I'll clue you in. Again. I'm a quarter owner in Fyra. We're missing three-quarters of the decision makers, none of whom *owe* you a thing. I'll take your offer for the formula to the board and we'll consider it. Period. That's how business works."

Her mouth was set so primly, he had the insane urge to kiss her. But they were just getting into the meat of this and he needed to hone his focus. Not lose it entirely.

So he grinned instead and waved off her protest. "Not in the real world, honey. You need to get out more if that's your best line of defense. Deals are done and undone across the globe based on exactly that. Companies don't make decisions. People do and rarely are they united."

"Fyra is," she insisted. "We're a team."

"I hope that's true," he said sincerely. "If so, then it's in your best interests to convince them to sell. How would they feel about their CEO not honoring this lingering debt?"

Her brows drew together but it was the only outward sign she gave that she'd heard the underlying message. This was business at its core and he was not leaving Dallas without that formula. It had become more than just about ensuring Fyra didn't take any of his market share. GB Skin was number one for a reason and he liked being the top dog. His products should be the best on the market and Fyra's formula would put him there—assuming it checked out like he thought it would.

Not to mention that Cass's stubbornness had piqued his.

"Threats, Gage?" Her laugh thrummed through him. "You gonna tattle to my partners about how naughty I am?"

He nearly groaned at her provocative tone.

"Nothing so pedestrian." He shifted a touch closer because he liked the scent of her, tightening the cross of his arms. Just to keep his hands where they belonged. "I wouldn't go behind your back to manipulate the other executives. This is your cross to bear, and I'm simply pointing out that you don't want this on your conscience. Do you?"

"My conscience is quite clear, thanks." Her gaze fastened firmly on his, she crossed her arms in a mirror of his pose, intentionally sliding her elbow across his. And then hung around, brushing arms deliberately. "I'll take your offer to the others. Shall I show you the way out or can you find it yourself?"

Heat flashed where they touched. "As you're late for a board meeting where I suspect one of the topics will be the offer in question, I'll see myself out."

She didn't move, still partially blocking the open doorway. On purpose. So he'd have to slide by her like he'd done when he entered the room, to show she had his number and that whatever he dished out, he should expect to have served right back. It almost pulled an appreciative chuckle out of him but he caught it at the last second. Cass had grown up in many intriguing ways and this battle was far from over.

No point in letting her believe she had a chance in hell of winning.

So close to her that he could easily see the lighter colored flecks of blue in her irises, he palmed those cutaway panels at her waist like he'd been itching to do for an eternity and drew her against him. Yes, she was still as warm as he remembered and he ached to pull the pins from her tight blond chignon to let it rain down around her shoulders.

He leaned in, nearly nuzzling her ear with his lips. Her quick intake of breath was almost as thrilling as the feel of her skin through the panels. Instead of pulling her toward him like he wanted to, he pivoted and hustled her back a step into her office.

"Tell the girls I said hi," he murmured and let her go. Though where he found the willpower, he had no idea.

She nodded, her expression blank. He was *so* going to enjoy putting a few more cracks in her newly found ice-goddess exterior when they next met.

Three

Cass blew out the breath she'd been holding. Which didn't help either her shakes or her thundering pulse.

That hadn't gone down quite like she would have hoped. She and Gage might be equals now but that hadn't afforded her any special magic to keep her insides under control.

But Gage had left and that seemed like a small win.

Except now she had to go into that board meeting, where Trinity had most definitely told the others who Cass was meeting with. So she would have to give them the whole story, including his ridiculous offer for the formula.

Of all the nerve. Telling her she owed him the formula because he'd given her a few pointers once upon a time. Oh, she owed him all right, but more like a fat lip. Fyra's success had nothing to do with Gage.

Well, the broken heart he'd left her with had driven her for a long time. But she'd succeeded by her own merit, not because he'd mentored her.

If anyone decided to sell the formula, it would be because it made sound business sense. Like she'd told him.
She squared her shoulders and went to her meeting in the
large, sunny room at the end of the hall.

The other three women in the C-suite ringed the conference table as the governing forces of the company they'd
dubbed Fyra, from the Swedish word for four. Alex Meer
ran the numbers as the chief financial officer, Dr. Harper
Livingston cooked up formulas in her lab as the chief science officer, Trinity Forrester convinced consumers to
buy as the chief marketing officer and Cass held the reins.

All three of her friends looked up as she entered, faces
bright with expectation.

"He's gone. Let's get started." Cass set down her phone
and tablet, then slid into her customary chair.

"Not so fast," Trinity said succinctly. "We've been sitting here patiently waiting for juicy details, remember?"

They'd all been friends a long time. Juicy details meant
they wanted to know how she felt about seeing Gage again.
Whether she wanted to punch him or just go in the corner and cry. What was he up to and had they talked about
their personal lives?

She didn't have the luxury of burdening her friends
with any of that because they were also her business partners. There was no room at this conference table for her
emotional upheaval.

"He wants to buy Formula-47. Offered one hundred
million," she said bluntly. Better to get it out on the table.
"I told him it wasn't for sale. That's the extent of it."

Harper's grin slipped as she wound her strawberry
blond ponytail around one finger, an absent gesture that
meant her brilliant mind was blazing away. "That's hardly
the extent. What's the damage? Did he hear about my formula from the trade article?"

"No." Cass hated to have to be the bearer of bad news, but they had to know. "His information was much more detailed. Which means the leak is worse than we thought."

Hearing her own words echo in her head was almost as bad as a physical blow.

"What's wrong?" Trinity asked immediately, her dark head bent at an angle as she evaluated Cass. "Did Gage get to you?"

Dang it. It had taken all of fourteen seconds for the woman who'd been Cass's best friend since eleventh grade to clue in on the undercurrents. That man had put a hitch in her stride and it was unforgivable.

"I'm concerned about the leak. That's it. Forget about Gage. I already have," she lied.

Trinity's eyes narrowed but she didn't push, thank God. Gage's timing was horrific. Why had he waltzed back into her life during such a huge professional catastrophe?

Alex, the consummate tomboy in a pair of jeans and a T-shirt, fiddled with her ever-present pen, tapping it against the legal pad on the conference table in front of her. "A hundred million is worth considering, don't you think?"

Instantly, Harper shook her head so hard, her ponytail flipped over her shoulder. Trinity and Cass scowled at Alex, who shrank under the heat of their gazes, but didn't recant her traitorous statement.

"Worth considering?" Cass's stomach contracted sharply as she took in the seriousness of Alex's expression. How could she be talking about selling so coolly? To Cass, it would be like selling her own child. "Are you out of your mind?"

"Shouldn't we consider a lucrative income stream when it's presented?" Alex argued. "We can't categorically dismiss that kind of paycheck."

They could when it was coming out of the bank account of the man who had destroyed Cass. Didn't that matter?

"Wait just a darn minute, Ms. Moneybags." Harper rounded on Alex, who shrank a bit under the redhead's scowl. "Formula-47 is my baby, not yours. I spent two years of my life perfecting it on the premise that we'd hinge our entire future strategy around the products we can create from the technology. If we sell it, we're giving up rights to it forever for a lump sum. That's not smart."

Alex tapped her pen faster against the legal pad. "Not if we retain rights and structure the deal—"

"No one is structuring deals," Cass broke in. "I only mentioned it because you needed to know. Gage's offer will vanish instantly if the leak shares the formula's recipe. And since we still don't know who it is, we have to focus on that first."

Alex firmed her mouth and nodded. "That's true."

"What did our lawyer say?" Trinity asked, raising her eyebrows as Cass blinked at her. "Didn't you just come back from Mike's office?"

"God, I'm sorry." Cass slid down in her chair an inch in mortification. Gage had wiped that entire meeting out of her head. "Mike doesn't think we can involve the police yet. The article didn't contain enough detail and wouldn't stand up in court as proprietary information. He advised us to file for FDA approval immediately, in hopes that will stem future information from being released prematurely. Until we find the leak, we can't be too careful."

She had to regain control *now*. Gage wasn't a factor. Period.

"I'm not ready." Harper shook her head mulishly. *Careful* and *thorough* might as well be tattooed on her forehead alongside her credentials, a valuable trait in a scientist who created the products with Fyra's label on them. "This is our first product that requires FDA approval. We can't rush it."

"So our lawyer gave us advice we don't plan to take." Pradas flat on the ground, Trinity leaned on the table. "What else do we have on the agenda that we need to get busy shooting down?"

"The leak is the only thing on the agenda," Cass said firmly.

Alex zeroed in on her. "What's your plan for fixing this problem, then?"

"I'm still working on it."

"You're working on it." Alex's sarcastic tone couldn't have conveyed her disbelief any more clearly. "You mean you don't have something laid out already?"

Cass froze her muscles, a trick she'd perfected over the years. She refused to let on that Alex's words had pierced her through the chest.

Alex's point wasn't lost on her. Cass should have a plan. But didn't, which was the last thing she'd admit to these women who were looking to her for leadership. "I've got some ideas. Things in the works."

"Things?" Trinity repeated incredulously.

Trinity and Alex glanced at each other and foreboding slid down Cass's spine. She was losing her edge. And everyone knew she didn't have a blessed clue how to handle this problem.

"I said I'll take care of it," Cass snapped and then immediately murmured an apology.

She couldn't believe how the meeting had deteriorated, how much it hurt to have Alex on the other side of these critical company issues. There were fractures in Fyra she hadn't known existed. Fractures in the relationships with her friends and business partners that scared her. Was

Alex disputing her ideas because she had lost confidence in Cass's ability to run Fyra?

And what was with that look Alex and Trinity had exchanged? Did they know Cass had lied about how much Gage had affected her? And Trinity hadn't defended Cass, not when Gage's offer had come up and not when Alex had attacked Cass for her lack of a plan.

It all rubbed at the raw place inside that Gage had opened up.

Cass cleared her throat and forced her CEO mask back into place. Emotions had no place in a boardroom, yet she'd been letting them run rampant thus far. It was much harder than she would have expected to shut it down given all the practice she had.

"I've got this," she said a little more calmly. "Trust me. Nothing is more important than finding this leak. Let me take care of it."

Trinity nodded. "Let's meet again on Friday. You can give us a progress report then."

Cass watched the other ladies stand and leave the conference room. No one said a word but the vote of no confidence rang out in the silence, nonetheless.

With the room empty, she let her forehead thunk the table but the wood didn't cool her raging thoughts.

She needed a plan.

But Gage had messed her up. Of course he was the reason she'd slipped up in the board meeting. Why had he picked today to dismantle her careful facade?

Her head snapped up. What if the timing wasn't coincidental? It had been bothering her how accurate his information was and how quickly on the heels of the trade article publication that he'd shown up. What if he'd planted someone in her company who was feeding him information and the mention of Fyra in the trade magazine had been designed to throw her off?

But why would he do that? He was already successful in his own right and he was willing to pay for the formula. It wasn't as if he'd put a mole in her company in hopes of stealing it.

Or was it?

She had to make sure. She'd never forgive herself if she left that stone unturned.

She also had to make progress on discovering who the culprit was and the faster the better. If the leak heard the formula was worth one hundred million dollars to GB Skin, it was as good as stolen. And Gage probably wasn't the only competitor willing to ante up.

Fyra needed Cass to step up, to lead this company. So she'd keep her friends close and her enemies closer, no matter what sort of distasteful cozying up to the CEO of GB Skin she'd have to do. After all, she *did* owe Gage Branson and it was time to pay him back.

He'd used her once upon a time. Turnabout was fair play in Gage's book, was it? It was time for Cass to wholeheartedly embrace that mantra.

Whatever Gage's game was, she'd uncover it. And maybe exact some revenge at the same time. Karma indeed.

Whistling as he rounded the Hummer's bumper, Gage went over his pitch as he strolled toward the entrance to Fyra Cosmetics only one short day after running into Cass in the parking lot. After she'd kicked him out, he'd really expected to have to push her for another appointment. When she'd called, it had been a pleasant surprise.

The 9:00 a.m. appointment had been another one. Nice to be Cass's first priority for the day. Apparently she'd thought about the logic of his offer overnight and was finally on board. Or the other executives had convinced her that selling him the formula did make for smart business, like he'd told Cass. Either way, the tide had turned.

Which was good because Arwen didn't like the hotel, and she'd let Gage know about it. Loudly. He'd have to take her on a weekend camping trip to the Hill Country to make up for all of this. Hopefully, he could melt a little of the ice in Cass's spine, close the deal and be back in Austin tomorrow.

Depending how things went with the ice melting, of course. If Cass was still as hot as he remembered under her new bulletproof CEO exterior, he might stick around for a couple of days. Arwen could rough it.

Cass didn't make him cool his heels like he'd thought she would. After yesterday, with all the power plays disguised as flirting and Cass not letting him run roughshod over her, he'd come prepared for battle. Hell, he'd kind of looked forward to another game of one-upmanship. It was rare that a woman could match him.

She appeared in the reception area looking gorgeous and untouchable in another sharp suit with a microskirt, this time in eye-popping candy pink, and she'd swept up her hair into another severe bun-like thing held by lacquered chopsticks that he immediately wanted to take apart. Why was that so hot?

He dredged up a memory of her old look from college, which had largely consisted of yoga pants and hoodies, and he'd liked that, too. But this was something else. Something elemental. He wanted to explore this new Cass in the worst way.

"Good morning, Mr. Branson," she said, though the frost in her tone told him she thought it was anything but. "This way."

The chilly greeting and use of his last name put a grin on his face. So she planned to cross swords after all. Excellent.

This time, he didn't even hesitate at the door of her office. No point in beating around the bush when the upper hand was still up for grabs. He waltzed into the middle of all that purple and plunked down into a chair. Happened to be the one behind the desk—Cass's chair—but he figured that would be enough to get her into the room.

It was. She followed him into the interior, and without batting an eye, she crossed to the desk and perched on it. Two feet from his chair. Gaze squarely on Gage, she crossed her stocking-clad legs with a slow and deliberate slide and let her stilettos dangle. The little skirt rode up her thighs almost to the point of indecency.

His tongue went numb as all the blood rushed from his head, pooling into a spectacular hard-on. One tiny push with his heel and Cass's chair would roll him into a proximity much better suited to enjoying the smorgasbord of delights inches away.

This was his punishment for stealing her chair? She clearly didn't get how corporate politics, particularly between competitors, worked.

"Thanks for coming on short notice," she purred and the subtle innuendo wasn't lost on him.

"Thanks for having me," he returned and cleared the rasp from his throat. Maybe she knew a little more about this game than he'd supposed. "You ready to talk details?"

"Sure, if you want to jump right into it." She cocked her head, watching him. "The others don't want to sell. But I'm willing to talk to them."

Instantly suspicious, he grinned and crossed his arms, leaning back in the chair so he could see all of her at once. She was something else. "Along with what strings?"

"Oh, nothing much." She waved a French-manicured hand airily and leaned forward, one palm on the desk. Her silky button-up shirt billowed a bit, just enough to draw his attention to her cleavage but not enough to actually show anything.

The anticipation of catching a glimpse of skin had his mouth watering.

"Name your price, Cass," he murmured and wondered what she'd do if he pulled her off that desk into his lap. "I'm assuming one hundred million wasn't enough?"

"Not quite. You also have to help me catch the leak first."

His gaze snapped back up to her beautiful face as her meaning registered. "Help you catch the leak? You mean you haven't already?"

Unacceptable. Hadn't she learned anything important from him? Yesterday he sure would have said so, but obviously she needed a few more pointers about how to run her business.

"I have a plan," she explained calmly. "And you're it. Until the leak is stopped, Fyra can't make a major decision like selling our formula. Surely you understand that."

He did. This was a wrinkle he hadn't anticipated. But what she was proposing—it meant he'd have to stay in Dallas longer than he'd anticipated. He ran a successful company, too, and it was suffering from his lack of attention. If he stayed, he'd have to ship Arwen home, which she'd never forgive him for.

"You should have already handled the leak," he groused.

"I know."

Her voice didn't change. Her expression didn't change. But something shifted as he realized how hard this conversation was for her. She hadn't wanted to admit that.

Disturbed at the sudden revelation, he stared at her and

his heart thumped strangely. He'd been so busy examining the angles, he'd failed to see this was actually just a baseline plea for help that she'd disguised well.

"Work with me, Gage. Together, like old times."

She wanted to pick up where they left off. Maybe in more ways than one. The simple phrases reached out and grabbed hold of his lungs. It echoed through his mind, his chest, and the thought pleased him. Enormously.

It was a redo of college, where he was her mentor and she soaked it all up like a sponge with a side of hero worship that made him feel invincible. That had been a heady arrangement for a twenty-four-year-old. But they weren't kids anymore.

And he didn't for a moment underestimate Cass. She'd suggested this for some reason he couldn't figure out yet. Which didn't keep him from contemplating that redo. Who was he kidding? He'd wanted her the moment he'd turned around in the parking lot yesterday and gotten an eyeful of grown-up Cass. If he hung around and helped her, it gave him an opportunity to get her naked again.

And he could ensure the problem with the leak was handled like it should have been from the get-go. Not to mention he could dig a bit to uncover her real motives here.

Her eyes huge and warm, she watched him and he was lost. Dang. She'd played this extremely well. There was absolutely no way he could say no. He didn't want to say no.

But a yes didn't mean he'd do it without adding a few strings of his own.

"I'll help you. Until Sunday. I have a meeting Monday that can't be rescheduled."

Her smile hit him crossways. And then it slipped from her face as he leaned forward oh-so-slowly. Mute, she stared at his hand as he braced it on the desk a millimeter from her thigh. He could slip a finger right under the hem of that tiny skirt. And his mind got busy on imagining where that would lead.

"But you have to do something for me," he murmured. He got as close to her as he dared, crowding her space where all the trappings of business melted away and they were simply man and woman.

She smelled classy and expensive, and instantly he wanted that scent on his own skin, transferred by her body heat as she writhed under him. He could lean her back against that desk and at this angle, the pleasure would be intense. The image made him a little lightheaded as his erection intensified.

"I already said I'd talk to the others about selling you the formula," she said a touch breathlessly, but to her credit, she didn't allow one single muscle twitch to give away whether she welcomed his nearness or preferred the distance. "*If* we catch the leak."

That ice-goddess routine needed to go, fast. That wasn't going to happen here. Not under these circumstances..If he wanted to take things to the next level, he had to go bold or go home.

"Yes, but you're doing that because deep down, you know you owe me. If I help you find the leak, you owe me again. Turnabout, sweetheart."

"What do you want?"

Oh, where should I start? "Nothing you can't handle."

The knowing glint in her gaze said she already had a pretty good idea what gauntlet he was about to throw down. They stared at each other for a long moment and her breathing hitched as he reached out and slid a thumb along her jawline.

"You have to take me to dinner."

Four

Cass's laughter bubbled to the surface in spite of it all. Gingerly she dabbed at her eyes without fear thanks to Harper's smudge-proof mascara. "That's what you want? Dinner?"

She'd been braced for…anything but that. Especially since she had the distinct impression he was working as many angles as she was.

His fingers dropped away, but her face was still warm where he'd stroked her. She missed his touch instantly.

Why had she thought sitting on the desk would give her an edge? Seemed so logical before she actually did it. Gage had taken her chair in deliberate provocation that she absolutely couldn't ignore. So she'd trapped him behind the desk and put all her good stuff at eye level. It should have been the perfect distraction. For *him*. The perfect way to spend the entire conversation looking down at him, imagining that he was suffering over her brilliant strategic move.

Karma, baby.

Instead, she'd spent half of the conversation acutely aware that all her good stuff was at eye level. He'd noticed, quite appreciatively, and it hit her in places she'd forgotten that felt so good when heated by a man's interest.

The other half of the conversation had been spent trying to stay one step ahead of Gage while feeding him the right combination of incentives to get him to agree to help. If he was up to no good, what better way to keep tabs on him than under the guise of working together to uncover the source of the leak? Besides, she hadn't done so hot at resolving the leak on her own. If they kept their activities on the down-low, no one had to know she'd outsourced the problem.

If they caught the leak—*and* Gage wasn't involved— she'd absolutely talk to the other girls about selling the formula. She hadn't specified what she'd say…but she'd talk to them all right. The conversation might be more along the lines of no way in hell she'd sell, but he didn't have to know that.

It was a win-win for everyone.

Crossing his heart with one lazy finger, he grinned. "Totally serious."

"Dinner?" She pretended to contemplate. "Like a date?"

"Not *like* a date. A date. And you're paying."

A God-honest date? The idea buzzed around inside, looking for a place to land, sounding almost…nice. She'd love to have dinner over a glass of wine with an interesting man who looked at her like Gage was looking at her right now.

She shook it off. She couldn't go on a real date with Gage Branson. It was ludicrous. The man was a heartbreaker of the highest order.

Instead, she should be thinking of how a date fell in

line with her strategy. A little after-hours party, just the two of them. Some drinks and a few seductive comments and, oh, look. Gage slips and says something incriminating, like the name of the person he'd planted at her company. The one who was feeding him information he could use to his advantage.

And she would pretend she wasn't sad it had to be this way.

Coy was the way to go here. But she had to tread very carefully with the devil incarnate. No point in raising his suspicions by agreeing to his deal right out of the gate. "What if I already have plans for dinner tonight?"

She *did* have plans. If working until everyone else left and then going home to her empty eight-thousand-square-foot house on White Rock Lake, where she'd open a bottle of wine and eat frozen pizza, counted as plans.

"Cancel them," he ordered. "You're too busy worrying about the leak to have fun, anyway. Have dinner with someone who gets that. Where you can unload and unwind without fear."

"What makes you think I need to unwind?" she purred to cover the sudden catch in her throat. Had she tipped him off somehow that she was tense and frantic 24/7?

His slow smile irritated her. How dare he get to her?

"Oh, I'm practicing my mindreading skills," he told her blithely. "I see that things are rough around here. You can't be happy that word got out about your unreleased formula. You're at a unique place in your career where you have millions of dollars and a large number of people's jobs at stake. You want to keep it all together and convince everyone that you have things under control. With me, you don't have to. I get it."

Something inside crumbled under his assessment.

Guess that shield she'd thought she'd developed wasn't so effective after all. How was he still so good at reading her?

Now would be a good time for that distance she should have put between them long ago. She unglued herself from the desk and rounded it, an ineffective barrier against the open wounds in her chest but better than nothing. Let him make what he chose out of her move.

"You can't come in here and throw around pop psychology," she told him, pleased how calmly she delivered it. "You don't know anything about me, Gage. Not anymore."

Arms crossed, he watched her from behind her own desk, still wearing a faint trace of that smile. "Yet you didn't say I was wrong."

She shut her eyes for a beat. Dinner was going to be far more difficult than she'd anticipated.

If Gage was involved in corporate espionage, catching him in the act was the only way to prove to the others she could lead Fyra through these difficult circumstances. Plus it got rid of him, once and for all. His hundred-million-dollar offer wouldn't be a factor and the leak would be stopped.

He'd get exactly what he deserved.

Then she could get started on getting over him—for real, this time. She could stop hating him. And stop being affected by him. And stop turning down every man who asked her out. The chaos inside with Gage's name written all over it had driven her for so long. Wasn't it time to move on? That was what *she* deserved.

"I'm not what you'd call a fun date," she said. "I have a very boring life outside of these walls. Dinner is a chance to discuss the leak. Strictly business."

A token protest. She knew good and well it was anything but.

"Is that really what you want, Cass?" he asked softly,

as if he already knew the answer. "Because it sounds to me as if you need a friend."

Of all the things she'd thought he come back with, that was not one of them. The laugh escaped her clamped lips before she could catch it. "What, like you're volunteering? I have lots of friends, thanks."

But did she really? This time last week, she would have said Trinity would take a bullet for her. They'd been friends for almost fifteen years. It still stung that no one had stood up for Cass in the board meeting, but Trinity's silence had hurt the worst.

Alex's defection was almost as bad.

Cass and Alex had met in a freshman-level algebra class. It had taken Cass four months to convince Alex she had what it took to be the CFO of a multimillion-dollar corporation and Cass had been right. Alex's lack of confidence and all the talk of selling hurt.

Cass was afraid the cracks in Fyra's foundation were really cracks in *her* foundation. The last person she could stomach finding out about the division in Fyra was Gage Branson, and it would be just like him to sniff out her weaknesses.

So she wouldn't show him any.

"There's always room for one more friend," Gage countered softly. "In fact, I changed my mind. Let *me* take *you* to dinner and you can relax for a while. Wear a dress and we'll leave our titles at the door."

There he went again, working his magic because that sounded like the exact date she'd envisioned. He was the last man on earth she should be envisioning it with, though. "How do you know that's what I need?"

"Cass. I know you. You can't have changed too much over the years. At least I hope you haven't."

Before she could figure out how to respond to that, he

rounded the desk and took her hand to hold it tight in his surprisingly smooth one. For a guy who'd always spent a lot of time outdoors, his skin should be rougher. It was a testament to GB Skin and the effectiveness of his products that it wasn't.

She stared at his chiseled jaw, gorgeous hazel eyes and beautiful face framed by the longish brown hair he'd always favored and something unhitched in her chest.

Gage had broken her so thoroughly because she'd once given this man her soul.

That hadn't been an accident. A mistake, surely, but not because she didn't realize what she was doing. She'd fallen in love with Gage willingly. He'd filled her, completely. Because he understood her, believed in her. Taught her, pushed her, stimulated her.

All of it rushed back and she went a little dizzy with the memories of what had been holy and magnificent about their relationship.

"Say yes," he prompted, squeezing her hand. "I promise not to mention how boring you are."

Despite everything, she laughed, oddly grateful that he had figured out how to get her to.

"Yes," she said. There'd really never been another choice. "But we split the check."

He couldn't be allowed to affect her. The good stuff about their relationship didn't matter because at the end of the day, Gage didn't do commitment and never would.

"That part's nonnegotiable," he said with a wicked smile. "I'm paying. After all, I bullied you into it."

Mission accomplished. He had no clue he'd spent this entire conversation persuading her into exactly what she wanted to do. For that alone, she returned the smile. "You haven't seen the price of the obscenely expensive wine I plan to order."

"I'll pick you up at eight," he said, clearly happy to have gotten what he wanted, though why he considered dinner such a coup was beyond her. He had an angle here that she hadn't yet discovered.

She watched him leave. That gave her nearly ten hours to figure out how to keep Gage at arm's length while cozying up to him. Hours she'd use to figure out how to pump him for information while keeping him in the dark about her motives.

Ten hours to figure out how to seduce answers out of Gage Branson without falling for him all over again. All she had to do was focus on his sins and the rest would be a walk in the park.

Gage knocked on Cass's door at seven fifty-five.

Nice place. A bit too glass-and-steel for his tastes but Cass's house overlooked a big lake with a walking trail around it. His own house in Austin was near a lake. Funny how their tastes in views had aligned all these years later.

She swung open the door wearing a sheer lacy dress that hugged her body in all the right places. Cranberry-colored, which was somehow ten times racier than red would have been, it rendered him speechless. When he'd told her to wear a dress, he'd fully expected her to wear anything but.

His body sprang to full attention. He could not get a handle on her.

"You're early," she said with an amused brow lift. "I like an eager man."

The blood that should have been stimulating his brain into a snappy response seemed to have vacated for a warmer locale in the south.

Cass wasn't a college student any longer. Not that he was confused. But he was having a hard time reconciling how *much* she'd changed. Cassandra Claremont, CEO, might be the most intriguing woman on the planet. She was also far more of a challenge because she seemed to have developed Gage-proof armor.

Dinner was supposed to level the playing field. Warm up that ice so he could get her used to the idea of selling him the formula because she recognized what she owed him. She might be willing to talk to the other ladies about the formula, but he needed her to convince them, not talk about it. For that, she had to be totally in his corner. How was he supposed to get her there when he couldn't get his feet under himself long enough to figure out what game she was playing?

"Uh…" *Brain not engaging.* He shook off the Cass stupor. "It's only early if you're more than fifteen minutes ahead. Technically, I'm right on time."

"Where are you taking me for dinner, Mr. Right-on-Time?" She cocked her head, sending her dangly diamond earrings dancing.

His body was not interested in food. At all.

"I'll let you choose," he allowed magnanimously. "Since you cancelled your previous plans."

Not for the first time, he wondered what she'd told the poor schmuck she'd ditched, who'd likely spent all day anticipating his date with Cass. Had she admitted to her date that an old boyfriend had unexpectedly come to town? A business deal had suddenly fallen in her lap that she needed to attend to? She had to wash her hair?

It probably didn't matter. She'd be forgiven for breaking the date regardless. Cass was a gorgeous, sophisticated woman who ran a multimillion dollar company and she likely had her pick of companions. Suave execs, successful doctors, cut athletes with Pro-Bowl or all-star credentials. The dating circles were wide open and she was most definitely sleeping with *someone*. A woman like Cass wouldn't be alone except by choice.

That burn in your gut? Feels a lot like jealousy.

Ridiculous. So Nicolas didn't get it right *all* the time.

Gage and Cass hadn't been an item for nearly a decade. Sure, he'd thought about her and wondered what might have been if he wasn't so averse to being tied down, but he hadn't spent all his nights alone since then either. Though lately, a couple of hours at the dog park with Arwen was more fun than wading through the pool of women in his circle. That was the one downside to guarding your freedom so ferociously—you went through eligible women pretty quickly.

"That's so generous of you to let me pick after leaving me so few choices otherwise," she said, infusing it with enough sarcasm to clue him in that she still wasn't clear on what she owed him.

"You always have choices," he countered. "One just might lead to a different place than the other."

"Well said." With a cryptic nod, she brushed past him onto the front steps, engulfing him in a delicious haze of jasmine and other exotic spices. On Cass, the scent was half "come and get me" and half "I'm untouchable." A thoroughly arousing combination.

Somehow, he managed to drive to the restaurant without veering off into a ditch. Or a shadowy hiding place between two buildings where he could ravish the cool beauty in the next seat. If he wanted her willing, he had to get back on track. But the ice in her spine seemed extra hard and cold tonight.

The restaurant was as highbrow as they came, making him glad he'd tossed a suit in his overnight bag, just in case. The maître d' led them to a secluded table in the back, exactly as Gage had instructed, and left them bless-edly alone.

Except Gage still didn't know how to play this dinner. Seduction or strategy? Which would get him an invitation through the front door of Cass's house at the end of the night? Because seduction might be the only way to get what he wanted in the end. A sated Cass might make for a much more reasonable Cass. But they did need to work together on the leak or the formula would be worthless. He couldn't ignore the need to discuss strategy.

Fortunately, what he apparently lacked in ESP, he made up for in charm and ingenuity. So he'd wing it. Like always.

Gage barely glanced at the wine menu before handing it over to Cass. "Since you called dibs on ordering the wine, here you go."

She arched one of those cool brows and took the leather-bound wine listing. The movement drew attention to her cleavage, where scarcely-contained nipples threatened to burst free of their cranberry lace cage at a moment's notice. A bead of sweat slid between his shoulder blades as he tore his gaze from her breasts.

"I was expecting more of an argument," she commented as if the sexual undercurrents didn't exist. "You're not a fan of wine, if memory serves."

No, but the fact that she recalled his preference put a good deal more warmth down south. As if he'd had room for more.

"I'll make an exception for you."

The more she drank, the less she'd remember to act like the ice goddess, or at least that had been the plan once upon a time when his faculties were in order. Back in her office, she'd seemed...brittle. As if she'd needed someone to pay attention to her. Cass was in sore need of a glass of wine and an orgasm, and not necessarily in that order.

That made up his mind. He wanted to give her a chance to relax, as he'd entreated her to. One of them should be able to anyway. Seduction first. And then they could talk leak strategy later. Much later.

With their food, Cass ordered a four hundred dollar bottle of wine—exorbitant, as promised—and once the waiter left to retrieve it, she folded her hands, contemplating Gage as if she'd found an amusing little puppy she didn't know whether to pet or send outside for peeing on the floor.

"Tell me something," she began in her boardroom voice that he should not find so sexy.

"Sure. I'm an open book." He spread his hands wide, earning a small, less-than-amused smile. She needed to drink more. Maybe her Gage-proof armor would fall off along with her inhibitions.

Once, they'd talked about everything under the sun and he'd enjoyed hearing her thoughts and soothing her through her angst. Just like he'd enjoyed being her mentor, shaping her, guiding her.

Maybe you hope to fall into that role again, with the hero worship and Pygmalion overtones, hmm?

Yeah. He did. And she needed his help to find the leak. Needed *him*. So what? Seduction *and* strategy, then. All of that worked together to get him the formula. Where was the harm?

"Why the interest in my formula?" she asked point-blank. "Other than the song and dance about how I owe it to you. For real. Why? You've expanded your retail reach enormously over the past five years and you just landed that endorsement deal. Something must have prompted you to show up on my doorstep."

"That's a fair question," he acknowledged, impressed that she'd done her homework on his company. And that's why he chose to answer her honestly. "It's simple really. My target consumers are starting to pay close attention to things like bar-fight scars and wrinkles. So I launched my own product. I don't want any competition."

"Gage, there are a hundred wrinkle creams on the market. Your competition is legion."

"No." He caught her gaze and held it. "There's only one person who's my equal."

"So this is a pride thing." Looking away, she sipped the glass of wine the waiter had placed in front of her and murmured her appreciation for the red blend. "You can't stand it when a competitor is primed to beat you."

He might as well be made of glass when it came to Cass and that was sexy, too. Dang if he could figure out why he was so drawn to her when all he should care about was whatever got him that formula.

Ignoring his own vile glass of headache in a bottle, he grinned because it would be pointless to argue when she clearly saw the truth. But that didn't mean they had to dwell on it.

Gage slid a palm across the table and captured her hand before she could prevent it. "Don't think of me as your competition, not tonight."

She glanced down at their joined hands but didn't snatch hers away. He could tell she was contemplating it, though, hopefully because she also felt the electricity between them—and it was working to loosen her up.

"But you are. Always and forever. We sell similar products or you wouldn't be here. Nor would you have been my mentor. Competition is not something you can will away."

"Maybe not. I can, however, ban all business talk until later. Then we're just old friends reconnecting. Like I told you in your office."

He had the distinct impression she didn't loosen up easily these days. If there was any competition going on tonight, that was it. And he didn't intend to lose this particular contest.

"I'm curious," she said, her gaze back on him but not nearly warm enough for his taste. "I never see you at trade shows. My email address is easy to locate on Fyra's website. If you have such an interest in reconnecting, why haven't we done so before now?"

A hot prickle walked across the back of his neck as he instantly recognized a spring-loaded trap, ready to close around his leg if he moved the wrong way. An unsettled feeling bled through his chest.

And in the end, *he* was the one to pull his hand back from hers, suddenly uncomfortable with the contact.

"I hate trade shows. They're stifling. And they're always on weekends when I'm...busy."

That had sounded much dirtier than he'd intended, especially when lately, his weekends had consisted of giving Arwen a bath or taking her to the lake so she could have fun practicing her pointer skills.

Cass watched him without blinking, silently waiting on him to stop stalling and get to the meat of her question, which was basically designed to force him to admit he'd developed an interest in her in order to get his hands on her formula.

Maybe it had started out as a little of both—seducing her to ensure she remembered what she owed him. He wasn't a saint.

But at this moment, he really did want to be a friend. None of her other so-called friends seemed to realize how brittle she was under her super-CEO costume. Someone had to banish the shadows of fatigue and uncertainty in her gaze. Give her a safe place to let her hair down, which would preferably be in his bed, like she'd once done.

Yeah. He'd like to pull those pins from the tight blond twist at her crown, all right. His lower half went rock solid as he imagined that fall of hair raining down around her bare shoulders as he peeled that lacy, sexy cranberry-colored dress from her beautiful body. It was crazy to be so hot for her again after not seeing her for so long—or to her point, after not actively pursuing reacquaintance for all these years.

He should have looked her up. Why hadn't he?

He blew out a pent-up breath. "Truth? I didn't drive up from Austin to reconnect over a drink. I want your formula. But that's just business."

Tonight was very personal.

Nodding at the wine bottle, she drained her glass and held it out for Gage to pour her another. "I'm surprised you'd admit it."

"I told you, I'm an open book. I don't mind being cagey when the occasion calls for it, but I don't have deep dark secrets." Who had time for that noise? Life was too short to care about other people's opinions, and that's all secrets were—things you didn't want others to know because you feared their judgment.

Cass leaned forward and the new angle did fascinating things to the deep V over her breasts. Not that he was a lecher, but come on. A lady didn't wear a dress like that if she didn't want her date to notice her spectacular breasts. And a lady who didn't want a man to imagine tasting her breasts definitely didn't *lean*.

"Really. No secrets?"

"Really, really." His tongue was still a bit thick.

"Sounds like we need to play a game of truth or dare, then."

Five

Cass held her breath as Gage's gaze flew to hers. It had been lingering somewhere in the vicinity of her cleavage, and the heat from his appreciation had been warming her uncomfortably for the better part of ten minutes. But what had she expected with such a daring wardrobe choice?

Gage's eyes on her body were far more affecting than any other man's hands would be.

Question marks shooting from the top of his head, Gage lifted a brow. "Yeah, truth or dare. That's what I was thinking, too. How did you know?"

She bit back the laugh. Even when he was being sarcastic, he was still charming. She wasn't falling for it. "I'm serious. If you don't have any secrets, should be an easy game."

And she could pump him for information about his involvement in the leak without raising red flags. It was brilliant.

Lazily he traced the rim of his untouched wineglass, watching her with undisguised calculation. But what all those equations added up to, she had no idea. The clink of silverware against china filled the sudden silence, along with snatches of conversation from other diners.

"You know how that game works, right?" he finally asked.

She waved dismissively. "Of course, or I wouldn't have suggested it. I ask you a question and if you don't choose to answer it honestly, you have to do whatever I dare you to."

"And you have to do the same." The once-over he slid down her body unleashed a shiver.

She'd considered that. Not enough, apparently. "Yeah, so? I'm not worried."

The waiter brought their dinners but instead of picking up a fork, Gage folded his hands in front of his plate of salmon and asparagus. "You probably should be. But now I'm insanely curious what you want to know that you feel you have to bury inside a game. You could just ask."

Her pulse tripped as she scrambled for a response. She was slipping. How had he seen through that ploy so *easily*? "That's no fun."

His laugh curled up inside her thickly. "It *so* can be, but it's all in the asking. No matter. I'm in. Truth or dare away. Truth for my first round."

Forking a bite of salmon into his mouth, he watched her expectantly and it bobbled her pulse again. This was why she sold cosmetics for a living instead of becoming an investigator. There was a skill to it apparently, one that she lacked. Too late to back out now.

"Have you ever…" She cursed silently. Thinking on the fly was one of her strong suits but not with Gage's hazel laser beams boring into her. *Say something.* "Cheated on your taxes?"

"That's your question?" He shook his head with a laugh. "I'm almost afraid to ask what the dare would be. But it doesn't matter because I have nothing to hide. As much as I think the corporate tax structure needs to be reworked in favor of businesses, no, I've never cheated on my taxes."

Taxes. Could she be more boring? Despite having warned him that she was not a fun date, she had a goal here and she needed to get on it by steering the conversation toward his ethics. "But you cheat at cards. All the time."

His slow smile did something X-rated to her insides. "That's only when we're playing strip poker, darling. And believe me, it's worth it."

The memory of messing around in college, using things like card games as foreplay, spiked through her. They'd always ended up naked and breathless. The anticipation had been drawn out over the length of a game she could hardly pay attention to because Gage had been revealing himself oh-so-slowly while she sat there in a similar state of vulnerability.

Kind of like now.

And she couldn't unthink it. Back then, when they'd finally come together, she'd exploded under his careful and thorough lovemaking. Because he had always thoroughly engaged her—mind, body and soul.

And that hadn't changed. The moment she'd recognized Gage in the parking lot, it felt as though she'd woken up from a coma. She hadn't realized how much she'd missed being so comprehensively engaged. How much she missed a man paying attention to her.

No. Not any man. This one.

Their gazes met over the table, burning up the atmosphere. Obviously he was recalling their hot and heavy times, as well, and his expression unleashed a shiver she couldn't control. Something unknitted inside, falling apart as if all the glue holding her together melted at Gage-point-five degrees.

They'd once been so close because they had so much in common. They'd shared the same goals, and she'd always been able to count on him to have the answers she sought. She'd counted on him to encourage her, to push her. Because he understood her.

It was so much more powerful now that they were equals. Gage Branson, CEO, was so much more attractive than he'd been as her mentor.

Fork suspended in midair, he tilted his head. "Weren't we playing a game?"

Cass blinked. The game. The suspicions. Her precarious position within Fyra. She bit back an unladylike swear word and took a fortifying sip of wine.

How had she fallen into Gage so easily that she'd forgotten what this dinner was supposed to be about? He'd cursed her with his magic voice and wicked personality, lulling her into believing they were former lovers reconnecting over a drink.

He wasn't on her side, not like he used to be. Maybe he never had been. As he was making love to her, he'd probably already be plotting his escape. Just like he'd almost assuredly plotted to steal her formula.

Gage Branson, CEO, wasn't any more of a good bet with her heart than he had been as a graduate student.

She steeled her spine against the good memories and dredged up the bad ones. She'd spent years working sixteen-hour days so she could fall into bed exhausted and actually sleep. Otherwise, she lay there in misery, aching over having lost the love of her life.

And here he was again, ripe for a comeuppance and

deserving of whatever she threw at him. She narrowed her gaze and shoved back the past. "We got off track. Sorry. Next question. Have you ever stolen anything?"

"I'm supposed to say whether I want truth or dare first." Warily, he eyed her. "What's with all these moral questions anyway? Admittedly, it's been a long time since I played truth or dare, but I seem to recall we always asked things like who was your first crush or have you ever gone skinny-dipping?"

"Those are great questions for eleven-year-olds. This is the adult version," she informed him pertly and was instantly sorry as something wicked flashed through his expression.

"Why didn't you say so?" His slow smile had all sorts of danger signs attached to it. "I'd like to take the dare, then."

She cursed. *Should have anticipated that he'd take the dare, dummy.* "I dare you to answer the question."

"Oh, no, honey," he said with a laugh. "It doesn't work like that. You promised me the adult version and I'm fully prepared to pay up for not answering. Lay it on me."

Clearly he expected the dare to come packaged in a thinly veiled sexual wrapper. So she indulged him with a sensuous smile. "I dare you to take your shirt off."

"Here?" He glanced around the crowded, high-class restaurant with a dubious line between his brows. "It doesn't seem fair to show up all these other guys. Can't you think of something else?"

Typical male machismo. Of course if his body still looked like it used to—and chances were high that it did—his point was valid.

"Chicken?" she asked sweetly. "You wanted the dare."

"I'd be happy to take my shirt off," he growled. "In the car. In your living room. In your office. No card game required. Pick another locale, sweetheart, and dare me to get naked to your heart's content. Unfortunately, there are both a dress code and health regulations in a restaurant. Which means your dare is invalid."

First the insistence he always paid his fair share of taxes and then he'd refused her dare because of *health regulations*? She bit back the noise of disgust. Barely. "When did you become such a boy scout?"

"I've never willingly broken the law." He shrugged. "So there's your answer since I can't take the dare. My turn."

"Your turn for what?" she asked, temporarily distracted by his claim to be a law-abiding citizen.

Honesty? Just because truth was the name of the game didn't mean he wasn't lying. But in reality, he'd never been anything but forthright in their relationship. Sure, he'd dumped her and broken her heart. But he'd been honest about it.

"To ask you a question." He finished off his dinner and chewed thoughtfully. "What's the name of the last guy you were in love with?"

Love. The word echoed through her chest cavity, which was still empty thanks to the last guy she'd fallen in love with. Her stomach rolled and the wine soured in her mouth.

Stupid game. She could lie. But he'd see through that as though he was reading her mind. And she couldn't take the dare—she'd bet his hundred million it would be something impossible like sit in his lap for five minutes or put her underwear in his pocket with her toes.

Why had she started this game? To prove he'd become someone untrustworthy, when she had no evidence of his involvement in the leak? To prove she wasn't affected by him any longer, when she'd only managed to prove the exact opposite?

Or some deeper reason that she couldn't admit, even internally?

Trapped and furious with herself, she stared at him as her frustration grew. And then she pictured the shock on his face if she blurted out *Gage Branson* in response to his question. That was perhaps what stung the most—he didn't even realize he'd detonated a landmine in her heart.

The emotional agitation inside boiled over. And that was unacceptable.

"Excuse me." She threw her napkin into the middle of her plate of uneaten chicken marsala and fled to the bathroom before the sob beating in her throat escaped.

What in the... Gage watched Cass do the hundred-yard sprint through the obstacle course of tables and waiters, presumably headed for the restrooms at the rear of the building.

She'd started this silly game. Was she really that upset he hadn't taken her dare? Why—because she wanted him naked and was too afraid to come right out and say it?

He shook his head and thought seriously about draining his untouched glass of wine to see if Cass made any more sense when he had a buzz. The subsequent headache would at least be more easily explained than the one Cass was giving him.

She didn't return for a long while. A little concerned, Gage followed her, hoping to find a female employee to check on her if need be. Except she was sitting on the velvet bench at the end of the long hallway, her vibe so edgy, he could almost feel the tension.

"Hey," he said softly as he approached. "What's up? Trying to skip out on me? I said I'd pay."

The joke didn't get the smile he'd hoped for. In fact, her expression remained completely blank. "I'm fine."

"Yeah. I can see that." Taking a chance that she'd welcome the company, he sat on the bench next to her.

She didn't move. He'd noticed she did that a lot, holding herself frozen. But this time, he was close enough to see the muscle spasms in her thighs as if she was fighting her body's natural instincts to flee in some kind of mind-over-matter contest.

"I'm sorry I didn't play the game fairly," he said sincerely. And gingerly, in case that wasn't the reason she was upset. Women and emotions were not his forte and he wouldn't be surprised to learn this was one of those situations where if he didn't know why she was upset—she sure wasn't going to tell him.

"You did." She stared straight ahead. "I'm the one who was playing unfairly. You were right, the dare wasn't valid."

Somehow, her admission of guilt managed to sound as if she felt it was anything but her fault. Which was a rare talent.

"Okay. You ready to get out of here, then?" He nodded toward the end of the hallway. "Or do you want to finish dinner?"

"What would be the point of finishing dinner?" she asked in a monotone that pricked the hair on the back of his neck.

This strange mood went well beyond her normal reserve. When he'd labeled her demeanor as *brittle* earlier, he'd had no clue how much more so she could actually become, as if he had to watch how heavily he breathed for fear of shattering her into a million pieces.

"The point of dinner is so I can spend time with you," he said. And…some other agenda items that had somehow slipped his mind in favor of the woman herself.

That earned him a sidelong glance. "I told you I wasn't a fun date."

"I'm having fun," he told her automatically and then had to clarify. "Well, I *was*. And then you disappeared."

Physically and mentally.

"That was fun?" She tilted her head toward the dining room, her eyes incredulously wide. "I made you drink wine, which you hate, and then foisted a teenagers' sleepover game on you. Which part did you find the most entertaining?"

"All of it." He grinned in spite of her mood and accepted her scowl with a nod. "You heard me. I have legs and I know how to use them. Trust me, I've got no problem walking out of a restaurant in the middle of a date. I don't waste my time on things that aren't fun."

"Really?"

"Honesty. It isn't just for breakfast anymore."

And finally, he scored a small laugh. Why did that make his chest feel so tight and full?

"I guess I'm done with dinner." She sneaked another glance at him and he pretended not to notice.

"But not with spending time together?" He resisted the urge to reach out. He wanted to touch her but he couldn't gauge if her mood had shifted enough to welcome it.

"Well…" She crossed her arms, hiding her hands underneath, as if she'd sensed that he'd been contemplating taking one of them. "We were supposed to be talking about the leak. I think we have to do that together."

Which wasn't an answer at all. "You know dinner wasn't about the leak. Don't be dense."

"I was giving you the benefit of the doubt," she countered. "I'm well aware that you're playing all the angles."

And that was the opportunity he'd been waiting for. Since her hands were still locked behind the cross of her arms, he opted to slide one chunk of hair from her cheek and lingered at her neck. Touching that beautiful alabaster skin had suddenly grown more important than breathing. So he indulged himself, letting his fingers play with her neck. And then he tipped her head back so he could meet her gaze.

A shield snapped over her expression. That look he recognized. The ice goddess returneth. Excellent. Now he could get started melting her, like he'd planned. Though the reasons that had felt so necessary at the beginning of the night weren't the same as they were now. At all.

"No angles," he murmured and drew her face closer. Almost within kissing distance. But not quite. "I asked you to dinner because I wanted to. You…interest me. I want to find out how you've changed since college. Discover what's still the same."

Cass didn't look away, challenging him with merely the glint in her eye. "So you can use it to your advantage."

God, that was sexy. In-charge, take-no-prisoners Cass was something else. His motor started humming. "Absolutely. I fully intend to use every scrap of information I learn to seduce you."

Not even a blink to show she'd registered that he'd shifted away from business and zeroed in on pleasure. Which was where they'd keep it if he had his way. Oh, he'd eventually wind his way back to the formula. But for now, it was all about Cass.

"I think you've forgotten that I specified this dinner should be strictly business. I was about to thank you for sticking to it."

Ah-ha. Her voice had grown a little huskier and it skated through his blood, raising the heat a notch. She wasn't as unaffected as she wanted him to believe.

"Sorry," he apologized without a shred of regret. "I

never agreed to that. But we're smart people. We can keep business and pleasure separate. Like we did in college."

He watched her expression smooth out, becoming blank. Which meant he'd hit a nerve.

"I can," she said firmly. "I'm not so sure about you."

"I'm good for it." *Press your advantage. Now.* "If you are, too, prove it."

Her gaze dropped to his mouth. "How?"

Heat and awareness shot through the roof. God, that dress clung to her curves like a second skin. Would it be terrible if he hooked both sleeves with his thumbs and yanked it down so he could feast his eyes on her beautiful bare breasts?

Gage tipped her chin up with a crooked finger to bring her mouth in range. But he didn't take it with his. Not yet.

"So, let me see if I've got this straight," Cass murmured, her breath mingling with his. "By your logic, if I kiss you, that'll prove I can separate business from pleasure?"

"Who said anything about kissing?" he countered. "Is that what's on your mind, Cass? Because I'm game if you think kissing me will make your point."

It was a dare and a challenge—guaranteed to get an in-control, powerful woman like Cass hot—and she caught both full force. Her mouth curved upward as she contemplated him. "I think it'll make your point, not mine."

"Oh?" Barely six inches separated their lips and he ached to close that distance. "What point is that?"

She leaned in, almost there but not quite, lips feathering against his, and it was more evocative than if she'd gone for it. Her perfume engulfed him in a sensuous wave that heightened the sparking awareness. Her breasts brushed his chest aggressively and he nearly groaned with the effort it took to keep his fingers from her dress.

One little signal and he'd slide his arms around her, pulling her into the fiercest kiss. The only prayer he had of cracking that ice was to give her something sizzling hot to grab on to with both hands.

Public place, public place, public place, he reminded himself furiously.

"Your point—if I recall—was that you'd use all the information at your disposal to seduce me," she murmured throatily. "I don't think you have a shot."

"Guess there's only one way to find out."

The irresistible draw between them sucked him in, and finally his arms closed around her and her mouth sought his. A scorching kiss ignited the pent-up emotions and desire Gage had been fighting since he'd first laid eyes on Cass in the parking lot of her building.

They twined together, shifting closer. As close as they could on the bench without turning the kiss into something too indecent for public consumption.

Yes. Oh, God yes. Her tongue darted out in a quest for his and he lost himself in the sensation of her hot flesh. She tasted of wine and familiarity, throwing him back to a time when she'd been a major part of his first round of freedom.

Memories zipped by of Cass spread out under him, hips rolling toward his in a sensuous rhythm, hair spread out, her gaze hot and full of anticipation and pleasure as they came together again and again. Memories of her laughing with him, challenging him, filling him.

He wanted her. Just like that. Right now.

He forgot about the hard bench and pulled her closer, nearly into his lap as he let the lace of her dress pleasure his fingers.

She tilted her head, sucking him deeper, her hands sliding across his back, gripping his waist. Driving him

wild with the need she'd enflamed with a simple touch.
He wanted to feel her again, feel like the world was his for
the taking, like life had endless possibilities. How had he
not realized that Cass had been such a huge piece of that?

Masterfully, purposefully, she kissed him, breaking
down everything he'd thought he was doing here. Everything went out the window: plans, strategy, formulas. Who
cared? This was pleasure at its finest and he wanted more.

Then she pulled back, separating from him before he
was ready, and his knees went weak. She smiled, her expression heavy with something he couldn't identify.

"Nice," she said conversationally. "And now it's time
for the business talk we've been avoiding. Join me when
you're done with the pleasure part of the evening."

She stood, swishing away from him on her dangerously sexy heels and sashaying out of the hall. The ice in
her spine appeared firmly in place.

Blearily, he watched her go, too floored to call out.
That had been hotter than he could have ever imagined.
Hotter than it had ever been with Cass in the past. Hotter
than he would have credited, given the ice-goddess routine she'd perfected.

He'd goaded her into kissing him in hopes of getting
past all that icy reserve, past her CEO exterior, past all
this business talk so he could seduce her into his bed. Instead of melting her, he'd learned he wasn't quite over
Cassandra Claremont. And she hadn't been affected at all.

That turnabout was anything but fair.

Six

Gage paid the tab and followed Cass out of the restaurant.

Thank God he was behind her. That gave her a good three minutes to get her shakes under control.

It wasn't long enough. By the time they hit the sidewalk and Gage gave the valet his ticket, she'd almost managed to stop hyperventilating.

That kiss still singed her lips. His touch still burned her back. Worse? She'd touched him, too. Her own fingertips had reacquainted themselves with Gage's broad shoulders, thick hair, muscular torso. They'd explored him thoroughly and she ached to memorize him all over again.

She was supposed to be seducing him so she could get some answers about his involvement in her company's problems. Somehow that hadn't happened. She had to get the advantage back. Pronto.

As they waited in tense silence for his Hummer to appear at the curb, she prayed he wouldn't try to corner her again, maybe in one of the shadowy alcoves off to the right, where he could back her up against the brick away from prying eyes and kiss her like that again. Because she could almost feel the bite of that brick against her back. Could almost feel his hands on her. His mouth.

That would be...too much. And it was all she could think about.

"Hi, Cass. I thought that was you."

The enthusiastic female voice on her right snapped her out of the fantasy where Gage had hiked up her dress as he kissed her in that shadowy alcove and... *Get a grip, for crying out loud.*

Cass turned. And her heart tripped as she came face-to-face with Fyra's accounting manager. Who was eyeing Gage with undisguised interest as she gripped her own date's arm.

"Hi, Laurie," Cass croaked before clearing her Gage-riddled throat.

"Fancy seeing you here," Laurie commented and gestured to the man with her. "This is my husband, Mark. You may remember him from the Christmas party? But I haven't had the pleasure," she said to Gage, sticking out her hand in expectation.

Oh, no. This was not the time or place to be caught with a rival CEO. They needed to play it cool and extract themselves without—

"Gage Branson," he announced cheerily, completely ignoring the elbow Cass had just shoved in his ribs.

Too late. She stifled a groan as Laurie's expression lit up.

"Not *the* Gage Branson of GB Skin? I'm a huge fan of your body wash. I use it all the time, but don't tell my husband," she said with a laugh.

Cass glowered at her but Laurie just shrugged. "What?

Ours is too flowery. Men's scents are more outdoorsy. Lemon and sage and such."

Gage grinned. "That's what I like to hear."

The mutual admiration club gained another member when Laurie's husband jumped into the mix to announce his own GB Skin product preferences. This was beyond uncomfortable. Not simply because it grated to hear that Gage had one-upped her, but also because he'd just kissed her.

Could Laurie and Mark tell? Of course they could— she was probably mussed, and she hadn't had a chance to slick on more lipstick. It was a cardinal sin to stand here on the curb with missing makeup. They'd probably noticed her naked lips the moment she'd turned around.

Okay, yes. She'd been kissing the CEO of GB Skin. Cass had kissed Gage. Strictly in the name of finding out whether he'd been the mastermind behind the leak, which had somehow turned into something else.

Her guilty conscience was probably seeping from her pores. She had to get out of here.

Cass gritted her teeth and broke in at an opportune moment. "Laurie, you know we welcome suggestions from employees on Fyra's products. Just send me an email with your thoughts about how to improve the scents in our body wash, and I'll get it into the right hands."

"Oh, I know I shouldn't be gushing over a competitor's products in front of my boss's boss." Laurie's giggle was the opposite of contrite. "But I figured it was okay to admit it. After all, I'm just using the products, not dating the CEO."

"Oh, this isn't a date," Cass interjected swiftly. "Mr. Branson is...uh—"

"Providing consulting services to Ms. Claremont," Gage finished for her smoothly. "Cass and I went to college together and she contacted me to ask for strategic advice."

"That's a pretty fancy dress for a business meeting." Laurie sighed a little over it. "I would love to be able to wear something that sexy."

Her husband murmured something in her ear and she laughed as the valet rolled up in a Lexus. "That's our ride. Nice to meet you."

The couple disappeared into the interior of the car.

"A consultant, Gage? Really?" Cass muttered as the valet parked the Hummer behind the Lexus. A horn blared behind her but she didn't take her focus off the traitor at her shoulder.

"Yeah." He opened her door and helped her into the monstrously high seat without asking. Which she appreciated because she hated needing help.

As he handed her up, she pretended she didn't notice that his fingers brushed her thigh and hung around a little longer than was absolutely necessary. Just like she was pretending she wasn't remembering what had happened a few minutes ago. But noticing was a little hard to stop once she'd opened that Pandora's box.

When he slid into his own seat, he glanced at her. "Would you have rather I corrected you? I can run up to the window of Mark and Laurie's Lexus and let them know it really *is* a date. I'm sure the company grapevine would catch fire as quickly as that news would travel."

"I get the point."

"Thank you, Gage," he mimicked in a high voice. "You're the best, Gage. Your quick thinking saved me, Gage."

A spurt of laughter burst out through her clamped lips. How dare he make her have a good time? He was not allowed to be funny and charming. And sexy. Or such a good kisser. There should be a law.

How in the world did Gage get her to have fun on this date that wasn't a date?

She sobered and crossed her arms. "It wasn't a terrible cover. Now you can come by in the morning to continue digging into the leak. The other girls know you were my mentor and they'll believe me if I say I'm consulting with you."

He shot her an amused once-over, brows raised and she resisted sinking down in the seat.

"Thank you, Gage," she said in a high voice, imitating him mimicking her because she was not about to admit she should have already thanked him. "You're the best, Gage. And so on."

She didn't like how masterfully he'd handled her. It was supposed to be the other way around.

"That's more like it." Oblivious to her sarcasm, he grinned and nodded out the windshield. "Where to?"

Everything rolled off him like water off a duck's back. She wished she had that skill; she had to work at making it *appear* as if she did, when in truth, nothing rolled off. He'd missed teaching her that back in college—how to not care about anything and always squeeze the maximum amount of fun out of everything.

Perhaps she needed to practice. Retreating wouldn't get her what she needed—answers. She threw her shoulders back.

"Turn at the next light," she instructed impulsively. "There's a great little area that overlooks the lake."

As it wasn't too far from her house, she often used the trail for jogging, though she'd never been there at night. The spot had nighttime assignation written all over it.

"Are you asking me to *park*, Ms. Claremont?" The innuendo in his tone was half amused and half *hell, yeah*.

She forced a laugh as he followed her directions and pulled into the parking lot. "I'm asking you to stroll. It's a walking path."

They could walk along the secluded moonlit path and she'd get him comfortable enough so she could ask a few pointed questions. And then when he least expected it, she'd move in for the kill.

It was no less than he deserved.

And she'd keep the reminder front and center, no matter how good it felt to be with him again. He'd kissed her. She'd kissed him back. No big deal. She didn't have to fall in love with every man she kissed. In fact, she'd never fallen in love with any man she'd kissed. Except one.

The key here was to work with Gage to find his connection to the leak and go on. A kiss was just a kiss. Emotions didn't belong in the middle of this and she'd make sure to keep it that way.

No problem.

She wished she didn't have to keep reminding herself of that.

"There's a gate with a keypad," she called over her shoulder as they slid from the car. "This part of the lake is only for residents. Follow me."

The area was secluded, with one dim light that illuminated only a small circle of the concrete lot. Trees marched away from the lot along the line of the path, sheltering it from the outside world.

"Sure." Gage's voice had deepened in the dark, skittering along her bare skin and burrowing underneath to heat up her insides, as if he'd whispered erotic instructions instead of merely agreeing with her.

Lights would be good here. Gage and the dark mixed like oil and water.

Except she didn't have any lights to turn on. The dark blanketed them both as they walked to the gate, wrapping them in a secluded bubble that felt entirely too intimate.

As she punched in the key code, Gage's presence swept along her back, igniting her nerve endings with sensuous heat. He wasn't physically touching her, but she could feel him, hear his breath. Maybe even sense the beat of his heart.

The urge to move backward, flush against his body, almost overtook her and she bit her lip. He'd be warm, solid. Her core flooded with sharp desire and she covered her gasp with a cough.

The key panel flashed red. Wrong code. Dang it.

"Problem?" Gage murmured and leaned forward, decimating the space between their bodies.

Who was she kidding? Gage and darkness went together like chocolate and peanut butter. The dark was where he did his best work, wove his best spells. Wreaked the most destruction.

"I...fat fingered it," she muttered back. "Give me a sec."

She got it right the second time. How, she'd never know.

The gate swung open on well-oiled hinges and that's when the moon blessed her with an appearance, washing the path and the lake below with a silver sheen. Perfect timing. Her nerves couldn't take much more and the dark would only tempt the devil to perform his black magic.

"There's a gazebo a few hundred yards up the path," she murmured. "We can talk."

Yes, talking. She grasped on to the concept like a lifeline, hoping the short walk would allow her to get her brain in working order again. If everything went according to plan, she'd have the solid proof she needed to implicate Gage in the leak and then she could drop him like a hot potato.

Gage, to his credit, strolled to the moonlit gazebo as instructed. The heady scent of man and sage wound through the stillness, distracting her. She never would have identified the faint herbal notes of Gage's aftershave without Laurie's comments in front of the restaurant and now it was all she could do to keep from sticking her nose in the hollow of his shoulder bone.

"So," she said as she glided up the gazebo stairs and leaned on the railing to peer out over the silvery lake. "You must have some great ears to the ground to have such detailed information about my formula."

He leaned against a post, arms crossed, and watched her as if the gorgeous panorama beyond the gazebo didn't exist. "Pardon me if I have very little interest in that subject right this minute."

She glanced at him and he wasn't even bothering to conceal his thoughts. Which must be very naughty indeed judging by the lascivious once-over he gave her. Answering heat gathered in her core, totally against her will.

All at once, she wished for a bunch of clouds to cover the moon. At least in the dark, she could pretend she didn't notice how he had such a beautiful body and gorgeous face, both of which had become more interesting with age. She shuddered as she recalled the way he'd kissed her. More heat flashed across her skin.

Why did he do that to her?

"It's a great subject," she corrected, ignoring the corkscrewing pulls inside her abdomen. "Very important. I'm just curious where you heard about it. If we're going to stop the leak, it might help to work our way backward."

"You think?" he murmured as he unwound from his

casual pose against the post to advance on her. "What if I want to talk about something else?"

She held her ground as he drew up within a hairsbreadth of touching her. "Like what?"

Without hesitation, he grabbed her hand, pulling her flush against him. Her body fell into alignment with his, nestling into the grooves like a mascara wand meeting eyelashes. His arms settled around her and somehow her head tipped back, exposing her throat to his hot perusal.

"Like how it would feel to kiss you when there's no danger of anyone interrupting us."

"Gage," she said and cursed the breathless delivery. She might as well announce how her core had gone liquid the moment his hard muscles came in contact with her curves. "Let go."

"Are you sure that's wise?" he murmured, holding her closer, which she would have sworn was impossible. "You sound a little faint. I wouldn't want you to collapse."

God, he felt good.

She needed to go on a real date, obviously, with a nice man who would treat her well and drink the wine she'd ordered. They'd have a pleasant evening ending with a romantic nightcap at her place and then he'd gently and attentively make love to her.

Above all, when she told him what to do, he'd do it.

"I'm okay. Thanks," she threw in before he started mimicking her again.

"*I'm* not okay." He bent his head to murmur into her ear. "And I like you where you are."

His breath on her skin and his hard thigh between her legs—hell, his voice alone—ripped through her in a whitehot streak of lust.

Insanity. She needed that nice man, pronto, so she could slake this thirst. A couple of rounds with Mr. Gentle-and-

Attentive and she'd be good for another year or so. Gage Branson wouldn't cause so much as a blip on her sex radar.

"This is supposed to be business only," she reminded him, but her voice cracked in the middle of the sentence and she doubted he was listening anyway.

"Hold still."

Eyes on her hair, he reached up and plucked one chopstick from her chignon, tossed it to the wooden slats under their feet and went for the other one as she yelped.

"What are you doing?" she protested as her hair spilled down her back.

"I couldn't help it." His own voice broke as he threaded both hands through the strands, winding up the locks around his fingers, a groan rumbling in his chest that vibrated her rib cage. "Your hair. It's so beautiful. Why do you put it up?"

"It's professiona—"

His mouth hit hers and stole the rest of her words as he kissed her into stunned silence. Hot and wet, his tongue slid through her lips and pleasured her relentlessly.

Tugs at her hair tilted her head back, and he took her deeper into the sensuous haze. She lost all sense of up or down, all sense period because, *oh, yes*, Gage was kissing her again and she wanted it.

The emotional tangle? Not on the agenda. If she could separate business from pleasure, she could surely separate pleasure from love. No broken hearts this time. She'd take a lesson from the King of Fun and have some.

Without warning, he pushed her against the wooden post. It wasn't brick biting into her back. Close enough.

His mouth drifted to her throat as his hands untangled from her hair to cup the back of her head, drawing her against his magic lips. She arched into him, and a moan escaped her throat, echoing in the still night.

All at once, his hands seemed to be everywhere, racing down her sides, at her shoulders. Pushing down the neckline of her dress. Her breasts sprang free of the fabric and he cupped one, bending to draw her taut nipple into his mouth.

She gasped. Exquisite. The pulls of his mouth and tongue buckled her knees but he had her. Yes, he did. He held her firmly in place as he pleasured her with his talented mouth. Shutting her eyes, she let the pleasure fork through her, damp heat gathering at her center until she thought she would burst if he didn't...

He did. One hand snaked under her dress and found her folds beneath the scrap of underwear. The barrier didn't exist to him. Clever fingers danced over her burning flesh, inside. Out.

Anyone could walk by. It heightened the pleasure... somehow. She hissed and opened wider, encouraging him to go deeper. Faster. Her breath came quicker as he drove her relentlessly, sucking at her breast, touching her intimately.

And then one final stroke shattered her resistance. She rode wave after wave of release, crying out at the strength and intensity of the pleasure he'd given her. *Gage.* Smart, funny, tender, amazing Gage. She'd missed him.

That was...not good. Oh, it had been *good.* But somehow he'd gotten below the surface, past her emotional armor.

When she floated back down from the heavens, he was watching her. He leaned in to set her dress back to rights, hands lingering, touching, pleasuring, and he murmured, "Take me back to your place. I want to do that again properly."

Again? She shook off the miasma of Gage and stared up at him, stricken with guilt. That beautiful face stared back at her and she longed to fall into him again without reservation, without fear. Without complications. Without agendas.

What was she *doing*? This wasn't the time to be playing around with fire, not with her career at stake and her company on the brink of disaster. Not when she wasn't sure she could actually stay emotionally uninvolved. She couldn't be vulnerable to him again, couldn't fathom how she'd pick herself up if he flattened her. *Could. Not.*

"I…can't."

And then her throat closed, forcing her to swallow the rest.

His expression blanked and he stepped back, releasing her. "Okay."

His tone said it was anything but. He didn't press her, though, which she was pathetically grateful for. Because if he had, he'd probably have broken down her resistance in about four seconds.

Yeah, she was a whiz at separating business and pleasure. The moment his flesh touched hers, all thoughts of business went out the window and she'd forgotten about digging for his secrets entirely.

That wasn't going to work. She had to get back in the game.

Gage dropped Cass off at her house with a terse goodnight.

They hadn't spoken at all after she shut him down. Apparently, she could flip the ice-goddess switch at will, melting in his arms for a gorgeous orgasm that nearly finished him off, as well, and then hardening her spine right back into place.

He was slipping if that hadn't gotten him an invitation into her bed. Cass had matured in many intriguing ways, but she'd also grown...distant. He had to figure out how to get rid of that space between them or he'd lose his bid for the formula. This was one competition he could not afford to lose.

When he got back to his hotel, frustrated and alone, Arwen greeted him at the door, leash in her mouth. He groaned. Last thing he needed right now. "All right."

Happily, she sniffed her way in the dark to the small park across from his hotel, zigzagging between clumps of bushes as she always did. It got a small smile from him. He hadn't been able to send her home and midnight walks in the park were due penance.

Unfortunately, Arwen didn't talk so he was left with his thoughts for company and they were anything but restful.

This thing with Cass was a problem. She was making him lose his focus on the end game. He still didn't know why she'd asked him to help her or what that silly game at dinner had been about, but one thing was for sure— he'd fully intended to find out. That was before she'd put on that cranberry dress and driven him to thorough distraction.

Of course, his solution to eliminating the distraction had been—and would continue to be—burning off their mutual, insanely hot attraction with a night of uninhibited passion. Then, with that out of the way, they both could concentrate on the business at hand: the leak.

He hoped. He couldn't deny he wanted Cass more fiercely than he could ever recall wanting a woman. Maybe more. He still ached with unfulfilled release and it was an unpleasant reminder that somewhere in the middle of all of this, getting his hands on Cass had started to eclipse getting his hands on her formula. Somehow, his plan to remind her of what she owed him had vanished and become a plan to reacquaint himself with Cass as a lover.

That was an even bigger problem. He was not going home without that formula. So far, he wasn't balancing his two agendas very well.

That changed *la mañana*.

Seven

"Hi, Melinda," he said easily to Fyra's receptionist the next morning. "I have a nine o'clock with Ms. Claremont."

"Good morning, Mr. Branson," she chirped. "She's expecting you."

Looked as though Cass had already cleared the decks for their leak discussion, which was masquerading as a "consulting" gig. The cover story had been quick thinking on his part, if he did say so himself.

He knocked on her open door. Cass was waiting for him, leaning on the front of her desk, arms crossed over a sleek pantsuit. Chopsticks peeked over the edge of her crown and dang if his fingers didn't curl at the sight of them, itching to yank them out.

He tore his gaze away. *Focus.*

"Ready to get to work?" Cass asked coolly as if last night had never happened.

"Sure." He grinned to dispel the heavy vibe and slid

into one of the chairs on the visitor's side of the desk. No power plays today. None of them had worked anyway.

Well…they'd worked to a degree. After all, he'd had Cass in his arms twice last night. That was progress. Very hot, very spectacular progress. His body sprang fully alert.

Focus, he reminded himself.

"I have a couple of thoughts I wanted to run by you," she said.

She seemed agitated, though he couldn't put his finger on what had given him that impression when she closely resembled an ice sculpture. A subtlety in her tone, maybe.

"Do any of them start with *Gage* and end with the word *naked*?"

Cass's mouth tightened. So that hadn't been the best tactic, even though he'd been kidding in an attempt to lighten the mood. Mostly. He could no sooner forget his outrageous attraction to her than he could leave without the formula. The dual agendas were supposed to complement each other, not be at war. It was killing him.

"Not in the slightest." The frost in her voice needed to go. "I've already done a couple of hours' worth of research. Now that you're here, I want to go over my notes with you."

Would she balk if he yanked her into his lap and kissed that frown upside down? Since the door was open, he resisted. But only just. And only for now.

It was better to deal with business during daylight hours. Probably.

"All right. Lay it on me. I am a fount of advice."

Her brow raised as if she didn't quite believe him. "I haven't even told you what I've got yet. How do you know you'll have anything valuable to contribute?"

"I'm motivated. Plus, you of all people should be aware of my résumé when it comes to that."

"Well, then. I'm dying to hear it, O Sage One."

Maybe her mood wasn't as volatile as he'd assumed if she was making jokes.

Memories of her, hot and pliant in his arms, damp heat against his fingers, all that hair like silk in his fingers… yeah.

It was totally worth taking a shot.

"My first piece of advice is to relax," he said smoothly. Cass hadn't moved an iota from her no-nonsense pose against the desk. Gage couldn't work his charm with her so uptight. "Second, I advise you to have dinner with me again tonight. But let's actually eat this time."

Other than a slight eye roll, she held herself impressively frozen with not even a leg tremor to give away her thoughts. "I can't display that on a presentation at a board meeting. I need results and I need them today."

"Then sit down and let's hash it out," he suggested with a nod at the other chair. "I'm starting to feel as though I was called to the principal's office the way you're towering over me."

With a piercing side eye aimed pointedly in his direction, she perched on the other chair but he had the distinct impression she didn't like the idea. He held his hands up in silent promise to keep them to himself, which she acknowledged with a muttered, "Yeah, we'll see."

The truth was he had as much of an interest in finding the leak and plugging it as Cass did—if nothing else, he wasn't prepared to hand over one single dollar until it was handled, or his investment would be worthless.

Nor could he afford to let the leak take the formula public. Then someone else might get the upper hand. The issues inside Cass's company needed to be resolved.

"Talk to me about your notes." When she hesitated, he

stuck his palms under his butt, and widened his eyes in an exaggerated *okay*? "Come on."

It was so subtle, he almost missed it. But he was watching her closely enough to pinpoint the exact moment she relaxed. The victory shot through him with a sharp thrill.

"My theory is that the leak came from someone in the lab. Has to be. No one else outside of the four founders knows how the formula works."

He'd considered that, too, and it was probably true, but she couldn't make broad assumptions. "Anyone could have hacked into your database or paid off a janitor to steal Harper's notes."

"True. But I don't think that's how it happened. So I'm thinking about planting some false information and watermarking the files. If it gets leaked, I can trace it back."

"Digital forensics? Like what banks use when they're hacked? That's expensive."

"Formula-47 is worth millions of dollars. Maybe billions."

Yes, absolutely. But you had to spend money where it made sense. "Regardless, you'd have to wait until the leak found the information and hope he or she didn't realize that the transferred files could be traced, then you have to assume the leak will decide to spill it, wait for the news to hit the industry and then try to track down who accessed the file on your server. You don't have that long."

Her lips pursed but she didn't give away anything else of her thoughts. "That's exactly why I wanted to run this by you. I knew you'd find the holes if there were any."

That small compliment from a tough customer like Cass held more weight than he would have imagined. It spread through his chest warmly. He could get used to that. Get used to combining business and pleasure in exactly this way, with a woman who could match him mentally and physically.

That's a new experience you can get behind.

Except it wasn't exactly new. This was like old times, but better because they were equals.

"It's not rocket science. I've just been around a while. Failed a lot early on and learned a few things. No big deal," he said, and he ducked his head.

She swept him with a once-over laden with—dare he hope it—some heat?

"You'll forgive me if I disagree. It's is a big deal. You're the CEO of a billion-dollar company for a reason. And I'm not. Also for a reason." Her self-deprecating shrug spoke volumes.

"Hey. You're being too hard on yourself."

Her gaze flew to his and something raw flashed in the depths, a stricken sense of anxiety. The brief spurt of emotion in her eyes sucked him in instantly, spreading through him with equal parts warmth and a desire to fix it. He almost reached out then to comfort her.

Because she needed him that way, too. And he liked being needed by a strong, independent woman like Cass.

It had nothing to do with sex, nothing to do with business—or even fun—and everything to do with why he'd recalled their relationship so fondly. Why he'd wanted to revive that between them. He liked being her go-to guy, being there for her. How had he walked away from that so easily?

Better yet, how did he keep it going now?

"Am I? How many times has one of your employees spilled company secrets?" she asked, and he didn't like how matter-of-fact she was about it.

She'd accomplished something really fantastic here at

Fyra. Insisting that a blip like the leak overshadowed that riled him up but good.

"That's not a yardstick," he insisted right back. "If it was, then you could also compare yourself to the CEOs of companies that went bankrupt or employed executives that ended up in orange jumpsuits. You're a star in comparison."

Her amused smile heated his blood unnaturally fast.

And if he could get Cass on the same page, this conversation could very well explode into something that didn't need words.

Cass let her smile widen.

She had Gage exactly where she wanted him. It had taken her a bit to shift the mood and even longer to convince Gage his charm was working on her. At this point, he was so busy flirting and shooting her heated glances, he was scarcely paying attention to the matter at hand—the leak. Advantage Cassandra.

Keeping it was another story.

"You really think so?" She leaned into him, letting her arm casually brush Gage's. His gaze darkened. "That means a lot to me."

"This is not the conversation I thought we were going to have." He shifted closer, crowding into her space and she almost flinched as the contact sang through her but caught herself in time.

That episode last night, up against the gazebo post, had kept her tossing and turning all night long. She couldn't forget it. She might never be able to jog by that gazebo again without reliving the feel of Gage's mouth on her flesh and the intensity of his heated gaze on her bare breasts as he watched her climax under his talented fingers.

It was enough to make her want to corner him, strip

him naked and let the passion between them come to conclusion. Where she got to watch *him* fall apart at *her* hands.

Which she totally planned to do...while extracting the information she needed. She could not, under any circumstances, let him dissolve that goal like he'd done last night. No more would she let her emotions run away with her. It was all business, all the time, especially while she was seducing him.

This was her career at stake, and the careers of her friends, poised to vanish into thin air if she didn't produce the name of the person responsible for disclosing company secrets.

Fyra was her life and no man could replace it. Especially not this one.

"This conversation is better," she said with a tiny smile guaranteed to pique his interest. "For example, I was just about to take your advice and ask you to dinner tonight. At my place."

That got his attention. He sat up so fast, his back teeth clacked together. "Don't toy with me, woman."

Oh, but he was so fun to toy with, especially as she gave him a taste of his own medicine.

"Does that mean you don't want to come?" she purred. "Or do you want me to tack the dinner discussion to the end of today's agenda?"

"Now I'm dying to know what topics we have to get through to reach that particular item."

"Business," she said firmly. "Then pleasure."

His hazel eyes lit up and a wicked smile spread across his face. "Just so you know, the fact that you label dinner at your place as pleasure warms my heart tremendously."

She held off the shiver because he didn't need to know he'd affected her *that* way. He *shouldn't* be affecting her that way. Her armor—the shield she easily employed with other men—seemed to soften far too easily when he was around.

"Business," she repeated. "We have to make more progress on the leak. The news broke on Monday. It's Thursday morning. I'm no closer to plugging the blabbermouth than I was then."

She'd done a considerable amount of digging this morning on her own and had found a couple of promising leads. Right before Gage had arrived, she'd ordered the most high-level background check money could buy on every last employee in this company. But he didn't have to know that. In reality, she didn't want him anywhere near her files or embroiled in a real discussion about her strategy.

His job was to tell her what his connection was to the leak. What strings he was pulling. Which angles he was playing. She needed to uncover every last secret, especially when he looked at her like he was right now, like he wanted to finish what he'd started last night in the gazebo.

Because as soon as she handed him over to the authorities, then she could remind herself with cold hard facts that he was the spawn of Satan. Somehow she kept forgetting that.

"It's a problem," he agreed far too easily.

Suspicious of his capitulation, she nodded. "Right. We find the leak and then we can think about pursuing a… personal relationship."

She caressed the term with her voice as suggestively as she could. She had to regain the upper hand.

"Oh, no, sweetheart," he growled. "You have it all backward. That orgasm last night? Only the beginning of what's in store for you. For both of us. It's an absolute necessity that we start there and then worry about the leak."

His heavy, masculine vibe snaked through the room,

engulfing her. Tempting her down the wrong path, where she craved that pleasure, that connection more than anything else. "That makes no sense."

His intense gaze zeroed in on her and she felt it deep inside, where he'd thoroughly woken up her latent sex drive. He didn't move, didn't touch her, and somehow that was more powerful than if he had.

"It's the only thing that makes sense. We're not going to get anything accomplished until this fire between us is extinguished. Admit it. You know it's true."

She hated to say it...but he might have a point. Worse, she couldn't think of one solid argument against it, but she had to try as a matter of principle. "That's your logic? We're not disciplined enough to work together so we should just screw around instead?"

He didn't flinch. "If you want logic, then do it for the best reason of all. You want to. And I want you, Cassandra."

His deep voice caressed her name, unleashing another wave of desire that grew very hard to contain. This was a seduction, plain and simple, but she'd lost track of who was seducing whom. Besides, dragging it out wouldn't change things. It was just sex. She wasn't going to fall for him again. Why deny herself what she wanted?

Maybe she'd failed thus far to get him to admit anything incriminating because she really needed to get him naked first. Naked and sated.

"I dug up some paper archives from Harper's research over the past few years that have names of the employees attached to each stage of the development. Can we at least pretend to do some work tonight?" she asked as the compelling force of his smile nearly drew her into his space, magnetically, like she'd transformed into a pile of metal pins straining toward him.

"Sure. If that's what turns you on, I'm game."

"Be at my place at seven." Her turf, her rules. And there was no way she'd let him get to her like he'd done last night. Ruthless detachment was the only way. "I'll bring the files and you bring the drinks since you're such a big baby about wine. I have until tomorrow to report progress back to the other executives. So we definitely have to do *some* work."

Hopefully she'd discover she did her best work between the sheets.

He grinned and saluted. "Wear something sexy and I'll read every one of those files word for word."

She'd removed all the proprietary information from the files and her employee's names were posted on the company website, so she had no qualms about sharing that information with him. With enough incentive, he might slip up and clue her in that he recognized one of the names. "It's a deal."

She just had to be very careful to ensure the only slipping going on was on his side.

Eight

Later that night, Gage picked up a bottle of cachaça, some limes and a bag of brown sugar, just in case Cass didn't have any on hand. Caipirinhas were a far sight more tolerable than margaritas, and women usually loved the way he made them. Plus the drink was about 85 percent alcohol, which gave a nice buzz but, because cachaça was distilled from sugarcane, the next morning didn't come with a busting headache.

On his way to Cass's house, Gage dropped Arwen off at a doggie daycare. With that heartbreaking task out of the way, he drove to Cass's house. She was worth a furious vizsla and the probability of an additional fee upon pickup after Arwen drove everyone at the daycare to the brink of insanity.

Cass opened the door, barefoot and clad in shorts that showed a mile of leg, thank the good Lord, and a fitted T-shirt that most women couldn't have done justice. On

Cass, it was legendary. She'd twisted her hair up in a messy waterfall of a hairdo that was somehow more suggestive than the chopsticks.

His mouth went dry.

"Hey," she said, opening the door wider, which lifted the hem of her T-shirt just a flash, revealing a slice of bare stomach. "Hope casual is okay. I thought low-key might help us get some work accomplished tonight."

Yeah, no. She needed a better mirror if she thought that what she had on was supposed to provide some kind of Gage repellant. Her toes were hot pink, for crying out loud, which drew his attention to her bare feet again and again.

"Oh, good," he said when he could speak. "I was worried I wouldn't be able to keep my hands off you. *Whew.*"

He mimed wiping his brow in relief and she shot him a sunny smile that heightened the flame inside his gut.

She motioned him inside and called over her shoulder. "Should we start on the paperwork first, then? Maybe later we can have a drink and relax."

Seriously?

"That was sarcasm," he said bluntly as he blew over the threshold, shutting the door behind him with a loud bang.

She whirled, clearly startled by the sudden noise, and smacked into his chest. Right where he wanted her. He set down his bag of goodies—caipirinhas had totally lost his interest.

"If you wanted me to keep my hands off you," he growled, hauling her into his arms. "A better plan would have been to move to Timbuktu."

He hustled her backward, against the wall, and shoved a thigh between her legs. Hard and high. She gasped, a throaty sound that crawled inside him and lit the fuse of a row of fireworks residing in his groin, threatening to explode without notice.

"In case you're not clear on this," he continued, nipping at her ear as he leaned in. The full body contact sang through him. "I want you. *Now.* Not later."

Her nipples pebbled against his chest as he rolled his hips to fit more snuggly against hers. Those shorts were made of much thinner fabric than he'd guessed and her heat engulfed his steel-hard lower half. Lust licked through his blood like a wildfire.

He needed her hot and pliant immediately, before he lost it. There was no way she would get the opportunity to leave him hanging like she had last night. Oh, he'd enjoyed every second of making her come against that post, moonlight spilling over her gorgeous body, while they were both fully dressed. It had ranked as one of the hottest experiences of his life. But tonight he deserved a turn, too.

He ached to reacquaint himself with her body, the way she tasted, the way she would respond to his touch. That T-shirt, soft under his fingers, promised delights underneath it and he was game to discover them.

No one was around and they had all night. He planned to make the most of it.

They gazed at each other and the ocean of desire in her eyes twisted through him. She was inside him already and he welcomed her with a sense of awe. How had she made him feel this way before they'd scarcely gotten started?

"I want you," he repeated hoarsely, but the phrase scarcely encompassed the sheer need he was trying to describe, as if he depended on her for his next breath. "And not because you're wearing a sexy outfit. Because you have a brain. Because you challenge me. Because I like being around you. Because—"

"If you're going to kiss me, shut up and do it."

"That might be the sexiest thing you've ever said."

Because it suited him, he tilted her head back and took her mouth with his, open and wet, pleasing them both with the force of his tongue. She tasted of fire and woman and he wanted more. So he went deeper, coaxing her to meet him with increased passion. No holding back. No ice goddess, not tonight.

Apparently of the same mind, she moaned and shifted against his thigh, her fingers working at his waistband. She pulled his shirt free and spread her palms across his back. Oh, yeah. *Heaven.* He'd captured his very own angel. Her touch raced down his spine and dipped into his pants, resting on his butt. She shoved, grinding his erection against her.

Nothing angelic about that.

Sensation exploded. In his body. In his head. She was taking over, taking her own pleasure, and he was hard-pressed to find an argument against it. Bolder now, she rubbed against his shaft, nearly finishing him off. He clawed back the release through will alone.

With her barriers down, she was hotter than he'd imagined. Duly noted.

With a groan, he fumbled with the hem of her shirt and finally, his fingers closed around it. Gone. Next? Bra. Also gone.

Her gorgeous breasts fell into his palms, heavy and hot. She was made for him, filling his hands perfectly. Locking his lips onto one erect nipple, he swirled his tongue around it as he worked the rest of her clothes into a heap, desperate to have her flesh against his. His pulse beat in his throat as she stripped him in kind, then urged him on with her hands against his thighs.

"Wait, darling," he murmured, and in moments, he'd sheathed himself with a condom.

Boosting her up against the wall, he slid into her heat and pinned her in place, reveling in the perfection of her tightness. *Yes.* Exactly where he belonged. Inside her.

She wrapped her legs around him and thrust her hips, drawing him deeper. And deeper still. She gasped out tiny moans of pleasure that drove him wild.

He needed to touch her…but he couldn't let go or she'd fall. From this angle, the sensation was unbelievable. Then she widened her hips, changing the pressure and his moans mingled with hers.

This wasn't the Cass he recalled. This woman was on fire, taking what she wanted, giving unconditionally. Finding his pleasure center easily and drawing him higher and higher, against his will. He'd planned to savor. To reclaim.

But this Cass, who was every inch his equal, was claiming him, wholly.

He couldn't hold back one second longer, but somehow managed to get a thumb between their bodies, stimulating her the way she'd always preferred and that set her off. At last. The ripples of her climax closed around him a moment before his answering climax exploded.

Sweet, blessed release. He shut his eyes and drove home one last time, drawing out the pleasure for them both. When he could feel his legs again, he swung her around and slid to the ground, still holding her in his lap. He tilted his head against hers, both of them breathless, chests heaving from exertion.

That had been…something else. Nothing like it had been before. It had been hot and erotic and the stuff of X-rated fantasies. She'd always been amazing but they'd never gotten so caught up that they couldn't make it to the bed. They were still in her foyer. He'd meant to be gentler, less frenzied. He'd envisioned a slow, sweet reintroduction to each other, but who could complain about a fast, unbelievably intense reintroduction?

Thankfully, they'd gotten that out of their systems.

"Maybe now we can concentrate," he muttered. But he didn't think so.

Cass ended up ordering pizza from the place around the corner. After the hallway gymnastics, her bones had melted away entirely and she couldn't stand long enough to cook. Gage had been amazing. Strong, tender, hot, sweet. Far more so than she'd expected or remembered.

True to his word, he got down to business and they read files while drinking a pitcher of the limey, sugary concoction he'd put together. It was delicious. But not as delicious as Gage. Or the conversation they fell into as they were reading. It was like old times—and her insides, which were not all that solid in the first place, mushed under the dual onslaught of sexy man and alcohol.

Names. She needed to focus on these names. She steeled her spine, hardened her heart and ignored all the sizzling sidelong glances he shot her way.

This was about sex and work. Only. After all, he'd practically dared her to prove she could separate business and pleasure. No emotions necessary for that.

She had Gage read the names out loud and as he did, she offered her impression of the person, their work ethic, any workplace drama she knew of. As she talked, she watched Gage carefully for any flicker of recognition. Nothing. Either he was very good at keeping his cards close to the vest or the leak's name wasn't on this list.

Of course, deep inside she recognized the possibility that he wasn't involved. The longer they spent in each other's company, the more she'd started to hope that he wasn't. Because if his interest in the formula was innocent, then it changed everything between them.

And she wanted that. Oh, how she wanted things to be different, with the possibility of throwing their agendas out the window and just connecting as man and woman.

It was madness. Gage could not be trusted under any circumstances and obviously sex had only confused things, not clarified them. She kicked him out before she started imagining things that were impossible, like asking him to stay and hold her all night.

He left without arguing, which dug under her skin and sat there irritating her for no apparent reason. Why? He'd done what she asked—what more could she want? Gage did not belong in her bed. That was reserved for men who wanted to stick around and he wasn't the type. A few days and then *gone*.

She knew that. But that didn't stop all the needy dreams during the long night where he curled around her in bed and stroked her hair and told her everything was going to be okay, that he was here for her and she didn't have to be strong with him. That he understood her and cared about her.

Clearly a dream—Gage Branson wasn't marriage material and she didn't need a man who whispered pretty lies in her ear about the state of things. There was no guarantee even one blessed thing in her life would turn out okay. The investigative work she'd done on her own time hadn't amounted to much and Gage hadn't given up any information either, which meant she was still at square one.

Around 5:00 a.m. she crawled from the big, lonely bed and tried to rinse Gage off her body and soul with a hot shower. It was Friday. Reckoning day. Trinity had scheduled a meeting with the four executives to hear Cass's progress report on the leak. It was shaping up to be a short meeting because she had nothing to report.

It took twice as long as normal to do her makeup, partly due to her shaking hands and partly due to the necessity of taking extra care to present her best "I've got this" face to the world. Then, she dressed carefully in a black suit with a knee-length skirt and red silk shell. The look radiated power and control and she needed both today.

By nine, the other ladies filed in to take their customary seats around the conference table. Cass had been in her chair for fifteen minutes, going over nonexistent notes, and calming her nerves. It should have been the other way around. Lots of progress, cool as a cucumber.

There was a distinct possibility she might throw up.

New fine lines around Harper's eyes spoke to the heightened level of stress on Fyra's chief science officer. She'd been clocking long hours in anticipation of presenting Formula-47 for FDA approval, perhaps in vain if Cass didn't get with the program. Trinity tapped one foot, impatient and ready to draw blood the moment someone presented their jugular. *Someone* was about to be Cass, she had a feeling. Eyes on her legal pad, Alex wore a slight frown, as if this boardroom was the last place she wanted to be and Cass had interrupted the CFO's more important agenda items for the day.

"Thanks for taking time from your busy Friday to hear my progress report," Cass began smoothly and squared her tablet, trying to get her emotions under control. She'd failed to do her job and her partners needed to know it, no matter how hard it was to admit she didn't have it all together.

If only she'd gotten some sleep last night, her emotions wouldn't be riding so close to the surface. If only she'd checked her mushy heart at the door when Gage came over, she could have gone all night with him and maybe extracted something useful. Instead, she'd kicked him out because she couldn't control anything, let alone herself.

"I'll cut to the chase," Cass said and met the gaze of each of her partners in turn. "I haven't found anything yet."

The three women's expressions ranged from disbelief to anger.

Alex spoke first. "What do you mean, you haven't found anything yet? You've had all week." She sank down in her chair an inch, as if Cass's news had physically added weight to her shoulders, which increased the general despair in the room. "This is awful. We should have involved the authorities from the beginning."

"We couldn't have," Cass reminded her. She cleared the catch from her throat. They'd had this discussion on Monday when the trade magazine had hit the industry and again on Tuesday in their board meeting. "Mike said the article was too vague, remember? We don't have any recourse but to investigate ourselves."

"Which has failed miserably." Alex crossed her arms and stared at Cass. "We trusted you with this. We could have all been working on it but you said you'd handle it. What, exactly, did you do all week?"

Cass took the harsh question without flinching. "I have a list of suspects. Everyone who's had their hands on Formula-47 over the past two years and could reasonably understand how it works."

The betrayer's name was on that list—she knew it like she knew her own face. How else would Gage's additional information about Fyra's yet-to-be-released product offering be so accurate? It was the only explanation. Now she just had to find a way to prove it. And convince the others to give her more time.

Trinity's chair squeaked as she swiveled it toward Cass. "So the article is too vague to involve the authorities, but when your old boyfriend shows up with more detailed information, that's not enough to go to the cops?"

Heat flushed through Cass's cheeks. Blushing? Really? She never did that. Thankfully, Harper's color-correcting foundation should hide the worst of it. "I'm working that angle. In case he's involved."

"Oh." Light dawned in Trinity's expression. "I thought that whole consulting thing was weird. I was convinced Gage was hanging around in hopes of swooping in for another chance to break your heart. It never occurred to me that you were the one working him. Good for you."

Alex's brows snapped together. "What, like you're sleeping with him to find out if he coordinated the leak? That's horrible."

A squeak of denial almost escaped Cass's clamped lips.

But she couldn't deny it. That was exactly what she was doing, but hearing it from Alex did make it sound horrible. Something sad crawled through her chest and she couldn't breathe.

Why? They were just fooling around anyway. Nothing serious was going on, so it wasn't as if he was going to get *his* heart broken. She wasn't even sure he had one to break.

And *how* in God's name had her friends figured out so quickly that she and Gage weren't strictly business associates this time around? Somehow this whole conversation had become a cross-examination of Cass's sex life.

"It's brilliant," Trinity insisted. "Men do stuff like that all the time and no one thinks anything of it. About time we turn the tables. Screw him and then screw him over, Cass."

Finally Trinity was defending her, and if only she hadn't been so enthusiastic about Cass's new status as a ballbreaker, it might have made Alex's accusations more tolerable.

"It's true," Cass admitted. "I'm keeping my eye on him from close quarters just in case he lets something incriminating slip."

"Was that before or after he seduced away your good sense?" Alex asked derisively. "You'll forgive me if I find your investigative techniques suspect. No one can fully separate business from sex. It's impossible."

Not for me.

Cass started to say it out loud, to defend herself against Alex's blatant charge that she'd compromised Fyra due to her personal relationship with Gage, such as it was. She should tell them unequivocally that she wouldn't allow a naked man to distract her from what she knew she needed to do.

But she couldn't say it. What if Gage *was* involved in the leak and she missed it because she was too busy daydreaming about him magically transforming into someone she could count on? That very possibility was exactly the reason the board meeting had descended into girl talk about the man Cass was boinking—because everyone thought she might be compromised.

Ridiculous. She was compartmentalizing just fine. The person responsible for the leak was keeping a low profile, that was all. If Gage knew anything about it, he'd trip up before long.

"Give me a few more days," she pleaded. "I know what I'm doing."

Throwing her pen down on her pad with considerable force, Alex shook her head. "No. We don't have a few more days."

Heart in her throat, Cass evaluated the other two girls,

who glanced at each other. Trinity shrugged. "I'm game for it. I kind of want to see what happens with lover boy."

Harper narrowed her gaze and flipped her ponytail over her shoulder. "Gage Branson treated you like dog food in college, Cass. While he's lighting your fire, don't fool yourself into thinking he's changed."

Red stained Harper's cheeks, likely as a result of holding back her legendary hot temper, which Cass appreciated. Alex's hostility was heartbreaking enough without adding another longtime friend to the other side of the fence.

"I've got that under control, too," Cass assured them, ignoring that sad ping inside that had only gotten worse the longer the conversation went on.

Of course Gage hadn't changed. Fortunately, Cass's eyes were wide open and soon she'd be watching him disappear down the highway. It was a fact, and wishing things could be different didn't mean she was fooling herself.

Alex's sigh was long-suffering. "This is a mistake. Have all of you forgotten that Gage runs a company that eats into our profits every stinking quarter? He's our competition, just as much as Lancôme and MAC."

And that was the bottom line in all of this. How fitting that Fyra's CFO would be the one to point that out. In marked contrast to the last time they'd been in this room, Alex's contrariness and lack of confidence had roots in reality, and that sobered Cass faster than anything else could have.

"No one's forgotten that, least of all me," Cass countered quietly. "Why do you think I'm cozying up to him? Give me a few more days."

"Fine," Alex conceded wearily. "I don't see how you're going to prove Gage is involved in the leak while he's got his tongue in your mouth, but whatever. We don't have a lot of choices."

As victories went, it felt hollow. With the leak still undetected, the company could come down like a house of cards. She got that. But it twisted her stomach to have her strategy so cold-bloodedly laid out for her. Yes, she'd planned to keep Gage close for exactly the reasons they'd discussed, but all at once, the idea didn't sit well. Gage had been...fun thus far. Almost like a friend. A confidante. Everything a lover should be. What if he *wasn't* involved?

She liked it better when her partners had been in the dark about her covert plans.

Abnormally quiet, they left the boardroom, and miraculously Cass made it all the way to her office before the shakes started. Nothing helped calm her nerves—coffee, water, a brisk walk at lunch. She had to get it together, had to find a way to produce results.

If Gage was involved in the leak, she had to figure out a way to prove it. To prove she could compartmentalize and that he wasn't affecting her ability to do her job, once and for all. She buckled down and pored over files and personnel records until she thought her eyes would bleed.

Around three o'clock, her phone vibrated and Gage's name flashed on the screen. She read the text message.

I'm in the parking lot. Ditch work and play hooky with me.

For God knew what reason, that put a smile on her face. That sounded like the perfect short-term solution to her problems.

Nine

The dark green Hummer sat in the same parking spot as it had the first time Gage had visited Fyra, under a large oak tree saved when the developers poured the concrete for Fyra's new building.

Shade nearly obscured the monstrosity of a vehicle, but Cass found it easily. With a heightened sense of anticipation, she dashed across the parking lot in hopes of hopping into the Hummer before anyone saw her.

After the unproductive day she'd had, the last thing she should be doing was leaving work at three o'clock. In her current mood, it was the only thing she could have done. Besides, this was exactly where she was supposed to be. She'd promised the others she'd make progress with Gage and the leak. No one had to know she was happy to see him.

Hooky. It used to be one of their favorite code words and it still had the same punch. Maybe more because she was skipping out on the enormous pressure inside the walls of her company instead of a boring lecture in a drafty hall. A little thrill shot through her as she clambered up into the passenger seat of Gage's car.

God, this sucked. She'd rather pretend they didn't have any more complications between them apart from where to go so they could spend an illicit couple of hours together. Strictly in the name of sex, of course. Instead, she'd spend their time together with both eyes wide open for any signs of his involvement in her company's troubles.

"Hey," Gage said, flashing her a mischievous smile. "I thought I was in for at least a couple of rounds of sexy text messages designed to get you out of your purple cave. Silly me. If I'd have known all it was going to take was one, I'd have been by at lunchtime."

"It's Friday." She waved it off as if she left early on Friday all the time, which was a flat-out lie. "I needed the break."

Especially if the break involved the man she should be sticking to like Velcro—and not because he was lickable. Which he was.

Concern filled his gaze as he pulled out of the Fyra lot. "Rough day?"

God, she was slipping. How had he realized that instantly? Gage shouldn't be the one person who saw through her, the only person who looked at her long enough to see her internal struggles.

She started to deny it but couldn't. What would be the point? "Yeah."

He drove in silence for a few minutes, but veered off the road after only a couple of miles. The Hummer rolled to a stop under the shade of a large oak tree near a deserted park.

"Come here," he commanded as he pulled her into his arms easily despite the gearshift and steering wheel.

She should have struggled more. Should have pushed him away. Sex only, nothing more. That's why she was here—for a much-needed release at the hands of a man very capable of delivering it.

But his soothing touch bled through her and nothing else could penetrate the little bubble surrounding her and Gage as he held her. *Nothing*, not the various parts of the car, not all the weight of Fyra's troubles, not the difficult past between them.

Everything faded under his tender strokes against her skin. She'd needed this, needed him. Needed someone to be there to catch her when she fell, to be on her side. His shirt was soft against her cheek and his woodsy scent filled her head, spreading the oddest sense of peace through her chest.

A tickle in her hair alerted her to the presence of his fingers a moment before both chopsticks slid free, releasing the tight chignon. Her scalp nearly cried in relief as her hair billowed down her back. He gathered the strands in his strong hands, winding them around his palms. Threading them through to his knuckles. Caressing her back.

It was relaxing and stimulating at the same time. How was that possible? But with the binding hairstyle gone, a weight lifted, almost as if he'd studied her and pinpointed precisely what she'd needed.

A groan rumbled in Gage's chest, vibrating her own, and in a snap, the atmosphere shifted. Awareness spread across her skin, sensitizing it. Switching cheeks, she rested her head in the hollow of his shoulder, but oh look, there was Gage's ear just a millimeter from her lips.

Grazing it lightly, she inhaled him, letting his powerful masculinity wash through her. The slow tide picked up speed, flowing like lava toward her toes, heating her in its wake.

Riding the flood, she arched her back, pushing her aching breasts against his chest, seeking more of his touch. She nipped at his throat, slowly working her way back to the tender lobe. When her teeth closed around it, he exhaled hard. It was ragged and thrilling, filling her with bold desire.

She licked him and oh, yes, he tasted amazing. *More.* And then his mouth was on hers and she drank from him, drawing out even more of that essence she craved. Hot and masterful, he kissed her back, meeting her tongue thrusts with his own, changing the angles to go deeper, and she moaned under the onslaught of sensation and Gage and everything she'd been missing for so long.

"Cass," he murmured against her mouth. "Let me take you to my hotel. It's five minutes away."

Five whole minutes? Too long. She didn't bother to respond and pulled him half into her seat as she went on a survey of that wicked, gorgeous body.

He sucked in a breath as she dipped into his pants and found the heated length of flesh she craved. So hard and thick and she wanted it. "Now, Gage. Don't make me wait."

With a curse, he pushed her hands off his body and moved from behind the steering wheel to slide into her seat, shoving her against the door. He promptly picked her up and resettled her on his lap, facing him, and watched her with a hooded, wicked glint to those hazel eyes as he pushed his palms against the hem of her skirt. The fabric gathered under his hands, riding up to her waist where he grabbed on and fitted their hips together, aligning his hard shaft against her center.

Perfect. Almost. Not enough. She rolled her hips, grinding against him and the answering shadow of lust shooting through his gaze heightened her own pleasure.

Without another word, he cupped her head with both hands and pulled her against his mouth, ravishing her with a long, wet kiss. Frantically, blindly, she worked at his pants until he sprang free into her eager hands. Her very own velvet-wrapped present. With her first stroke, his head fell back against the seat, flopping his too-long hair against his forehead and he groaned, eyes tightly shut.

That was…inspiring. She did it again, awed that she could command the body of such a powerful man.

"Back pocket," he rasped. "Hurry."

She wasted no time rolling on the condom. Pushing up on her thighs, she guided him to her entrance and plunged until they joined fully in one swift rush. They moaned in tandem as he flung his arms around her to hold her in place, rocking her so sensuously, so soul deep, she felt tears pricking at her eyelids. He filled her body, filled her head, filled every millimeter of *her*.

"So good." His breath fluttered in her ear as he read her mind. "Open for me."

To demonstrate, he widened her hips, nestling himself even closer to her.

Slowly, more slowly than she'd thought possible for a man on a mission, he drew her mouth to his and laid his lips against it. Savoring. He explored her as if they had all the time in the world, and as if she wasn't about to scream, and just as she thought she'd come out of her skin if he didn't move, he thrust his hips, driving deeper inside her.

She gasped and the rush overwhelmed her, pounding in her chest, at her center. Her vision darkened as he slid home again and again, and then his thumb found the true center of her pleasure, swirling against it with exactly the right pressure to set her off like a lit stick of dynamite.

The release rolled through her thickly, gathering power as she exploded over and over. She slumped against his chest as he cried out her name hoarsely, tensing through his own climax.

He held her gently, wrapped tight in his arms as if he never planned to let go. She sank down into the ocean of Gage. He surrounded her and she couldn't kick her way to the surface. Didn't want to. This was sheer bliss and it wasn't just due to the sex.

It was Gage. Only him.

"That was amazing," he murmured into her hair. "Now can we go to my hotel?"

"No." She snuggled deeper into his embrace, her nose against his neck where it smelled the most like well-loved man. "Take me home. And stay."

A mistake. He'd cracked open something inside her that should have been sealed shut.

Except she was so tired of pretending she didn't feel anything. So tired of bottling up her emotions and trying to prove she had it all together when in fact, she didn't.

Gage didn't care. He was leaving soon anyway, so why keep up pretenses? It was kind of freeing, knowing how it would end. She didn't have to worry about him breaking her heart because she wasn't going to give it to him. He didn't have to know she harbored all these feelings for him.

"That sounds like an idea I can get behind," he growled. "Or on top of, in front of, against the wall, in the shower. All of the above."

Too late to take it back now. And besides, she should have had the presence of mind to invite him deliberately. Because what better way to keep tabs on him than if they were together around the clock? That's where her mind *should* have been at.

"Stay the weekend. I know you have to go back to Austin Sunday night but until then? We'll order lots of takeout and never get dressed."

"That's a deal, Ms. Claremont."

His slow, sexy smile felt like a reward and she planned to grab her spoils with both hands. She'd spend the weekend enjoying herself and, as a bonus, she'd make solid progress on investigating Gage's involvement in the leak, just like she'd promised her partners. With the man in question in her bed, surely she could sneak a glance through his phone or keep an ear out in case he talked in his sleep. It was the best of both worlds and she didn't even have to feel guilty about it because she was looking out for Fyra first and foremost.

The other stuff—the emotional knot—wasn't a factor. She wouldn't let it be. She had to buckle on her armor a bit tighter while around Gage, that was all.

Gage untangled their clothes, hair and bodies, helping her resituate everything and then climbed back into the driver's seat. Fortunately, the park was still deserted or that would have been a helluva show.

She had one short weekend to get results on her quest for a name…before the other girls made a motion to relieve her of her position as head of the company she'd helped build from nothing.

Gage stopped by the hotel to pick up Arwen and his luggage, then checked out while Cass waited for him outside.

When he got back to the Hummer, he opened the back to stow his bags and waved for Arwen to hop in. That's when he realized this was not going to go well. She sat on her haunches and stared at the sky, the ground, a bug flying by. It was her way of saying she wasn't riding in the back like chattel.

"Don't be ridiculous," he growled. "There's a human in the front seat. You're a dog. Ride in the back. That's what they make this part of the vehicle for."

Nothing. He shook his head. They both knew she wasn't just a *dog* and this was one of the worst times in recent memory for her to remind him of it. He treated her like she was human, and she lapped it up as her due in true lady-of-the-manor style. Just because Gage had a real human to spend time with for a change didn't alter the fact that he'd spoiled her rotten due to his own lack of companionship over the years.

"What's going on?" Cass asked, her hair still loose and delicious around her shoulders.

The sight of her in that passenger seat, where she'd so sweetly offered him a fantasy weekend four seconds after giving him what he'd already thought was the ultimate encounter—amazing. He couldn't wait to dive in again.

"Arwen. In the car. Now," he muttered. "I've got a date with a shower and a wet woman and you are not going to mess it up." Louder, he called, "Just having a discussion about the proper place for a dog. One sec."

Extra motivation must have done the trick because he manhandled Arwen into the back on the first try and shut the hatch before she could leap out, which he wouldn't put past her. She gave a mournful cry that he heard even with all of the doors closed.

When he climbed into the driver's seat, Arwen had already weaseled in between the front seats, paws on the gearshift. She stuck her nose in Cass's face, clearly bent on discovering all the secrets of the woman who had usurped her spot.

Uh-oh. Arwen had never deigned to check out a woman

Gage had brought into her world. Usually she ignored them. Of course, Gage always introduced her to someone off Arwen's turf and it was rare that Arwen saw the same woman twice. Gage couldn't even remember the last time he'd had a woman in the Hummer, let alone at the same time as the vizsla.

"She's so sweet," Cass exclaimed as she rubbed Arwen's ginger head enthusiastically, earning a smile from the dog.

Gage eyed Arwen suspiciously and with no small amount of shock. She never approved of anyone female, let alone someone she'd already singled out as a rival. "Yeah, that's one word for her."

Arwen muscled her way into the front seat, right onto Cass's lap before Gage could grab her collar or even warn Cass that forty pounds of dog was coming her way.

Great. It wasn't as if Cass was wearing a fifteen-hundred-dollar suit or anything—not that he'd shown much more care when he'd crumpled it up around her waist. But still. There was a place for Arwen and it wasn't on top of Gage's...date. Former lover. Current lover. Partner in crime. Whatever.

"Sorry," he threw out. "Arwen, get in the back!"

"It's okay." Cass shot him a smile as she rearranged Arwen's paws off her bare legs. "I don't mind. It's not that far to my house and she's used to riding in the front, I would imagine."

"She is. Doesn't mean she should get her way." He started the car with one last warning glare at the dog who was predictably ignoring him. "I can drop her off at a pet hotel on the way."

Both woman and dog shook their heads.

"That's not necessary," Cass said, patting Arwen's back. "She's welcome in my backyard. I have some sad little hydrangeas that would probably benefit from being eaten."

"Really?" This time, he eyed Cass suspiciously. "She'll dig up your grass. I'm not kidding."

"So? She's been cooped up in a hotel all week, hasn't she? My yard overlooks the lake and there are always lots of birds. No reason why she can't have a nice weekend, too, is there?"

Arwen's ears perked up at the mention of birds and that seemed to decide it. Casually, as if it had been her idea all along, the dog picked her way to her own seat and lay down on it without bothering to glance at Gage.

A little dumbfounded, he drove toward Cass's house and wondered what had just happened. "Okay. Thanks. Apparently that plan got the thumbs-up from Her Royal Highness."

And from Gage. He snuck a sidelong peek at Cass. There'd always been something special about Cass but he hadn't realized her skills included dog whispering.

Warmth spread through his chest. Did Cass have any clue how much he appreciated her good humor over his bad-mannered dog? The invitation to let Arwen skip the dog hotel had earned *mucho* points with both man and beast. And neither of them gave points easily.

Arwen heartily approved of Cass's massive backyard. The moment Cass set down the bowl of water, Gage's diva of a dog gave Cass an extra nose to the hand, which was the equivalent of a rare thank-you. Would wonders never cease?

Gage followed Cass into the house, mystified why she'd be so welcoming of his dog. And why his dog was so welcoming of the woman.

Cass needs a big, fat thank-you. Immediately.

"Show me to your shower," he commanded, his body already hardening in anticipation of a hot and wet Cass.

She raised a brow. "That's the first thing you want to do? Take a shower?"

"You say that as though I'll be by myself."

"In that case…" She pivoted on one stiletto, then climbed the wide hardwood planked staircase at a brisk trot.

He raced after her, effortlessly taking the stairs two at a time, laughing as she ducked into a room and then popped back out as if to make sure he was following her. As if he'd be foolish enough to lose her.

"You're not getting away that easily," he promised as he entered what was clearly her bedroom. He made short work of whirling her into his arms so he could strip her slowly for a much-needed round two.

When her gaze met his, it was full of promise and his breath hitched in his chest as he drew off her suit one luscious piece at a time. Never one to hold back, she got him out of his clothes lickety-split and when they were both bared to each other, he picked her up and carried her into the en suite bathroom he'd spied earlier.

She flung her arms around his neck, her own breath coming faster as she nuzzled his ear. Heat swept across his skin. Would he ever get tired of her? Usually he was done by now. Once, maybe twice, was generally enough with one woman.

Not this one. She kept drawing him back and he kept not resisting.

Gently, he set down the armful of long-legged blonde on the black granite vanity so he could turn on the water in the shower. Six showerheads spurted to life and he let them run in the cavernous enclosure that had the perfect seat for what he had in mind.

Cass perched on the counter, blinking at him dreamily, and it was so sexy, he crossed back to her while the water heated. He wanted to touch her.

Stepping between her legs, he gathered her against him, flesh to flesh. She clung to him, wrapping her limbs around his waist. Her hair was still down, golden and curly against her back, tempting. So he indulged himself in what had become one of his favorite sights—her hair wound up in his fist.

A six-foot-long mirror spread out behind the vanity and Gage had a front row seat for viewing the gorgeous woman reflected there. Sensation engulfed him, sending a blast of blood to his groin so fast, it left him lightheaded. He groaned and his eyelids drifted shut. *No bueno.* There was no way in hell he was missing a minute of this.

Prying his eyes open, he gorged himself on the sight of the lovely naked woman in the mirror, and the man who was poised provocatively between her legs. And that's when he realized this was the first time he'd seen Cass fully unclothed. They'd made love in a couple of inventive spots that had been, oh, so very hot, but it hadn't given them the time to undress.

This was a first. And he planned to enjoy every second of it.

Reverently, he soaked her in. Then he was kissing her, delving into the moment with every fiber of his being. She made him ache, down deep inside where it couldn't be salved. Except by her.

They undulated together, physically and in their reflection. Steam from the shower gave the picture of the two of them a dreamlike quality, and it was the most erotic scene imaginable.

When they'd both shuddered to an intense, unbelievable release, he gathered her in his arms and took her to

the shower, where he ministered to her like a slave doting on his mistress. It was as much an act of making love
as what had happened on the vanity, though the thorough
washing could never be remotely construed as sex. Didn't
matter. Here in the shower as he rubbed soap over her
skin and slicked shampoo through her hair, he wanted to
make her feel as good as she made him feel, to connect
on a higher level. Maybe somehow, he could open her up
enough to know the ice was gone for good.

He couldn't stand it if things went back to being frozen between them.

Because he liked this Cass. More than he should. Far
more than he had in college. This time was totally different, but he couldn't put his finger on what caused it to
be that way. When he was inside her, his heart beat so
fast, he thought it might burst from his chest, and when
he wasn't with her, he thought about her. And not just
about the physical stuff, though that was never far from
his mind. No, he thought about how she'd come into her
own as a woman. As a CEO. She'd grown far beyond his
decade-old counsel.

The water grew cool and he shut it off, drying her tenderly. When he swiped the last of the water away, she
grazed his cheek with her hand and lifted his lips to hers
for the least suggestive kiss of his life. There was nothing sensual about it, just her laying her lips on his, and he
couldn't have ended it to save his life.

Finally, she pulled back with a smile.

"Get dressed and let's eat something," he suggested,
shocked at the roughness of his voice. He'd like to chalk
it up to the explosive encounter on the vanity but that had
happened thirty minutes ago. He suspected the source was
Cass. Always Cass.

"Tired of me naked already?" she asked saucily.

"Never. I need nourishment if I want to have any hope of keeping up with you."

Dinner consisted of Chinese takeout eaten at the long island in Cass's kitchen. They sat on barstools, legs entwined and heads bent together as they laughed over failed attempts to use the included chopsticks.

Later that night, after a worthless attempt to watch a romantic comedy on Cass's wide-screen TV, he curled around her in her big fluffy bed, skin to skin. Moonlight poured in from the large triple bay window opposite the bed, where Cass had drawn the curtain to reveal the silvery lake. It was a million-dollar view but he only had eyes for the woman in his arms.

He stroked her hair, letting her essence wind through him and he had to know.

"Cass," he murmured. "Why did you agree to talk to the others about selling the formula?"

She stiffened and he regretted bringing it up. But weren't they at a place where they could be honest with each other? He hadn't sniffed out her agenda so far; the only thing he hadn't tried was flat-out asking.

"It doesn't matter. We haven't found the leak yet."

The bleakness in her voice reached out and smacked him. "We will. We'll spend all day tomorrow on it."

"Yes. We have to. Otherwise, I'll lose my job."

"What? They can't fire you. You own one-fourth of the company."

"Yeah," she allowed. "But if they say I'm out, I'm out. It's a vote of no confidence. I'd sell them my share and find something else to do with my life. That's the downside of being on a team."

He rolled her to face him in the dim moonlight. "You're not giving yourself enough credit. You've done amazing things with Fyra *because* you're a team."

He'd never been part of anything and he felt the lack all at once. Cass and her friends had been together for a long time. Longer than he'd known her. He'd never connected with anyone like that.

What would it be like if he did? If he hung on to someone longer than a couple of nights? Not as business partners, but as lovers. Would it always feel like this, like he felt with Cass? As though he could never get enough, never get tired of her, never run out of things to talk about?

It couldn't. Could it? Maybe for other guys who didn't have promises to their long-lost brothers to keep. Who would he be if he settled down?

She gave him a small smile. "Be that as it may, if I don't plug that hole, Fyra's profits could plunge. I have to answer to the whole company, as well as my executive team. Who are also my friends."

She was making herself accountable, like a great CEO should. It was inspirational and a little moving.

Her firm resolution spoke to something inside that he had no idea was there. Awed at the wash of emotion, he took in the serious expression on her beautiful face and everything shifted.

Cassandra Claremont wasn't just a fun distraction. He was starting to fall for her. How was that possible? He'd never let his emotions go like this. And what was he supposed to do with it—offer her his heart? Make her a bunch of promises?

Fall was definitely the right word. He'd fallen so far out of his depth, he'd need a thousand-foot ladder to climb his way out.

A bit panicked, he tried to get back on track. "So we'll find the leak. That's the only answer."

Get that squared away and then get the formula. That's what he was doing here. The crazy talk, that wasn't him.

He had nothing to offer Cass but a few laughs and a hundred million dollars. Then he'd go home and be done here. Like always. Like he was comfortable with.

She smiled. "Easier said than done, apparently."

"Double down, sweetheart." He kissed her temple. "I'm still a good bet. Get some sleep so we can spend all day tomorrow finding your name."

"I've heard that one before," she said wryly.

She'd meant it as a joke, but it sat heavy on his chest. He'd spent far more time focusing on pleasure than he had business with absolutely no thought to how their lack of progress might be affecting her. He could do better.

"Really. You can count on me. I promise we'll get there."

She didn't argue, though he understood why she might have a case for not believing in him.

As she drifted off to sleep, he gathered her in his arms and tried not to think about how natural it felt to be her go-to guy, how it made him want to stick to the problem until it was solved. How it made him want to stick to her.

Coupledom. Love. Living with someone under the same roof, sharing a bed, bank accounts—that was definitely an adventure Nicolas had never gotten to have. Gage had been avoiding anything that even remotely looked like that under the pretense of living life to the fullest on behalf of his brother. But in reality, the whole concept made him want to run screaming in the other direction.

Or at least it used to. He'd developed the strangest urge to stop running.

And he was truly daft if he thought for a moment that settling down was in the cards for someone like him.

Ten

A mournful howl woke Cass in the morning. She blinked. Sunlight streamed through the window and Gage's heavy arm pinned her to the bed.

Arwen apparently wanted them both to know she was awake and bored. But only one of them seemed to notice. Gage still slept like the dead, a fact she'd not forgotten. He'd never been the type to let the pressures of life keep him from something he enjoyed as much as sleep. He'd need a dictionary and autocorrect to spell *stress*.

One of the many reasons he fascinated her. It was a trick she'd like to learn. She openly evaluated his beautiful face, relaxed in sleep. How did he shut off everything inside so easily? Or was it more a matter of truly not caring and therefore, there was nothing to shut off?

The latter, definitely. She'd lost count of the number of times she'd labeled him heartless. It was starting to ring false. Any man who clearly loved his dog as much as Gage did couldn't be heartless. And he'd been so sweet in the Hummer yesterday before rocking her world, then again last night.

She shook her head. And therein lay his danger. Instead of uncovering his involvement in the leak, he'd uncovered *her*, in so many ways, reminding her why she'd fallen for him in the first place. He'd taken everything she'd dished out and come back for more.

He lulled her into believing he might be someone different this time around, someone who would be there tomorrow and the next day, growing closer as they grew older. Someone who could be trusted. She had no evidence of that.

Didn't stop her from yearning for it, though.

Gage stirred awake and smiled sleepily at her. "Morning, gorgeous. You better stop looking at me like that or we're going to get a very late start on our investigation. That's our top priority for today, no ifs, ands or buts."

"Oh, that's a shame. I do enjoy your butt." She snickered as he waggled his brows.

And somehow, she ended up under him and panting out his name before she'd scarcely registered him moving.

Finally, they rolled from bed at nine o'clock, the latest she'd gotten up since…college as a matter of fact. Gage was truly a terrible influence on her.

But then he took over her Keurig and brewed her a giant cup of coffee, exactly the way she liked it, which hadn't changed in a decade, but still. How had he remembered that? Trinity never remembered that Cass hated sugar in her coffee, and Trinity had watched Cass make it every weekday morning for years and years.

Gage elbowed her aside as she tried to put some breakfast together, insisting on scrambling eggs and frying bacon himself, despite never having set foot in her well-equipped kitchen before. Of course, she rarely set foot in it either. The pan he'd scrounged up from under the Viking range didn't even look familiar.

After Gage filled a plastic bowl with food for Arwen, they sat outside on the flagstone patio at the bistro set she'd purchased shortly after buying the house five years ago, and yet had never once used. It was a gorgeous morning full of fluffy clouds flung across a blue sky, but Cass was busy watching the man across from her as he tossed an old tennis ball he'd pulled from Arwen's bag. The dog raced after it time and time again. In between tosses, Gage shoveled eggs and bacon into his mouth in what was clearly a practiced routine.

It was all very domestic and twisted Cass's heart strangely.

She'd dated a guy… Tyler Matheson…a year or so ago and she'd have said it was bordering on serious, but she'd never once thought about inviting him to her house for the weekend. It had felt intrusive. As if men and her domain should be kept separate at all times. When they'd broken up, Tyler had accused her of being cold and detached, but she'd brushed it off as the ranting of a rejected man, just like she'd ignored the hurt over the unkind, unnecessary accusation during what should have been an amicable split.

Now she wasn't so sure he'd been wrong.

In contrast, Gage had flowed into her life effortlessly. As if he'd always been there and it was easy and right. As if they'd picked up where they'd left off. She'd been holding her breath for almost a decade, waiting for her heart to start beating again. And now it was.

She stared at him as if seeing him for the first time.

She'd never gotten over Gage Branson and chalked it up to having endured such a badly broken heart. But that wasn't it at all. She'd never gotten over him because she was still in love with him.

She shut her eyes for a beat. That was the opposite of a good thing. And this was a really bad time to discover it. He might be involved in the leak. Hell, he might have even orchestrated it and at this rate, she'd never find out. If he flat out denied involvement, she'd never believe him. He'd proven he couldn't be trusted personally, so what was to say he could be trusted professionally? She would not give him the opportunity to destroy her or her business all over again.

Even if he got down on one knee and proposed, which would happen when monkeys learned to pilot a stealth bomber, she'd say no. Her own self-preservation overrode everything.

"I did some more digging into our files. Ready to talk through them?" she asked after she cleared the emotion from her throat. Not only was it a horrible time to discover she still had very real, very raw feelings for him, it would be a disaster to tip him off. God knew what he'd do with it. Twist it around and say she owed him something.

He glanced at her, ball in hand, as Arwen barked to show her displeasure at the interruption. He threw it to the far end of Cass's property, a good hundred yards, and managed to make it look effortless. Like everything else he did.

"Sure. We've got all day and most of tomorrow. Let's make good use of it."

That was her deadline to somehow work through her emotional mess, too. A day and a half to get him out of her system for good and move on.

"I'm curious." She drank deeply from her coffee mug for fortification. "When I talked to you about planting false information, you seemed to know a lot about how digital forensics works. How did that come about?"

The best way to get him out of her system was to prove his involvement in the leak. Then she wouldn't have to remind herself he wasn't trustworthy. Because he'd be in jail. Her heart squeezed. Surely that wasn't going to be the result of all this.

But even if it wasn't, Gage's presence in her life was still because of the formula. He wasn't falling in love with her. He was only here to squash his competition.

Gage shrugged. "You learn stuff over the years. I read articles and such. But really, the reasons that wouldn't have worked are common sense."

Carefully, she raised her brows. "How so?"

"Because. Like I said, you don't have that kind of time. And you're assuming that the person responsible for the leak would actually be transferring files. What if they take handwritten notes? Memorize files? Take photographs? There are dozens of ways people can access information, especially if the person doing it is authorized in the first place."

All said very casually, while still throwing Arwen's ball. She'd watched him over her coffee cup, growing more frustrated by the minute at his clear hazel eyes and relaxed expression. He was supposed to be letting his guard down enough to say something he shouldn't.

Maybe he hadn't because she was being too subtle.

"Is that how you'd do it?" she asked, just as casually. Good thing she had a lot of practice at keeping her voice calm even when her insides were a mess. "Take photographs?"

"For what? To steal proprietary information?" He laughed and she'd swear it was genuine, not the kind designed to cover nervousness. "No reason for me to resort to underhanded tactics. If I want something, I buy it."

Yeah, as she well knew. Her coffee soured in her mouth. The problem with this line of questioning lay in the fact that she didn't have a clue if Gage was blowing smoke to distract her from his crimes or truly not involved in the leak.

How would she ever know for sure?

Maybe she was still being too subtle and the best way to resolve this was to flat out ask *Gage, are you involved?*

Surely she could read him well enough to recognize truth in his response. She opened her mouth to do it, once and for all, when his phone rang.

Frowning, he glanced at the screen. "Excuse me a sec. Someone from this number has called a couple of times but never leaves a message. Otherwise, I wouldn't take it."

Cass nodded as he stepped away from the table, her pulse pounding in her throat. So close. She'd almost blurted out the million-dollar question and she hated being forced to wait now that she'd made up her mind to go this route. But Gage ran a billion-dollar company. Of course people were vying for his attention.

She'd hoped to get her hands on his phone at some point this weekend, but snooping through his private life felt a little dirty, so she hadn't. So far. If he gave her any reason to, though...

Gage thunked back into his chair, his expression completely transformed from the relaxed, easygoing one he'd worn earlier. Thunderclouds had gathered in his eyes, turning his entire demeanor dark. "I have to leave. I'm sorry to cut our weekend short."

"What's wrong?" she asked before she thought better of it. They weren't a couple. They didn't share their problems. And no amount of yearning for that type of relation-ship would change things.

"Something's happened." Bleakly, he met her gaze, and suddenly it didn't matter if they weren't a couple. She reached out and captured his hand. In comfort, solidar-ity, she didn't even know. She just couldn't stop herself from touching him.

"What, Gage?" she asked softly, envisioning an acci-dent involving his parents, a fire at his production facility. The pallor of his skin indicated it must be something bad.

"That was… I don't know for sure yet. I have to go home." He scrubbed his face with his free hand as he gripped Cass's with his other. "Someone I used to date died. Briana. That was her sister on the phone."

"Oh, I'm so sorry." Cass's heart twisted in sympathy. The woman must have been someone special for Gage to be so visibly upset. The thought of him caring about a woman so deeply set her back a moment. Was she miss-ing something here? When had Gage become the com-mitted sort?

"Thanks, I hadn't spoken to her in a long time. A year and a half."

Cass eyed him. "Then why would her sister have called you, if you don't mind me asking?"

Maybe *that* was the million-dollar question. Her cu-riosity burned. What if he truly had turned into some-one who stuck around, growing close to this woman, and she'd been the one to dump him? Maybe *he* was nursing a broken heart.

After all, they'd never really talked about what the fu-ture between the two of them could look like. Maybe everything was within her reach if she just—

"She called because Briana had a son." Gage blinked. "My son. Or so she says."

* * *

Gage's two-story house overlooked Lake Travis just outside of Austin. It was one of the main reasons he'd bought the house several years ago and the water had always spoken to him. After driving straight home from Dallas in less than three hours—a record—he stood on the balcony, hands braced on the railing surrounding the enclosure and stared at the gray surface of the lake without really seeing it, wishing like hell the view didn't remind him of Cass.

But it did because her house was similarly situated near White Rock Lake in Dallas. He should be there with her right now, but wasn't because his world had shifted into something unrecognizable, where a paternity test was suddenly a part of his reality.

The woman who had called him was on her way over to discuss that very thing. It was bizarre. If what she'd said was true, he'd fathered a child with Briana.

Briana Miles. The name conjured up the image of a diminutive brown-haired waitress he'd met at a sports bar not far from his house. Beautiful girl. She'd come home to Austin after five years in LA and had started waiting tables so she could put herself through college, hoping to graduate without debt.

They'd struck up a conversation because Gage had expressed curiosity about how the University of Texas had changed in the almost ten years since he'd exited graduate school. That had led to a great couple of days that had ended amicably. He hadn't heard from her since.

The doorbell pealed through the house, and Gage opened the door to a short brown-haired woman with the swollen eyes and messy ponytail. Lauren Miles shared features with Briana and he could see their family resemblance even though he hadn't laid eyes on her sister in a year and a half.

"Come in," he said woodenly.

"The courier dropped off the results of the paternity test you took." She handed Gage the sealed envelope with her free hand. "I guess it's true that if you have enough money, you can get anything done quickly."

He ripped the envelope open and his vision went a little gray. No question. He was a father.

Lauren perched on his couch but he couldn't sit down, not until he got the most important question answered.

"Why?" he burst out as he absently paced the strip of hardwood between the couch and the fireplace. "Why didn't she tell me? I would have helped her with the medical bills. Paid for diapers and teddy bears. I would have—"

His throat seized.

Liked to be involved. But he couldn't finish the thought, not with the way his chest had gotten so tight that he couldn't breathe. All this time. Briana had been raising a baby without his help. Without even bothering to tell him he'd fathered a son. He'd have supported her if he'd known. She shouldn't have had to worry about anything.

And now it was too late.

Lauren bit her lip. "I argued with her about that. I really did. But she insisted you wouldn't want the baby and she was scared you'd make her have an abortion."

Gage's vision blacked out for a long minute. Rage tore through his chest and he thought he'd lose it if he couldn't punch something. *Make* her terminate her pregnancy?

Life was precious, so precious. That core belief was the one sole gift Nicolas's death had given him. The fact that Briana didn't know that about him infuriated him. Except how could he blame her? It spoke to the shallowness of their relationship that she'd assumed he wouldn't want his son.

Gradually, he uncurled his fists and breathed until he could speak.

"Fine, okay. I get that she didn't tell me because she—wrongly—assumed I wouldn't support her decision to raise her child. Nothing could be further from the truth. The baby is my responsibility and I appreciate the fact that you've come to me so I can do the right thing."

His vision went dim again as he processed what the *right thing* actually translated into. After years of cutting all ties with women as quickly as possible, one had managed to hook him with the ultimate string. For a guy who had no practice with commitment, he was about to get a crash course.

He was a father. A *single* father. His child's mother was dead and he had to step up. His carefree days of living life to the fullest had just come to a screeching halt with a set of brakes called parenthood.

And he'd never even held his son. What was he going to do?

All at once, he wished he'd asked Cass to be here with him. It made no sense. But he wanted to hold her hand.

"About that." Lauren scooted to the edge of the couch, brow furrowed as she leaned closer to Gage. "I'd like to formally adopt Robbie."

"Adopt him?" he parroted because his brain was having a hard time processing. Lauren wasn't here to pass off Briana's son to his father?

"That's actually why I contacted you, to discuss the paperwork that my lawyer is drawing up. You'll have to sign, of course, because you're the legal father on record. But it's just a formality," she said quickly. "I'm not asking for any child support or any split custody. He'd be all

mine and you can go about your life. I'm sure you're totally unprepared to be a father."

It was as though she'd read his mind.

Something that felt an awful lot like relief washed
through him. He'd give her money, of course. That was
nonnegotiable. But Lauren could pick up where Briana
left off and all of this would go away.

And the relief kicked off a pretty solid sense of shame.
"So you want me to sign away all rights to my kid?"

"Well, yeah. Unless Briana was wrong and you are
interested in being a father?" she asked tremulously, as
if afraid of the answer, and tears welled up in her eyes.
"You've never even met Robbie. I love him like my own
son. He's a piece of Briana and I can't imagine giving
him up. It would be best if he stayed with the family he's
always known."

"I don't know if that is best," he admitted and his stomach rolled.

He should be agreeing with her. He should be asking
her for papers to sign. Right now. What better circumstances could he have hoped for than to learn he had a
son but someone else wanted him? It was practically a
done deal.

But he couldn't. Somehow, he'd developed a fierce need
to see this kid he'd fathered. He needed it to be real, and
meeting his flesh and blood was the only way he could
sign those papers in good conscience.

"I didn't know my son existed before today," he heard
himself saying as if a remote third party had taken over
his body and started spitting out words without his per-
mission. "And you're coming in here like it's all already
decided. How can I know what's best for him? I want to
meet him first."

Gage had a significant number of zeroes padding his

bank account, which wouldn't be hard to figure out, even for a casual observer. This could still be an elaborate ploy for a seven- or eight-figure check. But he didn't think so.

She nodded once. "Can it be in the next couple of days? Briana didn't have much, but her estate needs to be settled. Robbie's future being the most critical part, of course."

Settled. Yeah, all of this needed to be settled, but unfortunately, this was the least settled he'd ever been. What an impossible situation. And he didn't have the luxury of shrugging it off like he normally did.

Grimly, Gage showed Lauren out and sat on the couch, head in his hands. And he didn't even think twice about his next move. He pulled out his phone and dialed Cass.

When he'd left her in Dallas, it was with a terse goodbye and a promise to call her, but he'd never imagined he actually would, at least not for personal reasons. It should have been a good place for them to break things off and only focus on the business of Fyra's formula. He'd planned for it to be the end, but nothing with Cass felt finished.

Besides, he needed someone with a level head who knew him personally to stand by his side as he met his son for the first time. Someone who wouldn't let emotions get the best of her. Someone he hoped cared enough about him to help him make the right decision. Someone like Cass.

Too late, he realized none of that actually mattered. He wanted Cass because *she* mattered. Yeah, it scared him, but he couldn't deny the truth. The formula had ceased to be the most important thing between him and Cass.

Cass answered on the first ring and he didn't even bother to try and interpret that. Too much had shifted since they'd last talked for petty mind games like guessing whether she'd missed him like he'd missed her. Or whether she'd realize the fact that he'd called her had earth-shattering significance. It did. She could do what she wanted with that.

"I need you," he said shortly. "It's important. Can you come to Austin?"

Eleven

Cass went to Austin.

There really wasn't a choice. Gage had said he needed her and that was enough. For now. Later, she'd examine the real reason she'd hopped in the car ten minutes after ending his call. Much later. Because there was so much wrapped up inside it, she could hardly make sense of it all.

When his name had come up on her caller ID, she'd answered out of sheer curiosity. You didn't drop something on a woman like a surprise baby and then jet off. Of course, she'd also been prepared for some elaborate plot designed to see her again so he could coerce her into either giving him the formula or getting naked, at least until he got tired of her again. She'd planned to say no and spend the weekend crossing the finish line on the leak's name.

She had to be close. The list of potentials wasn't *that* long.

But instead she'd found herself saying yes to the surprising request to accompany Gage as he met his son for the first time. He wanted *her* to be by his side as he navigated this unprecedented situation. The sheer emotion in his voice had decided it. What if Gage wasn't involved in the leak and she missed her chance to find out what might happen between them?

Cass held Gage's hand as they mounted Lauren Miles's front steps and wondered not for the first time if he'd literally come apart under her grip. The new, hard lines around his mouth scared her, but the fragility—that was ten times worse. As if the news he'd fathered a child had replaced his bones with dust. One wrong move and he'd blow away in a strong wind if she didn't hold on tight enough.

Just this morning, they'd been drinking coffee on her back porch and she'd been desperate to work him out of her system. So she could let him go and move on. Clearly that wasn't happening. But what was?

Less than four hours had passed since she received Gage's troubling and cryptic phone call and their arrival on this quiet suburban street. The slam of a car door down the way cracked the silence. It felt as if there should be something more momentous to mark the occasion of entering the next phase of your life. Because no matter what, Gage would never be the same. His rigid spine and disturbed aura announced that far better than any words ever could.

"I admire what you're doing," she told him quietly before he rang the doorbell. "This is a tough thing, meeting your son for the first time. I think you'd regret signing the papers if you didn't do this first."

The fact that he'd asked her to come with him still hadn't fully registered. Because she didn't know what it meant.

"Thanks." Gage's eyelids closed and he swallowed. "I

had to do it even though I feel like I'm standing on quicksand. All the time. I needed something to hold on to."

He accompanied the frank admission by tightening his grip on her hand. He meant her. She was the one holding him up and it settled quietly in her soul. In his time of need, he'd reached out to her. She wished she could say why that meant so much to her. Or why the fact that he was meeting this challenge head-on had softened her in ways she hadn't anticipated. Ways that couldn't be good in the long run.

But what if there was the slightest possibility that they might both put down their agendas now that something so life altering had happened? That hadn't felt conceivable in Dallas, but here...well, she was keeping her eyes open.

He rang the doorbell and a frazzled woman answered the door with a baby on her hip.

"Right on time," the woman said inanely, and she cleared her throat.

Gage's gaze cut to the baby magnetically and his hazel eyes shone as he drank in the chubby little darling clad in one of those suits that seemed to be the universal baby uniform.

"I'm Lauren," she said to Cass. "We haven't met."

"Cassandra Claremont." Since she wasn't clear what her role here was, she left it at that. She and Lauren didn't shake hands as there wasn't any sort of protocol for this situation, and besides, they were both focused on Gage. Who was still focused on the baby.

"Is this him?" he whispered. "Robbie?"

"None other." Lauren stepped back to let Gage and Cass into the house, apologizing for the state of it as she led them to the living room.

A square playpen sat off to one side of the old couch surrounded by other baby paraphernalia that Cass couldn't have identified at gunpoint. All of it was tiny, pastel and utterly frightening.

That was when Cass realized she knew nothing about babies. She'd always known they existed and murmured appropriately over them when other women who had them entered Cass's orbit. But this was a baby's home, where the process of living and eating and growing up happened.

Gage had told her in the car on the way over that the baby's aunt was seeking to adopt Robbie. Really Cass was floored Gage hadn't signed the papers to give up his rights on the spot. Why hadn't he? The solution was tailor-made for a billionaire CEO who thought commitment was the name of a town in Massachusetts. Give up your kid and go on living life as though it was one big basket of fun with nothing to hold you back.

Sounded like Gage's idea of heaven to her.

The fact that he was here meeting his son instead... well, she wouldn't have missed it for anything in the world.

Crossing to the mat on the floor, Lauren set the baby upright in the center of one bright square and motioned Gage over. "Come sit with him. I can't honestly say he doesn't bite, but when he does, it doesn't really hurt." She laughed without much humor. "Sorry, that was a lame joke."

Then Gage knelt on the mat and held out a hand to his son. The baby glanced at the stranger quizzically but then reached out and grasped his father's finger with a small baby sound.

Cass forgot to breathe as a wave of tenderness and awe and a million other emotions she couldn't begin to name broke over Gage's expression, transforming it into something that tugged at her soul. She almost couldn't watch as the moment bled through her, blasting away the last of her barriers against a man whom she could never call heartless again. It would be a lie.

His heart was all over his face, in his touch as he ruffled his son's fuzzy head. In the telltale drop of moisture in the corner of his eye.

She couldn't watch and she couldn't look away as her own heart cried along with Gage. That's what love looked like on him and she wanted more of it.

Thirty minutes passed in a blur as Gage held his son in his strong arms and laughed as the baby pulled at his father's too-long hair. He pumped Lauren for information, demanding details like what Robbie ate, whether he'd taken his first step, what he did when he rolled over. Robbie's aunt answered the questions to the best of her ability but it soon became clear she hadn't spent every waking minute with the boy like his own mother had.

A somber cloud spread over the four of them with its dark reminder that this wasn't strictly a happy occasion of father meeting son. Gage had a decision to make and he needed to make it soon so Robbie could get settled in the home where he'd live for the next eighteen years with his permanent parent.

Lauren announced it was Robbie's nap time. She left the room, disappearing into the back of the house to perform the mysterious ritual of "putting him down" and returned after ten minutes, her eyes puffy and red, as if she'd been crying.

"He's so precious." She sniffed. "It's so unfair. I can't tell you how it breaks my heart that he's lost his mother."

"It's hard for me, too," Gage admitted quietly. "My son should have a mother. Yet if Briana hadn't died, I might never have known about Robbie."

It was the most brutal sort of turnabout and it was definitely not fair play. But Cass couldn't argue that fate had set that pendulum in motion. And the swings had widened to encompass her, as well.

Gage held out his hand to Lauren. "Thank you for opening your home to him."

"I wouldn't have done anything else." Lauren shook Gage's hand solemnly and didn't let go as she caught his gaze to speak directly to him. "I love him. He's my nephew, first and foremost, and we will always share that bond of blood. But you're his father. That's something I can't be to him and I'm prepared for whatever decision you make. Please, take twenty-four hours, though. Make a decision you can live with forever."

Nodding, Gage squeezed Lauren's hand and turned to go, ushering Cass out the door ahead of him. His touch on her back was firm and warm and it infused her with the essence of Gage that she'd be a fool to pretend she didn't crave.

The best part was she didn't have to pretend. Instead of spending the weekend working Gage out of her system, something else entirely was happening and she couldn't wait to find out what.

He drove back to his mansion on the lake and helped her out of the Hummer, leading her up the flagstone steps to the grand entryway flanked by soaring panes of glass... all without asking if she planned to stay.

No way in hell was she going anywhere.

Throwing a frozen pizza in the oven passed for dinner, and an open bottle of Jack Daniel's managed to intensify the somberness that had cloaked them since leaving Lauren's house. They pulled up bar stools at the long, luminous piece of quartz topping the island in Gage's kitchen and ate.

Or rather, she ate and Gage stared into his rapidly diminishing highball filled with whiskey.

"I'd ask if you were okay," Cass commented wryly, "but that would be ridiculous under the circumstances. So instead I'll ask if you want to talk about it."

"He looks like Nicolas." Gage tossed the last of his Jack down his throat and reached for the bottle. "Robbie. He's the spitting image of my brother at that age. My mom had a shrine to her firstborn lining the hallway. Literally dozens of pictures stared down at me for eighteen years as I went between my bedroom and the bathroom. Today was like seeing a ghost."

"Oh, Gage." *More alcohol needed, stat.* Her own Jack Daniel's disappeared as she sucked the bottom out of her glass through a straw. "That's…"

She didn't know what it was. Horrible? Morbid? Unfortunate? Gage had talked about Nicolas in college on occasion, so she knew the tragic story well. It had shaped a family into something different than might have been otherwise.

"It's a miracle." A small smile lit up Gage's features. "I never would have imagined… My son is a gift that I don't deserve. A piece of myself and my brother all wrapped up into one amazing little package."

The love and tenderness she'd seen at Lauren's house when he looked at his son appeared again in his expression, and it pierced her right through the heart. It was breathtaking on Gage, a man she'd longed to look at *her* that way, a man she'd been sure didn't care about anything. The fact that he'd shown a capacity for it was a game changer.

And she had a strong feeling she knew what that look signified. "You don't want to give up Robbie."

Gage shook his head. "I can't. It never sat quite right with me anyway, but once I saw him… I don't need twenty-four hours to decide. He needs me."

He wasn't going to walk away from his son. And she'd never been more proud of someone in her life.

That burst Gage's dam and he started talking about Robbie. How was it possible that a man becoming a father before her very eyes could be so affecting? But it was. Gage's decision opened up a part of her inside that flooded with something divine and beautiful.

They drifted to bed where they lay awake, facing each other in the dark, as she listened to Gage's plans for his impending fatherhood. There was no subject too inane, from the color of the walls in his son's new room to what kind of car Gage would buy him when he turned sixteen.

Cass smiled and bit back a suggestion that he let his son pick out his own car. Far be it from her to interrupt his flow. This was his way of working through it and her job was to be there for him. It was nice to be needed by the one man who had never needed her. Heady even.

"Thank you," he said abruptly. "For coming on short notice. For holding my hand. For not heaping condemnation and a sermon on top of me. I had to figure this out and I couldn't have without you."

What, like he was expecting her to shake her finger at him and give him a lecture about accepting responsibility? She shook her head. "You're giving me too much credit. I just responded to a phone call. You did the hard part."

"No. I don't do hard." His voice went scratchy but he blazed ahead. "I get out before anything difficult happens. Back at your house, that was supposed to be about burning off the tension so we could focus. It wasn't supposed to be the start of something. I don't do relationships. You know that, right?"

That was the first time she'd ever heard him admit he had a commitment problem. Admitting it was the first step toward curing it, right?

"Yeah. I knew it wasn't anything more than sex."

"What if I want it to be?" he asked, sincerity warming his voice and curling through her in the dark. It was as if he'd read the same question in her heart and voiced it out loud.

"What if you do?" she heard herself repeat when she should have been saying *so what?* Or *this is goodbye right now.* "Have things changed?"

Please, God. Let that be true and not a huge mistake.

His hand found hers, threading their fingers together, and the rightness of it drifted through her like a balm. She could listen to him talk all night long if this was the topic.

If she hadn't gotten in the car when he asked her to come to Austin, she'd never have gotten to watch this monumental shift in Gage.

"So many things," he repeated quietly. "I'm not even sure how yet. The formula… I wasn't going to give up. I wanted it and I was going after it. But somewhere along the way, I started to want more."

The earth shifted beneath the bed, sliding away faster and faster as her mind whirled, turning over his words, searching for the angle, the gotcha. "What are you saying, Gage? That you want to keep seeing each other?"

He spit out a nervous laugh. "Why not? I like spending time with you. I'm pretty sure the feeling is mutual or I'm much worse at this kind of thing than I think I am."

"You have a lot going on right now," she said cautiously. "Maybe this isn't the best time to be talking about this."

"I *am* worse at this than I thought if I'm not making myself clear. Let's see how it goes. I'll come up to Dallas. You drive to Austin. We talk on the phone during the week. Maybe a video chat late at night that involves some dirty talk. I don't know. I've never done this before."

She could envision it. Perfectly. Sexting during a conference call and naughty emails and rushing to throw her overnight bag into her Jaguar for a Friday night dash to the Hill Country in anticipation of a long weekend in Gage's bed.

But for how long? And what would happen when he ditched her again, as he surely would? "I don't know how to do that either."

His sigh vibrated through her rib cage. "Yeah. Robbie changes everything."

That was so not what she'd meant. "Why, because you think you being a father is a turn-off? Think again."

"It should be. My life will never be the same. It's ridiculous to even say something like 'let's see how things go.' I already know where I'm going. Play dates, preschool, the principal's office and Cub Scouts."

He was committing to his child. Didn't that give her some hope he might want to commit to her, too?

"Maybe it's not so ridiculous." Had that just come out of her mouth? It was madness. But honest.

"Stop humoring me," he said flatly. "I get it. Everything is up in the air, which is unfair to you. Besides, you might want to think about whether you'd like to be in the same boat as Briana. I don't know how she got pregnant. I used protection every single time."

Yeah, that had occurred to her. But he'd gotten it wrong. She was in a whole boatload of trouble regardless because she wasn't mother material. She ran a million-dollar company for crying out loud. Any conversation she and Gage had about seeing where things could go included a future with a baby no matter what. Now that she'd thought of it, she couldn't *stop* thinking about it.

But there was no point in heaping condemnation on him, especially not when it sounded as though he was doing a pretty good job of that on his own. "Of course you did, Gage. It was an accident. It happens all the time, even to smart, careful people."

Her heart twisted as they talked about subjects that shouldn't be a part of his reality. Gage embraced this challenge in a way she'd never have guessed—the king of disentangling himself from anything that smacked of the long-term had changed when she wasn't looking. Really and truly changed, which she'd just spent a considerable amount of effort denying over the past week.

What if she *could* trust him with her heart this time? A world of possibilities might be open to her. To both of them.

It gave her a lot to think about.

In the morning, she awoke before Gage. His sleeping form was close enough to touch but she didn't dare do it. He'd only slept for a couple of hours last night, which she knew because she'd been holding him when he'd finally drifted off.

Their conversation had meandered to every subject under the sun—how they'd gone without their first year in business, what kind of spices you could add to ramen noodles to make them taste like something other than cardboard, the first splurge purchase they'd made when their companies finally turned a profit.

It was like the old days, except Gage hadn't even tried to kiss her. Last night hadn't been about sex, a fact she appreciated. But at the same time, she couldn't help but try to categorize the night.

A turning point, perhaps. But one thing she did know for sure—she had to answer that million-dollar question about Gage's involvement in the leak. Soon.

Twelve

Cass entered this new phase of her relationship with Gage with equal parts caution and greed. She soaked up every second of laughing with him over Robbie's antics as Gage visited his son at Lauren's house, and she helped Gage shop for nursery items.

No task required to prepare Gage to take custody of his son was too small for her involvement, apparently. She didn't mind. Except for the part where they never picked up the conversation about where things were going. Whether there was a goodbye in their future or not. Was she simply a hand to hold until he found his footing?

Eventually, that question would have to be answered. But she was content, for now.

She shuttled between Austin and Dallas enough times over the next week that she could pick out roadside elements as mile markers. That weed formation meant it was an hour and thirty-six minutes until she'd be in Gage's arms again. The pile of rocks by the exit sign meant she'd see Gage's beautiful hazel eyes light up at the sight of her in seventeen minutes.

In between, she ran her company and hired a private detective to look into the leak. If she hadn't been so distracted, she would have done so earlier. The move was enough to satisfy her partners into giving her more time. And enough to satisfy herself that if Gage was involved, she'd find out before things went too far. She hoped.

On Friday, one week after she'd snuck out early to get busy with Gage in his Hummer—totally by accident, in her defense—she spent an hour at the end of the day frantically whittling down her email in anticipation of spending the weekend in Austin with Gage.

Her phone rang. Speak of the devil.

"Hey, sexy," she purred.

"It's done," he said. "The last of Briana's estate is settled and Robbie is officially mine."

She swallowed. Hard. "That's great news!"

Just in time for the weekend. They'd expected it to take a few more days, but Lauren had been instrumental in pushing things through once she saw how serious Gage was about being a father. She could have made Gage's life a living hell and he'd said he was grateful she'd chosen to take the high road for Robbie's sake.

Except now it was real. Gage was a single father.

Now that the estate was settled, Robbie would come to live with Gage permanently. Lauren would still be a huge part of her nephew's life, and she and Gage had already discussed potential arrangements for holidays. Gage's parents had put their house in Houston on the market and planned to move to Austin so they could spend their golden years with their new grandson.

The only person who didn't have her future mapped out was Cass.

"So I guess Lauren is bringing Robbie over tonight?" she asked. She'd planned to drive to Austin tonight to spend the weekend with Gage.

Things had just come to a head. What did Cass know about dating a single father? If things progressed, was she really ready to be a mother? The thought frightened her. She had a demanding job. She couldn't be calm and cool around a baby. The timing wasn't great for any of this.

One step at a time. What better way to figure out what came next than to spend time with the man and his child?

"No, she asked if she could keep Robbie until Monday so she could say goodbye, just the two of them. I couldn't say no."

"That was sweet of you."

Her heart opened a little more with each glimpse of the man Gage was becoming as he met this challenge. Each time, she had to reprogram a bit more of her thinking. She wasn't sure what to do with the result.

"So instead of you driving here, I'm coming to you. You've already put far too many miles on your car in the past week. Turnabout is fair play," he reminded her in case she'd forgotten about his strong sense of tit-for-tat. "I'll be there in three hours."

She ended the call with a smile and drove home instead of to Austin. The reprieve gave her time to review the email she'd received a few minutes ago from the background-check company. They'd finally completed new scans of all her employees.

Thirty minutes later, she kicked back on her sofa with her laptop, the report and a list of cross-referenced employees who worked in the lab. The scans she'd ordered included arrest records, of course, but that wasn't necessarily a good indicator of someone's propensity toward corporate espionage. A better one was financial records such as property owned and debt, which was the section of the report where she focused her attention.

Someone with a mountain of outstanding bills might be a prime candidate for thievery, particularly in light of what the formula was worth to someone like Gage. He'd never buy it from a shady Fyra employee, but the culprit might not realize that.

But Cass knew that about Gage. The thought settled into her mind as if it had always been there. Of course that was true. Why would he have bothered to come to Fyra's CEO with an offer to buy the formula if he planned to buy it on the black market?

Or was she missing the big picture?

Everything was mixed up in her head and the addition of his new status as a committed father wasn't helping. She just didn't know whether she trusted Gage or not.

Cass refocused and noted two lab employees with outstanding mortgages that seemed quite large for what Fyra paid them. Also not a blinking sign that pointed to criminal activity. But a curiosity all the same, considering neither of them were married according to the scan. Inheritance, maybe, but Cass couldn't be too careful.

Next, she moved on to her employees' former employers and known associates. GB Skin leaped off the page almost instantly. Cass's gaze slid to the employee's name. Rebecca Moon. She worked for Harper as a lab analyst. She'd worked for Gage before coming to Fyra. Also in his lab.

It wasn't uncommon. Many of Fyra's employees had previously worked for Mary Kay, too. That didn't make them criminals, just people with skill sets companies in the cosmetics industry sought.

But no one from a competitor had approached Cass about her formula, except one.

Cass sat up and started from the beginning of Rebecca's report. The picture was not pretty. She had a wide swath of credit card debt totaling well over a hundred grand and outstanding medical bills from—Cass tapped the line once she found it—her ex-husband's many elective procedures. So Rebecca had gotten divorced but was still saddled with an ex's debt.

Shaking her head over the things people did to each other, Cass eyed the woman's known associates and a sense of foreboding grew in her stomach. All of the people linked to Rebecca had addresses in Austin. Not a big deal. The woman had lived and worked in Austin when she was employed by GB Skin.

It just seemed odd that Rebecca Moon hadn't made any friends in Dallas in the...seven months she'd worked for Fyra. Not one person from her new neighborhood had asked her to lunch via text message or friended her on Facebook?

The background check hadn't extended to Rebecca's friends' information. So there was no way to know if the people she'd interacted with online and made phone calls to were employed by GB Skin—but logic would dictate that she'd made friends at Gage's company and kept them.

If Gage had found that out somehow, would it have been a temptation to lean on that connection? *No*, she couldn't assume that. Could she?

Her stomach rolled again as she recalled how convenient the timing had been when he'd first shown up at Fyra. Yes, she knew the drive between here and Austin was easy. Someone could conceivably hop in the car with little planning and be here before lunch. It didn't mean Gage had known about the formula *before* the information hit the trade magazine, or that he'd used the leak as some kind of leverage to get her to agree to sell.

But still. Gage had been convinced Cass owed him something. But then he'd stopped reminding her of it. The formula rarely came up these days. Why, because he knew Rebecca Moon was going to steal it for him?

That was a stretch. But Cass couldn't get it off her mind. A leak was one thing, but the threat of the culprit doing additional harm was very real. As was the possibility she'd been played by the master, just like she had been in college.

She would drive herself crazy with that line of thinking. She used her time to thoroughly peruse the rest of the report but Rebecca was the only lead she had.

Who better to contradict whether he'd discovered the perfect mole in Cass's company than Gage himself? There was absolutely no reason she couldn't bring this information to him and get his explanation. They could be straight with each other. He'd talk to her and tell her she was being silly and then maybe she'd tell him that she'd hired a private detective. With the detective on the job, she and Gage could focus on each other. See what their relationship might look like with all the agendas put away.

Because if she couldn't trust him with business, what could she trust him with?

Halfway through the last page of the report, a knock on the door startled her. *Gage.*

She let him into her house and drank in the man's beauty and masculinity as she stood frozen in the foyer where he'd made love to her for the first time in a decade. A million powerful emotions washed over her. She'd tried to keep her distance. Tried to keep her heart where it belonged—in her chest and shielded from Gage—but as she looked at him, images flew at her, of him as he held his son, as he laughed with her, as he made love to her.

The addition of his baby had shifted things. Far more so than she'd have anticipated, and not the way she'd have thought. Gage was a father now. Did that mean he'd changed his thinking about commitment? Was he ready to find a woman to settle down with?

But he still said things like *let's see how it goes. We're having fun. You owe me. Turnabout is fair play.* He'd distracted her from the leak again and again with his talk of pleasure before business. Had he been afraid she'd find something?

Ask him about Rebecca. Go on.

The wicked smile he treated her to fuzzled her mind and then he swept her into a very friendly embrace that promised to get a lot friendlier.

She pulled away and crossed her arms over the ache in her midsection that wouldn't ease. This was why she shouldn't let her heart take over. Emotions only led to problems.

"That was fast," she said brightly.

He raised one eyebrow quizzically. "Not fast enough, clearly. What's wrong?"

"I'm hungry," she lied. Of course he'd picked up on the swirl of uncertainty under her skin. "I waited for you to eat."

"I had Whataburger on the way. I'll hang out with you in the kitchen while you eat something, if you want."

"Sure." Then they could talk.

Except she couldn't seem to segue into *by the way, did you happen to set up a deal with one of my employees to steal my formula for you?*

Gage sat on a bar stool and chatted about Robbie, absently sipping a highball with a splash of Jack Daniel's in it. As she woodenly ate a very unappetizing sandwich that didn't sit well in her swirly stomach, she couldn't stand it any longer. The best approach was to ease into it, perhaps.

"When are we going to check in with each other?" she asked during a lull in Gage's conversation. Because of course their relationship, the leak and the formula were all tied together. Without one, the others didn't exist, and it was time to get all of it straight. "About how things are going."

"Now?" he suggested mildly. "Is that what's bugging you? You don't have to dance around it if that's on your mind. How are things going, Cass?"

Right, jump straight to her as if she could possibly articulate what was going on inside. She made it a habit of pretending she didn't have any emotions and she certainly didn't spend a lot of time cataloguing them for others when she didn't fully understand them herself.

Besides, this was about Gage. About whether he'd planted a mole in her company. Whether he'd invented a relationship with her to get his hands on her formula. Whether he'd become a man she could trust.

She scowled. "I wanted to know how it was going from your chair."

He took in her dark expression without comment. "It's working. But it's only been a week and Robbie will be a big part of my life come Monday. So I guess I'm still seeing how things go."

And somehow, his perfectly legitimate response plowed through her nerves like water torture. "What does that mean? Once you become a dad, you might decide two is enough?"

It would be exactly what she'd been expecting. *Sorry, this thing between us has run its course.* That's what she'd prepared for.

His brow furrowed and he abandoned his drink to focus
on her. "No, it means it's a complexity in an already shaky
situation."

"Shaky how?" she whispered. "Do you have something
you need to tell me?"

Oh, God, what was she going to do if he came right
out and confessed? He was bound to have some kind of
rationale, like he'd only planned to use Rebecca to gather
information for leverage or he'd say that technically, he
hadn't done anything illegal.

"Cass, you're trembling."

Clearly concerned, he tried to grip her hand but she
yanked it away, whacking her nearly empty wineglass and
sending it clattering across the granite bar. Gage, bless his
honed reflexes, caught the stemware before it shattered
on the travertine tile below, but the trail of wine across
her light brown counters would stain.

Good. Something to occupy her hands while she gained
control again. *No emotions*, she scolded herself. *Brazen it
out. Don't let him know what's going on inside.*

"You didn't answer my question," she said, pleased at
how calmly she delivered the statement. And how coolly
she wiped up the spilled wine with careful, even strokes.
"If our situation is shaky, what's making it that way?"

"The formula, for one. I was expecting you to tell me
to go to hell when I called about Robbie. But you didn't."
He watched her closely but she refused to meet his all-
knowing gaze.

She would never have told him that. He'd needed her.
Maybe she should have told him to go to hell twenty times
since then, but dang it, she'd wanted to believe in him.
In them.

Yes, it meant something that she'd come when he called.
She'd been hanging around, thinking she'd hold on to her

heart and dip one toe in, but really, she was pathetically, predictably wishing for him to fall in love with her. Just like last time.

But he'd given her no reason to trust him, no reason to believe that could ever happen. Becoming a father didn't automatically make Gage Branson someone he wasn't and that's why he wasn't suddenly spouting promises and pretty words. *Let's see how things go* was code for *I've found my Ms. Right-Now.* Until he got tired of her. Until something better came along. It was all fun and games until someone's heart got broken.

Or worse, until she found out exactly how good he was at keeping business and pleasure separate. A little thing like corporate espionage wasn't supposed to get between them while they were burning up the sheets.

Before she could argue the point, he skewered her with those gorgeous hazel eyes and she felt it all the way through her soul. He'd burrowed under her barriers, winding his way through her heart despite all her vows to refuse him entrance. At the end of the day, she was the problem here. Because against all odds, she *had* started to trust him in spite of it all. And she shouldn't have.

"You came when I needed you." He held her gaze and wouldn't let go. "And we fell into something that I was hoping would continue. I meant it when I said I wasn't ready for it to end."

The rawness in his voice sliced through her. She wanted to believe him. Believe *in* him. The past week had been so amazing and surprising and deep, and sex had only been a small part of that.

When had she lost her "it's only sex" mantra? When had this become a relationship and not just sticking to a man to learn his secrets?

Unfortunately, she could pinpoint it exactly. It had happened the moment she'd answered Gage's call and he'd said, *I need you.*

He'd ruined her for other men—Gage Branson was it for her. She realized that now.

And she had to know once and for all if she could trust him.

"Rebecca Moon," she blurted out and his expression darkened so rapidly that the rag fell from her suddenly numb fingers.

"Yeah, what about her?"

"So you admit you know who she is?" Cass squawked.

"Of course I do. She used to work for me," he acknowledged without a scrap of shame. "My company isn't so big that I've lost the ability to keep track of my people. Especially those who worked in Research and Development."

"Used to work for you?" she prodded. "But not anymore?"

Gage stood, unfurling to his full height a good three inches above Cass. He crossed his arms, leaning a hip against the bar casually, but his frame vibrated with tension.

"Since I'm pretty sure we both know she works for Fyra now, it sounds like you're the one who has something you need to tell me."

This was her opening. The other Fyra executives were counting on her to solve the company's problems and the last thing she wanted was for her team to accuse her of letting her feelings for Gage get in the way of justice. Alex, in particular, was already poised to lambast Cass. She had to pull this thread.

"I'm sure there's a rational explanation." She resisted the urge to back away. "But Rebecca's in a lot of debt and maintains contact with people in your area. You can see how someone might think that's a suspicious combination. It just looks bad, Gage."

"Bad how?" he asked softly. Lethally. "What exactly are you trying to say?"

The pressure of his accusatory expression pushed on her chest, stealing her ability to draw in air. He was going to make her spell this out. She swore. "Come on. You agreed to help me identify a probable suspect for the leak but have spent almost every second distracting me from that goal. Almost as if you wanted to steer me away from any evidence pointing to a name."

Of course she was the dummy who'd fallen for it. Half of the fault lay with her.

"You seem to forget that I had an interest in finding the leak, as well. The formula is worthless otherwise."

She waved it off. "Only if you don't have another way to get your hands on it."

"Cass." He huffed out a sigh of frustration. "We agreed you'd talk to the others about selling when we found the leak. We haven't yet. What other possible way would I get my hands on it?"

Did he think she was born yesterday? "Turnabout is fair play, right? That's what you said when you demanded I sell you the formula less than twenty-four hours after its existence was leaked to the industry. Tell me the timing is a coincidence."

"It's a coincidence." His knuckles went white as he contemplated her with clenched fists. "But you don't really think so, do you? You suspect that Rebecca's the leak and I'm pulling her strings like some kind of corporate raider puppet master. You think I've paid her to steal the formula."

"Well…in a nutshell, yeah." It didn't sound so concrete

coming from Gage's mouth and she wavered. He didn't look guilty. He looked furious. "Are you denying it?"

"Hell, yes." A muttered expletive accompanied the declaration. "Though why I have to is the real question here."

Instantly, her hackles rose. Was he that out of touch? "Really? It's confusing to you why I might have a problem trusting you?"

Obviously, he didn't see anything wrong with being there for her and giving her a place to get away from all the pressures of life, being understanding and strong and wonderful…and then taking it away at a moment's notice. Like he had the first time. "You dumped me in college like yesterday's trash with *no explanation*. I can't—"

She shouldn't have brought that up. Not now.

"No explanation?" He stared at her, his expression darkening. "Our relationship is one of my fondest memories, or I wouldn't have rekindled it. But it ended at the right time, once it had run its course. We talked about it. That's what I said."

"Oh, you said that all right. But you might as well have said, 'It's not you, it's me.' Either way, it's a lame line designed to brush off the person you're tired of." All of this had been bottled up for far too long. It came rushing out—the formula and the baby and *let's see how it goes* all muddled together into a big emotional mess she couldn't control. "Surely you didn't think it was an actual reason."

He'd broken her and she wasn't letting him do it again. Not personally. Not professionally.

"Wait just a minute." He threw up a hand as if to ward off the barrage of words. "We had a lot of fun in college. But that's all it was—fun. Are you saying you expected an opportunity to talk me out of it when I said it was time to move on?"

"No," she countered. "I expected that you'd figure out

you loved me as much I loved you and ask me to marry you."

She'd thrown up wall after wall to prevent a repeat of those feelings. Unsuccessfully. Because at the end of the day, that was still what she wanted.

And she knew now it was an impossible dream.

"Marriage?" The pattern of Cass's granite counter-tops blurred as Gage processed that bombshell on top of the Rebecca Moon accusation. "You wanted to get married? To *me*?"

Of all the things he'd thought about their time together, her in a white dress and diamond rings and…other to-gether-forever stuff that he couldn't even fathom right now—none of that had ever crossed his mind. None of that had ever crossed his mind with *anyone*, let alone back in college when he'd just begun to spread his wings.

He'd vowed to himself, and to Nicolas, to have the quintessential college experience—drink a lot of beer, sleep with a lot of women, have a lot of esoteric conver-sations at coffee houses with foreign exchange students. No one got *married* in college.

He and Cass had totally different viewpoints on their history. How was he only discovering this now? *And* in the midst of a conversation where apparently, he was being accused of planting an employee at Cass's company. His temper simmered again, which was not a good sign. He never got angry. Mostly because he never had much of an emotional investment.

Looked as if he was going to experience yet another first with Cass.

"I guess this is news to you," she said and her voice broke.

There were no tears, no hard lines around her mouth,

but he could tell she was upset about their relationship ending. *Still* upset. The bitterness radiated from her and he caught it in the gut.

"Completely. Jeez, Cass. We were kids with our whole lives—our whole careers—ahead of us."

But that wasn't true now. If that was what she'd wanted then, what had she wanted this time around? The same? While he was trying to reconcile and explore these new, unprecedented feelings she'd evoked, had she been waiting for a proposal? The thought put his chest into a deep freeze and none of the beating and breathing that should have been going on inside was working.

She crossed her arms over her abdomen as if to protect herself. From him. "So what's different this time that makes you say things like *let's see how it goes*? Am I suddenly more palatable now that I have power and money? Or is my allure strictly related to your bottom line?"

His anger mounted. How dare she accuse him of not only consorting with a former employee to steal from Fyra but then playing other angles, too. As though he'd faked his attraction and feelings for Cass strictly because of her formula?

"My offer to buy your formula is legitimate and legal. And I didn't bring up extending our affair because of it," he told her truthfully.

Maybe the affair had started as a way to make sure the odds fell in his favor. But that had changed a long time ago. She had their relationship all wrong—the first one and the second one—and somehow he was the bad guy in all of this. As though she'd had expectations of him that he'd stomped all over and God forbid he be given a second chance.

"Then why?" she pushed, her expression darkening

more with each passing second. "Why keep seeing each other? Why not end it like you always do?"

Because…he had all these feelings he didn't know what to do with. Because he liked being around her. Because he couldn't imagine saying goodbye.

But all at once, he couldn't spit that out. Heaviness weighed down his chest. If they didn't say goodbye, what then? He wasn't marriage material.

"Yeah, that's what I thought," she said derisively when he didn't answer her. "You haven't changed. You're another broken heart waiting to happen."

Another broken heart? Something snapped inside.

All this time… Cass had been in love with him. And he'd broken her heart because he'd ended their relationship, despite never making any promises. No wonder she'd been so frosty and uptight at first. Obviously, their past had colored her agenda and explained why he could never put his finger on what she was up to. Why he could never find his balance with her.

"Are you still in love with me?" he demanded.

She laughed but it sounded forced and hollow. "Boy, someone sure packed their industrial-sized ego for this trip down memory lane. What do you think?"

That cool exterior was a front, one she did better than he'd credited, but he knew the Cass underneath it. Very well.

Sarcasm meant he'd hit a nerve.

"I think you didn't deny it." Eyes narrowed, he evaluated her.

Of course, that question would remain unanswered because, at the end of the day, she didn't trust him. And he was still angry about it. The unfounded accusations about Rebecca Moon still stuck in his craw and he was having a hard time getting them loose. "I guess I should have ended things. Especially if you're convinced I'm out to steal from you."

"It doesn't matter," she cut in swiftly. "We both know your interest in me starts and ends with my formula. So I'll make it easy for you. This...whatever it is...is over."

So that was it? Because of how things had ended between them the first time, she chose to believe that he was involved in the leak and didn't have any intention of listening to him. She was operating under a decade-old hurt and refused to give him an opportunity to explore what he wanted this time. That was crap and he was calling her on it.

"What if I asked you to extend our relationship because I want to see what happens when we don't end things right away? It's totally unfair of you to say *adios* when I'm genuinely trying to figure this out. Almost as unfair as accusing me of being involved in the leak with literally no proof."

She stared at him, her eyes huge and troubled. "Yeah, well turnabout is fair play, Gage. Spend the next decade thinking about *that*."

Thirteen

Gage drove back to Austin, his mind a furious blur. Cass had found the ultimate way to get him back for breaking her heart—by accusing him of betraying her.

Turnabout is fair play.

If it had happened to anyone else, he'd have appreciated the irony.

As it was, his chest ached with unprocessed emotions. If it wasn't for the layer of mad, he might understand what had just happened. But he couldn't get the heaviness in his chest to ease or the anger to abate. She hadn't believed him when he said he wasn't involved. Because she didn't trust him.

In Cass's mind, he was guilty simply because he hadn't fallen to one knee and declared undying love. Stealing a competitor's secrets was apparently as much a crime to her as not proposing. It was ridiculous. He cared about Cass. Of course he did. Who suggested they keep seeing each other? *Gage*. Who had called Cass when he'd been at his absolute lowest? Still him. Didn't she get that he'd been falling for her all along and had kind of freaked out about it?

Obviously not.

He'd given as best as he knew how. And his best wasn't good enough.

Fine. That was the way it should be, anyway. Clearly this relationship business wasn't for him. But what if that meant he couldn't be a father either? What if he was completely flawed in some way?

Gage spent the remainder of the drive home nursing his wounds and then drowned them in a quarter of a bottle of Jack Daniel's. He tried to go to bed, where it smelled like Cass and everything good and hopeful in his life, and that was the breaking point.

He vaulted out of bed, scaring the bejesus out of Arwen, who was enjoying the rare treat of sleeping at Gage's feet. Head cocked at a curious angle, she watched him throw on jeans but elected to stay put when Gage stormed from the room.

Twisting open the whiskey again, he got started on what was probably a vain attempt to drink enough to forget the stricken look on Cass's face when she'd said *this is over*.

He'd hurt her. He got that. But it had happened a long time ago. This was all on her and her inability to forgive and forget. There was no reason for Gage to reevaluate anything, yet here he was, doing it anyway.

He groaned and let his head fall into his hands. Who was he kidding? He'd screwed up, too.

Whether it was fair, whether he'd made mistakes with Cass due to his unquenchable desire to best his competition, whether Robbie made his life unduly complicated—

none of that mattered. He'd lost something precious and he missed her. Cass should be in his arms at this moment and she wasn't and it sucked.

Before he dissolved into an unmanly puddle of regret, he palmed his phone and flicked through pictures of Robbie. The boy's face was so reminiscent of Gage's brother, it was almost eerie. Genetics. That's all it was, not a message from beyond the grave.

He's going to be a handful.

Gage smiled. Yeah, his son was pretty great. What did Nicolas know about kids, anyway? It was a sobering thought. His brother had guided him for so long. Who would be the voice of his conscience now that Gage was moving toward something new and different?

You'll figure it out. After all, you already know what not *to do.*

He definitely knew that. Gage would raise Robbie with no boundaries. Carpe diem and full speed ahead, unlike how his own parents had raised him. If Robbie wanted to run with scissors, Gage would put plastic tips on the sharp ends and lead the way. If Robbie wanted to climb trees—or mountains—Gage would be behind him every step, ready to catch him when he fell.

He'd say yes to every "Hey, Dad, can I…?"

Mom and Dad didn't put restrictions on you to keep you from having fun.

Yeah, he knew that. They loved Gage, fiercely, even to this day, despite their disappointment that none of Gage's childhood limitations had resulted in a son who played it safe. He lived his life unapologetically, reveling in all the experiences Nicolas couldn't.

Like falling in love?

Gage drained the highball and flipped it over instead of

refilling it like he wanted to. When his conscience came up with gems like that, it was time to lay off the sauce.

Except the thought wouldn't go away.

For his entire adult life, he'd avoided anything that smacked of permanence. Even with Cass, who made him feel alive and amazing and as though he wanted to be around her all the time. He couldn't just come out and commit. Why?

Because he feared losing someone who mattered—like his parents had. God, why hadn't he ever realized that? With Robbie, it had been easy. There hadn't even been a choice in his mind. But he had control over whether he committed to Cass and he'd exercised it by walking out the door instead of fighting for what he wanted.

You live life to the extreme but it costs you. You have no personal relationships. No one to lean on. What are you going to do when parenting gets hard?

Gage frowned. His parents were moving here. His mom would give him advice.

The same woman you just vowed not to emulate when raising your son? Good thinking. Besides, don't you want someone to be there for you who gets you? Who's your equal? Someone you can count on and vice versa?

"Shut up, already. I get it," he muttered. "I messed up with Cass and instead of figuring out how to fix it, I'm sitting here arguing with a ghost."

But was it even possible to fix it? Cass's frozen routine was a safeguard against *him*, after all. He'd started their relationship solely with the intent of leveraging their attraction to get his hands on her formula, and she was forcing him to reap what he'd sown. Which was no less than he deserved. The rift between them was as much his fault as hers.

He'd wanted something more and had been too chicken

to lay it all on the line, disguising his thirst for Cass as a drive to beat the competition.

And by the way…if you've never done permanent, never been in love, never figured out how to sacrifice and be selfless, you know being a father will be that much harder.

His chest squeezed again. Nicolas was right. Gage's closest companions were Arwen and his conscience disguised as his long-gone brother. He had no idea how to do relationships. And he needed to. Gage couldn't be a good father if he flitted between commitment and freedom. He'd already realized that but now he knew how to fix it.

He had to learn how to stick. He *wanted* to. Cass and Robbie were both worth it.

Somehow, he had to prove to Cass that she could trust him this time. That he wasn't responsible for the leak.

He wanted Cassandra Claremont in his life, living it alongside him, giving him the ultimate experience he'd yet to have.

But as difficult as it was to admit, Gage had no basis for figuring out what it took to be a good partner or a good father. He'd never had a relationship before—with *anyone*, his family, a lover…what was different this time? What could he offer Cass to convince her to give him one last chance?

After a long night of tossing and turning, Gage sat up in bed as the perfect answer came to him.

Phillip Edgewood.

Cass frowned as she listened to the detective spout more rhetoric about how the investigation was ongoing, nothing concrete to report, blah, blah. She switched her phone to the other ear but the news didn't get any better.

At the end of the day, Rebecca Moon either wasn't the culprit or she had been very, very savvy about her movements over the past few weeks. Nothing pointed to the woman as the source of the leak, nothing pointed to a link between her and Gage, and Cass was tired of beating her head against this wall.

She was even more tired of missing Gage and wondering why she was beating her head against that wall, too. The man wasn't interested in a relationship—which she'd known from day one. She'd done everything in her power to keep her emotions out of it, trying to convince herself she was sticking to him like glue so she could keep tabs on him.

It hadn't worked. She'd fallen in love with him all over again thanks to those quiet moments when he was the man she longed for, who believed in her but didn't care if she wasn't strong and capable 24/7, who'd demonstrated his ability to commit to his son.

None of that mattered. She couldn't trust him and that meant they were through. Forever.

That hole in her heart? It was there for good.

It almost would have been better to find evidence that Gage had been the one whispering in Rebecca's ear. At least then Cass could hate him for being a sleaze. Instead, she'd had to cut ties because, after it was all said and done, he only cared about the formula. When she'd told Gage it was over, he hadn't argued. Because he knew he'd end things eventually, so why not now?

A knock on her open door dragged her attention away from the detective's disappointing phone call and the regret burning in her chest. Alex stood in the doorway. Cass waved in the CFO and held up one finger in the universal "give me a minute" gesture as she told the detective to keep digging.

Alex sauntered into her office, but Cass could tell this wasn't a friendly visit.

"We need to talk," Alex said before Cass had even set the phone on her desk. "The prelim quarterly numbers are not looking good."

Cass bit back the groan. When it rained, it poured. "And now you're going to tell me they're down due to the leak, right?"

The hard line of Alex's mouth didn't bode well. "I don't think we can directly pin it on that. But it's clear we've got a problem, and not having that breach buttoned up isn't helping."

The accusation of fault hadn't been verbalized but it came through loud and clear. This was all on Cass and Alex wasn't pulling any punches. As the CEO, the buck stopped at Cass's chair and she should have found the leak's name long ago.

Helplessness welled up and nearly overflowed into her expression.

Push it back. Her throat was already so raw from watching Gage walk out of her life that she hadn't thought it could get much worse. Turned out she was wrong.

"I'm working on it," she said smoothly. Or what she thought would pass for smooth, but Alex scowled instead of lightening up.

"You've been saying that for weeks. I'm starting to wonder whether you've got a secret agenda you've failed to share with me."

Oh, God. She'd landed in turnabout hell. This was shaping up to be a redo of the conversation she'd had with Gage last week, except she was the one in the hot seat.

Being accused by *Alex*, who had been Cass's friend for years and years. They'd suffered through exams together in college, through Alex's man troubles, and of course, Cass's singular experience with Gage. Later, she and Alex had worked around the clock together, poring over financial statements for places to cut and bonding through the difficulties of starting a brand-new company.

Except Alex was in Cass's office in her capacity as one-quarter owner of that company. It was her right to call Cass onto the carpet. But she did not have the right to make this about something other than Cass's inability to do her job.

"I don't have a secret agenda. Don't be ridiculous."

"Why are you always so dismissive of me?" Alex's unmanicured fingernails drummed against her leg in a restless pattern as she stared at Cass with a small frown. "I run this company alongside you, not beneath you."

Confused, Cass shook her head slightly.

There was more here than a reproach about Cass's performance on the job. This was personal. She did not get the lack of trust and animosity wafting in her direction. It wasn't as though she'd done something horrible to her friend that would make all of this justified. Not like what Gage had done to Cass, for example.

"What are you talking about?" Cass asked. "I'm not dismissing you. I—"

A brisk knock at the door cut off the rest and Cass glanced up sharply to see Melinda, Fyra's receptionist, hovering in the hall outside her office, practically wringing her hands.

"Sorry to interrupt." Melinda's eyes were so wide, it was a wonder they didn't fall out of her head. "But not really. You've got a visitor and, well, he's not the kind of person you make wait around. Besides, I'm afraid he's disrupted the entire office and I thought—"

"Who's the visitor?" Cass asked as patiently as possible.

The timing was the worst and whoever it was could wait. She wanted to get to the bottom of what was going on with Alex, once and for all.

"Phillip Edgewood," Melinda blurted out. There might have even been swooning. "*The* Phillip Edgewood. The *senator,*" she stage-whispered in case Alex and Cass lived under a rock and might not know the popular United States senator. "He's even dreamier in person than he is on TV. Oh, and Mr. Branson is with him."

Cass stood so fast, her chair shot across the low-pile carpet and crashed into the wall. "You could have told me that first. Send him back right away."

A compact. There was a compact around here some-where. Pulse thundering, Cass fished blindly through her desk drawer, fingers closing around three lipstick tubes, a bottle of Fyrago perfume and then a foundation brush before she finally located the powder case. She flicked it open and used the mirror to slick on a fresh layer of lip-stick, which predictably went on crooked because of how badly her hand was shaking.

Gage was here. In this building. He'd come to apolo-gize, to throw himself at her feet. To declare his undy-ing love...

Now *she* was the one being ridiculous. Her heart de-flated. Gage wouldn't have shown up after a week of radio silence with a US Senator in tow if he was here to step back into her life. He was here about the formula.

Business. Of course. The man separated business and pleasure like a pro.

"Hot date?" Alex asked wryly and Cass peeked over the compact.

God, she'd forgotten all about Alex and, lucky girl, she was about to witness Cass's complete breakdown.

"Actually, Gage and I aren't seeing each other any-more. We —"

He swept into the room and she forgot to breathe. The sharp, dark navy suit he wore would make an Italian tailor weep. His too-long hair was somewhat tamed and smoothed back, leaving his gorgeous face the focal point it should be.

She scarcely noticed the handsome dark-haired man at his elbow. Because next to Gage, Phillip Edgewood might as well have been invisible.

"Ms. Meer." Gage nodded to Alex as she rose. "This is my cousin, Phillip Edgewood. Phillip, Alexandra Meer, Fyra's chief financial officer."

The CFO and the senator shook hands politely, exchanging pleasantries while Cass shot Gage a look and hissed under her breath, "Senator Edgewood is your *cousin*? Since when?"

"Since I was born?" he suggested mildly. "His mother and my mother have been sisters for almost sixty years."

"You never mentioned that."

He shrugged, messing up the lines of his gorgeous suit, which was a shame. "I never mentioned a lot of things. Which, not so coincidentally, is why I'm here."

With that cryptic comment hanging in the middle of everything, Gage repeated the introductions between Cass and Phillip and swung his attention back to Cass. "Phillip has graciously agreed to help Fyra navigate the FDA process required to get your formula to market. I came by with him today so you could meet him personally and get the ball rolling. Oh, and he'll also help you grease the wheels at the patent office. The sooner you get going, the sooner the leak will become a nonissue."

Cass's mouth fell open. "We're not—I mean…what?"

"That's amazing, Gage," Alex said, with a withering glance at Cass. To the senator, she said simply, "Thank you. We're honored to have such expert assistance."

"Yes, of course." Cass nodded woodenly, her faculties still scattered. "Thank you. We appreciate the assistance."

And now she sounded like a parrot instead of a savvy executive. Gage *still* fuzzled her mind.

The senator smiled at Alex, and it took over his entire body, as if he was lit from within. Charisma radiated from him like the corona around the sun. Cass started to get an inkling of what the fuss over him was all about.

"It's no problem," Phillip said, but he was looking at Alex as if Cass didn't exist. "Is there somewhere we can go to talk? And of course, we should include your chief science officer."

"Dr. Harper Livingston," Alex interjected, and the two of them were off, their conversation deep in the details.

Looked as if Alex was more than willing to stay in the senator's orbit, though he was hardly her type. They were a study in contrasts with Alex's face bare of cosmetics and clad in a gray shirt and jeans. Senator Edgewood wore Armani and power, and not necessarily in that order.

They excused themselves to Alex's office, leaving Gage and Cass staring at each other.

"What was that all about?" Cass demanded. "Waltzing in here with a US senator and throwing him at Fyra like some kind of peace offering."

"You say that like it's a bad thing." Gage shoved his hands in his pockets. "Does that mean it didn't work?"

"That's what it was?" A little stunned, Cass sank into her chair. She'd been about to grill him on his angle. Without reason apparently. "A peace offering?"

"Yeah. I needed an 'in,' in case you wouldn't see me otherwise. Phillip was my trump card." He grinned and she fought to keep from smiling back. Too many unanswered questions for that.

"But why did you ask him to work with us on the FDA process? If we file for approval, that's a pretty clear indication we're not going to sell it. To you or anyone."

"That's why I did it. I don't want your formula anymore, but this seemed like the only way you'd believe me. Now it's not a factor between us." He took her hand and held it without making any other move, but that alone connected them. "I owe you, and turnabout is fair play."

"You owe *me*?" She shook her head, still dazed. "You've got that backward. You've been quite clear that it's the other way around."

"That was before I fell in love with you."

Her breath caught and she drank in the emotion spilling from his gaze. Love. Tenderness. All of the things she'd witnessed in his expression when he looked at his son. The same emotion she'd dreamed of seeing directed at her. And now it was.

Shell-shocked, she stared at him. "I...what?"

"Oh, am I stuttering again? Let me start over."

He swept her into his arms and laid his lips on hers, infusing his warmth into her dark and frozen soul. Everything thawed instantly, blooming under his talented mouth as he kissed her senseless. All of her feelings for this man surged to the surface, spilling out of her heart in an endless flow. He was in love with her, and all of the sharp, painful places inside smoothed out as she united with him, body and soul.

No. No, no, no. She wiggled away, breathless and still fuzzled because, *oh my God*, she wanted to dive back in and forget the past miserable week had happened. But it *had* happened.

"When did you decide this?" she demanded, but he just grinned and yanked her back into his embrace.

"For such a smart lady, you're being very slow to catch on," he murmured into her ear. "I'm not letting you go again. So you might as well forget about throwing up your walls. I'll keep knocking them down until you admit you're in love with me, too."

"Why would I do that?" She scowled but he just kissed the line between her brows.

"Because I'm sticking around this time. Forever," he promised and crossed his heart, catching her gaze. The depths of sincerity in his expression put a slow tingle in her midsection. "And I'd like to know up front where we stand. No seeing how it goes. No agendas. Just two people in it for the long haul."

"That's not what you want." Eyeing him suspiciously, she tried to cross her arms, but he wouldn't loosen his grip on her waist enough to give her room. "You want the formula, not me. So what exactly is all this Gage-speak supposed to mean?"

He pursed his lips and contemplated her. "Here's the thing. I haven't given you any reason to trust me. So I've spent the past week convincing Phillip to clear his schedule, and then I cleared mine. Because I want you to go to market with your formula so we can compete head-to-head. May the best CEO win."

That sounded more like Gage. There was a gotcha in there somewhere. A yet-to-be-named angle she couldn't see. "Now you're just talking crazy."

"No, I'm finally sane, thanks to you." Tenderly, he tucked a chunk of hair behind her ear. "You *have* moved past my mentorship. Far past. And turnabout is fair play. Show me what you've learned since then. I fully expect you to win."

It was as if he'd opened her heart and read the words she'd longed for him to say like a script. Where was this stuff coming from? Because if he kept going, she was going to completely lose all her safeguards against a bad decision.

But it was far, far too late for that. She'd been sliding toward Gage since the moment she'd recognized him in the parking lot of her building.

"Oh, I see." She didn't. But she had to keep fishing. His real agenda was buried in these well-delivered lines somewhere. "You've given up your bid for the formula and forgiven the debt you've claimed I owe you. Out of the goodness of your heart."

"That debt never existed." His small smile wiped the one from her face. "In fact, I owe you. Because I didn't know I had such a bad habit of turning a blind eye to what was happening around me. Briana had a baby without me cluing in. You were in love with me and I didn't know. You didn't tell me because I was too busy pushing you away. And then when you did tell me, I handled everything wrong. I should have admitted I was falling for you then. But instead, I clung to my freedom, not realizing it was meaningless. I'm a serial idiot."

This couldn't be real. All her dreams of being with Gage forever were not on the brink of coming true. Her life was not a fairy tale and he was not the guy he was claiming to be.

"So you've climbed aboard the commitment train?" She shook her head. "I'm sorry, Gage, but I can't buy that."

"Then you're going to feel very silly once I do this."

He pulled a small box from his jacket pocket and flipped the hinged lid to reveal something that might look like a diamond ring to someone whose vision wasn't instantly blurry with tears.

His arm dropped from her waist and he pulled the band from its velvet nest to slide it on her finger. "That's the sound of the conductor yelling 'All aboard.' I love you and I want to marry you."

She went a little lightheaded. "You know that if the

senator is helping us get the formula to market, marrying me won't get you access to it, right?"

Gage just smiled. "No agendas here. Mine *or* yours. You know if you marry me, you have to trust me. No more dates where you pump me for information, or sleepover games designed to figure out my angle. When you have questions, we have to talk about things like rational adults. And when we spend time together, it'll be because we can't be apart."

Guilt crushed through her chest. "Did you know the whole time?"

"No. I figured out later that all the strange questions were because you suspected I was involved in the leak from the very beginning. It's okay. I realized why you thought that was necessary. I hadn't given you any reason to trust me, which I hope I'm fixing right now."

Finally, it started to sink in. He'd taken soul-searching to a whole other plane. And somehow figured out how to claim her heart in the process with a simple thing like forgiveness. She'd held him at arm's length, convinced he would break her heart, when instead he'd offered his up with no strings attached.

She shoved back the flood of emotion for a second time. Or was it a third? She'd lost count because he'd done exactly what he'd predicted he would—knocked down her barriers against him.

"No agenda," she repeated dumbly. "Then why *marriage*? You could hardly say the word the last time this came up."

He took that with surprising grace and nodded. "I've spent years running from anything that smacked of commitment under the guise of living life to the fullest and experiencing new heights. I've done it all, except one thing. You're my ultimate experience, Cass. Just you. Everything feels better when I'm with you. Why would I keep running from that?"

"Because you're a serial idiot?" she choked out, and he laughed, pulling one from her, as well.

That was the benefit of falling in love with a man like Gage. She was botching up his marriage proposal and he still managed to pull it off.

"I am a serial idiot. I hope that means we're a perfect match," he said, his voice clogged with emotion she'd never heard before. "Because it would be dumb of you to take a chance on me. I'm going to immediately drop a baby in your lap. That's a lot to ask. I get that. But if you hand me that ring back, I'm only going to keep coming around until you say yes."

It was real. The man she loved had just asked her to marry him. She curled her hand around the ring, holding it tight against her palm. "The best thing about us is that we're equals. Guess that means I'm a serial idiot, too, because I never fell out of love with you."

Yes, clearly she'd gone mad because she never would have imagined admitting that in a million years. Never imagined being a mother. Never imagined she'd be this happy.

Strangely, Gage becoming a father had been the tipping point. She could trust that he'd stick around this time because she'd seen what he was capable of with Robbie. What it looked like when he loved someone. She knew it was possible and could finally believe it was happening to her.

A smile split his face and when he kissed her, he nearly split her heart, as well. Good thing. All the emotion inside was too big to be contained in that little bitty organ. Looked like she was getting her happily-ever-after.

Epilogue

Phillip Edgewood threw a hell of party. His status as one of the nation's most eligible bachelors coupled with his deep Texas roots afforded him a wide circle of acquaintances. Gage had never socialized with his cousin. Shame it had taken him so long to reach out to a man he'd known since childhood. They'd had lunch a couple of times since that day Gage had shown up out of the blue to ask for help, and they might even be on the way to becoming friends.

But tonight, Gage only had eyes for his date. Cassandra Claremont put the Hollywood celebs, Texas oil royalty and glittery society wives in attendance at Phillip's fundraiser to shame.

And Gage had been apart from his fiancée for five long minutes. He crossed the crowded ballroom to the bar, where Cass laughed over something Alex had said. That was a welcome sight. Cass had mentioned she and Alex were at odds over Fyra's strategy and that Alex had been the main one speaking out against Cass's leadership.

Whatever had happened to cause the rift appeared to be repaired, which Gage knew was a load off Cass's mind.

"Ladies," he murmured as he came up behind the most gorgeous woman in the room, wrapping his arm around her.

He couldn't touch her enough. Sometimes he did it just to assure himself he hadn't invented this fantasy out of thin air. But every time he reached out, she reached back. Commitment had its perks. Lots of them.

"Alex, you look fantastic," he commented truthfully as Cass's arm circled his waist in kind. "Did you do something different?"

Cass smacked him playfully. "Spoken like a true man. Of course she did. It's a formal party and we spent two days getting ready for it."

The two women exchanged smiles and piqued Gage's interest. "Sounds like there's a story there."

He'd been privy to nothing as Cass had told him to butt out. Repeatedly.

"A boring one," Alex assured him with a careful nod, likely in deference to the gravity-defying swept-up hairdo that drew attention to her lovely face. "Cass volunteered to give me a makeover, that's all."

"That's all?" Cass squealed incredulously. To Gage, she said, "The woman works for a cosmetics company and never wears the stuff. So I taught her a few tricks and voilà."

Alex blushed becomingly. "It's not that I didn't want to wear makeup. But every time I did, I felt like I was trying too hard."

Phillip appeared at Alex's side, which was the most likely cause of her blush. They made a cute couple and Phillip deserved some happiness after the untimely death of his wife several years before. Of course, the senator and the CFO both brushed off their association as "working together" to secure Fyra's FDA approval. They weren't fooling anyone.

As their host whisked Alex off to the dance floor, Gage nestled his fiancée closer.

"So things are good between you now?" he asked.

Cass nodded. "Yeah. We had a heart-to-heart and she admitted she was feeling left out. I have a tendency to deal with issues on my own, and apparently that comes across as...cold."

Gage stuck his tongue in his cheek. "You don't say."

"No, really," she insisted, oblivious to Gage's sarcasm. "I was acting like the title of CEO meant I had to do it all with no help and as if letting anyone see that I was uncertain was like some big crime. I ended up confessing that to all the girls when I told them I hadn't found the leak and you weren't involved. It was a real turning point and now we're 100 percent united. I have you to thank for helping me learn that."

"Me?" That was a genuine surprise. "You're the one who's been mentoring me in how to do this long-term thing. What did I teach you?"

"That it's okay to use your head and your heart." She smiled. "In all things. I couldn't have fathomed becoming a mother otherwise."

Robbie had warmed to Cass instantly, so much so that his son cried inconsolably when Cass had to go back to Dallas on Sunday nights. It was only temporary until they could figure out the logistics of moving an entire company's headquarters. And until they finished arguing about whose company was doing the moving.

"I told you we're a perfect match," Gage insisted. "I don't know what took you so long to get wise to how good we are together."

Guess it turns out you can live life to the fullest with one woman, after all.

Gage smiled. Nicolas was right once again. Cass was the ultimate experience and he couldn't wait to get started on forever.

* * * * *

SNOWBOUND SURPRISE FOR THE BILLIONAIRE

MICHELLE DOUGLAS

To my Romance Authors' Google Group – thank you, ladies, for your wisdom, your support and your friendship.

CHAPTER ONE

ADDIE SAUNTERED DOWN to Bruce Augustus's pen, keeping her head high and her limbs loose while her lungs cramped and her eyes stung. There was probably no one watching her, but just in case.

She rounded the corner of the pen where the galvanised iron shelter finally hid her from the homestead. Pressing the back of her hand to her mouth, she swung herself over the fence, upturned the feed bin, collapsed down onto it and finally gave way to the sobs that raked through her.

The huge Hereford stud bull—ex-stud bull, he'd been retired for a few years now—nuzzled her ear. She leant forward, wrapped her arms around him and cried into his massive shoulder. He just stood there, nuzzling her and giving off animal warmth and a measure of comfort. Eventually though he snorted and stamped a foot and Addie knew it was time to pull herself together.

She eased away to rest back against the wooden palings behind and scrubbed her hands down her face. 'Sorry, Bruce Augustus, what a big cry baby you must think me.'

He lowered his head to her lap and she scratched her hands up his nose and around his ears the way he loved. He groaned and rocked into her slightly, but she wasn't afraid. He might be twelve hundred pounds of brute animal strength, but he'd never hurt her. They'd been hanging out since she was eight years old. She'd cried with him when her mother had died two years ago. She'd cried with him when her father had died four months ago.

And she'd cried with him when her best friend, Robbie, had died.

She closed her eyes. Her head dropped. Robbie.

Finally she'd thought she'd be free to keep her promise to Robbie, had practically tasted the freedom of it on her tongue. But no. Flynn Mather in his perfect suit and with his perfectly cool—some might say cold—business manner had just presented his contract to them all. A contract with an insidious heartbreaking condition.

She stood and turned to survey the fields that rolled away in front of her, at the ranges way off to her right, and at the stands of ancient gum trees. She propped her arms on the fence and rested her chin on them. In early December in the Central West Tablelands of New South Wales, the grass was golden, the sky was an unending blue and the sun was fierce. She dashed away the perspiration that pricked her brow. 'How long do you think Robbie would've given me to fulfil my promise, Bruce Augustus?'

Of course he didn't answer.

She made herself smile—might as well practise out here where no one could see her. 'The good news is we've found a buyer for Lorna Lee's.'

A sigh juddered out of her. She and two of her neighbours had joined forces to sell their properties as a job lot. Frank and Jeannie were well past retirement age, while Eric and Lucy were spending so much time in Sydney for four-year-old Colin's treatment their place was in danger of falling into wrack and ruin. Addie and her father had helped out all they could, but when her father had died it was all Addie could do to keep on top of things here at Lorna Lee's. One person really did make that much of a difference. And when that person was gone…

She stared up at the sky and breathed deeply. No more

crying today. Besides, she'd already cried buckets for her father.

She leant a shoulder against Bruce's bulk. 'So our gamble paid off.' Putting the three properties together for sale had made it a more attractive venture for at least one buyer. Flynn Mather. 'Your new owner is a hotshot businessman. He also has a cattle station in Queensland Channel country—huge apparently.'

Bruce Augustus snorted.

'Don't be like that. He knows his stuff. Says he wants to diversify his portfolio.' She snorted then too. Who actually spoke like that? 'And he plans to expand the breeding programme here.' She practised another smile. 'That's good news, huh?'

The bull merely swished his tail, dislodging several enormous horseflies.

'We have a buyer. I should be over the moon.' She gripped the wooden paling until her knuckles turned white. 'But you know what I'd really like to do?' She glared at gorgeous golden fields. 'I'd like to take that contract and tell him to shove it where the sun don't shine.'

Bruce Augustus shook his head, dislodging the horse flies from his face. Addie grabbed the plastic swatter she'd hung on a nail by the fence and splattered both flies in one practised swat. Bruce Augustus didn't even flinch. 'That's what I'd like to do with Flynn Mather's contract.'

Two years! He'd demanded she stay here for *two whole years* to oversee the breeding programme and to train someone up. He'd made it a condition of that rotten contract.

A well of something dark and suffocating rose inside her. She swallowed. 'That means spending Christmas here.' She straightened and scowled. 'No way! I'm not some indentured servant. I'm allowed to leave. I'm *not* spending Christmas on the farm!'

The anger drained out of her. She collapsed back onto

the feed bin. 'How am I going to stand it, Bruce? How am I going to cope with two more years in this godforsaken place, treading water while everyone else gets to live their dreams? When am I going to be allowed to follow my dreams?'

Robbie hadn't lived her dreams. She'd died before her time. Leukaemia. But Addie had promised to live them for her. Dreams of travel. Dreams of adventure in exotic lands. They'd marked out routes on maps, made lists of must-see places, had kept records of not-to-be missed sights. They'd planned out in minute detail how they'd office temp in London, work the ski lifts in Switzerland and be barmaids in German beer halls. They'd teach English as a second language in Japan and save enough money to go trekking in Nepal. They'd even taken French and Japanese in high school as preparation. Robbie had become too sick to finish her studies, but on her better days Addie had done what she could to catch her up with the French—Robbie's favourite.

But now...

But now Robbie was dead and Addie was stuck on the farm for another two years.

She dropped her head to her hands. 'You know what I'm afraid of, Bruce Augustus? That I'll never leave this place, that I'll get trapped here, and that I won't even have one adventure. I'm scared that I'll get so lonely Aaron Frey will wear me down and before I know it I'll find myself married with four kids and hating my life.' And if that proved the case then Robbie should've been the one to live. Not her.

She glared at a bale of straw. 'All I want is to see the world. Other than you, Bruce Augustus, there's nothing I'll miss from this place.' Not now that her parents were dead. 'Of course I'd come back to see you, and Molly Margaret and Roger Claudius and Donald Erasmus too. Goes without saying.'

She tried to battle the weariness that descended over her, the depression that had hovered over her since her father's death.

'If it were just me I'd tell Mather to take a hike, but it isn't just me.' She stood and dusted off her hands. Jeannie and Frank deserved to retire in comfort and ease. Little Colin with Down's syndrome and all the associated health challenges that presented deserved a chance for as full a life as he could have, and his parents deserved the chance to focus on him without the worries of a farm plaguing them.

'You're right, Bruce. It's time to time stop whining and suck it up.' She couldn't turn Flynn Mather away. Given the current economic climate there were no guarantees another buyer could be found—certainly not one willing to pay the asking price. Flynn hadn't quibbled over that.

She let out a long slow breath. 'The pity party's over. I have a contract to sign.' She kissed Bruce Augustus's nose, vaulted the fence and set off towards the main house—chin up and shoulders back, whistling as if she didn't have a care in the world.

Flynn watched Adelaide Ramsey saunter back towards the house. He rested his head against the corrugated iron of the shed and swore softly. Damn it all to hell!

Looking at her now, nobody would guess all she'd confided to her bull.

He moved around to glance in the pen. The bull eyeballed him and his head lowered. 'Yeah, yeah, I'm the villain of the piece.'

One ear flicked forward. 'The problem is, Bruce Augustus—' What a name! '—I have plans for this place, big plans, and your mistress knows her stuff. She knows this place better than anyone on the planet.' Her expertise would be key to his success here.

The bull snorted and Flynn shook his head. 'I can't believe I'm talking to a bull.'

When am I going to be allowed to follow my dreams?

It had been a cry from the heart. His chest tightened as if in a vice. He couldn't afford to lose Addie and her expertise, but he didn't traffic in other people's misery either. He didn't want her to feel trapped here. He scratched a hand through his hair. Was there something he could offer her to soften her disappointment, something that would make her want to stay?

His phone rang and the bull's head reared back. Flynn knew enough about bulls to know it was time to beat a hasty retreat. He glanced at the caller ID as he moved away and lifted the phone to his ear with a grim smile, turning his steps towards the Ramsey homestead—his homestead once she signed the contract.

'Hans, hello,' he said to the lawyer.

'Good news, Herr Mather. The will is due to go through probate in two weeks' time. After that the premises you're interested in will go on the market and you can bid for them.'

His heart beat hard. His smile turned grimmer. 'Excellent news.'

'I take it you will be in Munich for Christmas?'

'Correct.'

I'm not spending Christmas on the farm!

Flynn straightened. 'We'll confer again soon.'

All I want is to see the world?

He snapped his cell phone shut and vaulted up the stairs to the veranda. Voices emerged from the front room.

'Look, lass, we know you want to leave this place too. We can wait to see if another buyer shows interest.'

'Don't be silly, Frank.' That was Adelaide. He recognised the low, rich tones of her voice. 'Who knows if another buyer could be found, let alone when?'

'Lucy, Colin and I need to leave as soon as it can be arranged. I know that sounds hard and I'm sorry, but...'

That was Eric Seymour. Flynn didn't like the other man, but then he didn't have a seriously ill child in need of surgery either. In the same circumstances he'd probably be just as ruthless.

You are that ruthless.

He pushed that thought away.

Eric spoke again. 'If you decide to turn down Mather's offer, Addie, then I'm going to insist you buy out my farm like you once offered to. I can't wait any longer.'

The bank would lend her the necessary money. Flynn didn't doubt that for a moment. But it'd put her in debt up to her eyeballs.

'Don't get your knickers in a knot, Eric. I intend to sign the contract. All of us here understand your situation and we don't want to delay you a moment longer than necessary. We want the very best for Colin too. We're behind you a hundred per cent.'

'Lucy and I know that.'

'But, love,' Jeannie started.

Time to step in. Flynn strode across the veranda, making sure his footfalls echoed. He entered the front parlour. 'I'm sorry. I had a couple of business calls to make.'

Addie opened her mouth, but he continued before she could speak. 'I get the distinct impression, Ms Ramsey, that you're not exactly thrilled with the prospect of being bound to Lorna Lee's for the next two years?'

'Addie,' she said for what must've been the sixth time that day. 'Please call me Addie.' Although she tried to hide it, her eyes lit up in a way that had his heart beating hard. 'Have you changed your mind about that condition?'

'No.'

Her face fell.

His heart burned. 'Obviously the offer of a very generous salary package hasn't quite overcome your objections.'

'Oh, I...' She trailed off. She attempted what he suspected was a smile but it looked more like a grimace.

He held himself tall and taut. 'So I've been mulling over some other bonuses that you might find more tempting and will, therefore, lead you to signing the contract without hesitation.'

She glanced at her neighbours, opened her mouth and then closed it again. 'Oh?'

'I want to make it clear that you won't be confined here. It's not necessary that you spend the entirety of the next seven hundred and thirty days chained to the farm.'

Her shoulders sagged.

'You will be entitled to four weeks of annual leave a year. Would an annual business-class airfare to anywhere in the world, return of course, sweeten the deal for you? I will offer it for every year you work for me—whether that's the two years stipulated in the contract or longer if you decide to stay on.'

Her jaw dropped. Her eyes widened, and he suddenly realised they were the most startling shade of brown he'd ever seen—warm amber with copper highlights that flared as if embers in a hearth fire. He stared, caught up in trying to define their colour even more precisely as Frank, Jeannie and Eric all started talking over the top of each other. Addie's expression snapped closed as if the noise had brought her back to herself and he suddenly discovered he couldn't read her expression at all.

She laughed and clapped her hands, and he was suddenly reminded of the way she'd whistled as she'd walked away from Bruce Augustus's pen. 'Where do I sign? Mr Mather, you have yourself a deal.'

'Flynn,' he found himself saying. 'Call me Flynn.'

'I have another offer slash request to run past you as well.'

She blinked. How on earth hadn't he noticed those eyes earlier? 'Which is?'

'I have business in Munich later this month.'

'Munich? Munich in Germany?' She rubbed a hand against her chest as if to ease an ache there.

'The same. The business that calls me there is moving more quickly than originally anticipated so I find myself in a bit of a bind. I promised my PA that she could have several weeks' leave over Christmas, you see?'

'Your PA?' Addie said.

He could tell she only asked from politeness and had no idea where he was going with this. He straightened. 'Would you consider accompanying me to Munich and acting as my assistant for three or four weeks?'

Her jaw dropped.

She wanted to say yes; he could see that.

She hauled her jaw back into place. 'Why would you offer that position to me? I've never been a secretary before or even an office assistant.'

'You keep all of the farm's financial records. You put together the marketing and PR documents. You have a filing system that's in good order. I don't doubt you have the skills I need.' To be perfectly frank what he needed was a lackey, an offsider, someone who would jump to do his bidding when it was asked of them.

'Germany, love,' Jeannie breathed. 'What an adventure.'

Addie bit her lip and peered at him through narrowed eyes. 'I expect I'd be on call twenty-four seven?'

'Then you'd expect wrong. You'll have plenty of time for sightseeing.'

Why didn't she just say yes? Or wasn't she used to good fortune dropping into her lap? If she didn't want it there were at least five other people ready to jump at the chance to take her place.

'I do have an ulterior motive,' he said. 'I want to learn all I can about Lorna Lee's breeding programme. That means I'll be spending a significant amount of time here over the course of the next two years. Once I'm up to speed I'll know what changes to implement, where an injection of capital will be most beneficial…where to expand operations.'

She frowned. 'Changes?'

He almost laughed at her proprietorial tone. 'Changes,'

he repeated, keeping his voice firm. Once she signed the contract, and after the obligatory cooling-off period, the farm would be his. 'As we'll be working closely together over the next few months, Addie—' he used the diminutive of her Christian name deliberately '—the sooner we get to know each other, the better.'

She stared at him as if seeing him for the first time. 'You actually mean to be hands-on at Lorna Lee's?'

It wasn't his usual practice, but he'd taken one look at this property and a knot inside him had unravelled. Lorna Lee's might, in fact, become his home base. 'That's right.'

She shook herself. 'Okay, well, first things first. Let's deal with the contract.'

That suited him just fine. He added in a clause outlining her new bonus before scrawling his signature at the bottom and moving across to the other side of the room.

Eric signed first. Frank and Jeannie added their signatures next. Jeannie held the pen out to Addie. She cast her eyes around the room once before taking the pen and adding her signature in turn.

Deal done.

Eric slapped his hat to his head. 'I'm off to tell Lucy the good news. We plan to be gone just after Christmas.'

Both Frank and Addie nodded.

Jeannie patted Addie's arm. 'I'm overdue for my nanna nap, love. We'll see you later. Why don't you come over for dinner?'

'Okay, thanks.'

Everyone left and as soon as the door closed behind them Addie's shoulders slumped. Flynn swallowed, hoping she wasn't going to cry again. He cleared his throat and her chin shot up and her shoulders pushed back. She swung around to face him. 'You mentioned you wanted another tour of the property today too, right?'

He nodded. He'd specifically requested that she accompany him.

'Would you like that tour now or do you have more business calls to make?'

She glanced at the cell phone he held. He stowed it away. Before he'd heard what he had at Bruce Augustus's pen, he'd thought he had her pegged—a no-nonsense, competent country girl.

When am I going to be allowed to follow my dreams?

Other than a desire to see the world, what were her dreams?

He shook off the thought. Her dreams were none of his concern. All he wanted was to reconcile her to the contract she'd just signed. Once that was done she'd be a model employee. A problem solved. Then he could move forward with his plans for the place.

'Now would be good if that suits you. I'd like to get changed first, though.'

She directed him to a spare bedroom, where he pulled on jeans, a T-shirt and riding boots.

When he returned, Addie glanced around and then her jaw dropped.

He frowned. 'What?'

'I just…' She reddened. She dragged her gaze away. It returned a few seconds later. 'I know you have a station in Channel country and all, but…heck, Flynn. Now you look like someone who could put in an honest day's work.'

He stiffened. 'You don't believe honest work can be achieved in a suit?'

'Sure it can.' She didn't sound convinced. 'Just not the kind of work we do around here.'

Before he could quiz her further she led him out of the front door. 'As you probably recall from the deeds to the properties, the Seymour farm extends from the boundary fence to the right of Lorna Lee's while Frank and Jeannie's extends in a wedge shape behind.'

He nodded. The individual farms shared an access road from the highway that led into the township of Mudgee,

which was roughly twenty minutes away. There was another property to the eastern boundary of Lorna Lee's. If
it ever came onto the market he'd snap it up as well. But, at
the moment, all up, he'd just acquired seven hundred acres
of prime beef country.

'The three individual farmhouses are of a similar size.
I expect you'd like one of them as your home base if you
mean to spend a lot of time here. Which one should I organise for you?'

He blinked. At the moment she was certainly no-nonsense and practical. 'I want you to remain at the homestead
here. You're familiar with it and it'll only create an unnecessary distraction to move you from it. I'll base myself
at the Marsh place.' Frank and Jeannie's. It was closer to
Lorna Lee's than the Seymour homestead. 'Next year I'll
hire a foreman and a housekeeper—a husband and wife
team ideally, so keep your ear to the ground. They can
have the Seymour house. There are workers' quarters if
the need arises.'

He didn't want her to move out of her family home? Addie
couldn't have said why, but a knot of tension eased out of
her.

They talked business as they made their way over to
the massive machinery shed. There'd been an itemised account of all farm equipment attached to the contract, but
she went over it all again.

Because he wanted her to.

Because he was now her boss.

And because he'd held the promise of Munich out to her
like a treasure of epic proportions and it shimmered in her
mind like a mirage.

She glanced at his boots. 'Were you hoping to ride
around the property?'

'I'd appreciate it if that could be arranged.'

'Saddle up Banjo and Blossom,' she told Logan, her

lone farmhand. Correction. Flynn's farmhand. She swung to him, hands on hips. 'You're wearing riding boots and you own a cattle station. I'm assuming you know your way around a horse.'

The man finally smiled. She'd started to think he didn't know how, that he was a machine—all cold, clinical efficiency.

'You assume right.'

For no reason at all her heart started thundering in her chest. She had to swallow before she could speak. 'I gave you a comprehensive tour of Lorna Lee's two weeks ago and I know both Frank and Eric did the same at their places. You and your people went over it all with a fine-tooth comb.' What was he actually hoping she'd show him?

'We studied points of interest—dams, fences, sheds and equipment, irrigation systems—but nothing beats getting to know the layout of the land like riding it.'

Question answered.

She rubbed the nape of her neck and tried to get her breathing back under control. It was probably the release of tension from having finally signed, but Flynn looked different in jeans and boots. He looked... She rolled her shoulders. Hot. As in *adventure* hot.

She shook her head. Crazy thought. Who cared what he looked like? She just wanted him to look after the farm, develop it to its full potential, while hoping he wasn't an absolute tyrant to work for. All of those things trumped *hot* any day.

Logan brought out the steeds and Flynn moved to take the reins from him. She selected an Akubra from a peg—an old one of her father's that had her swallowing back a lump—and handed it to him, before slapping her own hat to her head. The afternoon had lengthened but the sun would still be warm.

She glanced at the two horses. She'd been going to take Blossom, but... She glanced back at Flynn.

He gazed back steadily. 'What?'

'What are you in the mood for? An easy, relaxed ride or—' she grinned '—something more challenging?'

'Addie, something you ought to know about me from the get go is that I'll always choose challenging.'

Right. 'Then Blossom is all yours.' She indicated the grey. 'I'll take Banjo.'

'Leg up?' he offered.

If it'd been Logan, she'd have accepted. If Flynn had been in his business suit she'd have probably accepted— just to test him. But the large maleness of him as he moved in closer, all of the muscled strength clearly outlined in jeans and T-shirt, had her baulking. 'No, thank you.'

She slipped her foot into the stirrup and swung herself up into the saddle. Before she could be snarky and ask if he'd like a leg up, he'd done the same. Effortlessly. The big grey danced but Flynn handled him with ease. Perfectly.

She bit back a sigh. She suspected Flynn was one of those people who did everything perfectly.

He raised an eyebrow. 'Pass muster?'

'You'll do,' she muttered, turning her horse and hoping the movement hid the flare of colour that heated her cheeks.

She led the way out of the home paddock and then finally looked at him again. 'What in particular would you like to see?' Was there a particular herd he wanted to look over, a particular stretch of watercourse or a landscape feature?

'To be perfectly frank, Addie, there's nothing in particular I want to see. I just want to be out amongst it.'

He was tired of being cooped up. *That* she could deal with. She pointed. 'See that stand of ironbarks on the low hill over there?'

'Uh-huh.'

'Wait for me there.'

He frowned. 'Wait?'

She nodded at his steed. 'In his current mood, Blossom

will leave Banjo in the dust.' And without another word she dug her heels into Banjo's sides and set off at a canter.

As predicted, within ten seconds Blossom—and Flynn—had overtaken them and pulled ahead. Addie didn't care. She gave herself up to the smooth easy motion of the canter, the cooling afternoon and the scent of sun-warmed grasses—all the gnarls inside her working themselves free.

'Better?' she asked when she reached Flynn again.

He slanted her a grin. 'How'd you know?'

'I start to feel exactly the same way when I'm cooped up for too long. There's nothing like a good gallop to ease the kinks.'

He stared at her for a long moment. She thought he meant to say something, but he evidently decided to keep it to himself.

'Munich,' she blurted out, unable to keep her thoughts in.

'What do you want to know?'

'What would my duties be?'

'A bit of office support—some word processing, accessing databases and spreadsheets, and setting up the odd meeting. If I want printing done, you'll be my go-to person. The hotel will have business facilities. There might be the odd letter to post.'

This was her and Robbie's dream job!

'But…' she bit her lip '…I don't know any German beyond *danke* and *guten Tag.*'

He raised an eyebrow. '*Auf wiedersehen?*'

Oh, right. She nodded. 'Goodbye.'

'Those phrases will serve you well enough. You'll find you won't need to know the language. Most Europeans speak perfect English.'

Wow. Still, if she did go she meant to bone up on as much conversational German as she could.

'You'll be doing a lot of fetching and carrying—Get me that file, Addie. Where's the Parker document, Addie?

Ring down for coffee, will you, Addie? Where're the most recent sales figures and costing sheets? Things like that.'

That she could do. She could major in fetching and carrying. 'When are you planning to leave?'

'In a week's time.'

Oh, wow!

He frowned. 'Do you have a passport?'

'Yes.' She'd had one since she was seventeen. Robbie had wanted one, and even though by that stage it had been pointless, Robbie's parents hadn't been able to deny her anything. She'd wanted Addie to have one too. Addie had kept it up to date ever since.

'Good. Now be warned, when we work the pace will be fast and furious, but there'll be days—lots of them, I expect—when we'll be twiddling our thumbs. Days when you'll be free to sightsee.'

It was every dream she'd ever dreamed.

She straightened, slowly, but she felt a reverberation through her entire being. There was more than one way to get off the farm. If she played this right...

'Naturally I'll cover your expenses—airfare and accommodation—along with a wage.'

A lump lodged in her throat.

'I meant what I said earlier, Addie. I want us to build a solid working relationship and I'm not the kind of man to put off the things I want. I don't see any reason why that working relationship can't start in Munich.'

If she did a great job for him, if she proved herself a brilliant personal assistant, then maybe Flynn would keep her on as his PA? She could live the life she'd always been meant to live—striding out in a suit and jet-setting around the world.

He stared at her. Eventually he pushed the brim of his hat back as if to view her all the more intently or clearly. 'Mind if I ask you something?'

'Sure.'

'Why haven't you said yes to Munich yet? I can tell you want to.'

She moistened her lips and glanced out at the horizon. 'Have you ever wanted something so badly that when you finally think it's yours you're afraid it's too good to be true?'

He was silent for a moment and then nodded. 'I know exactly how that feels.'

She believed him.

'All you have to do is say yes, Addie.'

So she said it. 'Yes.'

CHAPTER TWO

FLYNN GLANCED ACROSS at Addie, who'd started to droop. 'Are you okay?'

She shook herself upright. 'Yes, thank you.'

He raised an eyebrow.

She gritted her teeth and wriggled back in her seat. 'When can we get off this tin can?'

They'd arrived at Munich airport and were waiting for a gate to become vacant. They'd been on the ground and waiting for fifteen minutes, but he silently agreed with her. It felt more like an hour. 'Shortly, I expect, but I thought you were looking forward to flying?'

'I've flown now. It's ticked off my list,' she ground out, and then she stilled and turned those extraordinary eyes to him. 'Not that it hasn't been interesting, but I just didn't know that twenty-two hours could take so long.'

Addie's problem was that she'd been so excited when they'd first boarded the plane in Sydney she hadn't slept a wink on the nine-and-a-half-hour leg between there and Bangkok. She'd worn herself out so much—had become so overtired—that she'd been lucky to get two hours' sleep over the next twelve hours.

He suspected she wasn't used to the inactivity either. He thought back to the way they'd cantered across the fields at Lorna Lee's and shook his head. Overtired and climbing walls. He understood completely.

A steward's voice chimed through the sound system

telling them they were taxiing to Gate Twenty-eight and to remain in their seats. Addie blew out a breath that made him laugh. Within twenty minutes, however, they'd cleared Customs and were waiting by the luggage carousel. Addie eased forward in one lithe movement and hefted a bag from the carousel as if it were a bale of hay.

He widened his stance and frowned at her. 'If you'd pointed it out I'd have got it for you.'

She blinked at him. 'Why would you do that when I'm more than capable?'

A laugh escaped him. 'Because I'm the big strong man and you're the dainty personal assistant.'

One side of her mouth hooked up and her eyes danced. 'You didn't tell me dainty was part of the job description.' And then she moved forward, picked his suitcase off the carousel and set it at his feet.

'Addie!'

'Fetch and carry—that was part of the job description and that I can do.'

He folded his arms. 'How'd you know it was my case? It's standard black and nondescript.'

She pointed. 'With a blue and green tartan ribbon tied to the handle.'

She'd noticed that? 'Adelaide Ramsey, I have a feeling you're going to be a handy person to have around.'

'That's the plan.'

Was it? Her earnestness puzzled him.

And then she jumped on the spot. 'Can we go and see Munich now?'

All of her weariness had fled. Her back had straightened, her eyes had brightened and she glanced about with interest. He swallowed and led the way out of the airport to the taxi stand. 'It'll take about forty minutes by cab to reach Munich proper.'

'It's so cold!'

He turned to find Addie struggling to pull her coat from

her hand luggage and haul it on, her breath misting on the air. 'December in Munich,' he pointed out. 'It was always going to be cold.'

Teeth chattering, she nodded. 'I'm counting on snow.'

She spent the entire trip into the city with her face pressed to the window. Flynn spent most of the trip watching her. She gobbled up everything—the trees, the houses, the shops, the people.

She flinched as they passed a truck. 'It's so wrong driving on this side of the road.'

They drove on the left in Australia. In Germany it was the opposite. It took a bit of getting used to. As he watched her an ache he couldn't explain started up in his chest.

He rubbed a hand across it and forced his gaze away to stare out of his own window, but it didn't stop him from catching the tiny sounds she made—little gasps and tiny sighs that sounded like purrs. Each and every one of them pressed that ache deeper into him.

Maybe that was why, when the taxi deposited them at the front of their hotel, he snapped at her when she didn't follow after him at a trot, but stood glued to the footpath instead. He turned, rubbing a hand across his chest again. 'What are you doing?'

She glanced around as if memorising the buildings, the street and its layout. 'This is the very first time my feet have touched European ground.'

He opened his mouth to point out that technically that wasn't true.

'I want to fix it in my mind, relish the moment. I've dreamed of it for so long and I can hardly believe...'

He snapped his mouth shut again.

She suddenly stiffened, tossed him a glance, and before he knew what she was about she'd swung her hand luggage over her shoulder, seized both of their cases and was striding straight into the foyer of the hotel with them.

For pity's sake! He took off after her to find her enquiring, in perfect German no less, for a booking in the name of Mather.

The concierge smiled and welcomed her and double-checked the details of the booking.

Flynn moved up beside her. 'I didn't think you spoke German?' It came out like an accusation.

'I don't. I learned that phrase specifically.'

'For goodness' sake, why?'

'I thought it might come in handy, and to be polite, but...' She swallowed and turned back to the concierge and glanced at his name badge. *'Entschuldigen Sie—'* I'm sorry '—Bruno, but I have no idea what you just said to me.'

The concierge beamed back at her. 'No matter at all, madam. Your accent was so perfect I thought you a native.'

'Now you're flattering me.' She laughed, delighted colour high on her cheeks. *'Danke.'* Thank you.

'Bitte.' You're welcome.

And from her smile Flynn could tell she knew what that meant. It was all he could do not to roll his eyes.

'Your hotel is sublime, beautiful.' She gestured around. 'And I can't tell you how excited I am to be here.'

The man beamed at her, completely charmed and this time Flynn did roll his eyes. 'And we're delighted to have you stay with us, madam.'

Given the prices they were charging, of course they were delighted.

Eventually Flynn managed to get their room keys and he pushed Addie in the direction of the elevator that silently whooshed them up four flights to the top floor.

Flynn stopped partway down the corridor. 'This should be your room.'

Her jaw dropped when she entered. 'It's huge!' She raced to the window. 'Oh, this is heaven.' She pointed. 'What's that?'

He moved to join her. 'That's called the Isartor. Munich

was once a gated medieval city. Tor means gate. Isar is the name of the nearby river.'

She stared at him. 'So that's the gate to the river Isar. It sounds like something from a Grimm's fairy tale.'

She turned back to fully take in her room. 'Oh, Flynn, I don't need something this big.'

'I have the main suite next door and I wanted you nearby.'

She glanced around more slowly this time and her face fell. 'What?' he barked.

'I thought there might be an adjoining door.' Colour flared suddenly in her face. 'I mean, it's not that I want one. It's just they have them in the movies and...' She broke off, grimacing.

He had to laugh and it eased the burn in his chest. 'No adjoining doors, but feel free to come across and check out the suite.'

Flynn had never thought too much about hotel rooms before beyond space and comfort. And most of the time he didn't waste much thought on the second of those. Space mattered to him though. It probably had something to do with the wide open spaces of the cattle country he was used to. He didn't like feeling hemmed in. It was strange, then, that he spent so much of his time in the cities of Sydney and Brisbane.

'Oh, my! You have a walk-in closet. *And* a second bedroom!' Addie came hurtling back into the living area. 'You have all this—' she spread her arms wide to encompass the lounge area, dining table and kitchenette '—plus all that.' She pointed back the way she'd come from the bedrooms and bathroom.

The suite was generous.

She bounced on the sofa. She sat at the table. 'And it's all lovely light wood and blue and grey accents. It's beautiful.'

He glanced around. She was right. It was.

She poked about the minibar and straightened with a frown. 'There's no price list.'

'The minibar is included in the overall price. It's the same for your room.' When he travelled he wanted the best.

'No-o-o.' Her jaw dropped. 'You mean, I can drink and eat whatever I want from it and it won't cost you a penny more?'

Heck! Had he ever been that young? *'Ja.'*

'Fantastisch!'

She sobered. 'Thank you for my beautiful room.'

He rolled his shoulders. He hadn't been thinking of her comfort or enjoyment, but his own convenience. 'It's nothing. Don't think about it.'

'Thank you for bringing me to Munich.'

'It's not a free ride, Adelaide.'

'I know, and just you wait. I'm going to be the best PA you've ever had.'

Her sincerity pricked him. 'Addie, go and unpack your bags.'

Without so much as a murmur, she turned and left. Flynn collapsed onto the sofa, shaking his head. He eased back a bit further. Addie was right. The sofa was comfortable. He'd be able to rest here and—

Out of the blue it hit him then that not once between the airport and now had he given thought to the reason he was in Munich. He straightened. He pushed to his feet. Twenty years in the planning all ousted because of Addie's excitement? Jet lag. He grabbed his suitcase and strode into the master bedroom, started flinging clothes into the closet. Either that or he was going soft in the head.

He stowed the suitcase and raked both hands back through his hair. The important thing was that he was here now and that finally—after twenty years, twenty-two, to be precise—he had the means and opportunity to bring down the man who had destroyed his family. He would crush George Mueller the way George had laid waste to his father. And he intended to relish every moment of that with the same gusto Addie had so far shown for Munich.

With a grim smile, he made for the shower.

A knock sounded on the door and Flynn glanced up from his laptop. Housekeeping?

Or Addie?

He forced himself to his feet to open it. Addie stood on the other side, but it was a version of her he'd never seen before. What on earth? He blinked.

'May I come in?'

He moved aside to let her enter, his voice trapped somewhere between chest and throat. She sauntered in with a pot of coffee in one hand and a briefcase in the other. She wore a black business suit.

Hell's bells! Addie had legs that went on forever.

She set the briefcase on the table and the coffee pot on a trivet on the bench, before turning. He dragged his gaze from her legs. 'Where did you get that?' He pointed so she knew he meant the coffee, not the legs.

'The breakfast room.'

She collected two mugs and leant down to grab the milk from the bar fridge. Her skirt was a perfectly respectable length, but... He rubbed the nape of his neck. Who'd have known that beneath her jeans she'd have legs like that?

He shook himself. 'What are you doing?' The words practically bellowed from him. 'And why are you wearing that?'

Her face fell and he could've kicked himself. 'Sorry,' he ground out. 'Jet lag. That didn't come out right.'

She swallowed. 'Flynn, I know this trip isn't a free ride. So—' she gestured down at herself '—like a good *dainty* personal assistant, I donned my work clothes, made sure to get the boss coffee and now I'm here to put in a day's work.'

'I don't expect you to do any work today.'

She handed him a coffee. Strong and black. She must've remembered that from their meetings at Lorna Lee's. 'Why not?'

He took a sip. It wasn't as hot as he'd have liked, but he kept his trap shut on that head. She'd gone to the trouble of fetching it for him. Besides, it was excellent—brewed to perfection.

'I'm here to work,' she reminded him.

'Not on the day we fly in. You're allowed some time to settle in.'

'Oh.' She bit her lip. 'I didn't realise. You didn't say.'

'Where did you get the suit?' Had she bought it especially for the trip? He hadn't meant to put her out of pocket.

'I have a wardrobe full of suits. When I finished school I started an office administration course. I had plans to—'

She broke off and he realised that whatever plans she'd made, they hadn't come to fruition.

'But my mother became sick and I came home to help out and, well, the suits haven't really seen the light of day since.'

Because she'd been stuck on the farm. *Trapped* on the farm. He recalled the way she'd pressed her face against the window of the taxi, the look on her face as she'd stared around the city street below. Why was she in his room ready to work when she should be out there exploring the streets of Munich?

'Flynn, I don't even know what it is we're doing in Munich.'

That decided him. 'Go change into your warmer clothes—jeans, a jumper and a coat—and I'll show you why we're here.'

Her eyes lit up. 'And a scarf, gloves and boots. I swear I've never known cold like this.'

'Wear two pairs of socks,' he called after her. 'I'll meet you in the foyer in ten minutes.'

Addie made it down to the foyer in eight minutes to find Flynn already there. She waved to Bruno, who waved back.

'Good to know you can move when necessary,' Flynn said, gesturing her towards the door.

Addie could hardly believe she was in Munich! She practically danced out of the door.

She halted outside. Which way did he want to go? Where did he mean to take her? Oh, goodness, it was cold! She tightened her scarf about her throat and stamped her feet up and down. 'It was thirty-three degrees Celsius when we left Sydney. The predicted top for Munich today is four!'

'In a couple of days you won't even notice.'

She turned to stare at him.

'Okay, you'll notice, but it won't hurt so much.'

'I'll accept that. So, what are you going to show me?'

'We're going to get our bearings first.'

Excellent plan. She pulled the complimentary map she'd found in her room from her coat pocket at the exact moment he pulled the same map from his.

He stared at her map, then at her and shook his head.

'What? I didn't want to get lost.' In rural Australia getting lost could get you killed.

'There's nothing dainty about you, is there, Addie?'

'Not if you're using dainty as a synonym for helpless,' she agreed warily. If it was important to him she supposed she could try and cultivate it, though.

He shoved his map back into his pocket. 'While we're on the subject, for the record I do not want you carrying my luggage.'

'Okay. Noted.' Man, who knew that negotiating the waters of PA and boss politics could be so tricky? 'Okay, while we're on the subject. When we're in business meetings and stuff, do you want me to call you Mr Mather and sir?'

His lip curled. 'Sir?'

Okay, she didn't need a business degree to work out his thoughts on that. 'So we're Herr Mather and his super-efficient—' and dainty if she could manage it '—PA, Addie.'

'Herr Mather and his assistant, Adelaide,' he corrected.

A little thrill shot up her spine. Adelaide sounded so grown up. It was a proper name for a PA. 'Right.'

Brrr…if they didn't move soon, though, she'd freeze to the footpath. She glanced at the map in her hand and then held it out to him. She could read a map as well as the next person, but she was well aware that the male of the species took particular pride in his navigational skills.

'You haven't been to Munich before?' she asked as he unfolded the map.

'No. What made you think I had?'

He studied the map and a lock of chestnut hair fell onto his forehead. The very tips were a couple of shades lighter and they, along with his tan, seemed at odds with all of this frosty cold. It made him seem suddenly exotic.

Deliciously exotic.

Delicious? She frowned. Well, she knew he was perfectly perfect—she'd known that the moment he'd stepped onto Lorna Lee's dressed in a perfectly perfect suit. He was also decidedly male. That had become evident the moment she'd clapped eyes on him in jeans and boots. She just hadn't felt all of that down in her gut until this very moment. She swallowed. Now she felt it all the way to her bones.

Flynn Mather was a perfect specimen of perfectly perfect maleness. In fact, if he'd been a stud bull she'd have moved heaven and earth to have him on the books at Lorna Lee's and—

'Addie?'

She snapped out of it. She swallowed. 'Sorry, brain fog, jet lag, the cold, I don't know.' What had they been talking about? She couldn't remember. She stared at the map and pointed. 'So where are we? What do I need to know?'

'Medieval walled city, remember?'

'Yep.' Nothing wrong with her memory.

'This circle here encloses the heart of the city. Most of our negotiations will take place within this area.'

She followed his finger as it went around, outlining where he meant. A tanned finger. A strong, tanned, masculine finger.

She had a feeling that perfectly perfect PAs didn't notice their boss's fingers.

'Our hotel is here.' His finger tapped the big blue star emblazoned with the hotel's name. 'Marienplatz—the town square—is the heart of it all and it's here…which is only a couple of blocks away.'

She jolted away from him in excitement. 'Oh, let's start there! I've read so much—'

She choked her words back. Perfectly perfect PAs waited to find out what was required of them. They didn't take the bit between their teeth and charge off.

'I mean only if it's convenient, of course, and part of your plan.'

He stared down at her and, while Munich was cold, the sky was blue but not as blue as Flynn's eyes. He grinned, and warmth—as if an oven door had been opened—encompassed her. 'You're trying really hard, aren't you?'

She couldn't deny it. 'Very.'

'I'd be happier if you'd just relax a bit.'

She bit her lip. 'I just want to do a good job and not let you down.'

'Wrong answer.'

She stared back at him. 'What was I supposed to say?'

'Noted,' he drawled and she couldn't help but laugh.

She could do relaxed…perfectly. 'To be honest, Flynn, I don't care which way we go, but can we move, please, before my feet freeze solid?'

He took her arm, his chuckle a frosty breath on the air. 'Right this way.'

He turned them towards Marienplatz. She stared at the shop fronts they passed, the people and the clothes they wore, the cars…but when she glanced up her feet slid to a halt.

'What now?' Flynn asked with exaggerated patience.

She pointed. 'Spires,' she whispered. *Oh, Robbie!* 'And green domes.'

'Pretty,' he agreed.

There was nothing like this in Australia. *Nothing.* A lump lodged in her throat. She'd never seen anything more beautiful.

'If you like those you should go to Paris. They have green domes enough to gladden every soul.'

No. She forced her legs forward again. She was *exactly* where she ought to be.

When they entered the town square, full of bustle and people on this bright chilly morning, and made their way to its centre even Flynn was quiet for a moment. 'That's really something,' he finally said.

All Addie could do was nod. Gothic architecture, sweeping spires, gargoyles and a glockenspiel were all arrayed in front of her. 'What more could one want from a town hall?' she breathed.

On cue, the glockenspiel rang out a series of notes. She and Flynn shared a glance and then folded their arms and stood shoulder to shoulder to watch. Addie had to keep closing her mouth as the jesters jested, the couples danced and the knights duelled. She watched as if in a dream, Flynn's shoulder solid against hers reminding her that this was all for real. She soaked it in, marvelled at it, her heart expanding with gratitude. The show lasted for fifteen minutes, and, despite the cold and the sore neck from craning upwards, she could've watched for another fifteen.

She spun to Flynn. 'Can you imagine how amazed the first people who ever saw that must've been? It would have been the height of technology at the time and—'

She suddenly realised she was holding his arm and, in her enthusiasm, was squeezing it. With a grimace and a belated pat of apology, she let it go. 'Sorry, got carried away.' It certainly wasn't dainty to pull your boss's arm out of its socket.

His lips twitched.

No, no—she didn't want to amuse him. She wanted to impress him.

She gestured back to the glockenspiel. 'And they call that the *New* Town Hall. I mean, it's gothic and—'

He turned her ninety degrees to face back the way they'd come. 'Oh!' A breath escaped her. 'And that would be the Old Town Hall and as it's medieval then I guess that makes sense.'

She turned a slow circle trying to take it all in.

'What do you think?'

He sounded interested in her impression. She wondered if he was merely humouring her. 'I can't believe how beautiful it all is.' She turned back to the New Town Hall and her stomach plummeted. An ache started up in her chest. 'Oh,' she murmured. 'I forgot.'

'Forgot what?'

'That it's Christmas.'

'Addie, there're decorations everywhere, not to mention a huge Christmas tree right there. How could you forget?'

She'd been too busy taking in the breathtaking architecture and the strangeness of it all. She lifted a shoulder. 'It's been such a rush this last week.' What with signing the contract to sell Lorna Lee's and preparing for the trip, Christmas had been the last thing on her mind.

Christmas. Her first ever Christmas away from Lorna Lee's. Her first Christmas without her father.

The ache stretched through her chest. If her father were still alive they'd have decorated their awful plastic tree—loaded it with tinsel and coloured balls and tiny aluminium bells and topped it with a gaudy angel. She'd be organising a ham and a turkey roll and—

A touch on her arm brought her back with a start. 'Where did you just go?'

His eyes were warm and soft and they eased the ache inside her. She remembered the way his eyes had blazed when she'd asked him if he knew what it was like to want something so terribly badly.

Yes, he'd known. She suspected he'd understand this too. 'The ghost of Christmases past,' she murmured. 'It's the first Christmas without my father.'

His face gentled. 'I'm sorry.'

'I've been doing my best not to think about it.' She stared across at the giant decorated tree that stood out at the front of the New Town Hall. 'I'm glad I'm spending Christmas here this year rather than on the farm.'

He nodded.

She turned back to him. 'Are your parents still alive?'

'My father isn't.'

Her lungs cramped at the desolation that momentarily stretched through his eyes. 'I'm sorry.'

He shoved his hands into the pockets of his coat. 'It was a long time ago.'

'Your mother?'

'My mother and I are estranged.'

She grimaced and shoved her hands into her pockets too. 'Oh, I'm sorry.' She shouldn't have pressed him.

He shrugged as if it didn't make an ounce of difference to him, but she didn't believe that for a moment. 'She's a difficult woman.'

She pushed her shoulders back. 'Then we'll just have to have our own orphans' Christmas in Munich.'

He opened his mouth. She waited but he closed it again. She cleared her throat, grimaced and scratched a hand through her hair. 'I, the thing is, I've just realised in the rush of it all that I haven't bought presents for the people back home.'

He stared down at her for three beats and then he laughed

as if she'd shaken something loose from him. 'Addie, that's not going to be a problem. Haven't you heard about the Munich Christmas markets?'

'Markets?' She wanted to jump up and down. 'Really?'

'Some are held in this very square. You'll find presents for everyone.'

'There'll be time for that?' She could send the gifts express post to make sure they arrived on time. Hang the expense.

'Plenty of time.'

She folded her arms and surveyed him. 'When are you going to tell me what your business in Munich is?'

'Come right this way.' He took her arm and set off past the New Town Hall. They passed what looked like the main shopping area. She slanted a glance up at him. 'We'll still be in Munich for the post-Christmas sales, right?'

'Never stand in the way of a woman and the sales. Don't worry; you'll have time to shop.'

Cool.

She shook herself. That was all well and good, but when were they in fact going to do any work?

Eventually he stopped, let go of her arm and pointed. She peered at the building he gestured to. It took her a moment, but… 'Ooh, a beer hall! Can we…? I mean, is it too early…?'

'It's nearly midday. C'mon.' He ushered her inside.

The interior was enormous and filled with wooden tables and benches. He led her to a table by the wall, where they had a perfect view of the rest of the room. He studied the menu and ordered them both beers in perfect German.

She stared at her glass when it was set down in front of her—her very tall glass. 'Uh, Flynn, you ordered me half a litre of beer?'

'We could've ordered it by the litre if you'd prefer.'

Her jaw dropped as a barmaid walked past with three litre tankards in one hand and two in the other.

'Bottoms up!'

He sounded younger than she'd ever heard him. She raised her glass. 'Cheers.'

She took a sip and closed her eyes in bliss. 'Nectar from the gods. Now tell me what we're drinking to?'

'This—' he gestured around '—is what we're doing here.'

It took a moment. When she realised what he meant she set her glass down and leaned towards him. 'You're buying the beer hall?' A grin threatened to split her face in two. That had to be every Australian boy's dream.

How perfectly perfect!

CHAPTER THREE

Dear Daisy

Munich is amazing. Gorgeous. And so cold! After a couple of hours out my face burned when I came back inside as if it were sunburned. Everything here is so different from Mudgee. I know it's not Paris, but it's marvellous just the same.

You know, it got me thinking about starting the blog back up, but...I'd simply be searching for something I can't have. Again.

You should be here in Europe with me. You should... Sorry, enough of that. Guess what? I finally found out what we're doing here. The perfectly perfect F is buying a brewery that has its own beer hall! How exciting is that?

We have our very first business meeting at eleven o'clock this morning. I'm going to wear that gorgeous garnet-coloured suit I bought in Sydney when we went to see Cate Blanchett at the theatre that time. I have no idea what I'm supposed to do in said meeting, but in that suit I'll at least look the part!

Wish you were here.

Love, Buttercup

ADDIE EXITED HER *Till the Cows Come Home* Word document, closed the lid of her laptop and resisted the urge to snuggle back beneath the covers. It was only seven a.m.

She could sneak in another hour of shut-eye. Flynn had said he didn't need to see her until quarter to eleven in his room, where the meeting was scheduled to take place, but...

She was in Munich!

She leapt out of bed, smothering a yawn. A brisk walk down by the River Isar would be just the thing. She wanted her body clock on Munich time asap. What she didn't want was any more of the crazy disturbed sleep like that she'd had last night.

A walk *in Munich* would wake her up, enliven her and have her bright-eyed and bushy-tailed for Flynn's business meeting.

Perfect.

Addie tried to stifle a yawn as the lawyer droned on and on and on about the conditions of probate and the details of the contract negotiations that were under way, plus additional clauses that would need to be considered, along with local government regulations and demands and...on and on and on.

Did Flynn find this stuff interesting?

She glanced at him from the corner of her eye. He watched the lawyer narrowly, those blue eyes alert. She sensed the tension coiled up inside him as if he were a stroppy King Brown waiting to strike, even as he leaned back in his seat, the picture of studied ease. She wondered if the lawyer knew.

She shivered, but she couldn't deny it only made him seem more powerful...and lethal, like a hero from a thriller. It must be beyond brilliant to feel that confident, to have all of that uncompromising derring-do. One could save small children from burning buildings and dive into seething seas to rescue battered shipwreck victims and—

'Make a note of that, will you, please, Adelaide?'

She crashed back into the room, swallowing. She pulled her notebook towards her without glancing at Flynn and jotted on it.

Am making notes about nothing so as to look efficient. Listen in future, Addie! Pay attention.

She underlined 'listen' three times.

Biting back a sigh, she tried to force her attention back to the conversation—the negotiations—but the lawyer was droning on and on in that barely varying monotone. If he'd been speaking German she'd have had a reason for tuning out, but he was speaking English with an American accent and it should've had her riveted, but...

For heaven's sake, the subject matter was so dry and dull that he could've had the most gorgeous and compelling voice in the world and she'd still tune out. She mentally scrubbed property developer off her list of potential future jobs. And lawyer.

She glanced at Flynn again. He wore a charcoal business suit and looked perfect. Didn't he feel the slightest effect from jet lag? Perhaps he really was a machine?

She bit back another sigh. Perhaps he was just a seasoned world traveller who was used to brokering million-dollar deals.

The figures these two were bandying about had almost made her eyes pop. She'd wanted to tug on Flynn's sleeve and double-check that he really wanted to invest that much money in a German brewery.

Sure, he was an Aussie guy. Aussie guys—and girls, for that matter—and beer went hand in hand. But there were limits, surely? Even for high-flying Flynn.

Still, she knew what it was like to have a childhood dream. Good luck to him for making his a reality.

She had a sudden vision of him galloping across the

fields at Lorna Lee's on Blossom. She leaned back. Did he really prefer this kind of wheeling and dealing to—?

'Record that number, please, Adelaide.'

She started and glanced at the lawyer, who barked a series of numbers at her. She scribbled them down. Was it a phone number or a fax number? For all she knew it was a serial number for... She drew a blank. She scrawled a question mark beside it.

In her pocket her phone vibrated. She silently thanked the patron saint of personal assistants for giving her the insight to switch it to silent. She slid it out and her lips lifted. A message from Frank. She clicked on it, eager for news from home.

This man of Flynn's wants to get rid of Bruce Augustus.

Her hand clenched about the phone. She shot to her feet. 'Over my dead body!'

The lawyer broke off. Both he and Flynn stared at her. She scowled at Flynn. 'This foreman of yours and I are going to have serious words.'

He cocked an eyebrow.

She recalled where they were and what they were supposed to be doing and cleared her throat, took her seat again. 'Later,' she murmured. 'We'll have our serious words later.'

But she messaged back to Frank.

If he does he dies. Text me his number.

Flynn stretched out a long leg, leaning further back in his chair, reminding her even more vividly of a King Brown. Addie pocketed her phone and kept a close eye on him.

'So what you're in effect telling me, Herr Gunther, is that there's going to be a delay in probate.'

When Flynn spoke she had no trouble whatsoever paying attention. The lawyer hummed and hawed and tried to squeeze his way out of the corner Flynn had herded him into, but there was no evading Flynn. She wondered if he'd ever camp drafted. She'd bet he'd be good at it. With those shoulders…

She blinked and shifted on her seat. She didn't care about shoulders. What she cared about was Bruce Augustus.

And getting off the farm.

She rolled her eyes. Yeah, right, as if she'd scaled the heights of PA proficiency today. She'd need to do better if she wanted this job for real.

You have a month.

'Are you familiar with the law firm Schubert, Schuller and Schmidt?'

The lawyer nodded.

'I've hired them to represent me. You'll be hearing from them.'

'I—'

Flynn rose and the lawyer's words bumbled to a halt. Addie stood too and fixed the lawyer with what she hoped was a smile as pleasantly cool as Flynn's. Thank goodness this was over.

'Thank you for your time, Herr Gunther. It was most instructive.'

Was it? Addie ushered the lawyer towards the door with an inane, 'Have a nice day, Herr Gunther,' all the while impatience building inside her.

The door had barely closed before she pulled her cell phone from her pocket and punched in Howard's number.

'What's he done?' Flynn asked as she strode back towards the table.

'Nothing you need to worry about. I'll deal with it.'

He opened his mouth and it suddenly occurred to her

what nicely shaped lips he had. It wasn't something she generally noticed about a man, but Flynn definitely—

'Hello?'

She snapped to attention. 'Howard, it's Adelaide Ramsey.'

He swore. 'Do you know what time it is in Australia?'

'I don't care what time it is.' That only made it worse. It meant Frank and Jeannie had been fretting till all hours. 'Now listen to me very carefully. If you harm one hair on Bruce Augustus's head, if you try to send him to the knackers, I will have your guts for garters. Do you hear me?'

'But—'

'No buts!'

'Look, Addie, I understand—'

'Have you ever owned a farm, Howard?' She shifted, suddenly aware of how closely Flynn watched her. She swallowed and avoided eye contact.

'No.'

'Then you don't understand.'

A pause followed. 'The boss has given me the authority to make changes, Addie, and Bruce Augustus is dead wood.'

Dead wood! She could feel herself start to shake.

'I have the boss's ear and—'

She snorted. 'You have his ear? Honey, I have more than his ear. I'm going to *be* your boss when I return home— you realise that, don't you? You do *not* want to get on the wrong side of me.'

Silence sounded and this time Howard didn't break it. 'Goodnight, Howard.' With that she snapped her phone shut and swung to face Flynn.

His lips twitched. 'Sorted, huh?'

Was he laughing at her? She narrowed her gaze and pocketed her phone. 'Absolutely.'

He lowered himself to the sofa. 'Can you tell me exactly why Bruce Augustus is necessary to Lorna Lee's future?'

'Because if he goes—' she folded her arms '—I go.'

He leaned forward and she found herself on the receiving end of a gaze colder than a Munich winter. 'We have a deal. You signed a contract.'

She widened her stance. 'You mess with my bull and the deal's off. There's a six-week cooling-off period to that contract, remember? You threaten my bull and I'll pull out of the sale.'

He leaned back. She couldn't read his expression at all. 'You mean that,' he eventually said.

She tried to stop her shoulders from sagging and nodded. She meant it.

'Why is he so important to you?'

She would never be able to explain to him what a friend the bull had been to her. It was pointless even to try. 'You said one of the reasons you wanted me to remain at Lorna Lee's was due to the affinity I have with the animals.'

'I believe the term I used was stock.'

'You can use whatever term you like—you can try and distance yourself from them—but it doesn't change what they are.'

'Which is?'

'Living creatures that provide us with our livelihoods. We have a culture at Lorna Lee's of looking after our own. I consider it a duty. *That's* where my so-called affinity comes from. When an animal provides us with good service we don't repay that by getting rid of them when they're past their use-by date. They get to live out their days in easy retirement. If that's a culture you can't live with, Flynn, then you'd better tell me now.'

He pursed his lips and continued to survey her. It took all of her strength not to fidget. 'I can live with it,' he finally said. 'Do you want it in writing?'

Very slowly she let out a breath. 'No. I believe you're a man of your word.'

He blinked. She held out her hand and he rose and shook it.

For no reason at all her heart knocked against her ribs. She pulled her hand free again, but her heart didn't stop pounding.

'Howard?' Flynn held his cell phone to his ear.

'Yes, I do. Just…don't touch the bull.'

He listened then. Obviously to the other man's justifications. She scowled. There were no justifications for—

'Howard wants to know if you're okay with him dredging the dam in the western paddock of the Seymour place…'

Oh, yes, that was long overdue.

'…extending the irrigation system on the southern boundary…'

There'd be money for that?

'…and installing solar panels on the roofs of all the homesteads?'

She swallowed and nodded. 'Those things all sound great. I don't have a problem with improvements.'

Flynn spoke to Howard for a few moments more and then rang off.

She swung back to him. 'When I return to the farm, who's going to be in charge—him or me?'

'I'll be in charge, Addie.'

Oops, that was right. Still, if rumour were anything to go by, Flynn didn't stay in any one spot for too long.

'You and Howard will have authority over different areas. You'll be in charge of the breeding programme. He'll be in charge of overseeing major improvements. I'll be overseeing the two of you.'

Unless she managed to change his mind by turning into the perfect PA. Which reminded her…

'I'm sorry I had that outburst in the meeting.'

He shrugged. 'It needed something to liven it up.'

It didn't change the fact that she should've had more presence of mind than to shout out during a business meeting. She bit her lip and glanced at him. 'So, you didn't find that meeting riveting?'

'Absolutely not.'

She sagged. 'I thought it might've just been me. Jet lag or something.' She retrieved her notebook and handed it to him. 'I'm really sorry, but my mind kept drifting off.'

He laughed when he read her notes—or lack of them.

'I promise to do better next time.'

He handed the notebook back. 'I only asked you to jot things down to keep myself awake.'

She wrinkled her nose. 'Are all business meetings that dull?'

'Not at all. Herr Gunther was just doing his best to bore and obfuscate.'

He'd succeeded with her. 'Why?'

'Because he favours one of my rivals and is hoping this other party can get a jump on me somehow.'

'There's a rival?'

'There're several, but only the one we need worry about.'

'Will this rival get a jump on you? Should we be worried?'

His eyes suddenly blazed and one of his hands clenched. 'I say bring it on. The harder and the dirtier the battle, the more satisfying it'll be.'

Really?

'Regardless of the cost, Addie, this is one battle I mean to win.'

She swallowed. Right.

'The upshot of the meeting is that there's been a delay in processing probate.'

The one thing Addie had fathomed from the meeting was that the person who'd owned the premises that housed the brewery and beer hall had recently died. Hence the reason the property would soon be on the market. The probate referred to the reading of this man's will so his estate could be finalised.

'Herr Gunther will try to draw that delay out for as long as he can, but we're not going to let him.'

That made them sound thrillingly powerful and masterful. She clapped her hands. 'So?'

He raised an eyebrow. 'So?'

'What next? Do we head over to these Schubert, Schuller and Schmidt's of yours and come up with a game plan?'

'They already have my instructions. You, Adelaide Ramsey, have the rest of the day off to do whatever you want.'

Really? That was the entirety of her work for the day?

'Go out and explore. Sightsee.' He glanced up when she didn't move. 'If I need you I have your mobile number. I'll call you if something comes up.'

Right. She gathered up her things.

'And, Addie?'

She turned in the doorway. 'Yes?'

'Have fun.'

Oh, she meant to, but she wouldn't be sightseeing in this gorgeous and compelling city. At least, not this afternoon. If she wanted to convince Flynn that she was perfect PA material, she had work to do.

Flynn barely glanced up from his laptop when the room phone rang. He seized it and pressed it to his ear. 'Hello?'

'Flynn, it's Addie. I wondered if you were busy.'

He closed the lid of his laptop, her threat to pull out of the sale still ringing in his ears. He wondered if she realised how fully invested in Lorna Lee's she was. And if he hadn't been aware of his own emotional stake in the place before, he was now. 'Not busy at all. What's up?'

'Would it be convenient to come over to show you something I've been working on?'

She'd been working? On what? 'The door's open.'

He replaced the receiver with a smothered curse and unlocked the door—stood there holding it wide open, like a lackey. Darn it! She wasn't going to pull out of their deal, was she? Lorna Lee's was small fry in the grand scheme of things, but…he'd started to think of it as a place he could hang his hat. He didn't have one of those. It was disconcerting to discover that he wanted one, but he refused to bury the need. Lorna Lee's would be perfect.

Addie came tripping in with her laptop under one arm and her notepad clutched to her chest. She'd swapped her saucy red suit for jeans and a long-sleeved T-shirt. She moved straight to the table and fired the laptop to life without a word, but a smile lit her lips and a pretty colour bloomed high on her cheeks. When she turned those amber eyes to him, their brightness made his heart sink.

If she loved her home that much he'd never be able to take it away from her.

Would she consider going into a partnership with him instead?

'I've spent the afternoon researching breweries and beer halls and—'

'You've what?' The door slipped from his fingers and closed with a muted whoosh. 'For heaven's sake, why?'

Her hands went to her hips. 'You're buying one, aren't you?'

'Specifically, I'm buying the premises.'

She waved a hand in the air. 'Semantics.'

He decided not to correct her.

'Bavaria is known for its fine beer. And, of course, Munich is famous for Oktoberfest.'

He rubbed his nape. 'Addie, why aren't you out there seeing the sights and experiencing the delights of Munich?'

She clicked away on her computer. 'I want to be useful.'

He closed his eyes and counted to three. 'What happened to "have you ever wanted something so bad", et cetera? This is a once-in–a-lifetime opportunity.'

She spun to stare at him. 'And buying a brewery and beer hall isn't?'

His mouth opened and closed, but no sound came out. He shook himself. 'C'mon.' He took her arm and propelled her out of the room, grabbing his coat and scarf on the way. 'Go put on a jumper and scarf and coat.'

'But don't you want to hear about the research I did and—?'

'Later.'

He waited outside her door while she grabbed her things.

'If you really want to be useful to me, Addie, then I want you out and about in Munich seeing and experiencing everything you can.'

She stared at him as they made their way down the stairs, struggling to get her arms into her coat. 'You want me to immerse myself in the culture?' She bit her lip. 'Are you hoping that whatever insights I gain might be helpful in your negotiations somehow?'

If she thought that was the reason then he'd play along. He held her coat so she could get her left arm in the sleeve. 'Yes.'

'Oh.' She glared at him. 'Then why didn't you say so?'

Because he hadn't been fool enough to think she'd waste the best part of a day researching breweries when it wasn't even breweries he was interested in.

Not that she knew that.

'Really, Flynn,' she harrumphed. 'You need to give your people better information.'

'Noted,' he said and had the pleasure of seeing her lips twitch. He wanted her to sightsee until she was sick of it. He wanted her to get the wanderlust out of her system so she'd settle back at Lorna Lee's without chafing at imaginary restraints.

They're not imaginary.

Whatever! She'd get four weeks' annual leave a year and plane tickets wherever she wanted. He didn't want her getting the wanderlust so completely out of her system that she refused to sell her farm to him.

She belted the sash of her coat all the more securely

about her when they stepped outside. 'It gets dark so quickly here. It's barely five o'clock.'

He missed Australia's warmth and daylight savings. Back home night wouldn't fall for another four hours. 'That's the joys of a northern hemisphere winter,' was all he said.

'Where are we going?'

He'd considered that while waiting outside her door. 'You said you needed to buy Christmas presents, and I expect you'd like to mail them home in time for Christmas.'

Her face lit up. 'The Christmas markets?'

Better yet. 'The *medieval* Christmas markets.'

Her eyes widened. 'Oh.' She clasped her gloved hands beneath her chin. 'That sounds perfectly perfect.'

He glanced down at her and something shifted in his chest. Silly woman! Why had she wasted her precious time cooped up inside? She didn't strike him as the type who'd be afraid to venture forth on her own.

I want to be useful.

He bit back a sigh. Yeah, well, he didn't want her crying on her own in Bruce Augustus's pen in the future. 'Just so you know,' he said, turning them in the direction of Wittelsbacherplatz—the site of the markets, 'this isn't some touristy money spinner.' Though no doubt it did that too. 'There's been a Christmas market on the site since medieval times apparently.'

Her jaw dropped when a short while later they passed one of the façades of the Residenz—a series of palaces and courtyards that had been the home of former Bavarian rulers. 'That's… It's amazing.'

He stared too. It was really something.

They turned down the next boulevard and her eyes widened as if to take in all the beauty. He totally sympathised. When they stepped into Odeonsplatz and she clapped eyes on St Peter's Church, she came to a dead halt. She glanced around, blinking at the Field Marshal's Hall. 'How can one city have so much beauty?' she breathed.

'What do you think?'

'Words can't do it justice. It's beautiful. I love it.'

He grinned then. 'Come right this way.'

Less than a minute later they entered Wittelsbacher-platz. It was purported to be one of the most commanding squares in Munich and at the moment it was alive with colour and bustle and the scent of Christmas. Not to mention row upon row of market stalls.

He glanced down at her and his grin widened. Breweries and Lorna Lee's were the furthest things from her mind and he pushed them firmly from his too. 'C'mon. Let's start down here.' He took her arm and led her down one of the alleys formed by the stalls.

They lost themselves in a whole new world. There were woodcarvers, glass-blowers and bakers. There were shoemakers, cuckoo clocks and gingerbread. There was noise and life and vigour, and he watched as it brought Addie alive and filled her with delight. They stopped to watch a medieval dance troop perform a folk dance, the scents from the nearby food stalls filling the air. When the dance was complete she took his arm and headed down a different alley. 'This is amazing! Have you ever seen anything so amazing? It's just…'

His mouth hooked up. 'Amazing?'

'Nutcrackers!'

He glanced from her face to the items she pointed to. An entire stall was devoted to small, and not so small, wooden soldiers.

'Colin would love these!' She selected four and paid for them all on her own, never once asking him to interpret for her. He shook his head. She definitely wasn't afraid of venturing forth on her own.

I want to be useful.

He had overcome that barrier now, hadn't he?

She oohed and aahed over chimney sweeps made from dried plums and almonds. She bought some gingerbread.

'Uh, Addie, I'm not sure you'll get that through Australian customs.'

'Who said anything about posting this home? It's for us now.' She opened the bag and broke off a piece. He thought she might melt on the spot when she tasted it. She held the bag out to him and lunch suddenly seemed like hours ago. He helped himself to a slice. She grinned at whatever expression passed across his face. 'Good, isn't it?'

He took some more. 'Really good.'

He bought them mugs of *glühwein* and they drank it, standing around one of the makeshift fires that dotted the square, Addie's holiday mood infecting him. He drank in the Christmas goodness and watched as she tried to choose a wooden figurine for Frank. 'What do you think?' She turned, holding up two carvings for his inspection. 'Father Time or the billy goat?'

He could tell by the way she surveyed the goat that it was her favourite. He didn't doubt for a moment that Frank would love either of them. 'The goat.'

He took her parcels from her so she could browse unencumbered. They stopped to watch a glass-blower shape a perfect snowflake—an ornament for a Christmas tree— but he preferred to watch her.

When was the last time he'd relished something as much as Addie was relishing this outing?

He frowned and tried to wipe the thought away. He didn't want to put any kind of dampener on Addie's mood. Not when she'd put in a full day's work on his behalf. He frowned again. He still didn't feel as if he'd got to the bottom of that yet.

'Oh, Flynn, look at that.'

He dutifully glanced at what she held out to him. It was an exquisite glass angel—ludicrously delicate and unbelievably detailed.

'Jeannie would go into ecstasies over this, but…'

'But?'

'It'd be in a thousand pieces before it ever reached her.'

He eyed it and then the packaging it came in. 'Not necessarily. It'd be well protected in its box with all of that tissue paper and sawdust around it. If we put it in another box with bubble wrap—' lots of bubble wrap '—and marked it fragile it should be fine.'

'You really think so?'

'The packaging and postage won't come cheap,' he warned.

'Hang the expense.' She bought it. It made her eyes bright. His shoulders swung suddenly free.

'Now who do you need to buy for?'

He blinked. Him? Nobody. 'I give bonuses, Addie, not Christmas gifts.'

'But surely you have friends who…' She trailed off.

Friends he hadn't spent enough time with over the last few years, he suddenly realised.

'I'm sorry. I didn't mean to make you sad.'

He shook himself. 'Not sad,' he countered. 'Wine. I've sent them wine. It's already been ordered.' One of his secretaries would've taken care of it.

She folded her arms. 'Surely there's a significant other out there you ought to buy some frippery for?'

He tried to look forbidding. 'I beg your pardon?'

She reddened. 'I'm not trying to pry.' She stiffened. 'And I don't want you thinking I'm putting myself forward for the position, mind, if there is a vacancy.'

Perhaps he'd overdone it on the forbidding thing. 'I'm not getting those vibes from you, Addie. If I were I'd make sure you were aware that I *never* get involved with employees.'

'Right.' She eased back a bit further to stare at him.

He rolled his shoulders. 'What?'

'Don't get me wrong, but you're young, successful and presentable.' She raised an eyebrow. 'Heterosexual?'

'As two failed marriages will attest.'

She shook her head. 'That doesn't prove—' Her jaw dropped. *Two failed marriages! Two?*'

'Which is why I make sure *no* woman ever expects a Christmas present from me. I'm not travelling that particular road to hell ever again.'

'Two—' She gulped back whatever she'd been going to say and shook herself upright, gave one emphatic nod. 'Fair enough. The short answer is there's really nobody you need to buy for.'

'Correct.'

'The long answer is there's not going to be a new mistress at Lorna Lee's.'

Had she been worried about that? It made sense, he guessed. In her place he'd have wondered the same. 'Who else do you need to buy for?'

'Eric and Lucy.'

She'd bought a present for their little boy. Wasn't that enough?

'To own the truth, Flynn, I'm starting to feel a little shopped out.'

No, she wasn't. She'd only said that because she thought he must be bored with the shopping. He opened his mouth to disabuse her of the notion.

'What I am is starved.'

He glanced at his watch and did a double take. Seven o'clock? How had that happened? 'C'mon, we passed a cute-looking traditional place on the way here.'

The cute place turned out to be a beer hall. Of course. But Addie didn't seem to mind. 'I'll have the pork knuckle with the potato dumpling,' she said to the waitress, pointing to the dish on the menu.

Flynn held up two fingers. *Zwei, bitte.*' He ordered two wheat beers as well.

'My research today informs me that one can't get more Bavarian than pork knuckle and dumpling.'

'Unless you settle for a plate of bratwurst,' he pointed out.

'I'll try that tomorrow.'

She stared at him. Eventually he raised his hands. 'What?'

'Aren't you even the slightest bit interested in all the stuff I've researched today?'

Not really. He didn't say that, though.

'For example, do you know how expensive beef is here?'

'Compared to Australian prices, beef is expensive throughout all of Europe.'

'You could make an absolute killing by supplying beef dishes at your beer hall. Beef sourced from your cattle station.'

He leaned towards her. She smelled of gingerbread and oranges. 'Why is doing a good job for me so important to you?'

'Oh.' She bit her lip and her gaze slid away. 'I, um…I was thinking that if I did a really good job for you, that you wouldn't mind providing me with a reference. A glowing reference I'll be able to use when I come back to Europe for real.'

'Addie, you are in Europe for real.'

She shook her head, her gaze returning to his. 'This is time out of time, not real life.'

What on earth was she talking about?

'When my two years are up on Lorna Lee's I'll be leaving to lead my real life.'

Her real life?

'And my real life is working my way through Europe at my leisure.'

Why was she so determined to leave a place that had nurtured her, a place she obviously loved, for a hobo temping trek around Europe? For heaven's sake, she'd be bored to death as a PA. Wasn't today's meeting proof positive of that?

'Unless of course you find that I'm the best PA you've ever had and decide you can't be doing without me.'

He laughed.

Addie glanced down at the table.

The waitress arrived with their beers and he lifted his glass in salute. 'To enjoying Munich.'

When she lifted her gaze he could've sworn her eyes swam, but she saluted him with her glass, blinding him with a big bright smile. 'To Munich.'

CHAPTER FOUR

FLYNN CLOSED THE door to his room and flung his coat and scarf on a chair. Pushing his hands into the small of his back, he stretched. His body ached, which didn't make a whole lot of sense. All he'd done was walk and talk, eat and laugh. It wasn't as if he'd been on muster.

He glanced at his watch and blew out a breath. Eleven p.m. He'd been walking and talking and eating and laughing for six hours. He moved to the window to stare down at the now quiet street below. He hadn't expected to enjoy Munich. He'd come here to get a job done. Enjoyment hadn't been on the agenda. Somewhere along the way, though, Addie's delight in the Christmas markets had proved contagious.

From his pocket he pulled the carved wooden bull he'd bought when Addie hadn't been looking. He'd meant to give it to her during dinner as a gesture of goodwill, a promise that Bruce Augustus would always have a home at Lorna Lee's, but, while there was no denying that Addie was good company, there'd been a shift in...tone, mood, temper? He hadn't been able to put his finger on it, but Addie had somehow subtly distanced herself and the carved bull had remained in his pocket—the right moment never presenting itself.

He frowned. It'd been a long time since he'd shared a convivial meal with a friend. Not that Addie was a friend—she was an employee—but it had him thinking about his real friends. Wasn't it time to enjoy the fruits of his labours and slow down on the cut-and-thrust? It wasn't a question he'd ever considered. Now he couldn't get it out of his mind.

He swung away from the window. What? A slip of a girl milked every ounce of enjoyment from a new experience and now he was questioning his entire way of life?

He shook himself. There was nothing wrong with being goal-oriented!

He rubbed his nape. But, when *was* the last time he'd enjoyed something as wholeheartedly as Addie?

He collapsed to the sofa. Maybe it was time to slow down. After he'd brought ruin down on Mueller's head, of course.

He recalled the peace that had filtered through his soul when he'd first clapped eyes on the rolling fields of Lorna Lee's. When he left Munich maybe he could focus on spending time there, working the land and building a home. The idea eased the ball of tightness in his chest.

First, though, he had to deal with Mueller. That fist clenched up tight again. With a growl, he headed for the shower.

It wasn't until he emerged, rubbing a towel over his hair, that Flynn noticed Addie's laptop and notepad sitting on the dining table. He paused, hesitated and then flipped open the notepad. Nothing. She'd obviously brought it along to make notes.

He eyed the laptop, rolled his shoulders and stretched his neck, first to the right and then to the left. He didn't care about the brewery. He only cared about ruining Mueller.

Still, he'd have to do something with the premises. The local council wouldn't allow them to remain idle. He'd need to provide them with assurances, make promises. Besides, it wouldn't hurt to look at the material Addie had gathered *in her free time*.

He seized the computer, planted himself on the sofa and fired it up. He'd be careful not to look at any personal documents. Clicking on the last word-processing document she'd been working one—the one titled Flynn's Brewery/Beer Hall—he read her rough notes.

He straightened. Actually, while some of her ideas were fairly basic, some of them were interesting and surprisingly savvy.

He opened her Internet browser to follow a couple of references she'd made in her notes. He pursed his lips, his mind starting to race. Once he'd bought the premises out from beneath Mueller, it wouldn't be too hard to establish another brewery there—the equipment belonged to the premises, which meant it'd meet local council regulations.

He grinned and lifted a foot to the coffee table. Mueller's finances were in a sorry state. He'd invested too heavily in improvements to the premises without securing a guarantee—*in writing*—that he'd have first option to buy if they ever came on the market. A gentleman's agreement didn't count in this situation. A harsh laugh broke from him. That was just as well. Mueller was no gentleman. He might be able to make a halfway decent offer on the premises, but Flynn would be able to offer three times as much.

He rested his head back and stared up at the ceiling, satisfaction coursing through him. Running a brewery on Mueller's premises? Talk about poetic justice. Talk about rubbing salt into the wound.

He glanced at the computer again. The idea of owning a brewery hadn't filled him with any enthusiasm except as a means to an end. It could just as well have been a sausage factory for all he cared. But now...

Addie's enthusiasm, he discovered, wasn't just reserved for her travels—it filled her notes too and some of it caught fire in his veins. Owning a beer hall could be fun. Hadn't he just decided he needed more fun in his life? He settled back and checked her word-processing file history and then selected a document titled 'Till the Cows Come Home.' He figured it'd have something to do with the beef industry. Her idea of using beef supplied from his cattle station to launch a cheaper beef menu had a lot of merit.

A document with a header of daisies and buttercups and cartoon cows appeared. He frowned. This looked personal. He went to close it when several words leapt out at him— Munich, Brewery and F.

Dear Daisy,
I know I've said it before, but I have to say it again— you'd love Munich as much as I do! I know it's not Paris, but beggars can't be choosers—isn't that what they say? Anyway, you'd have a ball, turning all the guys' heads in one of the traditional Bavarian costumes the barmaids wear—very sexy.

We'd have to build up our arm muscles, though, before embarking on a barmaid career here. You wouldn't believe it, but I saw one girl carrying ten litres of beer—five litres in each hand—and she didn't even break a sweat. Amazing! I love the beer halls.

Hmm...wonder if F would leave me here as a tavern wench?

He grinned. Not a chance.

Speaking of which, the perfectly perfect F is perfectly cool and collected in business meetings too. Extraordinary that someone actually enjoys those things.

Still...I wish...with all my heart I wish you were here.
Love Buttercup.

Buttercup, huh?
So who was Daisy?

PS I've decided against starting the blog up again and—

Flynn jerked upright and hit 'quit' in double-quick time. He wasn't going to read Addie's private diary! Sheesh!

He stared at her computer screen, went to close down the internet browser when, on impulse, he typed 'Till the Cows Come Home' into the search engine. A page with a background of daisies, buttercups and cartoon cows loaded. He checked the archives. The very first post was dated six years ago. He read it. He read the next one and the one after that, battling the lump growing in his throat. He read into the wee small hours until he could no longer battle fatigue. In the morning when he woke he picked up where he'd left off.

Addie had posted every day for eighteen months, but the blog had been defunct for the last four years. He stared at the wall opposite. Was it an invasion to read her blog like this? If she'd truly wanted privacy she'd have kept a diary instead, right? As she did now. He scrubbed a hand down his face before shutting off the computer and pulling on a pair of sweats.

She'd published it in a public forum. After all, that was what a blog was—a way of reaching out and connecting with other people. Only…comments had been left but Addie hadn't responded to any of them.

Who was Daisy? Addie had bared her soul in that blog—her pain and heartbreak when her friend—Daisy—had died of leukaemia.

He could ask her.

Or you could keep your fat trap shut.

None of it was his business.

So why did it feel as if it were?

He jerked around at the tap on his door. A quiet tap as if the person on the other side was being careful to not disturb him if he were still asleep. Instinct told him it'd be Addie. Asleep? Ha!

He pulled in a breath, careful to keep his face smooth, before opening the door. Addie had started to turn away, but she swung back and her smile hit him in the gut. 'Hey, good morning.'

'Morning.'

She eyed him carefully. 'You okay?'

He cleared his throat. 'Yep. Fine. All's good with me.'

She blinked and her brow furrowed and then she shook it all away. 'Sorry to disturb you, but I wondered if I could grab my laptop. I left it here yesterday. I forgot to collect it when we got back last night. Speaking of which, I laid down for just a moment and bang! I was out for the count. Jet lag's a killer, huh?'

He strove for casual, for normal, when all he really wanted to do was haul her in his arms and hug her tight, tell her how sorry he was about Daisy. He cleared his throat. 'Jet lag? But you stayed awake all day yesterday, right?'

She snorted. 'One could hardly call whatever I was in that meeting with the lawyer awake.'

He laughed, when he'd thought laughing would be beyond him.

'Fingers crossed, though, that the body clock is on local time now.'

He suddenly realised they both still stood by the door. He strode back into the room, seized her laptop and notepad and then swung back and thrust them at her. He didn't invite her inside. He hoped a bit of distance would help him get his thoughts and impulses under control and ease the burning in his chest when he glanced at her.

Everything he'd read, it was none of his business. That, however, didn't mean he could just push it out of his head, disregard it or forget it. It was still too close.

She clasped the computer and notepad to her chest. 'Is today still a free day?'

He nodded. Tomorrow he'd have a meeting with his lawyers, but it was only for form's sake—to keep him abreast of what they were doing and where they were at. They'd been quietly beavering away on his behalf for the last few weeks.

'Okay, well, while I have a chance to ask, what would you like me to prepare for tomorrow?'

'Nothing.' In fact, she wouldn't even need to attend.

'You haven't given me so much as a letter to type up yet!'

But she wanted to help, to be useful. He leaned against the door. 'You want the truth?'

She stuck out a hip and nodded.

'Many of these kinds of negotiations are about appearances.'

She stared at him as if waiting for more. 'Okay.' She drew the word out.

'While we're here I want—need—to appear powerful, in control and ruthless.'

She lifted a shoulder. 'As you're all those things then I don't see the problem.'

She thought him ruthless?

He rubbed his nape. Of course she did. He was all but forcing her to spend the next two years at Lorna Lee's. 'I know I am and you know I am...'

'Ah, but you need the people you're negotiating with to know that you are too.'

'And the sooner, the better. How do you think I can best achieve that?'

'By dressing smartly in expensive suits and staying in swish hotels?'

'And having lackeys.'

Her face cleared. 'I'm your lackey!'

'Not literally, you realise.'

'But *they* don't know that.' She chewed her lip. 'So I just have to dress smartly, say "Yes, Mr Mather" and "No, Mr Mather" at the appropriate times, fetch you coffee when you demand it, email London when you tell me to, and ring New York when you deem it necessary.'

'Now you're getting the hang of it.'

She beamed at him. 'I could do that with my eyes closed.'

He frowned.

'Except I won't, of course.'

'I have perfect faith in your abilities, Adelaide.'

She stared at him for a moment before shaking herself. 'So you don't have plans for this afternoon and this evening?'

'I…'

'Because I'm going to try and get us tickets to the ice hockey.'

He stared at her.

'Sport is a universal language, Flynn.'

In her diary she'd called him perfectly perfect and it hadn't sounded like a compliment.

'So you never know. A passing comment that you saw the Red Bulls in action could swing a negotiation your way, or create a useful connection. It'll also show you're interested in the community and that won't do you any harm.'

Perfectly perfect?

'You make a strong case,' he allowed. 'But here…' He fished out his credit card. 'Charge the tickets to this.' He didn't want her out of pocket.

'But—'

'Legitimate business expenses,' he declared over the top of her protests.

'Oh!' She took a step back and then gestured to what he was wearing. 'I've interrupted your morning run.'

'Just going to hit the hotel gym for an hour.'

She rolled her eyes. 'Flynn, for heaven's sake!'

'What?'

'Look out the window.' She pointed.

He turned to stare, but he didn't know what he was supposed to be looking at.

'The sun is shining,' she said as if speaking to a six-year-old. 'Fresh air.' She slammed a hand to her hip. 'What is wrong with you? If you're going to buy a Munich business the least you can do is breathe in the Munich air.'

Did she know how cold it was out there?

'Instead of some perfectly temperature controlled recycled air that's free of the scent or taste of anything.'

There was that word again—*perfectly*.

He thrust out his jaw. 'It's convenient.'

'But is it interesting? Does it teach you anything? Is it fun?'

That last stung.

She shook her head. 'Give me five. I know the perfect jogging trail.'

He opened his mouth to refuse. *Dear Daisy…* He closed it again. 'You jog?'

'Under sufferance. I'll meet you in the foyer in five minutes.'

It took her six, not that he pointed that out as she called a *guten Morgen* to Bruno. An altogether different emotion gripped him when he surveyed her legs in their fitted track pants. Addie didn't have a classically beautiful shape—her hips were too wide and her chest too small—but it didn't stop him from wondering what it'd be like to drag those hips against his and—

Whoa! Inappropriate. Employee. Jeez.

'C'mon, we're going to jog by the river. I went for a walk down there yesterday. It's gorgeous.'

It took them three minutes to reach it. She made them go across the bridge and down to the park on the other side. 'See, what did I tell you?'

She stretched her arms out wide and he had a sudden image of her sprawled beneath him, tousled and sultry and—

Why did he have to go and read 'Till the Cows Come Home'? Why did he have to see Addie in a whole new light?

For a moment he was tempted to tell her she could jog on her own, that he was going back to the hotel.

Wish you were here,
Love Buttercup.

He bit back an oath. She didn't deserve that from him. She'd had enough grief in her life without him adding to it. All he had to do was get his hormones in check.

'You really need to get the kinks out, don't you?'

He turned to find her, hands on hips, surveying him. What was so wrong about being perfectly perfect? What the hell did perfectly perfect mean anyway?

'I know it's cold but breathe it in.' She took a deep breath and so did he. 'Can you smell it?'

He knew exactly what she meant. Could he smell the land? Yes. He could smell the brown of the river and the green of the grass and the tang of sap and bark and tree. The air was thinner than home, and colder, but invigorating too. Without another word she set off down the path at a jog.

He set off after her, breathing in the cold air and trying not to notice how her hips moved in those track pants.

She set an easy pace. He could've overtaken her if he wanted, but, for reasons he refused to delve into, he chose not to.

He wasn't sure for how long they jogged, maybe ten minutes, when she pulled up short and pointed to an upcoming bridge. 'Look, it has statues on it like something out of *Lord of the Rings.*'

As they approached he noticed the detail and workmanship. He was about to suggest they go up onto the bridge to discover whom the statues commemorated when she grabbed his arm and pulled him to a halt. She pointed to her right. 'Look at that,' she breathed. 'Isn't it the most splendid building?'

Splendid described it perfectly.

'The first thing I did when I got back from my walk yesterday was find out what it was.'

He really should've done more homework before landing here. So much culture and history just outside his door and he hadn't even been aware of it. *What is wrong with you?* What indeed?

'Do you know what it is?'

A lump blocked his throat and he couldn't have explained why. He shook his head.

'It's home to the state parliament so I guess it should be grand, *but...*'

He understood her *but—but I've never seen anything like it before; but there's nothing like this in Australia; but it's outside my experience and I'm in a foreign country and it's amazing and exciting and an adventure.*

All the total antithesis of the reason he was here.

'Are you okay, Flynn?'

Apparently he was perfectly perfect for all the good it did him. He glanced down at her. The exercise had brightened her cheeks and eyes. A well of yearning rose up inside him. How had she held onto her excitement and joy and hope in the face of all her grief?

'Flynn?'

He shook himself. 'It's just occurred to me that I've been working too hard.'

'One should never work so hard that there's no time for this.' She gestured to the parliament building, the bridge and river.

He made a vow then. As soon as he'd vanquished Mueller, he'd find his excitement again. He'd make time to feed his soul with adventure and joy the way Addie did.

After the meeting with Flynn's lawyers the next day, which Addie had insisted on attending despite Flynn's assurances that she needn't, Addie needed a shopping trip. She'd endured forty minutes of boring, boring, boring. The four men had talked figures and had used phrases like 'projected outcomes', 'financial prognoses', 'incorporated portfolios' and 'Regulation 557' until she'd thought her brain would leak out of her ears and her feigned interest would freeze into a kind of rictus on her face.

The shopping, though, sorted her out.

She let herself into her room, collapsed onto the sofa and grinned at the assortment of bags that surrounded her. Oops. She might've gone a little overboard.

Oh, what the heck? She leapt up and tipped the contents of one of the bags onto the bed. Slipping out of her jeans, she tried on her new outfit and raced to the mirror. 'You'll never believe this, Robbie, but I have a cleavage!'

Her? A cleavage? She grinned, and then grinned some more, literally chortling. She turned to the left and then to the right before giving her reflection a thumbs-up. She'd only ever be able to wear it for fancy dress, but—

The phone rang.

She lifted it to her ear. 'Hello?'

'I need you in here. Right now.'

Flynn. 'But—'

There was no point speaking. The line had gone dead.

What on earth? She glanced down with a grimace, but headed next door without delay. She'd barely knocked before the door was yanked open.

'I...' Flynn did a double take. 'What on earth are you wearing?'

'It's a traditional Bavarian costume.'

'It's gingham!'

'The skirt of the dirndl is gingham,' she corrected. Blue-and-white gingham to be precise. 'The blouse is white and the bodice of the dirndl is royal blue.' Lord, she was babbling, but she could barely form a coherent sentence when Flynn stared at her chest like that. Her hand fluttered to her cleavage in an attempt to hide it. She cleared her throat. 'What's the emergency?'

He snapped to and swore, but he grabbed her arm and pulled her into the room. 'You're not even wearing shoes,' he groaned.

'I can go change.'

'No time.'

She wanted to shake him. 'For what?'

A heavy knock sounded on the door. He moved her away from it with another smothered curse. 'There's no time to explain, but just follow my lead. I need deadpan, no surprise. Cool, smooth and efficient.'

'Roger,' she murmured back.

He planted himself at the table with a file and his computer and then gestured towards the door. 'Please let Herr Mueller in.'

'Herr Mueller,' she repeated under her breath as she moved to the door. 'Herr Mueller?' she said when she opened it.

A pair of bushy eyebrows rose as they stared down at her. 'Yes.'

'Please come in.'

He took in her attire and twinkling eyes transformed a gruff face. 'You look charming, *fräulein*.'

She smiled back. 'I'm afraid you've rather caught me on the hop.'

'And I've been rewarded for it.'

What a nice man. 'Do come in, Herr Mueller. Mr Mather is expecting you.'

Those lips firmed and the bushy eyebrows lowered over his face when he entered the room. She swallowed and recalled Flynn's demand—cool, smooth and efficient. She gestured towards the table.

'Hello, Flynn.'

'Herr Mueller.' Flynn didn't rise or offer his hand. He didn't ask the other man to sit. He simply leaned back and crossed his legs. 'You wanted to talk. Well, talk.'

Her head rocked back. This was no way to do business,

surely? She gripped her hands in front of her. At least it wasn't how he'd done business with her or Herr Gunther or Herrs Schmidt, Schuller and Schubert.

The air in the room started to bristle and burn. She surged forward. 'Coffee?' she asked, hoping to ease the way.

'That would be appreciated,' Herr Mueller said with a forced smile.

'No coffee,' Flynn said with a glare, his voice like flint.

She realised then he didn't mean no coffee for him. He meant no coffee full stop. She blinked at his rudeness and choked back her automatic rebuke. His room. His rules. Fine, no coffee.

She had no idea what to do with herself—where to sit or where to stand. She decided to remain right where she was—behind Herr Mueller. She'd promised Flynn deadpan but now she wasn't sure that she could deliver. At least back here Herr Mueller wouldn't witness her shock.

Flynn would. If he bothered to glance her way. At the moment he was too busy summing up his…adversary, if that was what Herr Mueller was, to pay any attention to her.

'I didn't want to talk,' Herr Mueller said and she suddenly realised that behind the heavy German intonation there was a thread of an Australian accent. 'I just wanted to see your face and it tells me everything I need to know.'

Malice flashed in Flynn's smile. 'Good.'

He was enjoying this? Addie wished herself anywhere else on earth. She'd even plump for Lorna Lee's. In fact, Lorna Lee's suddenly seemed like a very attractive option.

'You're determined to ruin me?'

'I am. And I'll succeed.' The words were uttered smoothly, ruthlessly, triumphantly. Addie stared down to where her toes curled against the plush pile of the carpet.

'You hold a grudge for a long time.'

'Only the ones worth keeping.'

She glanced from one to the other. What on earth were they talking about?

'You may succeed in your aim, Flynn—'

'I have every intention of succeeding, George, and I'll relish every moment of it.'

She shivered and chafed her arms.

Herr Mueller frowned and leaned towards him. 'What you don't realise yet is that in the process you'll lose more than you gain. Are you prepared for that?'

Her head lifted at the pity in the older man's voice.

'No doubt that's what you'd like me to think.'

The older man shook his head. 'Despite what you think, I was sorry to hear about your father.'

Flynn laughed, but there was no humour in it. Herr Mueller turned to leave and Addie did what she could to smooth her face out into a calm mask. He held his hand out to her and she placed hers in it automatically. 'It was nice to meet you, Fräulein...'

'Ramsey. Adelaide Ramsey.' She tried to find a smile but she suspected it was more of a grimace. 'Likewise.' She leapt forward to open the door for him. '*Auf wiedersehen*.'

When the door shut behind the older man she swung back to Flynn, hands on hips. 'What on earth was that all about? My parents would've had my hide if I'd ever been as rude as you just were.'

'You were obviously raised more nicely than me.'

She gaped at him.

'By the way, Addie, you need to work on deadpan.'

'While you need to work on your manners! That man would have to be seventy if he's a day. Would it really have killed you to offer him a seat and a cup of coffee?' She dragged both hands back through her hair, paced to the door and back again.

Those hateful lips of his twitched. 'I've shocked you to the core, haven't I?'

'I may not know much about wheeling and dealing but that's no way to do business.'

'And yet it's exactly how I mean to conduct myself while in Munich, Addie. You don't have to like it.'

Like it? She hated it.

His face grew hard and cold. 'So you have two choices. Either shut up and put up or jump on the first plane back to Australia.'

She almost took the second option, but remembered her promise to Robbie. *Of course I'll see the world. I'll visit all of the places we've talked about.* The places they'd always meant to visit together. It hit her then, though, that they'd never considered—let alone discussed—what that promise might eventually cost.

When did the price become too high?

'You didn't come here to buy a brewery, did you? This isn't about making some boyhood dream come true.'

He laughed—a harsh sound. 'A boyhood dream? Where on earth did you get that idea? The brewery is only important insomuch as it's currently Mueller's. Make no mistake, though, I mean to take it from him.'

She took a step back. 'You came here with the express purpose of ruining him.'

'I did.'

She stared at him. 'It's Christmas, Flynn.' Who planned revenge at Christmas?

'I told you I was ruthless. And if I remember correctly you agreed with me.'

True, but... 'In business dealings, not personal ones.' And Herr Mueller was obviously personal. Nor had she thought Flynn ruthless to this level. She'd just thought him one of those perfectly perfect people who got everything they wanted with nothing more than the click of their fingers.

But Flynn wasn't perfect. He was far from perfect.

He leaned forward as if he'd read that thought in her

face. 'Think whatever you want, but I'm not the Scrooge in this particular scenario.'

Oh, as if she was going to believe that! 'What do you do for an encore—steal candy from babies?' she shot back.

He straightened and he reminded her of a snake readying itself to strike. 'As you haven't left yet I take it you've chosen to put up and shut up?'

Her stomach burned acid. 'Yes,' she said shortly. 'You're right. I don't have to like it, but... Are you sure that man deserves to be ruined?'

He rocked back on his heels. 'One compliment and he completely charmed your socks off. I credited you with more sense.'

The criticism stung. 'He was polite. I was polite back.'

'You were certainly that.'

She folded her arms. 'He seems nice.'

His lips twisted. 'Appearance is everything in these games, remember?'

So he'd said, but it suddenly occurred to her that she might not be the one wearing the blinkers. 'He reminded me of—'

'Let me guess—Santa Claus?'

'The grandfather of an old school friend.' Robbie's poppy. 'A nice old man.' Who'd seen too much heartache.

She walked to the window, blinking back tears. When she was certain she had herself in hand, she turned back to Flynn. 'What did Herr Mueller do to you to deserve this?'

'That's none of your business. And,' he continued over the top of her when she went to speak again, 'for the third and final time—put up and shut up or...'

His *or* hung there like a black threat. She swallowed the rest of her questions. 'Will you need me for the remainder of the day?'

'No.'

Without another word, she left.

CHAPTER FIVE

ADDIE REEFED OFF her apron and pulled the dirndl over her head, leaving them where they fell. She tugged on thick jeans, thick socks and her thickest jumper. She wound a scarf around her throat, seized her coat and slammed out of the hotel.

If she stayed she'd only do something stupid like stride back over to Flynn's room and fight with him. And then he'd send her home.

She didn't want to go home, but…

She buried her hands deep in the pockets of her coat and hunched her shoulders against the cold. Why on earth had he let her go prattling on about marketing strategies for beer halls and import deals that could be struck, huh? She must've sounded like a right idiot! Had he been laughing at her the entire time?

She scrubbed her hands down her face before shoving them in her pockets again. Jerk! Why hadn't he told her the real reason he was in Munich from the start?

Because it was easier?

Because he knew it was wrong and felt uncomfortable about it?

She snorted. He didn't have enough sensitivity for discomfit.

She stomped down the street, but it didn't ease the tension that had her coiled up tight. It didn't answer the question of why her discovery left a hole gaping through her.

What she needed was a long gallop over rolling fields. Rolling fields. Lorna Lee's.

She slammed to a halt and lifted her face to the sky. She was going to have to spend the next two years working for this man? If she did him some perceived wrong would he then turn on her and try to destroy her? Would she for ever have to watch herself? Bite her tongue?

Ha! As if biting her tongue were a skill she possessed.

She set back off. In her pockets, her hands clenched. She had a feeling it was a necessary PA skill, though, and if she wanted to travel the world as a PA it'd be a skill she'd better master.

She wrinkled her nose. She stomped on for a while longer before thinking to take stock of her surroundings. When she did she came to a dead halt. She hadn't paid much attention to the direction her feet had taken her—other than to stay on well-lit streets. It grew dark early in Munich at this time of year.

This time of year...

Somehow she'd wended her way behind Marienplatz and now she stood on the edge of the square—facing the awe-inspiring Gothic magnificence of the New Town Hall. The enormous Christmas tree twinkled and glittered. The coloured lights and Christmas decorations strung up all around the square winked and danced, and on the balcony of the Old Town Hall a folk group sang a Christmas carol. Beneath awnings the Christmas markets were a feast of sound and scent and movement.

It was Christmas. In exactly one week.

Back home Jeannie would've put up her and Frank's tree. There'd be presents wrapped beneath it in brightly coloured paper. The ham would've been ordered and the Christmas pudding made. Addie twisted her hands together. Frank, Jeannie and her family had shared Christmas lunch and spent Christmas afternoon together for as long as she could remember. She scuffed a toe against the ground. They'd miss her father so much this Christmas Day. Maybe it'd been selfish to come to Europe.

Especially as this would be their last Christmas on the farm.

She scratched her head and rolled her shoulders. It didn't have to be. She could invite them for Christmas next year, couldn't she? Flynn wouldn't mind. Or would he?

She plonked herself onto a bench when a family vacated it and rested her elbows on her knees to frown down at the ground. She'd thought Frank and Jeannie had wanted to leave the farm—it *had* become too much for them—and to move into a retirement village with its easier pace. An email she'd received from Jeannie this morning, though, had left her feeling uneasy. Oh, Jeannie had been cheerful, full of neighbourhood news and Howard's progress with all of his 'new-fangled' ideas, but the cheer had sounded forced when she'd spoken about leaving.

Addie rested back and stared at the Christmas tree. If she was going to be stuck on the farm for another two years Frank and Jeannie could stay with her until they found exactly the right place to move into, couldn't they? She folded her arms. She'd probably have to get Flynn's approval—he with the noteworthy absence of Christmas spirit and lack of the milk of human kindness.

She ground the heels of her boots together. It wasn't precisely true, though, was it? He'd been kind to her. He'd taken her to the medieval markets. It'd seemed important to him that she enjoy herself. If he truly was ruthless then that didn't make sense.

Did he have an ulterior motive?

She snorted. Talk about fanciful, because, if he did, heaven only knew what it could be.

She bought a mug of *glühwein* and sipped it, appreciating the way it warmed her from the inside out. Back home at Lorna Lee's they'd be sipping ice-cold beer in an attempt to cool themselves. For the teensiest moment she wished herself on the homestead veranda surrounded by people she trusted and understood.

Addie didn't so much as clap eyes on Flynn for the following two days. She'd returned to her hotel room after her glass of *gluhwein* to a terse message on her voice mail informing her that he wouldn't require her services for the next two days.

It made her paranoid. Why had he brought her to Munich if he didn't want her to do anything? She rang home to speak to Jeannie and Frank, and then Eric, Lucy and Colin. She wanted to double-check that Howard had followed Flynn's directive about Bruce Augustus. She wanted to know that everyone was okay and that nothing dire was going down.

With everything at home seemingly perfect and her fears allayed, Addie went sightseeing. She visited Schloss Nymphenburg—the summer palace of the former Bavarian rulers—where she promptly went into raptures. The palace was the most exquisite building she'd ever seen. But it was the grounds that transported her.

Her jaw dropped as she viewed them from the balcony and her soul expanded until it almost hurt. Formal avenues stretched away, the central one leading down to an ornamental lake with a fountain. Flowerbeds lined the avenues. The colour must be spectacular in spring. Beyond the formal gardens, far beyond, green fields extended for as far as she could see. How perfect they'd be for cantering across, for leaving the cares of the world behind.

She'd spent a long time there—an hour in the palace itself and the rest wandering through the grounds. Did Flynn really mean to forgo all of this in the pursuit of his mean-spirited revenge? There were so many marvels and wonders to enjoy if he'd only stop for a moment and—

Stop it! Trying to understand him was fruitless. He'd have his reasons.

And as he'd pointed out, she didn't have to like them.

She glared up at a sky almost as blue as his eyes and hoped those reasons kept him awake at night.

She visited the Residenz, the palace in Munich—a series of gorgeous buildings and courtyards. The museum of grand rooms depicting differing architectural styles and works of art—paintings, sculptures, tapestries, porcelain and more—blew her away. To think people had once lived like this.

It became a bit too much so she spent the rest of the day in the English Gardens—one of the largest urban green spaces in Germany. She stared at frozen streams and dark green spruce trees and marvelled at how different they were from the creeks and gums back home. She ate bratwurst and drank hot tea and wished Flynn had chosen to join her rather than whatever nefarious plan he was no doubt putting into action instead.

Maybe if he had more fun in his life he'd let go of his grudge and focus on the future rather than...

She snorted. Yeah, as if that were going to happen.

Why are you being so hard on him?

She almost spilled her tea when that thought hit her. Was she being hard on him? She swallowed. Why—because he'd been rude to a man she'd taken a liking to? That hardly seemed fair.

She chafed her arms. No, it wasn't that. It was the hardness that had appeared in his eyes, their coldness when they'd stared at Herr Mueller. It had chilled her, frightened her. She took a sip of tea to try and chase the cold away. Still, wasn't that her problem, rather than Flynn's? He might in fact have a very good reason for his...hatred.

She set her mug down, her stomach churning. That was Flynn's primary emotion towards Herr Mueller. Hatred. She had no experience with it. And she didn't want any either, thank you very much.

Why did he feel so strongly?

She dragged a hand through her hair. The likelihood of finding that out was zilch. She wasn't sure she even wanted to know.

She returned to the hotel that evening to another terse message from her enigmatic employer informing her that a meeting was scheduled for the following morning and to meet him in the foyer at 9:45 on the dot. 'And let's see if this time you can keep your face halfway impassive.'

She poked her tongue out at the telephone, but raced over to the wardrobe to make sure her little black suit was all in order. Looking the part of the perfect PA might help her act like the perfect PA.

'Good morning, Adelaide.'

Addie leapt up from the chair she'd taken possession of in the foyer ten minutes ago. She'd made sure to arrive early. 'Good morning.'

She bit back a sigh. Flynn looked disgustingly crisp and well rested—perfectly perfect. 'Are you Mr Mather or Flynn at the meeting?' she asked, following him out to the taxi rank.

'I'm Flynn when you address me directly. I'm Mr Mather when you refer to me to a third party.'

She moistened her lips. 'And who might these third parties be?'

He flicked a wry glance in her direction. 'Herr Mueller and his lawyers.'

So they were meeting with the big guns.

'Is that going to be a problem for you?'

She didn't flinch at his sarcasm. 'I don't care what you say or threaten me with, I'm not going to be rude, Flynn.'

The words shot out of her, unrehearsed. She stiffened and waited for him to turn with those eyes and freeze her to the spot. Instead his lips twitched as he opened the cab door for her. 'Try, at least, to keep your shock in check.'

She scooted across to the far seat. 'I've had time to prepare,' she assured him.

Those blue eyes of his rolled a fraction. 'I'm hoping you won't have to say anything at all.'

Fingers crossed.

He remained silent after that. He didn't ask what she'd done for the last two days and she didn't ask him. Who knew five minutes could take so long? She spent the time practising being impassive and keeping her fingers *lightly* clasped in her lap.

They emerged from the cab and she recognised the offices of Flynn's legal team. They were on his turf, then. She smoothed a hand down her hair. How exactly did he mean to ruin Herr Mueller? How did one go about bankrupting someone? She had no idea. It wasn't something they'd taught at secretarial college—at least, not during the brief time she'd attended. Mind you, she could count all the ways disaster could strike at Lorna Lee's—drought, flood, a worldwide drop in beef prices, an outbreak of foot and mouth disease. Flynn, she supposed, planned to be Herr Mueller's natural disaster.

'Addie?'

She half tripped up a step. 'Yes?'

'Tell me your role today.'

She pulled in a breath, eyes to the front. This man had bought Lorna Lee's and was going to expand it in exciting ways. He'd offered her incentives and bonuses to stay—a generous wage and the promise of international air travel. He'd brought her to Munich, he'd taken her to Christmas markets and he'd helped her to shop. She owed him some measure of loyalty. 'My role today is lackey— super-efficient PA and lackey. When you say jump I ask how high.'

'And?'

Oh! 'And I will do my best to keep a straight face, keep my thoughts to myself and to follow your lead.'

'Excellent.'

She followed him into the building with a sigh and tried to stop her shoulders from sagging. It all sounded perfectly perfect. As long as she could pull it off.

During the first twenty minutes of the meeting, Addie learned precisely how to bankrupt a man. What one did was buy out from beneath him the building he'd leased for the last eighteen years and had spent a ludicrous amount of money improving, with the sole intention of not leasing the building back to him. Apparently a verbal agreement had existed between the deceased owner and Herr Mueller for Herr Mueller to buy the premises at a reduced price, but there was nothing in writing. Likewise, all of the equipment that Herr Mueller had spent so much money investing in was now considered part of the premises—owned by the estate and not by him.

'I had a verbal agreement with Herr Hoffman that this building would be mine!' Herr Mueller slammed a hand down to the table.

'Present the documentation to support your claim and I will gladly cede the tender to you.'

She swallowed. Dear Lord, Flynn sounded controlled and deadly.

'It was a gentleman's agreement.'

'Herr Mueller, I don't for one moment believe you a gentleman.'

Addie nearly swallowed her tongue. How on earth did Flynn expect her to keep her face unreadable when he said things like that?

'As far as I'm concerned that building is up for grabs to the highest bidder.'

No points for guessing who the highest bidder would prove to be. She bit her pen, glancing from one man to the other.

'You have no love for German culture! What do you know about brewing techniques or—?'

'I know how to turn a profit. If you want the premises all you need to do is outbid me.'

That cold hard smile! She tried not to flinch.

The only hope she had of keeping her promise was to think of something else. To tune out of the conversation while keeping her ears pricked in case Flynn called her name. She pulled her notepad towards her.

Think, think, think! What was something that bored her to tears? She'd maintain a veneer of impassivity if she were bored to tears.

Artificial insemination!

She wrote that at the top of the page. In the last couple of years there'd been developments in the techniques used for the artificial insemination of breeding stock. Not to mention the collection of bull semen. She bit back a sigh. It could be hard work inseminating a herd of twitchy heifers. Her record was four hundred and eighty-seven. In a single day. Her arm—her whole body—had been aching by the end of it. But, with an injection of funds maybe they'd be able to explore the newer methods.

They might prove quicker. She tapped the pen against her chin. Would they prove as successful, though? She jotted down some pros and cons. She'd need to do some intensive research, check a few websites and talk to some people in the industry. She scrawled down a few names, added a couple of websites to the list.

She bit the end of her pen. The improvements at Lorna Lee's didn't have to be confronting or intimidating. They could be exciting. Think what Flynn's injection of capital could do for the place. They'd be able to increase their output. A smile built through her when she thought of all of the sweet spring and autumn calves they could have. Calving was her favourite time of year.

Who knew? Maybe in a couple of years they'd really start to make a significant mark on the Australian stage. Lorna Lee's had a good reputation, but it couldn't compete with the bigger stud farms. Not yet. But if they could win a ribbon—a blue ribbon—at the Royal Easter show, Sydney's biggest agricultural show, then interest in their stock and breeding programmes would increase tenfold.

She imagined standing there, holding the halter of a magnificent bull—one of Bruce Augustus's grandbabies—as a blue ribbon was placed across his back. What a moment that would be.

Flynn glanced across at Addie when the lawyers started droning on about ordinances, injunctions and directives. His lips twitched at the dreamy expression she wore. It was a thousand times better than her indignation and disapproval, and it warmed something inside him. He'd missed her vigour and enthusiasm over the past two days. His smile widened when she started to slouch in a most un-PA way, her chin resting on her hands. What on earth was she thinking about?

He glanced at her pad, edged it around so he could read the notes she'd made. She didn't even notice, too deep in her daydream or whatever it was. He read what she'd jotted down and almost choked. He had to hide his mouth momentarily behind his hand. Artificial insemination? He coughed back a laugh. What crazy notion made her think she wanted to be a secretary or personal assistant instead of working at Lorna Lee's?

He nudged her. She immediately straightened.

He rose. She shot to her feet, gathering notebook and pens and slipping them into her briefcase.

'Gentlemen.' He glanced at the lawyers. 'You can stay to thrash this out to your hearts' content, but my resolution is fixed. Unless Herr Mueller can offer a higher bid on the property than I can, I will be buying it.'

This was supposed to be the day of his greatest triumph and all he could think about was taking Addie to lunch and listening to her sightseeing adventures.

'So you're serious in your intent, Flynn?' George Mueller said. There was no desperation in his eyes, only sadness.

'Deadly serious.'

Again, no triumph. The thing was...Mueller did look a lot like...well, Santa Claus. Flynn hardened his heart, deliberately reminding himself what the other man had done to his father. Without another word he turned and left, aware of the click-click of Addie's heels as she followed him.

When they reached the street he didn't hail a cab, but turned left in the direction of their hotel. He glanced at Addie, who kept easy pace beside him. 'Artificial insemination?'

She grimaced. 'I was trying to think of something that would help me keep my face straight, would help me look calm and bored.'

It hadn't succeeded, but he didn't tell her that. Inattentive was a hell of a lot better than 'shocked to the soles of her feet'. He still remembered her flinch when he'd told George that he didn't consider him a gentleman. It had been an almost physical rebuke.

It irked him that she thought so badly of him.

And it irked him that *that* irked him.

They needed to talk. He gestured her into a coffee shop.

'A debrief?' she asked.

'Something like that.'

He moved to a table, but Addie walked right up to the counter to peer at the cakes and sweets on display. 'Ooh, look at all of that!'

'Would you like something to eat?'

'You bet.'

And again she made him grin. Effortlessly.

'I'm on a mission to try every German delicacy I can.' She ordered a cappuccino and apple strudel with cream. After a moment's hesitation Flynn did the same.

'So?' She sat and folded her hands on the table. 'What do you need to debrief me about?'

There was no point beating about the bush. 'Howard isn't taking too kindly to you checking up on him.'

She laughed. 'The others are razzing him, huh? Good for them.'

Their order arrived and he swore her mouth watered as the strudel was placed in front of her. She lifted her spoon and took a bite. 'So good,' she moaned.

He followed her lead. Hell, yeah, it was better than good.

She took a second bite. 'But you can tell Howard not to get his knickers in a knot. I wasn't checking up on him. I was checking up on you.'

He choked on apple and pastry. When she slapped him on the back she did it so hard he almost face-planted the table. He glared at her. 'Me?'

She shrugged and ate more strudel.

'You want to explain that?'

'Not really. You won't like it.' She set her spoon down with a clatter and folded her arms. 'But I can see you're going to insist.'

Too right.

Her eyes—the expression in them—skewered him to the spot. 'I might've agreed when you said you were ruthless, but I didn't believe it. Not really.' She blew out a breath and shrugged. 'You were sort of ruthless in getting your own way about me staying on at Lorna Lee's, but you did sweeten the deal.'

Exactly.

'It wasn't until I saw how emotionless and cold and... hateful you were towards Herr Mueller that I believed it.'

She was right. He didn't like it.

'And then you said I wasn't needed for the last two days and it got me wondering if...'

'What?' He shoved apple strudel and cream into his mouth in the hope it would rid him of the bad taste that coated his tongue.

She waited until he'd finished eating before speaking

again. 'It made me wonder if there was some deeper game you were playing with me and Lorna Lee's.'

His stomach churned.

'I started thinking you might've wanted to get me away from the place for a while.'

That was what she now thought of him? He pushed his plate away.

'I thought you might have something devastating planned and didn't want me there when it happened.'

He leaned towards her. 'Addie, Lorna Lee's is mine. Once the cooling-off period is over I can do with it whatever I darn well please.'

'In another three and a half weeks.'

Was she counting down the days? He sat back. 'Why would I jeopardise our contract like that?'

'You're a man who likes to get his own way.' She sipped her coffee. 'You told me yourself that you don't like to wait when you want something.'

'We all like getting our own way, there's nothing unique about that, but why would I ask you to stay at the farm if I was going to do something to it that would get you offside?'

'Because you are ruthless.' She set her cup down. 'And I don't doubt for a moment that you think you know better than me.'

He stared at her. His ruthlessness had really shocked her, hadn't it? It had made her question his entire ethos.

He fingered the carved wooden figure in his jacket pocket. He'd carried it around with him for the last two days. He pulled it out now and set it on the table between them. 'I bought this for you as a symbol of our verbal contract about your bull, Bruce Augustus.'

She reached out and picked it up, turned it over in her fingers. 'It's beautiful.'

He recalled the warmth that had spread through him when she'd told him she believed him a man of his word. She didn't now, though. Now she thought him some kind of power-hungry, revenge-driven monster. 'I'm ruthless only where Herr Mueller is concerned.'

She glanced up. She opened her mouth, but closed it again, her eyes murky and troubled. He recalled the way he'd told her it was none of her business.

He swore under his breath. Addie didn't flinch at that. She didn't even blink. Bred to country life, she was used to swearing and expletives. What she wasn't used to was explicit rudeness. And hate.

'Herr Mueller destroyed my family.' He hadn't known he'd meant to utter the words until they left him.

Her jaw dropped. 'How?'

He dragged a hand across his nape. 'He and my father were business partners. They owned a pub in Brisbane.' Bile burned his stomach. 'Unfortunately you're not the only person to find him charming and benevolent. My father thought the same. That's the thing about conmen, Addie. They're plausible. It's a trick of the trade—that along with their charm.'

She gripped the carving in her hand and held it to her chest. 'What happened?'

He convinced my father to invest all of his money in their enterprise and then fleeced him of the lot.'

'But...but that's awful!'

'He sold up, made a killing and came to Germany, where his father's people were.'

'And your father?'

'He killed himself.'

Her hand reached out to cover his. 'Oh, Flynn.'

She didn't say anything else. Probably because there wasn't anything else to say.

'After that my mother became bitter.'

'How old were you when your father...?'

'Twelve.'

Her hand tightened about his. 'That's criminal!'

'Exactly.' He removed his hand from hers before he did

something stupid like clasp it, hold it and not let it go. 'And while I don't have the proof to put him in jail where he belongs, I can ruin him.' He clenched his hand. 'And I will.' And he'd show no mercy.

'I meant…' She swallowed. 'What Herr Mueller did is dreadful but… It was a terrible thing, your father leaving you and your mother alone like that.' She moistened her lips. 'I know money is important, but people are more important.'

A fist tightened inside Flynn's chest. 'He thought he'd failed us. The man he'd looked up to almost as a father had betrayed him. It was all too much.' His father had become a shadow, a wraith.

He dragged a hand down his face, remembering his father's attempts to explain the situation to him and his mother. He recalled her tears and the drawn, haggard lines that had appeared on her face. His father's pallor and hopelessness had burned itself onto his soul. Those things still had the power to scorch him, to shrivel what small amount of contentment he reached for. George Mueller was responsible for that.

He glanced across at her and tried to find a smile. 'Addie, my father had been so full of life. My mother was always a difficult woman, but when my father came home in the evenings he made everything better. He'd make us laugh and make everything seem carefree and merry and full of promise.' When his father had died, life had never been the same again and it was time for Herr Mueller to pay.

'Why didn't your father fight? Take him to court?'

'Mueller was too clever. He didn't leave a paper trail and he left the country before we'd even realised it. Hell, Addie, he used to come around for dinner. He'd laugh and joke and act like one of the family.' His twelve-year-old self had loved George Mueller. 'But he left without a single word of goodbye. The financial records at the bar were destroyed by fire.' Nothing had gone right for his father. 'There was nothing my father could do.'

'I'm sorry, Flynn.'

He shook his head. 'I didn't tell you this for your sympathy.' Though he knew her sympathy was real. 'I told you so you'd understand my attitude towards that man. So you'd understand why I can't let him profit from my family's misery.'

She nodded, but he could tell she didn't understand. Not really. Addie had experienced grief, but not hatred. In her world one let bygones be bygones. And he couldn't help but be glad of that.

Addie pulled her strudel back towards her. She'd lost her appetite completely, but she could tell Flynn wanted them back on an even footing—didn't want her making a fuss. She understood that. She'd appreciated her friends' and neighbours' condolences when her father had passed, but it had grown old hat real quick too. She realised she still held the carving of Bruce Augustus tightly clenched in her hand. She set him down on the table by her plate. 'Thank you for my carved Bruce Augustus.'

'I thought you'd like him.'

'I appreciate what it represents more.' She pulled in a breath. 'I do trust that you don't mean harm to Lorna Lee's. I do trust that you'll keep your word.' She did trust that he wouldn't hurt her the way—

She cut that thought dead in its tracks.

'That means a lot to me, Addie.'

She believed that too. And that seemed the strangest thing of all.

She spooned strudel into her mouth, made herself chew and swallow. 'Can I be nosy for a bit?' She wanted to get rid of the tight, hard look around his eyes and mouth.

'You can try.' But he said it with the hint of a smile that gave her the courage to persist.

'It's just that I thought you'd grown up on a cattle station, that you'd grown up with money. Now obviously that's not the case. So how did you get from there to here?' To think she'd thought everything had simply fallen into his lap in a perfectly perfect fashion. How wrong she'd been.

'After my father died my mother moved us to Bourke to be nearer her sister.'

Bourke was a small township in the far west of New South Wales. It must've been quite the culture shock to the Brisbane boy.

'In my teens I started doing a bit of jackarooing during the school holidays and on weekends and found I had a knack for it.'

She'd never believed for a moment that hard body of his came from hours spent in the gym.

'I also discovered a talent for the rodeo circuit. I started with camp drafting and breakaway roping and progressed to bareback bronc and bull riding.'

Bull riding? Whoa! Now that was tough.

'You can make a pretty packet on the rodeo circuit. I saved up and by the time I was nineteen I'd bought a small property. I made improvements to it using my own blood and sweat and then sold it for twice the price. Rinse and repeat. At the same time I did a business course by correspondence, made a couple of investments that paid off.'

She stared at him. 'So you're really the epitome of the self-made man.' The twice-married self-made man. What had *that* been about? Not that she had any intention of getting that nosy.

It was none of her business.

And she had no intention of thinking about Flynn in *that* way.

'Once all of this is over, Addie, I mean to draw a line under the whole affair and concentrate on living the life I want.'

A niggle of unease shifted through her. She wasn't convinced that hate could be dealt with so easily. What was more, something about Flynn's story didn't ring true. Not that she thought he was lying. She didn't doubt that he believed all he'd told her, but...

She couldn't put her finger on it. Just that something didn't feel right.

'And what is the life you want?'

'Maybe I'll decide to turn Lorna Lee's into one of the world's most renowned stud properties.'

That'd keep him out of trouble.

He pushed his plate away and met her gaze with a defiant glare. 'I'm going to make my home at Lorna Lee's.'

Really?

'And...'

'And?'

He shook his head and leant back. 'Somewhere along the way, Adelaide Ramsey, you fired me with your enthusiasm. I want to create a successful brewery business here in Munich. I want my beer hall to be one of the best.'

Her jaw dropped. 'No?'

'Yes.'

He grinned at her. She grinned back. 'Flynn, what are your plans for Christmas Day?'

His nose curled. 'Spare me, Addie. As far as I'm concerned, it's just another day.'

She'd bet he hadn't had a proper Christmas since he was twelve years old. She shook her head. 'Wrong answer.'

CHAPTER SIX

FLYNN LEANED BACK, his face an interesting mix of conflicting emotions—politeness and an evident desire not to hurt her feelings battled with bull-headed stubbornness and resentment.

Politeness?

Extraordinary that he took such efforts to don it for her.

No, not extraordinary. She could see now it was his rudeness to Herr Mueller that was really out of character.

'Addie, forgive me, but I don't *do* Christmas.'

Just as he didn't do marriage or romantic relationships any more?

She shook herself. 'Ignoring it won't make it go away.'

He blinked.

And she wasn't above using a little emotional blackmail. She leaned towards him. 'I was going to try and ignore Christmas this year, because…but…'

He reached out to still the hand that worried at the carved bull.

She stared at his hand resting on hers. 'But I find I can't.' She glanced up and suddenly it was real emotion and not an attempt to manipulate pity that gripped her. 'I can't ignore it in this beautiful city, Flynn. Christmas is everywhere and—'

'I'm sorry I thought—'

'No, don't be sorry. I'm happy I'm here. It's an amazing place and I'm having a fabulous time.'

'So what's the problem?'

She scratched the back of her head. She glanced down to hide the tears that threatened her composure. His grip on her hand tightened, but she couldn't speak until the ache that stretched her throat had receded.

When she was certain she had herself under control she glanced up and his eyes softened as they searched her face. He lifted his other hand and she thought he'd reach out to touch her cheek. It shocked her how much she wanted his touch, but he lowered it back to the table.

She moistened her lips, swallowed. 'It seems wrong for me to take so much pleasure in all of this, to be enjoying myself so much when my father died only four months ago.'

'He wouldn't want you falling into a pit of depression. He'd be glad to know you were enjoying yourself.'

'What makes you so sure? You didn't know him. You never met him.'

'Maybe not, but I've come to know his daughter and she has a good heart. She does right by the people in her life even when it's at the expense of her own dreams, and she's done it without losing her sense of humour. She's a lovely woman with a zest for life that has taught me a thing or two. It only follows that your father would be a good man too.'

She bit her lip to stop it from trembling, her chest doing a funny 'expand and cramp' thing. She didn't know what to say. 'Thank you.'

'Life goes on and there's no shame in you finding pleasure in that life, Addie. It doesn't mean you don't miss him or wish he was still here.'

'In my head I know the truth of that, but…'

She eased back, removing her hand from beneath his. His touch had sent a swirling, confusing heat dancing through her and she wasn't sure how much more of it she could take. 'This might seem ridiculous to you, but I know I'll miss him more on Christmas Day. Ignoring the day and pretending it doesn't matter or telling myself that I'm not celebrating it this year isn't going to change that fact.'

He pinched the bridge of his nose between thumb and forefinger.

'I suspect you know what I mean. I suspect it's why you don't do Christmas.'

He glanced at her and his eyes darkened.

She grimaced in apology. 'The thing is, I don't see that it's working for you.'

His head reared back.

'I'm not saying this to be mean,' she added quickly. 'Just trying to work out my best way forward.'

'You think it'll all magically go away—the pain and grief and disillusion—if you celebrate Christmas?'

His face twisted as he spoke and her heart throbbed for him. At twelve his life had been turned upside down. She suspected it hadn't been on an even keel since.

Did he think that it would help ease the burn in his soul if he slayed the dragon Herr Mueller represented?

She tried to find a smile from somewhere. 'I know Christmas is touted as a time for miracles, but, no, I don't believe it'll all magically go away.' She rested her elbows on the table. 'Heavens, though, wouldn't it be nice?'

He stared at her and the faintest of smiles touched his lips and it occurred to her that she didn't see them as perfectly perfect any more. Instead she saw them as intriguing and with the potential to sate some ache inside her. She blinked and forced her gaze away. He'd been married. *Twice.* The gulf of differences that lay between them almost stole her breath. He had all this experience with romantic relationships while she had none.

Well, not precisely none. But she'd had to make sacrifices where romance was concerned, her duty to her parents and the farm coming first. She didn't regret that, but she wasn't going to now go and develop a crush on Flynn. *That* would be stupid.

'So why put in the effort of celebrating at all?'

She shook herself. 'Because if you don't, you're not giving the good stuff a chance to get through.'

He stared at her but he didn't say anything.

'I think it comes from the same place as your desire to bring down Herr Mueller.'

His eyes narrowed. She suspected a more sensible mortal would stop now, but she pushed on. 'It seems to me that you think if you vanquish him all will be well again—justice served and the world put to rights.'

'You don't think that the case?'

'No.' Her stomach rolled. 'But I can't explain why not. I just can't help feeling you'll lose something of yourself in the process. For the life of me, though, I haven't worked out what that might be.'

He brought one finger down to the table between them. 'You think it's wrong to want justice?'

'You don't want justice, Flynn. You want payback.' If he wanted justice he'd have spent his time finding the proof to put Herr Mueller on trial instead of making the money and acquiring the power to destroy him. 'What you really want is to bring your father back, but you already know that's impossible.'

'Addie—' he spoke carefully '—do you really think this is the way to go about convincing me to celebrate Christmas with you?'

Oh! She could feel her cheeks heat up. 'Sorry, I...' How on earth had they got onto the subject of Herr Mueller again? 'So...' She grimaced. 'You knew that's what I was doing—trying to get you to celebrate Christmas with me?'

He kinked an eyebrow.

Of course he had. She lifted a shoulder. 'I was going to be all pathetic and use emotional blackmail.' She wrinkled her nose. 'Instead I was just pathetic.'

'There's nothing pathetic about grief.'

'Flynn, it's my first Christmas as an orphan.' Awful

word! She met his gaze squarely. 'It hurts me to know that my children will never know their grandparents.'

'You don't have any children.'

'Not yet, but I will.' One day. 'And I don't want to sit at home on Christmas Day moping and feeling sorry for myself.'

He didn't say anything.

She hauled in a breath. 'So will you celebrate the day with me?'

'I…'

'Something I've learned over the last couple of days is that sightseeing is more fun if you have someone to share it with. Someone you can nudge and say, "Check that out!" and they can say, "I know. Amazing, isn't it?" back to you. Bearing witness together. A friend. I have a feeling Christmas will be the same.'

He still didn't say anything.

She folded her arms and glared at him. 'Oh, for heaven's sake. It's only Christmas. It's not like I'm asking you to marry me.'

He scowled. 'I don't want something all hushed and reverent.'

'Me neither.' She suppressed a shudder. 'I was thinking of something cheesy. The kitschier, the better.' Loud and rowdy. A revel. A party.

His scowl eased a fraction. 'Do I have to buy you a present?'

She feigned outrage. 'Of course you do.'

He thrust out his jaw. 'I bought you that bull.'

Suddenly she wanted to laugh. 'I'm high maintenance. I want one of the dried plum and almond chimney sweeps that abound at the markets and a pair of mittens.'

His scowl vanished and his laugh lifted her heart. '*That* I might be able to manage. Just call me Saint Nick.'

She wanted to hug him.

Heavens, wouldn't that have him backtracking at a million miles an hour? 'Well, Saint Nick, if you're serious, tell me your plans for the brewery.'

Addie and Flynn spent the next morning touring one of Munich's premier breweries.

'Of course, it's five times larger than the Mueller brewery,' Flynn said as they pushed through the rotating door into their hotel.

Addie crammed in beside him. 'It was all terribly interesting, though. Who knew—?'

She suddenly realised that she was pressed up against Flynn's side as they moved the five or so steps it took to get from the street and into the hotel foyer. She became excruciatingly aware of the hard leanness of his body beside hers, the slide of his hip and thigh, their contained strength, and the firmness of the shoulder pressing against hers. Her thighs tingled, her knees trembled and she stumbled. His arm slid about her waist and he kept her upright without any apparent effort at all, which only weakened her knees further. 'Careful,' he said.

'Sorry, klutz,' she managed, her voice emerging more breathlessly than the moment warranted. 'I, uh…I should've waited and taken the section behind.'

He shrugged. 'We were talking.'

And then the door emptied them into the foyer and they moved apart. Addie busied herself straightening her jacket.

'You were saying?' Flynn said.

She had been? Oh, yes. 'I was just going to say how interesting I found the brewing process, and what fun you're going to have getting up to speed on it all.'

He shook his head. 'I'll just hire the best in the business to brew the beer and oversee production.'

As he had with her? Her shoulders went back. Did he think she was one of the best in the cattle-breeding business?

Was she? She'd never thought about it before. Surely not? She—

She bit her lip. She had a lot of experience, though, and—

'What on earth is going through your head?'

She shook herself. 'Crazy thoughts. Artificial insemination.' It had become their shorthand for her daydreaming flights of fancy.

'Well, if you can drag yourself away from such things I think you'll find our intrepid concierge is trying to catch your attention.'

She glanced over to Bruno and waved to let him know she'd be with him in a moment.

'I have an afternoon of email and phone calls—nothing you can help me with,' he added when she opened her mouth. 'A shopping-centre development in Brisbane that I'm investing in.'

Right.

'So you have a free afternoon. Will you be okay?'

Ever since she'd mentioned that sightseeing would be more fun with a companion, he'd been awfully solicitous. Too solicitous She tossed her head. 'Of course.'

'What will you do?'

'Shopping. Just good old-fashioned girly clothes and make-up shopping. I might even get a haircut.' Her fringe was starting to fall in her eyes.

'Do you have plans for this evening?'

'Not yet.'

'Then don't make any. There's something I think you might enjoy.'

She glanced up into the blue of his eyes. She wasn't sure who moved closer to the other, but suddenly they were chest to chest and the air cramped in her lungs. The air shimmered. His hand lifted as if…as if to draw her closer.

His eyes snapped away. He eased back, clasped her shoulder briefly, but even through the layers of her coat, her jacket and her blouse she could feel the strength in his fingers. 'Meet me down here at six.'

She nodded, unable to push out a sound.

He disappeared up the stairs, the breath eased out of her and she sagged.

'Fräulein Addie?'

She snapped upright and moved over to the reception desk. '*Guten Tag*, Bruno.'

'*Vielen dank*. Look!' He held up a pamphlet. 'I think I have found just the place for you and Herr Mather to spend Christmas. Look, here and here.' He opened the pamphlet and pointed.

Her jaw dropped. 'This is perfect, Bruno. I mean, simply perfect!' She took the pamphlet and flicked through it, her smile growing.

'You would like me to book it for you and Herr Mather, yes?'

'Yes, please! Oh, Bruno, you're worth your weight in gold.'

'I will book a car for you too.'

'Gold and rubies,' she declared. She'd have to buy him a Christmas present for this.

'You're most welcome. It was a pleasure. All part of the service. Also, while you were out these arrived for you today.' He handed her a business-size envelope along with a parcel.

They'd be from home! 'Ooh, thank you. *Danke.*'

He beamed at her. '*Bitte.*'

Addie raced up to her room. She recognised Jeannie's handwriting on the parcel, but the envelope had a typed label. She shrugged off her coat, dropped the envelope to the coffee table and tore the parcel open.

Fruitcake! Jeannie had sent her a slab of home-made fruitcake. A great well of longing opened up inside her. How she missed them!

She laughed over the enclosed letters—Jeannie's full of news of the farm and local doings. Frank had enclosed the local paper along with a photograph of a complacent Bruce

Augustus as, quote: 'still the farm mascot'. She kissed the photo. Colin had sent her a drawing of a Christmas tree. She propped it up on her bedside table. She folded her arms and beamed. Her dear, dear friends. 'Merry Christmas,' she whispered, realising that a part of her would be at the farm with them on the day.

She turned to the large envelope and laughed when she pulled out a sheaf of accounts. There wasn't even a note enclosed. Poor Howard. He must think her an awful bully. Or, more like, Jeannie and Frank had bullied him into sending them to her.

Later! She tossed them back to the coffee table. She wasn't wasting a perfectly good afternoon on accounts. Not when she could hit the department stores.

Addie was waiting for him when Flynn strode into the foyer. She leapt up the moment she saw him, a smile lighting her face and anticipation making her eyes sparkle. Something inside him lifted. She looked ludicrously Christmassy in a red wool swing coat, the colour complementing the colour in her cheeks.

He flicked the lapel. 'Let me guess—a bargain-basement buy on your shopping trip today?'

She stuck her nose in the air. 'I'll have you know that there was nothing bargain basement about this particular number.' And then she grinned. 'But I couldn't resist.'

'Good. It suits you.'

Her grin widened and she took his arm, leading him out of the side door rather than the revolving one. But he was no less aware of her now than he had been when they'd stepped into the revolving door earlier. It didn't stop him from hoping she'd keep hold of his arm, though.

Which could be a bad thing.

Or it could be entirely innocent and innocuous.

Yeah, right.

He ignored that.

She stopped when they reached the footpath. 'Right, which way?'

He turned them in the direction of Marienplatz. He glanced down at her. 'Aren't you going to grill me about where we're going?'

She glanced up from beneath thick, dark lashes. Her new haircut somehow emphasised her eyes. His heart slammed against his ribs. He swallowed, but he didn't look away. 'Would it do me any good? Besides—' she shrugged '—I like surprises.'

She probably didn't get too many of those living on the farm. He suddenly questioned the fairness of asking her to stay on as he had. His lips twisted. He hadn't asked. He'd forced her hand. *Ruthless.*

'Also, I like to surprise other people.'

He shot back to the present.

'And so I don't want to spoil your fun either.'

He stopped dead and stared down at her.

She touched a hand to her face. 'What?'

He kicked his legs back into action. 'Nothing. We don't have far to go,' he added to forestall any questions.

He led her across the road and down a side street. 'And here we are.'

She glanced at the building they'd stopped in front of and her mouth formed a perfect O. 'Where are we?'

'Peterskirche—the Church of St Peter.'

'I visited Frauenkirche the other day. It was amazing.'

He made a mental note to visit it as well. He'd seen the twin soaring towers multiple times, had used them on more than one occasion to orient himself, but he'd yet to go inside.

'Peterskirche is the oldest church in Munich.'

'It's beautiful.'

'My guidebook tells me it's in the Rococo style. C'mon.' He urged her forward. 'We're going inside.'

There were lots of people inside already. He found them

a seat about halfway down the nave. 'Are we going to attend a mass?' she whispered.

He pointed to the front. She craned her neck to look and then her face lit up like a little child's. 'A concert?'

'A Christmas concert brought to you today by your friendly Munich Philharmonic.'

She started to bounce. 'A proper orchestra?'

'The best in Munich,' he promised. He had no idea if they were or not, but it seemed a pretty safe bet.

As he'd guessed, the concert proved a hit with Addie. What he hadn't expected was how much her delight would make his chest swell, or how much he would enjoy the atmosphere and the Christmas music for himself. When it was over they just sat there and let the church empty around them.

'Magical,' she finally whispered, turning to him.

'Stunning,' he said, turning more fully towards her. 'I couldn't believe how high those violins soared in the last piece.'

She clasped his arm. 'Or how those cellos could make your chest feel hollow and full at the same time. It was so beautiful I nearly cried.'

He stood, dragging her with him. He didn't mean to. He didn't mean for his arm to slide about her waist either, but she didn't pull away. Her hands rested against his chest. The searing brown of her eyes felt like whiskey in his veins and when that gaze lowered to his mouth he swore he started to smoke and smoulder.

His grip tightened. Her breath hitched and her fingers curled to grasp the lapels of his coat. He wanted to kiss her. He had to kiss her. Kissing her would be like soaring with that extraordinary music.

Hunger and heat filled her eyes. Her lips parted.

He drew the scent of her into his lungs, hunger roaring through his every cell and sinew. His gaze locked onto those lips—so inviting, so promising. He lowered his head until their breaths merged, letting the tension build inside him.

What do you think you're doing?

He froze. Acid burned his stomach.

He dropped his arms from around her, straightened and tried to take a step back, but her fingers still gripped his coat anchoring him to the spot. A breath shuddered out of her and then comprehension dawned in her eyes. She snatched her hands away and tossed her head. 'That's right. I remember—two ex-wives and no canoodling with the hired help.'

She turned, eased out of the pew and headed for the arch of the doors. He set off after her, not reaching her until they were outside. She stood on the steps looking everywhere but at him. A fist tightened in his chest. 'I'm sorry, Addie, that was my fault. I got caught up in the moment.'

She glanced at him and sort of wrinkled her nose. 'Yeah, well, you weren't the only one.' And it made things sort of all right between them again and the fist loosened, though he didn't know how it could, given the intensity of what had just passed between them.

Almost passed between them, he corrected.

He gestured in the direction of the town square. 'You want to go get a bite to eat? Maybe some *glühwein*?'

'Food, yes. *Glühwein*, no. I don't need that kind of heat flowing through my veins at the moment.'

She had a point.

He fell into step beside her. She didn't take his arm. He glowered at the footpath. 'You're more than the hired help, you know?'

'It was just a turn of phrase. I know I'm one of the *most* important cogs in your wheel.'

She'd said it to make him laugh only it didn't. He scowled. She wasn't a cog.

'So tell me about the ex-wives.'

He rolled his shoulders, tightened the belt of his coat and shoved his hands into his pockets. 'Nosy, aren't you?'

'Nosy is better than hot and bothered.'

Ah.

'Besides, you said back at Lorna Lee's that you wanted us to get to know each other.'

Yeah, but he hadn't meant...

He glanced down at her and let the thought trail off as a new thought struck him. 'It seems to me that you know me better than I know you.'

She snorted as they broke onto Marienplatz. 'How do you figure that one?'

'Herr Mueller.'

'Oh.'

The sights, sounds and scents of Christmas surrounded them. He glanced about and shook his head. It was so Christmas-card perfect it was as if Munich were the very place Christmas had been invented.

'I'll make a deal with you, Flynn.'

He snapped back to her.

'You buy me a hot chocolate—' she pointed to a street vendor '—and ask me any question you want and I'll answer it.'

Deal.

'And then you'll tell me about your ex-wives.'

His hands went to his hips. 'You're getting two for the price of one.'

Her smile widened. 'Ooh, is there a juicy story to be had, then?'

Hardly.

'Tell you what.' Her eyes danced and it was almost impossible to resist her. 'You get the hot chocolates and I'll grab some doughnuts.'

'Whatever,' he muttered. 'Anything for some peace.'

They found a vacant bench and sipped their hot chocolates. 'C'mon,' she ordered. 'Fire away. Ask me a question.'

Fine. 'What I'd like to know is why you're so gung-ho to leave Lorna Lee's, when you obviously love the place, to travel the world as a PA when you obviously find the work as dull as ditch water?'

'Whoa.' She lowered her mug to her lap. 'Now that's a two-or three-pronged question.'

'I'm happy to get a two-or three-pronged answer. Don't forget,' he added, 'you'll essentially be getting two stories from me. Two wives, remember?'

She snorted. 'How could I forget? Two for the price of one.'

He wished, but they'd been far more expensive than that.

'Okay, Lorna Lee's is the only place I've ever known, the only place I've ever lived, other than a few months in Dubbo where I attended secretarial college. I want to experience something else, something wildly different.'

He understood that, but, 'It doesn't necessarily follow that different is better.'

'Maybe. Maybe not. I'd like the chance to find that out for myself.'

He got that too, but what if in the future she regretting burning her bridges at Lorna Lee's?

'As for the PA bit? Well, I might've been wrong there. When you wear jeans and work boots every day the lure of those little suits can be hard to resist.'

She could say that again. She looked great in those little suits.

'I've been thinking about it. I think bar or restaurant work might suit me better.'

It'd be a waste of her talents.

'Or maybe even retail. I like working with people and I like being on my feet all day.'

How come, then, did he get the impression she'd choose Bruce Augustus's company over people's most days?

'It's not the how of it. Just the fact that I get out there and see the world.'

'You don't have to stop working at Lorna Lee's to achieve that. Four weeks' annual leave a year, free air travel.'

She offered him the bag of doughnuts. He took one. She did too and bit into it. The sugar glazed her lips. He stared and an ache started up inside him before he could wrench his gaze away.

'When we were growing up my closest friend and I used to dream of all the places we'd visit once we were old enough to leave Mudgee. We ordered travel brochures and made up itineraries. We'd spend hours at it. We…'

She trailed off and some instinct warned him to remain silent, not to push her.

A couple of moments later she shook herself. 'When we were sixteen, though, Robbie got sick—leukaemia.'

His every muscle froze. Robbie was Daisy!

'We still made our plans. We were convinced she could beat it.'

But she hadn't and his heart bled for the woman seated beside him, the woman who still mourned her childhood friend.

'She died when we were eighteen.' She sipped hot chocolate and stared out at the square, at the crowds and the stalls and the decorations, but he knew she didn't see them.

'Addie, I'm sorry.'

'Thank you.' But she said it in that automatic way. She glanced at him. 'Before she died I promised that I'd make our dream come true. And that's what I mean to do.'

A chill chased itself down his spine. Couldn't she see how crazy it was to focus on this childhood dream to the detriment of everything else in her life? Living the life Robbie had dreamt of wouldn't bring her back. And Addie deserved better than to be living someone else's dream.

CHAPTER SEVEN

'ADDIE?'

Addie glanced up to find Flynn scratching a hand through his hair. 'Yes?' she said, instead of now demanding the ex-wife story. She'd asked for it because she'd hoped it'd cool the heat stampeding through her blood. She'd wanted him to kiss her so badly her fingers had ached with it. She still did.

'I understand how heartbreaking it must've been to have lost your friend.'

She snapped away to stare out at the square with all of its Christmas glory, but the lights and festivities had lost their charm. Did he understand? Really? She thought of his face and how it had come alive when he'd described his father and thought that maybe he did.

It didn't change the fact that she didn't want to talk about Robbie. Not to him. Not to anyone. All of them had tried—Mum and Dad, Jeannie and Frank, even Robbie's mum and dad—but some things went too deep. Besides, what was there to say? Robbie was gone. She'd died far too young. End of story. Nothing any of them could do would bring her back. So she didn't answer Flynn now.

'But,' he said.

She stiffened. But? No buts! She glared at him to indicate the conversation was over.

'But,' he repeated, evidently oblivious to her silent signals. 'How old were the pair of you when you made these plans?'

'What's that got to do with anything?'

'Sixteen?'

'We'd been making travel plans since we were twelve.' He just stared at her. She glared and shrugged. 'These particular plans?' The particular itinerary Addie meant to follow? She shrugged. 'Nearly seventeen.' That 'nearly' mattered. Every single day had mattered.

'You were only children.'

'And, again, what's that got to do with anything? We were on the cusp of adulthood.' And talking about that itinerary had fired Robbie with enthusiasm, with the desire to get well, with hope.

'You made a plan to see the world at sixteen, which you turned into a pact at eighteen. The point I want to make is that you can fit that promise into your life the way you see it now rather than how you viewed it then.'

What on earth?

'Like ninety-nine per cent of teenagers the world over, you dreamed of independence and getting away from school, home and all the usual restraints. What could be more attractive and exciting than descending upon Europe? What you're not factoring in, however, is the way your world is now, the way your life has changed.'

'I'm not sure what you're getting at.' Her stomach scrunched up tight. 'And frankly, Flynn, I'm not sure I'm interested.'

His eyes narrowed. 'Just for a moment let's imagine Robbie had lived. You're both nineteen and about to embark on a working holiday around Europe for a year.'

That wasn't hard to imagine. She'd imagined it a thousand times. It didn't stop Flynn's words from tearing something inside her.

'Before you can leave, however, your mum gets sick and you have to stay at home to help look after her and the farm. Would Robbie have held that against you?'

'Of course not!' How could he even think such a thing?

'Right, so, hypothetically speaking, your trip has been delayed for a year, but during that time Robbie has met someone and fallen in love and she wants him to come on your working holiday too. Are you okay with that?'

It wasn't the way they'd envisaged it. She busied herself scrunching closed the bag of doughnuts, not understanding her sudden urge to hit the man beside her.

'And three months into your trip she falls pregnant and suddenly she wants to go home and marry her guy and have the baby and be near her mother.'

She gaped at him.

'Are you going to hold that against her?'

She couldn't answer him. The lump in her throat had grown too big. She couldn't even shake her head. Even blinking hurt. But…

If only that were true! If only Robbie were alive in the world with a man who adored her and a couple of rug rats.

If only.

She closed her eyes and fought for air. Her lungs cramped but she refused to let them get the better of her. She focused on relaxing them rather than fixing on the pain screaming through her, the sense of loss. Eventually she was able to swallow. 'I would do anything for that to be true, but it's impossible, and talking about it like this doesn't help, Flynn. It's cruel, as if you're deliberately taunting me with what should've been.'

His eyes darkened. 'I'm not trying to hurt you. It's the last thing I want to do. I'm trying to show you that you'd have been prepared to alter the plan to accommodate changes in Robbie's circumstances. If she was half the friend to you that you were to her—'

'Don't you doubt that for a second!'

Her hands fisted. He stared at them and nodded, half smiled. 'The pair of you must've been a force to be reckoned with.'

The anger evaporated out of her on a breath. Her shoulders sagged.

'I'm just saying she'd have been prepared to alter the plan to allow for changes in your circumstances too.'

'What changes?' She whirled on him. 'I haven't fallen in love, no ankle biters, and I still have my health. Nothing has changed for me. Nothing!'

'How can you say that? Your parents died and the entire responsibility for Lorna Lee's fell to you.'

'Not for long.'

He reached out to grip her shoulders and it reminded her of that moment back in the church. The moment they'd both best forget.

'I don't know why you're so hell-bent on hiding from it, but you love Lorna Lee's. You love the breeding programme, the land, Bruce Augustus, Blossom and Banjo and all of the people there.'

'That doesn't mean it's my destiny.' Robbie had never had the chance to leave, but Addie wasn't letting her down.

'Travelling the world won't bring her back, Addie.'

She thrust out her chin. 'Perhaps not, but it makes me feel closer to her.'

His grip tightened. 'And when it's done—when you've visited all the places you spoke about—what then? What will you be left with?'

The question shocked the breath out of her. She had no answer for it. It wasn't a question she'd ever considered. 'I'm not sure that matters.'

'I think it matters most of all. I think if Robbie had lived, and as the two of you matured, it's something you'd have considered.'

Why was he so worried about her, concerned for her? And why did his hands hold so much warmth? She glanced at his lips and moistened her own. 'Are you sure you wouldn't reconsider having a brief holiday affair with an employee—just this once, Flynn?'

He let her go as if she'd burned him. 'Lord, you're incorrigible.'

All of this talk about Robbie had reminded her of the mischief they'd got into. Of course, it was far more innocent mischief than what she had planned at this current point in time. Heat stirred through her. She shifted on the bench. 'The thing is, I like you as a person and I really like your body. I'd really like to…'

His face told her he caught her drift. It told her how seriously she tempted him too. She lifted one shoulder. 'I understand you're not looking for a commitment. I'm not looking to be tied down either.'

Those words didn't ring quite true. She frowned before shrugging it off. 'I haven't…you know…in a long time. But there's no one I'd rather break the drought with than you.' She shrugged again. 'I think we could keep it uncomplicated.'

He stared down at her and temptation raced across his face, desire simmered in his eyes. He cupped her face in his hands and her blood thumped. Would he kiss her?

Instead he pulled her in for a hug. 'Uncomplicated? Not a chance. Addie, I've never been more tempted by anything in my life, but…'

But he was going to say no. Her eyes burned. She blinked hard against the warmth of his woollen coat.

'It won't make the pain of missing Robbie go away.'

No, but it'd help her forget for a little while.

She summoned her strength and pushed away from him. 'I take it that's a no, then?'

He hesitated and nodded.

She pushed upright and dropped the bag of doughnuts into his lap. 'I'm going to go back to the hotel now.' She shook her head when he stood and went to take her arm. 'I'd like to be alone for a bit.'

She didn't wait for him to say anything. She just turned and walked away.

* * *

It was still early when Addie returned to the hotel.

She peeled off her clothes and had a shower, but it didn't ease her body's prickle and burn or the ache in her soul.

She drank the complimentary beer and ate the complimentary crisps. The crisps crunched satisfyingly in her mouth, but the beer didn't make her drowsy as she'd hoped it would.

She settled on the bed, piled the pillows at her back and watched television for a while.

Would it be awkward when she saw Flynn tomorrow?

Oddly enough she didn't feel embarrassed or self-conscious about what had taken place between them, or hadn't taken place, more to the point. Men asked for what they wanted all the time. She didn't see why women couldn't do the same. She'd asked a question and he'd said no. End of story.

She had no intention of asking the question again, though. He needn't be concerned on that head.

She blinked and realised she'd lost her place in the television show. She clicked the TV off with a sigh. Her gaze travelled across the room, passed over Jeannie's parcel and then zeroed back. Fruitcake! A taste from home.

She settled on the sofa with a slice, relishing the rich scent of brandy-soaked fruit. Yum! How many times as a youngster had she helped Jeannie make the cake, and the giant pudding that'd be brought out on Christmas Day?

An ache stretched through her. Her eyes burned. She bit into the cake.

After a moment she pulled Howard's accounts towards her. If she wasn't going to sleep, she might as well do something useful.

It took less than a minute to realise these weren't accounting records from Lorna Lee's. She hadn't a clue what they were for. One of Flynn's lackeys from the city must've sent them, but why address them to her rather than him?

Was she expected to do something with them? She checked her email to see if any instructions or explanations were forthcoming. Nothing.

She shrugged. She might as well check through them. If anything were designed to put her to sleep then accounts should do the trick.

She glanced down the list of figures, toted them up and frowned. Hold on…

She totalled the amounts again. They didn't add up. The figures in the total columns were pure invention. Money had gone missing—significant amounts of money. Were these accounts for one of Flynn's current business concerns? She reached for the phone and went to punch in his room number when she caught sight of the clock. It was one o'clock in the morning. She replaced the receiver and slid the accounts back into their envelope, tapping it against her chin.

This could wait till morning. She didn't want Flynn jumping to conclusions about the reason why she might be calling at such an hour. Besides, knowing Flynn, this was probably an issue he already had well in hand. She rolled her eyes. Of course he'd have it in hand! He hired the best, remember? Some lackey somewhere would've already emailed him about this.

With that sorted, she slid into bed and turned out the lights. And stared at the darkness and the clock as the night crawled by.

Addie rang Flynn at eight o'clock on the dot.

'Addie, there're no meetings planned. The day is yours to do with what you will.'

No *Good morning, how are you today?* Just crisp, impersonal instructions. 'Good morning to you too, Flynn. How did you sleep?' some devil prompted her to say.

He didn't answer.

'Me? I slept the sleep of the righteous, which, as it turns out, isn't so good after all.'

A choked sound resonated down the line.

'Look, Flynn, I don't want you to think there's going to be a repeat of last night's proposition. It's over and done with as far as I'm concerned and I'm not the type to flog a dead horse.'

Air whistled down the line. 'I can't believe you just described me as a dead horse.'

To her relief, though, his voice had returned to normal.

'Moving on. Yesterday I received a package containing some accounts. They were addressed to me and I thought they must be from Howard, but they're not from Lorna Lee's. I'm guessing they must be for you.'

'I've been expecting those.'

Good, so he knew what they were about, then. 'Can I drop them over in half an hour?'

'By all means.'

She was careful to dress in as unthreatening a manner as possible—jeans and a loose long-sleeve T-shirt. She didn't want him thinking she had sex or seduction on her mind.

They were *very* firmly off her mind. And if that wasn't entirely true then they were very firmly off the agenda and that was almost the same thing. It resulted in the same outcome. No sex.

She bit back a sigh and went to grab a pot of coffee from the breakfast room.

Flynn opened his door two beats after her knock. He scanned her face. She stared back, refusing to let her gaze waver. 'The coffee smells great,' he eventually said.

'Let me in and we might even have a chance to drink it while it's hot.'

He half grinned and stood aside to let her enter. She immediately moved to fill two of the mugs sitting on the sideboard, but her heart pounded unaccountably hard. Darn it! Why couldn't he be dressed in one of his suits rather than jeans? She handed him a mug, trying to not look at him directly, but, man, he filled out a pair of jeans nicely.

'Addie, about yesterday evening…'

'Do we really need to do this, Flynn?'

He blinked.

'I'm fine with it. If you're not, then that's your concern, not mine. I will apologise, though,' she added, 'if I made you feel uncomfortable.'

'Blunt as usual.' He sipped his coffee. 'Okay, we'll draw a line under last night and—'

'Wait.'

He stilled.

'You still haven't told me about the ex-wives.' She moved to the sofa and sat. 'It was part of our deal, remember?' And she wasn't letting him off the hook.

'You want to talk about my ex-wives now?'

'Sure, why not?' She wanted one hundred per cent proof that he was a man she should stay away from, romantically speaking. He might be one seriously hot dude, but that didn't mean he was the kind of guy she should be fantasising about. The more weapons she had in her armoury, the better, because the longer she surveyed the long-legged, lean-hipped beauty of the man, the greater the yearning that built through her. She wanted it gone.

Flynn couldn't believe that Addie wanted to discuss his ex-wives at all, let alone right at this particular moment. Not with the spectre of last night hanging over them.

Nothing happened last night.

'I mean, you said you had no work on today.'

He'd said *she* didn't have any work on today. It wasn't exactly the same thing.

She kinked an eyebrow. 'And I know you're a man of your word.'

Oh, for heaven's sake! He threw himself down into the armchair opposite. What the hell—it'd do him good to re-live past mistakes. It'd remind him not to make those same mistakes in the future.

And last night he'd been in danger of making a very big mistake. Huge. Even with his gut telling him what a big mistake it'd be, letting Addie walk away had been one of the hardest things he'd ever done.

But he had done it.

And he'd continue to do it.

'I married Jodi when I was nineteen.'

Addie's jaw dropped and all he could think of was kissing her. The deep green of her shirt highlighted the rich darkness of her hair, which in turn contrasted with the amber of her eyes. He dragged his gaze away to stare into his coffee

'That's so young,' she said, evidently trying to get her surprise under control. 'I was way too young—' she tapped a finger to her head '—in here at nineteen to marry.'

'As it turned out so were we. We just hadn't realised it.' He could see now that he'd been searching for the family he'd missed since he was twelve. He'd tried to recreate it with Jodi—the first girl he'd ever become serious about— but it just hadn't taken.

'What happened?'

'We met while I was on the rodeo circuit. She was a city girl doing a stint in the country.' A gap year like that was popular in some circles. 'We mistook lust for love and, believe me, there was a lot of lust, but in the end it burned itself out.'

He glanced across to find Addie had her nose buried in her mug. He shifted on his chair. Perhaps lust wasn't the wisest thing to be talking about with Addie. He cleared his throat. 'It turned out she hated country life. She never took to it. I'd bought the first of my properties but I was still making a lot of money on the rodeo circuit and I wasn't prepared to give those things up yet. We started fighting. A lot. One day she left and that was that.'

'Wow.'

'It lasted all of thirteen months.'

'I'm sorry,' she offered.

He shook his head. 'With the benefit of hindsight I can see now it was inevitable. She's happily remarried with a little girl. We've made our peace with each other.'

'Well, that's something, don't you think? We live and learn. It's the way of things.'

He raised an eyebrow.

She nodded and grimaced. 'Okay, I'll stop with the platitudes.'

'I'd appreciate that.'

She kept her mouth firmly shut. He rolled his shoulders. 'Besides, I didn't learn my lesson as I did marry again.'

'How old were you this time?'

'Twenty-seven.'

She shrugged. 'Twenty-seven is old enough to know your own mind and have a proper understanding of what you're doing. I don't see how that's repeating a mistake.'

He scowled. Matrimony was a mistake, full stop.

'Who was she, then? Rank, name and serial number, please.'

He didn't smile. Nothing about this episode in his life could make him smile. 'Her name was Angela Crawford.'

He stared at Addie. She stared back and then pursed her lips. 'Is that name supposed to mean something to me?'

'Crawford and Co Holdings Pty Ltd?'

'Oh.' She sat up straighter. 'Oh! You mean Crawford Cattle?'

'One and the same. Angela is the daughter of Ronald Crawford.'

'Who's in charge of...like, everything.'

Exactly. The Crawfords owned one of Australia's largest and oldest cattle empires.

'Wow, were the family in favour of the match?'

He nodded. 'I was Ronald's head stockman for a while. I already owned a decent holding of my own, but I wanted more experience. And Crawford paid well.' It had allowed him to expand his operations too. Crawford had bankrolled a couple of Flynn's ventures—projects that had paid off handsomely for the both of them.

'Angela came home from university and I'd never met a woman like her before. She'd been born and bred to country life, but she had polish and sophistication too that...' That he'd lacked and had hungered for.

'I've seen her in the society pages. She's beautiful.'

He couldn't read the expression in Addie's eyes. Somewhere between last night and this morning they'd shut him out.

'Yes, she was beautiful, but it wasn't just that. I was twenty-seven—I'd met a lot of beautiful women. We...'

Addie leaned towards him, her expression intent. 'You?'

'We could converse on the same topics for hours. I mean, I didn't know about art and music or antiques, but we both knew about cattle and horses and business and she laughed easily. She made me laugh easily.' And that had been no mean feat back then. 'She could make a room light up just by entering.'

Addie's shoulders inched up towards her ears. 'You fell hard.'

'Like a ton of bricks. I couldn't find fault with her.' Not that he'd wanted to. 'As far as I could tell we wanted exactly the same things out of life.'

He laughed.

Addie swallowed. 'Why is that funny?'

'Because, at heart, we did want the same things. She just didn't want them with me.'

She straightened. 'Then why did she marry you?'

'Because the guy she really loved was already married.'

She sagged back against the sofa and winced.

'That's not the worst of it,' he said, driving home nails that would remind him for a long time to come that he and matrimony were not a happy mix. 'The man she was in love with owned the farm that bordered mine. The farm we moved to once we were married.'

Addie had drawn her legs under her but now her feet hit the floor. 'No!'

'She married me to be closer to him. She married me so she would have access to him. It took her two years, but she broke up his marriage and ours. And all of that time she played me so beautifully I never had a clue.'

Addie set her mug down as if she had no stomach for coffee. He didn't blame her. He set his mug on the table too.

'What a dreadful thing to do.'

Yep.

'But, Flynn, it wasn't your fault. I mean, you can't blame yourself for trusting her. For heaven's sake, you loved her!'

Which only went to prove what a fool he was. 'I should've seen the signals sooner.'

'What would that have achieved?'

He blinked.

'I mean, it wouldn't have prevented what happened, would it?'

Probably not.

'It wouldn't have stopped you from being hurt.'

No, but maybe he wouldn't have felt like such a fool.

'Mind you, if I was ever betrayed like that I'd be pretty darn bitter.'

The thought of anyone taking advantage of Addie like that made his gut burn.

'You're being wrong-headed about the marriage thing, though.' She leaned towards him and he tried to ignore the enticing shape of her lips. 'The whole "I'm not suited to it" stance is just nonsense. The first was simply a youthful mistake that could've happened to any of us if we didn't have good people around to give us wise advice. And the second...'

She shook her head and shuddered. 'You did nothing

wrong. You have nothing to blame yourself for or to be ashamed about.'

It didn't feel that way. He sat back and folded his arms. 'It didn't stop my heart from being shredded, though, did it?'

'No,' she agreed slowly. 'And I expect I'm not the girl to change your mind on the whole marriage-stance thing anyway.'

For no reason at all his heart started to pound.

'I'm really sorry she did that to you, Flynn, but you know what? Karma'a a hellcat. Angela ought to be shaking in her designer boots when it comes to call.'

He laughed. He couldn't help it.

'You know, if you married one of these beautiful Munich women that'd make the local government authorities look on your tender with a more favourable eye.'

What beautiful Munich women? The only woman he'd seen in Munich that he could recall in any detail was Addie. And marriage? He must've looked seriously appalled by the prospect as Addie burst out laughing. 'At least the desire for revenge hasn't addled your brain completely.'

He tried to scowl. When that didn't work he tried to frown. Then he simply gave up. 'Enough. Where are these accounts?'

'Oh.' She pulled a sheaf of papers from an envelope she'd thrown earlier to the sofa beside her. 'Did you have one of your lackeys send them to me?'

'Nope.'

'Because they're dodgy.' She handed them to him.

What on earth?

She pulled another sheet of paper from the envelope. 'To the best of my knowledge, these are what the figures should say.' She placed the sheet on the coffee table and turned it around so he could read it. 'Which according to my calculations leaves a shortfall of this.'

Whoa. He stared at the amount she indicated. It was just shy of two hundred and twenty thousand dollars.

She glanced into his face and bit her lip. 'I, uh, figured this was something you'd already be on top of, but maybe not.' She cleared her throat. 'If these records are for one of your companies or, what do you call them—going concerns? Then someone is lining their pockets at your expense. They're cooking the books and not all that expertly either, I might add.'

Addie was a hundred per cent on the money.

She glanced at him again. 'Do you know which of your going concerns these figures refer to?'

'No, but...' He leaned over them, his finger running down the list of figures. There was something familiar about them. A niggle teased at the edge of his consciousness, but it slipped out of reach when he tried to seize it.

'Do you have any idea why they were sent to me rather than you?'

He stiffened. 'Can I see the envelope?'

She handed it to him without a word.

He glanced at the postmark. 'This wasn't sent from Australia, Addie. It was sent locally.' He handed it back to her, a grim smile coursing through him. 'From Munich.'

She took the envelope but, rather than study the postmark, she continued to stare at him. 'You've worked it out, haven't you?'

He leant back, his hands clasped behind his head. He let his grin widen. 'I have indeed. The reason these accounts are so familiar and yet unfamiliar is that they're over twenty years old.'

She blinked.

'These accounts are from the business my father and Herr Mueller owned. The man is now toast.'

Her eyes widened.

'This—' he lifted the documents '—is the proof I need to bury George Mueller.'

* * *

Addie gazed at Flynn and it wasn't a trickle of unease that shifted through her but an entire flood. 'Who would send them to me?'

'He'll have cheated more than just my father. He'll have left a trail of victims straggling in his wake. Someone has obviously decided it's time for karma to pay Herr Mueller a call.'

Addie scratched her head and frowned up at the ceiling.

'How did you so quaintly put it—he ought to be shaking in his shoes?'

That had been in relation to his evil witch of an ex. What she'd done had been...

Desperate.

Yes, and despicable. And selfish, callous and harmful. She deserved karma.

And Herr Mueller doesn't?

Of course he did. If what Flynn said was true. It was just... *If!* Flynn was so prejudiced against the other man she had trouble believing in his objectivity. She had trouble believing Herr Mueller was the man Flynn painted him to be.

'We have work to do today after all, Adelaide.'

She snapped to attention, but her heart sank at the triumph alive in Flynn's face, the satisfaction in his eyes.

'We're going to pay Herr Mueller a visit.'

Yippee.

'Can you be ready to leave in forty minutes?'

'Do you need me to prepare anything other than myself?'

'No.'

'Then yes.'

She went to gather up the accounts, but his hand came down on hers. 'Leave those with me, Addie. I'll take care of them.'

With a shrug she removed her hand from beneath his,

hoping he hadn't noticed the way her breath had hitched at the contact. She moved towards the door.

'And, Addie?' She turned. 'Wear that little red number, if you don't mind?'

'Right.'

Man, she hated being a PA. She really, *really* hated it.

CHAPTER EIGHT

THEY CAUGHT A cab to Herr Mueller's brewery. Flynn didn't hesitate when it deposited them on the footpath, but strode straight into Reception as if he knew the place, as if he owned the place.

Of course he knew the layout of the building. She'd seen him poring over the floor plans.

But he didn't own it yet, regardless of how he acted or the expression on his face.

She kept up with him effortlessly. She figured that was a lackey's duty and she at least had the legs for that, although she suspected she didn't have the stomach for what was to come.

Is this how you really want to live your life? Because it didn't matter if she were a PA, a barmaid or a shop assistant, she'd still be a lackey.

She hadn't been a lackey at Lorna Lee's.

You will be now.

She shook the thought off. In a smooth motion she slid past Flynn. *'Guten Tag,'* she said to the woman behind the reception desk. *'Sprechen Sie Englisch?'*

'Yes, ma'am.'

She smiled. Partly in relief, but most because she was determined to keep things polite. Or, at least, as polite as she could. 'My name is Adelaide Ramsey and I'm Mr Flynn Mather's personal assistant.'

A flare of recognition lit the other woman's eyes when Addie mentioned Flynn's name.

'We don't have an appointment, but we're hoping, if it's not too much trouble, for Herr Mueller to see us, briefly,' she added as an afterthought. She'd like to keep this meeting as brief as she could.

The receptionist directed them to nearby chairs and asked them to wait.

Flynn raised an eyebrow at Addie as if to mock her, laugh at her. She simply stared—or rather, glared—back. With something almost like a smile he moved to stare out of the window. So she didn't sit either. She just stood there clasping her briefcase in front of her with both hands and staring down at the green linoleum that covered the floor.

Flynn best not try telling her what to wear at Lorna Lee's or he'd get an earful. *Wear the little red number.* Why hadn't she told him what he could do with the 'little red number' instead?

Because you like the way his eyes gleam and follow you around whenever you wear it.

Oh, she was pathetic!

'Herr Mueller would be delighted to see you now.'

Addie snapped to attention and followed the receptionist and Flynn down the corridor to a large office. *'Danke,'* she said to the other woman before she closed the door behind them.

Herr Mueller sat behind a massive desk, looking as mild and Santa-Claus-like as ever. He gestured them to seats. This time Flynn sat so Addie did too.

'To what do I owe this pleasure?'

She had no doubt whatsoever that Herr Mueller wasn't delighted to see them; that their being here gave him no pleasure at all, but he put on a good front all the same and she wanted to nudge Flynn and tell him this was how things should be done.

Flynn didn't answer him. He merely clicked his fingers at Addie.

Clicked his fingers as if she were a dog!

She gritted her teeth. What on earth had happened to, 'May I have the relevant documentation, Adelaide?' She wouldn't even demand a please or thank you.

Lackey, remember? Impressions of power, remember?

Gritting her teeth harder, she slapped the relevant documentation into his hand. He didn't thank her. He didn't so much as glance at her.

He'd notice her if she got up and tap-danced on the table.

You can't tap-dance. And you have no right to judge him like this either.

She glanced down at her hands. How would she feel if someone had financially ruined her father and made him so desperate he committed suicide? Would she act any differently from Flynn? Twelve years old. Her heart burned. He'd just been a little boy.

Flynn didn't speak. He pulled the accounting records from the file. These were photocopies. The originals were in the room safe back at the hotel. Just as slowly he spread them out on the desk, making sure they faced Herr Mueller.

'These were delivered to my assistant yesterday. As you'll see they're accounting records from the pub you and my father owned in Brisbane back in the nineties.'

Herr Mueller didn't say a word. He didn't blanch. He didn't shift on his chair. His eyes remained fixed on Flynn's face and they weren't cold and hard. She couldn't make out the emotion in them—sympathy, perhaps, or regret?

Her stomach lurched. She had an awful premonition this meeting wasn't going to go as well as Flynn hoped.

It was never going to go well!

Maybe not, but she sensed it was going to go badly in a totally unexpected way…in a way Flynn hadn't planned on. She wanted to urge him to his feet and bundle him out of here.

Ha! As if that'd work.

'These records provide incontrovertible proof that you

were robbing the business and my father blind.' Flynn sat back and smiled a grim, ugly smile. 'This is the proof I need to start criminal proceedings against you, Herr Mueller, which I fully intend to do. I'll ruin you and then I'll see you in jail.'

Herr Mueller still didn't move. Addie's heart hammered against her ribs. She wished this were one of those meetings where she had to struggle to stay awake. Where she made notes about artificial insemination or, better yet, irrigation systems. That'd be perfect.

Herr Mueller steepled his fingers and met Flynn's gaze steadily. 'Your father was an extraordinary man, Flynn. So exuberant and full of life.'

One of Flynn's hands clenched. 'Until you crushed it out of him.'

'I loved your father, Flynn, but I couldn't stop him from self-destructing. If my own father hadn't suddenly fallen ill I'd have stayed to try and help you and your mother, but as it was I had to return to Germany.'

Addie suddenly recognised the emotion in his eyes. Affection. Her mouth dried.

'You ensured you left before charges could be brought against you. Don't try and wrap it up in familial duty.'

'There's an extradition treaty between our two countries, Flynn. If your father had wanted to press charges, he could have.'

'You'd destroyed the records, made it impossible for him to prove what you'd done. For a long time I thought you hadn't done anything technically illegal, just ethically and morally. But regardless of technicalities and legalities, you robbed him of everything he had—convinced him to sign papers he never should have. But these records show proof of evident wrongdoing in black and white. The records obviously weren't destroyed after all.'

'Your father loved you very much, Flynn, and I remember how much you looked up to him. Love, however, does not always make us strong. He would've hated for you to think badly of him.'

Herr Mueller's gaze shifted to Addie. 'It was I who sent you those documents, Fräulein Ramsey.' That gaze moved back to Flynn. 'It wasn't me who was embezzling those funds, Flynn. It was your father.'

Flynn shot to his feet. 'That's a dirty, filthy lie!'

'Son, you have no idea how much I wish it were.'

'You're going to shift the blame to save your own skin? I'm not going to let that happen. We're leaving, Adelaide.'

Addie shot to her feet too, her knees trembling. Herr Mueller gathered up the papers and handed them to her. Her hands trembled as she took them. She briefly met his gaze and an ache stretched through her chest. In them she recognised the same concern and affection for Flynn that coursed through her. *'Auf weidersehen,'* she whispered.

'Good day, Fräulein Ramsey.'

'Now, Adelaide!'

She turned and left.

Flynn didn't speak a single word as they exited the building. She glanced up at him, not liking the glitter in his eyes or the thunder on his brow. Christmas carols spilled onto the street from a nearby store and while it might be the season it seemed utterly incongruous to this moment. She swallowed and shifted her weight. 'Would you like to go for a coffee?'

'No.'

It was too early to suggest a beer. She glanced around. They weren't too far from the English Gardens. Maybe Flynn would like to walk off some steam.

She opened her mouth. 'No,' he snapped before she could get the suggestion out. She closed her mouth and kept it closed this time. He hailed a cab. She climbed in beside him wordlessly. When it deposited them at their hotel she entered the elevator without a sound. She followed him into his room, biting her lip, biting back the questions that pounded through her.

She watched as Flynn's jacket landed on the sofa. His tie followed. He turned, noticed her for what she suspected was the first time since he'd hailed the cab. 'What are you doing here?' he all but snarled.

'Awaiting instructions.'

'Go. Leave.'

She turned to do exactly that and then swung back. 'This situation is not of my making so what right do you think you have to speak to me like that?' She dropped her brief-case and strode up to him. 'And while we're on the sub-ject, don't you *ever* click your fingers at me again. Got it?'

He blinked.

'I know this is stressful for you and, believe me, I'm sympathetic to that, but it doesn't give you the right to treat people like they're insignificant or have no worth. Is this how you regularly treat your employees, Flynn? Because you can't pay me enough to put up with that.'

He stared at her and something in his shoulders un-hitched. He nodded. 'Point taken, Adelaide, you're right. I'm sorry.'

So far so good.

He frowned and spread his hands when she continued to stare at him. 'What?'

'You're supposed to add that it'll never happen again.'

A glimmer of a smile touched his lips and something in her chest pitter-pattered. 'It'll never happen again. I prom-ise.'

She found herself smiling. 'Thank you.'

He shook his head and collapsed into the armchair. 'You're really not lackey material, you know that?'

She bit back a sigh. That was becoming increasingly evident.

He turned his head from where it rested on the back of

the chair. 'I know you'll have trouble believing this, but Mueller's lying.'

She pushed his jacket aside and perched on the edge of the sofa. His pallor and the tired lines fanning out from his eyes caught at her. 'Let's say that's true and that all we have are some doctored accounts.' His gaze speared to hers and she had to swallow. 'How—?'

'How can I prove it was Mueller who doctored them?' He raked both hands back through his hair. 'Yes, therein lies the rub.'

She shook her head. 'That's not what I mean.' He stilled and glanced back at her. 'I mean, how can you be sure Herr Mueller isn't telling the truth?' She held up a hand to prevent him from going into fly-off-the-handle mode. 'I'm not trying to challenge you. I like you, Flynn. You're smart and you work hard.' She admired that. 'Generally you're good-natured and you've offered me a wonderfully attractive bonus to stay on at Lorna Lee's because you want me to be content and settled there. That tells me, as a general rule, that you care about people. I feel as if we've almost become friends.'

'Addie—'

'No, Flynn, let me finish. I feel you need to hear this and there's no one else to say it. Because of all of the things I've just outlined, my loyalty lies with you regardless of what first impressions I may have gained from Herr Mueller.'

He rested his elbows on his knees, his eyes intent on her face. Her heart hammered, but she met his gaze squarely. 'If you are going to ruin this man you need to be very certain of your facts. I mean, how will you feel in five years' time if you find out you were wrong?'

His jaw slackened.

'What actual proof do you have, Flynn? What your father told you when you were twelve years old? Truly, what do any of us know about our parents' greater lives when we're young? We just love them unconditionally and depend on them completely. We're totally biased.'

He leapt out of his chair and paced the length of the room. 'My father was a good man.'

'I believe you. But sometimes good people make bad decisions.'

He didn't say anything. He didn't even turn. She moistened her lips. 'Has there been a shadow of impropriety over any of Herr Mueller's other dealings since that time?'

Flynn waved that off. 'If my father had been embezzling funds why didn't Mueller have him arrested? Answer me that.'

'He said he loved your father.'

His snort told her what he thought about that.

She pressed a hand to her brow and dragged in a breath. 'I have another question.'

'Just the one?' he growled, throwing himself back into the armchair.

'When your ex, Angela, betrayed you like she did—'

'She was never mine.'

'When she did what she did, she hurt you and her family and tore another woman's marriage apart so…'

'So?'

'Did you go after her like this and make sure she paid for what she did?'

He hadn't. She could see the answer in his eyes.

'So if you didn't try to get your revenge on her why is Herr Mueller different?'

His face twisted and he leaned towards her. 'He killed my father.'

'No, Flynn, he didn't. Your father killed himself.' Her heart quailed as she said the words. 'That responsibility rests solely with him.'

He stabbed a finger at her. 'He drove my father to it.'

'Maybe, maybe not.' She twisted her hands together.

'It's a big question, a big accusation. Do you really want to get it wrong?'

'I thought you said you were on my side?' His lips twisted. 'Or do I need to pay you more to earn that kind of loyalty?'

She ignored that. He was simply trying to get a rise out of her. 'You know what I think?'

'I can hardly wait to hear,' he bit out.

'I think your anger and your bitterness towards Herr Mueller has provided you with the spur to succeed, to reach a position of power where you can make him pay. But are you sure it's really him you're angry with?'

He leapt up, hands clenched, his entire body shaking. It took an effort of will not to shrink back against the sofa. 'I will get you the proof you need. My father *wasn't* a thief!'

'I don't need the proof, Flynn. You do.'

The air in the room shimmered, but with what she wasn't sure. 'I think what you went through when you were twelve years old was dreadful, Flynn, horrendous. I want to horse-whip the world for putting you through that.'

The storm in his face died away.

'You need to remember, though, that you're not twelve years old any more. Nobody—and I mean *nobody*—can put you through that again.'

He stared at her as if he didn't know what to say. She swallowed and rose. 'Would you like me to leave now?'

'I think that would be a very good idea.'

She collected her briefcase and left, walked into her room and promptly threw herself across her bed and burst into tears.

Flynn glanced up at the knock on the door. It'd be Addie. For the previous two mornings she'd turned up at nine o'clock on the dot to report for duty. He'd given her both days off to sightsee.

Today wouldn't be any different. 'Come in.'

'Good morning.' She breezed in wearing a chic navy suit and bearing the customary pot of coffee. He wondered if it gave her a kick to dress up in her office clothes. She set the coffee on a trivet on the table in front of him. 'Did you have a good day yesterday?' she asked.

'Yes.' It was a lie. He tensed, waiting for her to quiz him about what he'd been doing or ask him if he'd found any evidence of Mueller's guilt yet.

He hadn't.

He thrust out his chin. He mightn't have known much at twelve, but he knew his father wasn't a thief!

But Addie didn't ask him anything. He shifted on his chair. 'What about you? Get up to anything interesting?'

'Oh, yes. I walked out to the art galleries, which was quite a hike. I spent hours there.' A smile lit her up from the inside out. 'I love holidays.'

He stared at her, transfixed.

'I like art but I don't know very much about it so I'm going to learn.'

She was?

'I ordered some books online. They should be waiting for me when I get home.'

'Good for you.'

'And then—' her eyes widened '—I caught a tram back to Marienplatz.'

He grinned. This woman could find fun in the most ordinary things. 'A day of art and trams, huh?'

Her eyes danced. 'And bratwurst and black forest cake.'

He'd have had more fun venturing forth with her.

You're not here for fun.

'What would you like me to do today? Any letters you'd like me to type and post? Any emails to send or meetings to set up?'

'Nothing's happening at the moment, Addie. Everything is quietening down for the Christmas break. Go out and enjoy the day.' He scowled. While he trawled more newspapers and business reports looking for dirt on Mueller. *All you have to do is ask and she'd help.*

Addie didn't notice his scowl. In fact she seemed totally oblivious to his inner turmoil. She stared beyond him and her eyes widened and her jaw dropped. He turned to see what had captured her attention.

'Snow!' She raced to the window. 'Flynn, it's snowing!' She bounced up onto her toes. 'I've never seen snow before.'

She turned and tore out of the room. 'Addie, wait!' He moved after her. 'It'll be freezing out. Take your coat.' But she was already clattering down the stairs. 'Silly woman. It's only snow,' he muttered.

He trudged back and collected his coat. He let himself into her room and collected her coat and scarf and then stomped down the stairs after her.

She turned when he emerged onto the street and her face was so alive with delight his grumpiness evaporated. He shook his head and tried to hide a grin. 'Jeez, Addie, you wanna freeze?'

He wound her scarf about her throat. For a moment their eyes locked. A familiar ache pulled at his groin. A less familiar one stretched through his chest. Fat flakes fell all around them; one landed on her hair. He brushed it off before he realised what he was about. Addie shook herself and broke the eye contact. With a shake of his head he held her coat out for her. She slipped it on and immediately moved out of his reach.

Neither ache abated.

She turned back to grin at him. 'You're lucky it's only just started snowing. If it'd been going for a while I'd have hit you with a snowball the moment you stepped out of the door.'

He'd welcome a cold slap of reality about now.

She eyed him uncertainly when he didn't say anything. 'I suppose this is old hat for you?'

He hadn't meant to rain on her parade. 'I've seen snow before. In America. Montana.' He injected enthusiasm into his voice. 'But I can quite safely say I've never seen snow while standing by the medieval gate of a European city.'

She grinned back at him and he was glad he'd made the effort. 'It's really something, isn't it?'

Yeah, it was. He nodded and then frowned. Why did he insulate himself so much from enjoying simple pleasures like these? What harm was there in enjoying them?

'You really don't need me today?'

At the shake of his head, she raced back inside.

Flynn remained on the footpath and noticed the way the snow had started to transform everything—frosted it. Munich was a pretty city and the snow only made it prettier.

'Oh!' Addie skidded to a halt beside him. 'Are you sure you don't need me today?'

She now had her handbag slung over her shoulder. 'Your day is your own,' he assured her. She'd go out and see something amazing, enjoy experiences outside her usual world, while he holed up in his room and—

I love holidays.

Addie's earlier words taunted him. When was the last time he'd taken the time for a holiday? His life revolved around work.

Work and revenge.

But seriously, would a day off here and there really kill him? A week off here and there even?

Addie took two steps away. Stopped. Swung back. 'I'm going to sit in a little café on Marienplatz. I'm going to sip coffee and eat pastries while I watch the square turn white.' She moistened her lips. 'Would you like to join me?'

He should say no. He should… 'Yes.'

She walked back to him. 'You're acting very oddly, Flynn.'

'Maybe I've had too much sun.'

'Or maybe you've been working too hard, but may I make a suggestion?'

'By all means.'

'I think you should put on your coat. It's cold.'

He started and realised he still held his coat. He reefed it on.

'A touch of the sun,' she snorted, setting back off. He kicked himself forward to keep pace beside her. 'Brain freeze more like.'

They didn't speak again until they were seated in an upstairs café. Addie had pounced on a window table. 'We'll have the perfect view of the glockenspiel when it ramps up to do its stuff.'

He glanced at his watch. 'That's an hour and a half away.'

She turned from staring out of the window and sent him a grin. 'I don't know about you, but I haven't anything better to do for the next ninety minutes.' She nodded towards the window. 'Look how pretty the square is.'

She was right. He leaned back and his shoulders started to relax. Ninety minutes of sipping coffee and nibbling pastries and watching the world go by? It had a nice ring to it.

They made desultory chit-chat over their first coffee. Addie told him about some of the art she'd seen the previous day and how it had affected her. When she asked him about his trip to Montana he told her about the mountains and the big sky country.

It wasn't until they were on their second cup of coffee—decaffeinated this time, Addie had insisted—when she turned to him abruptly. 'I've been thinking about what you said to me the other night.'

His cup halted halfway to his mouth. Which night? He set it back to its saucer.

'You asked me what I'd have left once I'd completed my mission—my promise to Robbie. After I'd seen it all through.'

His heart ached at the trouble in her eyes. 'Addie, I had no right to ask such a question. I—'

'No, your question came from a good place. I just found it a bit confronting at the time, is all. It felt as if you were suggesting I break faith with Robbie, break my promise. I can see now that's not what you were doing. You were saying that it would be okay for me to modify the plans we made back then to fit them into my life now, if that's what would make me happier. You were saying that Robbie wouldn't mind me doing that, that she'd understand.'

That was exactly what he'd been saying. He'd wanted to ease the pressure she put on herself. He'd wanted to bring her a measure of peace.

She gave a soft half laugh, but the sadness of her smile pierced his chest. 'You were saying I could dream other dreams too and that wouldn't mean I was being unfaithful to the first dream or to Robbie.'

'It's natural to dream, Addie, and there's no reason why you can't have two, five or ten dreams.' Hell, she could have a hundred if she wanted.

'By doing that—and please be honest with me, as honest as I was with you in your room after our meeting with Herr Mueller.'

His heart thumped when she glanced up at him, but he nodded.

'If I dream my other dreams, if I envisage a different life for myself now than I did when I was sixteen, am I not letting Robbie down? Am I not being false to her memory?'

'No.'

She stared at him. 'It seems wrong to dream when she no longer can.'

He dragged a hand down his face and forced a deep breath into his lungs. 'Addie, being true to yourself won't mean you're being false to Robbie's memory. You'll only be letting her down if you see that promise through at the expense of your own happiness. That'd make a mockery of all that you and Robbie shared.'

'Oh!' Her jaw dropped. 'That has an awful ring of truth.'

He leaned towards her. 'Because it is true. If your situations had been reversed, would you want Robbie to make ludicrous sacrifices just to tick off an itinerary that didn't hold the same allure or promise for her any more? Of course you wouldn't.'

Very slowly she nodded, but behind the warm amber of her eyes her mind raced. He sat back and waited for whatever would come next, determined to do what he could to set her mind at rest. This woman didn't have a malicious bone in her body. She shouldn't be tying herself in knots over this. She should be running out into the snow with outstretched arms every day of the week—figuratively speaking. She should be living her life with joy.

'You see?' she finally said. 'Our time here has been a revelation.' She broke off a corner of an apple Danish and popped it into her mouth. 'Please, no offence, but I've discovered I don't like being a PA.'

'None taken.'

She shrugged. 'Apparently loving the clothes doesn't mean loving the job.'

He laughed.

She sighed. 'I have a feeling I wouldn't enjoy being a barmaid or a shop assistant that much either.'

'Like I said, you're not really lackey material.'

'Also, if I were working a nine-to-five job here, I'd be staying in the outer suburbs, as that'd be all I could afford, which would mean a commute into the city. That means that at this time of the year I could be leaving home while it's still dark and then not getting home again until it's dark.'

'That's true.'

'I've been lucky. I've had more free days since we've been here than work days *and* I'm in the heart of things. It occurred to me I'd rather visit all the places on my list as a vacationer rather than as a working girl.'

Mission accomplished. 'And experience its delights to the full without other distractions and responsibilities weighing you down.'

She nodded.

He straightened. 'So what's the problem?'

She ducked her head, but not before he'd glimpsed a sheen of tears. In one fluid motion he moved from sitting opposite to sitting beside her. He took her hand. 'Tell me what's really troubling you, Addie.'

She gripped his hand tightly. 'I write to Robbie. A lot. In my diary. I've written to her every day that we've been here. That probably sounds silly to you.'

'Not at all.'

'It makes me feel closer to her. And…' A sob broke from her.

He slipped an arm around her shoulders and pulled her against his chest. She cried quietly and unobtrusively, but her pain stabbed at him. He found himself swallowing and blinking hard.

Eventually she righted herself, pulled out a tissue and wiped her eyes. He swore at that moment to go out and buy handkerchiefs and to always have one on hand.

She didn't apologise for crying and he was glad.

'I don't want to lose that sense of closeness.' She glanced up at him. 'I'm afraid of forgetting her, Flynn.'

It fell into place then—her single-minded focus. 'Heck, Addie, you're not going to forget her! You'll never forget her. It'd be like trying to forget a piece of yourself. She'll always mean what she meant to you, even as new people come and go in your life.' He cupped her face. 'You don't have to lose that sense of closeness. Sure, write to her about Munich. And about Paris and London and Rome when you visit them too, but you should be telling her about your life—the things that are happening at home and the plans you're making and your dreams.'

And then he let her go before he did something stupid like kiss her.

She blinked. She straightened. 'You know, you could be onto something there.' Then she grimaced. 'Except I can't tell her what my dreams are if I don't know what they are myself.'

He wanted to touch her. He sat on his hands instead. 'So you work out what it is you really want.'

'How?'

That question stumped him. 'Why don't you ask Robbie for her advice?'

She stared at him and then a smile broke across her face. It was like morning breaking over rolling green fields. 'Perfect answer.' She reached across and kissed his cheek. *Danke.*'

'You're welcome.' Though he had a feeling he only thought the words. He couldn't seem to get his lips to work.

CHAPTER NINE

ON CHRISTMAS MORNING Flynn met Addie in the foyer at ten o'clock as she'd instructed. The moment she saw him she beamed at him. When her eyes lit on the brightly coloured gift bag that he carried, which held three even more brightly coloured presents, she rubbed her hands together. 'Ooh.'

'Will I take that for you, sir?' the concierge asked with a grin.

He handed it over. 'Please.'

'I'd also like to take this opportunity to thank you, Herr Mather.' The concierge—Bruno, wasn't it?—nodded towards the reception desk. A bottle of schnapps and an assortment of chocolates stood amid torn Christmas paper.

They'd bought him a Christmas gift? He shook his head. *Addie* had bought him a Christmas gift. 'Merry Christmas, Bruno.'

'Merry Christmas, sir.' And then his gift bag was whisked away.

'Did we buy everyone in the hotel Christmas gifts?'

'Scrooge,' she shot back, which told him they had.

And then she wrapped her arms about him in a hug. It wasn't meant to be sexy. It wasn't that kind of hug. But it sent the blood racing through his veins and his skin prickling with heat, and it was sexy as hell.

She released him. 'Merry Christmas, Flynn.'

Lord, those eyes! They danced with so much excitement her cheeks were pink with it. Beneath the foyer lights her dark hair gleamed. In that moment he swore that regardless of how hokey a Christmas Day she'd planned, he would not rain on her parade. He would pretend to enjoy every moment of it.

Who knew? In her company there mightn't be any need for pretence.

'Merry Christmas, Addie.'

She slid her arm through his and pressed it against her side. 'C'mon, the car's already here. Let the festivities begin!'

He rolled his eyes, but grinned too. 'Where are you taking me?'

She seemed to grin with her whole body. 'You'll see.'

Their driver—Otto—was promptly handed a gift of fruitcake and spiced biscuits and wished a very merry Christmas. Within two minutes of their journey starting, Addie had wormed out of him that he was a retired chauffeur whose family was scattered. Driving on Christmas Day stopped him from getting too lonely. Oh, and he was looking forward to a family reunion next year.

Flynn shook his head. She might not be lackey material but she had a way with people. It wouldn't hurt him to take a trick or two from her book and apply it to his business life.

For the next hour, they drove in what Flynn calculated to be a roughly southerly direction. They passed through the outer suburbs of Munich until they'd left the city behind, advancing through smaller towns and villages. When they came to a town bordering a large lake, Otto stopped so Addie could admire it. She leapt out of the car and then just stood there. 'It's so beautiful,' she breathed.

Flynn stared down at her, evidently trying to memorise the view. 'Yes,' he agreed. Very beautiful.

'The landscape here is so different from home. I...' She flashed him a grin and then opened her mouth in a silent scream of delight. 'I can't believe I'm here!'

He held the door open for her as she slid back into the car, fighting the growing overwhelming urge to kiss her. Kissing her would be a bad thing to do.

Why was that again?

He scratched his head. Um…

Addie thumped his arm and pointed out of the window as the car climbed an incline. 'Look! It's a whole forest of spruce and pine and Christmas trees! It's like something from Grimm's fairy tales.'

She was right. They were surrounded by Christmas trees. He sucked in a breath. They were going to end up in the great hall of some castle, weren't they? There'd be a roast pig with an apple in its mouth and mulled wine. An oompah band would be playing and carollers would be carolling and everything would be picture-postcard perfect. *That* was where she was taking him.

His shoulders started to slump. All of it would highlight how far short his own Christmases had fallen ever since his father had died.

He passed a hand across his face, glanced across at Addie and pushed his shoulders back. He would not ruin this day for her. He'd enter into the spirit of the thing if it killed him.

'Are you ready, Ms Addie?' Otto rounded a curve in the road and as the forest retreated the view opened out. Flynn's jaw dropped. Otto pulled the car over to the verge. Addie's hand on Flynn's arm urged him out of the car. He obeyed.

'Oh, wow!' she murmured, standing shoulder to shoulder with him. 'I don't think we're in The Shire any more, Mr Frodo.'

Flynn smiled at her *Lord of the Rings* reference, but she was right. All around them soared spectacular snow-covered mountains. Dark forests dotted the landscape here and there along with sheer cliff faces. It all glittered and sparkled, fresh and crisp in the cold sunlight. He drew air so clean and fresh into his lungs it almost hurt. 'This is spectacular.'

'The Alps,' she said, somewhat unnecessarily. 'That's where I'm taking you for Christmas, Flynn.'

He thought of the cheesy medieval castle he'd conjured in his mind. It could still eventuate. He glanced down at her. 'Perfect,' he said. And then he blinked. 'What? To the very top?'

She laughed and pushed him back towards the car. 'All will be revealed soon enough.'

Fifteen minutes later they entered a town full of chalets and ski shops. 'Garmische-Partenkirchen,' Addie announced proudly. 'Try saying that five times without stopping.'

He frowned. 'The name's familiar.'

'The winter Olympics have been held here.'

'Of course!'

There wasn't a medieval castle in sight. She took him to a chalet. 'We're going to dine with twenty-four select guests on one of Germany's finest degustation menus.'

His mouth watered.

'I have a feeling there won't be a mince pie or plum pudding in sight.'

He glanced down at her. Wouldn't she miss those things?

'And there'll be a selection of wines from the Rhone Valley.'

Better and better. He took the proffered glass of schnapps from a waiter.

Addie did too and then she leaned in closer. 'We've been living on bratwurst, pork knuckle, sauerkraut and apple strudel. I thought it time we tried something different.'

Really? Did she really prefer this to a medieval castle?

They were led into a long room with an equally long picture window that looked out over those glorious soaring alpine scenes. They were both quiet as they surveyed the panorama.

'What made you choose this?' He turned to her. It was

suddenly important to know why. She hadn't done this just because she'd thought it was what he'd prefer, had she? His hand clenched about his glass of schnapps. He didn't want her to make those kinds of sacrifices for him.

Her brow creased. 'You don't like it?'

'I love it.'

Her brow cleared. 'When I looked into all the options available I initially started with traditional, but…' She stared down into her glass. 'Well, you see, Jeannie sent me some fruitcake from home and I suddenly realised that if I went traditional I'd spend most of the day missing them.'

She glanced up and the expression in her eyes skewered him to the spot.

'I knew I'd spend the day grieving for my father and I figure I'm already missing him enough as it is.'

Question answered. He pulled her in for a light hug. She rested against him for a moment and he relished it. When she pushed away from him he let her go again. He didn't want to, but he did it all the same.

'I don't mean to ignore it, though,' she said. She tipped her glass towards him. 'To absent friends. To my parents and your father and Robbie.'

He tilted his glass. 'To absent friends.'

She straightened. 'Now, I wouldn't advise you to imbibe too freely of the wine as the day doesn't end with the meal.'

He laughed, but he didn't pester her for details. He'd let the day unfold at the pace Addie had planned for it. And he'd enjoy every moment.

The meal was amazing. They sat at a table for six with a French businesswoman, her Austrian ski-instructor husband and a retired British couple from Bristol. Everyone was in greatest good humour. The wine flowed and the conversation flowed even faster. The food was amongst the best Flynn had ever sampled.

By three o'clock he swore he couldn't fit another morsel in. Not one of the petits fours or another sip of dessert wine. He turned down the brandy. So did Addie. 'I'm sure I say this every Christmas,' she groaned, 'but I have never been so full in my entire life and I swear I'm not going to eat for a week.'

They'd moved into the adjoining lounge area—a room of wood panelling, comfy sofas and a roaring fire. A picture window provided the perfect views of snow-covered mountains and ski runs. Some guests had remained talking in the dining room, some had moved in here with him and Addie, while others had adjourned to the rooms they had booked in the chalet.

Flynn collapsed onto a sofa, slumping down into its softness. He could suddenly and vividly imagine spending a week in the Alps with Addie.

He promptly shook himself upright. Crazy thought!

A bell sounded. People rose. He glanced at Addie and she grinned back. 'Are you too full to move?'

He shook his head. He'd actually been contemplating the pros and cons of braving the cold for a walk.

'Excellent. Phase Two begins.'

'Please tell me it doesn't involve food.'

'No food.'

Two small mini-buses were parked at the front of the chalet. He and Addie were directed to one of them. They drove for three minutes before pulling up again. 'We could've walked,' he said as they disembarked.

'Ah, but we may in fact appreciate the ride home later.'

He stared at the building in front of them and then swung to her. 'This is the Olympic centre. Are we getting a tour?' That'd be brilliant!

'In a manner of speaking. We get to test the facilities out.'

What was she talking about?

She laughed and urged him forward. 'We're going ice-skating, Flynn.'

They had a ball. After a mini-lesson, they were left to

their own devices. They fell, a lot, but he still figured that he and Addie picked it up pretty quickly.

'I'm going to be black and blue,' he accused her, offering his hand to help her up after another spill.

'Go on, admit it, you're having fun.'

'I am.' He held her hand a beat longer than he should have. He forced himself to let it go. He gestured around the ice-rink stadium. 'This was an inspired idea, Addie.'

'It's my one gripe with Christmas,' she said. 'There's never enough physical activity, and when I eat that much I need to move.' She glanced at him. 'You're like me in that regard—you like to jog every day, et cetera. So I figured you'd appreciate a bit of exercise too.'

She was spot on.

'Watch this.' She performed a perfect, if somewhat slow, pirouette. 'Ta-da!'

'You're obviously destined to become a star.'

She laughed and moved to the railing for a rest. 'I'm glad you've enjoyed it. I'd hoped you would. You see, the second bus went skiing.'

Skiing!

'And snowboarding.'

Snowboarding!

'And doesn't that sound like a whole trailer-load of fun?'

It did.

'But, of course, the weather conditions couldn't be guaranteed and if visibility had been poor the skiing would've been cancelled. This seemed the safer option.'

'The skating's been fun.' He wouldn't have given this up for anything. Not even to try his hand at snowboarding.

'But this might be the moment to let you know that overnight accommodation and a day on the ski slopes tomorrow is an option open to us. I had Housekeeping back at the hotel pack you an overnight case.'

He stared at her. She had? He moistened his lips. A whole day on the ski slopes.

'I didn't know what your timetable was like.' She shrugged. 'And I didn't want to pressure you, but...'

A grin built inside him. 'No, Addie, that is most definitely an option we should avail ourselves of.'

'Yes?'

'Yes.'

'Woo-hoo!' She jumped as if she meant to punch the air, but her skates shot out from beneath her. He grabbed her, yanking her back towards him and she landed against his chest, gripping his arms tightly when he wobbled too.

It brought her face in close and as their eyes met the laughter died on their lips. An ache swelled in his chest, his groin throbbed and he could barely breathe with the need to taste her.

Her gaze lowered to his lips and an answering hunger stretched through her face when she lifted her gaze back to his.

Once. Just once, he had to taste her.

His hands moved from her waist to her shoulders. Gripping them, he half lifted her as his lips slammed down to hers. Heat, sweetness and softness threatened to overwhelm him. She tasted like wine and cinnamon and her lips opened up at the sweep of his tongue as if she'd been yearning for his touch and had no interest in pretending otherwise.

Heat fireballed in his groin. Desire surged along his veins and his lungs cramped. It was too much. He couldn't breathe. He let her go and took a step back feeling branded...feeling naked.

They stared at each other, both breathing hard, both clutching the railing with one hand for balance. And then she reached forward with her free hand, grabbed the lapels of his jacket and stretched up to slam her lips to his.

It knocked the breath out of him.

She explored every inch of his lips with minute precision, thoroughly and with relish. He wanted to moan, he wanted to grab her and...and make her his!

Her tongue dared his to dance. He answered the dare and took the lead, but she matched him kiss for kiss, her fire and heat rivals for his. They kissed until they had no breath left and then she let him go and stepped back. 'I... I've been wondering what it'd be like, kissing you.'

Sensational! 'Satisfied?'

'Uh huh.' She nodded. 'Oh, yes.'

Kisses like that, though, could open a whole can of worms and—

He jolted back when she touched his face. 'Christmas kisses don't count, Flynn.'

They didn't? Her eyes told him there'd be no more Christmas kisses, though.

Good thing. He bit back a sigh.

'Race you across to the other side.'

She set off. He set off after her. Afterwards he couldn't remember who had won.

They returned to Munich on Boxing Day evening, after a day of skiing and snowboarding. Flynn had even contemplated staying for another night and day. Addie had wanted to jump up and down and shout, 'Yes!'

But then she'd wondered if either of them would have the strength to resist another night of sitting by a log fire, the winter warmth and holiday freedom and the lure of following it through to its natural conclusion.

She figured Flynn must've had the same thought. And the same fear. She knew now, in a way she hadn't on that night when she'd propositioned him, that if they made love now her heart would be in danger and Flynn had made it plain where he stood on the relationship front. She had to respect that.

Even if he was being a great, big, fat, wrong-headed fool about it.

'What are you frowning at?' Flynn demanded as the elevator whooshed them up to the fourth floor.

'Oh…uh, just tired.'

'I don't believe you.'

He was too in tune with her. She scratched her neck. 'I was thinking about Frank and Jeannie.'

'Problem?'

'Not really, but would you mind if they stayed at the farmhouse with me for a while when I get back?'

'Why?'

'They're having trouble finding the right retirement village.'

'What would they do on the farm?'

Do? She frowned at him. 'Nothing.'

'Then why…?'

He let the sentence hang. 'The why is because they're my friends.' She wanted to thump him. 'The benefits are that Jeannie's a great cook and Frank has a wealth of knowledge and experience I could call on if it's needed.'

The elevator door opened and Flynn stepped out. 'You have more experience at breeding techniques than anyone else in the district.'

'And Frank has more when it comes to pasture management, crop rotation and weed and pest control,' she said, keeping step beside him.

'I'd hazard a guess that Howard knows just as much about those subjects.'

'In Queensland Channel country maybe, but not in Mudgee.' She glared at him. 'Why is this an issue? It's not like they wouldn't be paying their own way.'

'It's an issue because I'm not running a retirement village at Lorna Lee's, Addie.'

She dropped her bag by her room door, folded her arms and widened her stance. 'We've talked about karma before, Flynn.'

'Yeah, and I'd better watch out, right?' He started to turn away.

'At Lorna Lee's we look after our own—whether they be human, animal or the land.'

He blew out a breath and turned back. 'How long would they stay?'

What was it to him? It was *her* house. 'A few months.' Maybe more. This should be up to her.

But it's not your house. Not any more. She swallowed.

'Okay, fine, yes. They can stay.' He glared at her. 'Happy?'

It occurred to her then that the answer to that might in fact be, No. She swallowed. 'Thank you.'

He slammed his hands to his hips. 'I was going to suggest that Room Service send up a plate of sandwiches and some hot chocolate, if you wanted to join me.'

An ache stretched through her chest. Did she dare?

'I still have your Christmas present in my case.'

That decided it. 'Give me half an hour to change and freshen up?'

With a nod he turned away.

Addie tripped into her room, a smile spreading through her. Had Flynn bought her something more than a dried plum and almond chimney sweep and a pair of mittens? Over the course of the last two days there hadn't been a suitable time to exchange their gifts. They'd done their best not to spend too much time on their own—especially after that kiss. They might not have actively sought out the company of others, but they'd tried to keep all of their exchanges public.

That kiss had happened in public.

Thanks heavens! Imagine where it would've led if they'd been somewhere private…intimate.

Like Flynn's room.

She shook that thought off. His bedroom in the suite next door was private—the door always firmly shut—but the rest of the suite was like the living room of a house. They'd be fine. As long as she remembered that she wanted to keep her heart intact and Flynn remembered he didn't sleep with his employees.

You don't have to be an employee. You wouldn't be an employee if...

She cut that thought dead and headed for the shower.

The phone rang as she pulled on a clean pair of jeans and a soft cashmere sweater in olive green that she'd bought on her shopping spree. Flynn had complimented her on it the first time she'd worn it. Which probably meant she should take it off.

She left it on and answered the phone.

'Fräulein Ramsey, it's Reception. There's a Herr Mueller to see you.'

What? She swallowed. 'I'll…' Um. 'I'll be right down.'

She led Herr Mueller into a small sitting room off to one side of Reception. She turned, gripping her hands together. 'I don't feel comfortable meeting you like this behind Flynn's back.'

'That does you credit, my dear, and I promise not to take up too much of your time.'

She sat and gestured for him to do the same. 'How can I help you?'

'I am very sorry—heartsick—at what Flynn experienced as a boy.'

That made the both of them.

'I did not know that Reuben, Flynn's father, would become so desperate as to take his own life. I hold myself partly responsible for that.'

Her stomach churned.

'I felt so let down and angry with him, and I let it blind me. I shouldn't have turned away from him so completely. It's not how friendship works.'

Her heart went out to the older man with his sad eyes and drooping shoulders. 'Herr Mueller, I don't believe you should take on that level of responsibility. I don't think anyone should.'

'Perhaps. Perhaps not. I do, however, understand Flynn's bitterness.'

She had no intention of talking about Flynn when he wasn't present.

'I understand it, but I will not let him take away everything for which my family has worked so hard.'

Flynn had made up his mind. She didn't see how Herr Mueller could stop him.

'Flynn is right. Reuben wasn't a thief—it wasn't he who stole the money.'

Her head shot up.

'It was his mistress—a barmaid at the pub called Rosie. Flynn and his mother never knew about her and I was grateful for that.' He sighed heavily. 'I'm afraid she had a cocaine habit that had spiralled out of control. Reuben covered up her misappropriation of funds as much as he could, but…' He shook his head. 'It couldn't go on and I'm afraid that when the money dried up she dumped him for someone younger and richer.'

She pressed a hand to her stomach. 'Why are you telling me this?'

He pulled a packet from his pocket. 'These are letters I found in Rosie's room after she left. They're the letters she and Reuben wrote to each other. There are also photographs. Some of them are quite…'

She winced and nodded.

'I didn't want either Flynn or his mother finding them.'

No.

'But it's obvious Flynn needs to see them now, needs to know the truth.'

She leapt to her feet. 'Oh, but—'

'The only question that remains—' he rose too '—is if this would come better from me or from you?'

Couldn't he see he was putting her in an impossible situation?

But when he held the packet out to her she took it, and then she turned and walked away without another word.

When she reached her room she sat on her bed. What to do? The moment she gave these letters and photographs to Flynn there'd be fireworks.

Big time.

Why couldn't Herr Mueller have just left them alone to have a nice Christmas?

She glanced at the presents she'd selected for Flynn, sitting on the coffee table waiting for her to take them across next door. She straightened. It was Boxing Day—a holiday and practically still Christmas. She wasn't going to let the past ruin today. Flynn hadn't had a proper Christmas in over twenty years.

She flung the packet into her bedside drawer. There'd be enough time for that tomorrow. Today was for presents and fun and relaxation. She collected up the presents and headed next door.

When Flynn opened his door at her knock, she had to reach right down into the depths of herself to find a smile. His lips twitched. 'You look beat.'

She seized hold of the excuse. 'The last time I was this bushed was when I went on muster when I was eighteen.'

'You went on a muster? But Lorna Lee's doesn't…'

'Oh, no.' She set his presents down, curled up into a corner of his sofa and helped herself to one of the tiny sandwiches on a platter sitting on the coffee table. 'It was on a station an hour north-west of us. A paying gig.' She shrugged. 'I wanted the experience.'

He folded himself into the armchair. 'Did you enjoy it?'

'Loved it.'

He stared at her. She shifted slightly. 'Would you be interested in mustering at my station every now and again just for the hell of it?'

Hell, yeah! Except… 'I…'

'Think about it.'

Right.

He rose. 'I ordered a pot of hot chocolate, but I'm going to have a beer.'

'Yes, please.'

After he was seated again a ripple of excitement fizzed through her. 'Present time!'

He laughed. 'You're like a big kid.'

'My father and I had a tradition of three presents. The first was something yummy, the second was something funny and the third was the real present.'

He glanced at the table where she'd lined up his presents, then at her, and his grin widened. He reached down beside his chair. 'One.' He lifted a brightly wrapped gift. 'Two.' A second one appeared. 'And three.'

She clapped her hands and beamed at him. 'My father would've liked you.'

They opened their first gifts—identical dried plum and almond chimney sweeps, of course.

Her second gift was a pair of woollen mittens—red and green with a print of fat white snowflakes sprinkled across them. Flynn grinned. 'They reminded me of the look on your face when you first saw it snowing.'

She clasped them to her chest. 'They're the best!' She'd treasure them.

'I'm almost frightened to open this,' he said when she handed him his second gift.

'I promise it doesn't bite.'

He tore open the wrapping to reveal a pair of lederhosen. He groaned and she laughed. 'I couldn't resist. Now it's your turn to go first.' She handed him his final present.

He tore off the wrapping paper and then just stared. She squirmed on her seat. She'd bought him a silver fountain pen. By chance when she'd been out walking one day she'd ambled into a quirky little shop that had specialised in all sorts of pens, including fountain pens. 'Do you like it?'

He pulled it free from his case. 'Addie, it's perfect. I'm not sure I've ever owned an object quite so beautiful.'

'I figure that given all the big contracts you sign that you ought to have a pen worthy of them.' She waved a finger at him. 'Now you have to promise to use it. You're not to put it away in some drawer to keep for good.'

He grinned. 'I promise. Now, here.' He handed her the final present.

She tried to open the paper delicately but in the end impatience overcame her and she simply tore it. Her jaw dropped. 'Oh!'

He leaned towards her. 'Do you like it?'

'No.' She shook her head. 'I *love* it!' He'd bought her a cuckoo clock—a marvellous and wonderful cuckoo clock. The local souvenir shops stocked them and they constantly fascinated her. Now she had one of her very own. 'Thank you!' She looked up. 'It's the best present ever.'

He grinned and he suddenly looked younger than she'd ever seen him. 'I wanted to give you a piece of Munich you'd be able to take home with you.'

Home…

She ran a finger across the little wooden frame of the cuckoo bird's house. 'You invited me along with you to Munich so I'd learn to really appreciate the things I have at home, didn't you?'

He shrugged and settled back in his chair. 'I hoped it would do that at the same time as ease your wanderlust.'

'It worked.'

'I'm glad.'

What he didn't know was that it had worked a little too well. She opened her mouth. She shook herself and shut it again. Tomorrow. There'd be time enough for all of that tomorrow.

She leaned forward and clinked her beer to his. 'Merry Christmas, Flynn. This has been a marvellous Christmas. Much better than expected. I'll never forget it.'

'I'll agree with each and every one of those statements. Merry Christmas, Addie.'

Addie drank in his smile and her heart twisted in her chest. It might, in fact, be the very last smile he ever gave her.

CHAPTER TEN

THE PULSE IN Addie's throat pounded when Flynn answered her knock on his door the next morning. She had to fight the urge to throw her arms around him and beg him not to hate her.

His gaze travelled down the length of her and his smile widened. 'I like your suits, Addie. I like them a lot, but I want you to know it's not necessary for you to don them every morning before you head on over here. I'll let you know in advance if we have a meeting.'

The pulse in her throat pounded harder. *Oh! Don't look at me like that.* As if he liked what he saw, as if she were a nice person. He wouldn't think her nice in a moment.

She gulped and moved into the suite on unsteady knees, setting the coffee pot onto the dining table as usual. She decided then that she hated her suits. She might burn them when she got home.

He frowned as if picking up on her mood. 'Is everything okay?'

She wiped her hands down her skirt and turned to face him. 'Not really.'

In two strides he was in front of her. 'Is everyone at Lorna Lee's okay? Jeannie and Frank? Bruce Augustus?'

His questions and the sincerity of his concern made her heart burn all the harder, made her love him all the more.

She straightened and blinked. Love? She swallowed. She didn't love him. She *liked* him a lot, but love?

He touched her arm. 'Addie?'

She moved out of his reach. 'It's nothing like that. As far as I know, everyone at home is fighting fit.'

She glanced at him. Had she fallen in love with Flynn? If so, did that change the things she needed to tell him?

She thought hard for a moment before shaking her head. She had to remember he didn't want her love—had warned her on that head more than once. Telling him she loved him would be his worst nightmare. She had no intention of making this interview harder for him than it'd already be.

She pushed her shoulders back. 'There are two things I need to tell you and you're not going to like either one of them. In fact, you're going to hate them.'

He stared at her. His brow lowered over his eyes and he folded his arms. 'Are you scared of me? Is that what this is about? You're scared I'm going to rant and rave and—'

'No.' She wheeled away to collect mugs, slammed them to the table. 'I mean, you'll probably rant and rave, but that doesn't scare me. It's just…'

He raised an eyebrow.

She bit back a sigh. 'It's just that you don't deserve it and I hate being the messenger.'

She pulled out a chair and fell into it. Flynn sat too, much more slowly and far more deliberately. 'You've been in contact with George Mueller.'

'He's been in contact with me,' she corrected, stung by the suspicion that laced his words.

'When?'

'Yesterday evening. I received a call from Reception that he was down there and wanted to see me.'

His face darkened. He leaned away from her, but his gaze didn't leave her face. 'Was that before or after our little supper?'

She swallowed. 'Before.' Her voice came out small.

The lines around his mouth turned white. 'And what right

did you think you had to withhold that piece of information from me?'

His voice emerged low and cold. She sensed the betrayal beneath his words and she wanted to drop her head to the table. 'I never had any intention of withholding the information from you. I just decided to delay it.'

'You had no right.'

'You don't even know what Herr Mueller spoke to me about yet.' She moistened her lips. 'Last night I hadn't worked out what I was going to do, so I made a judgment call. You obviously think it a bad one, but it's done now. In future it's probably a good idea to choose your PAs with more care, because I feel as if I'm in way over my head here, Flynn.'

He leapt out of his chair and wheeled away. 'You know how important closing this deal is to me. I can't believe you'd deliberately hold back something important and jeopardise negotiations.'

She stood, shaking. 'You don't even know yet what it was that Herr Mueller and I discussed, but you immediately leap to the worst possible conclusions. Can't you see how your obsession with this has clouded your judgment?'

He spun back. 'Clouded?' he spat.

'Yes!' she hollered at him. 'You've made it clear on more than one occasion how important this vendetta is to you.' So important he'd rather chase after it than live his life, enjoy his life.

He took his seat again. 'Sit,' he ordered, his voice containing not an ounce of compromise.

She sat.

'And now you will tell me everything.'

Her stomach churned. Her mouth went dry. She had to clear her throat before she could speak. 'Herr Mueller told me you were right—that your father didn't steal the money.'

A grim smile lit his lips. One hand clenched. 'I'm going to crush him like a bug.'

She closed her eyes. 'There is no easy way for me to tell you what he said next.' She opened them again. 'He said the thief was a barmaid called Rosie. He said that Rosie was your father's mistress.'

Flynn shot out of his chair so quickly it crashed to the floor. It barely made a sound against the thick carpet. He stabbed a finger at Addie. 'That is a dirty, filthy lie.'

Addie folded her arms. For the first time he noted her pallor and the dark circles beneath her eyes. 'Was your father really such a paragon of perfection?' she whispered.

'He wasn't a thief and he wasn't a cheat!'

'Even if he had been both of those things, it doesn't mean he wasn't a good father.'

What on earth was she talking about?

She stared at him, her amber eyes alternately flashing and clouding. 'You love him so much that I think he must've been a wonderful father, but you did say what a difficult woman your mother always was. Would it really be such a stretch to believe that he found comfort elsewhere?'

It went against everything Flynn believed in.

'This is the version of events Herr Mueller relayed to me. I don't know if they're lies or not. I'm just telling you what he said.'

He righted his chair and sat, nodded once in a way that he hoped hid the ache that stretched through his chest. She glanced at the coffee pot and he leaned forward and poured her a mug.

She curled her hands around it. 'Thank you.'

This situation wasn't of her making. He knew how much she hated it. She'd never pretended otherwise. But she'd no right to hold this back from him. 'Go on.' His voice came out harder and curter than he'd meant it to. When, really, all he wanted to do was reach out and take her hand and tell her how sorry he was that he'd dragged her into his sordid game. She must be wishing herself a million miles away. He dragged a hand down his face.

'He said Rosie had a cocaine problem. She stole money from the pub—lots of it—and when he realised your father tried to cover it up. Of course, the money dried up at that point and Rosie apparently dumped him for someone younger and richer.' She pulled in a breath. 'Herr Mueller said he felt betrayed by your father and turned his back on him. He says he regrets that now and wishes he'd done things differently.'

This was all a fantasy, a fiction. 'And you believed him?'

Addie met his gaze. 'I don't think it matters what I believe. It's what you believe that's important.'

Had she and George been in this together from the start? Had George promised her that she could see the world if she came and worked for him?

She reached down into her briefcase and pulled out a package. 'He gave these to me. He says they're letters your father and Rosie wrote to each other. And photographs. I haven't looked at them. They're none of my business.' She set them on the table. 'I can't help feeling they're none of yours either.'

His head snapped up. She grimaced and shrugged. 'Mind you, you're talking to the woman who wouldn't read the letters her parents left behind when they...' She trailed off with another shrug.

Flynn seized the package and waved it at her. 'Letters can be forged. Photographs can be doctored.'

She swallowed. 'True.' But he could see that in this instance she didn't believe they had been.

'What else did he say?'

She nodded at the package. 'He said he took those so you and your mother wouldn't find them, wouldn't find out about Rosie. And...' she pulled in a breath '...he wanted to know if I thought this news would come better from him or from me.'

'So you made another judgment call?'

She glanced down at her hands. 'I'm sorry if I made the wrong one.'

Was she?

She straightened. Her pallor tugged at him. 'Flynn, you have your father on a pedestal—an impossibly high one. I'm not even sure if you're aware of that. Why? Is it because the last time you truly felt safe was when your father was alive? I understand about honouring the dead, but—'

'Oh, yes, you know all about that, don't you?' He wheeled on her, wanting—needing—her to stop. 'Honouring the dead, putting them on pedestals! Look at what you've done to Robbie.'

She stood too. 'Yes, I did put her on a pedestal. I didn't know how else to deal with my grief, but you showed me how doing so had narrowed my view. You helped me realise I was in danger of making a big mistake. I'm working on it, trying to put it into some kind of perspective and make it better. And you have to learn to do the same.' She lifted her arms. 'Is this really what your father would want from you?'

His scalp crawled. 'Don't you presume to tell me what my father would want from me. You didn't know him and you don't know George Mueller!'

Her eyes flashed and she strode forward to poke him in the chest. 'What happens to us when we're young can leave scars—big, ugly, jagged ones. But I'm here to tell you that you're a grown man now—a grown man with the backing of a powerful financial empire you've built yourself. Nobody and nothing can take your achievements away from you. It's time to recognise that fact. It's time you stopped chasing demons and trying to slay imaginary dragons. It's time you started acting like a man!'

All he could do was stare at her.

'If your father was the paragon of perfection that you claim, then so be it. But paragons don't kill themselves,

Flynn. In which case he wasn't perfect. In which case deal with it and move on.'

He wanted to smash something. He wanted to run away. He wanted—

He strode away from her towards the window, dragging both hands back through his hair. The street below had become alive with cars and people.

If Herr Mueller wasn't guilty...

He shook that thought off. Of course he was guilty! This was just his latest attempt to save his neck. He opened the window to let in a blast of icy air, but it did nothing to clear the confusion rolling through him.

He might be a grown man, but the terror and confusion when he'd learned of his father's death still felt as raw and real to him now as it had when he'd been twelve years old. He gripped the window frame so hard the wood bit into his hand. He'd tried to bury that scared little boy when he'd made his first million. It hadn't worked. He didn't doubt for a moment, though, that taking George Mueller down would quieten the demons that plagued him.

'The ball is now in your court,' Addie said. 'What happens now is up to you.'

He knew that if it were up to her she'd have him walk away. Well, it wasn't up to her. He slammed the window shut and spun around, cloaking the war raging inside him behind an icy wall. 'You said you had two things to tell me. What's the second thing?'

Her gaze slid away. 'You know what?' She seized her briefcase. 'I think you should consider what Herr Mueller had to say and we can discuss the other issue tomorrow. I—'

'Don't presume to tell me what I should do.'

She dropped her briefcase back to the floor, pushed her shoulders back and met his gaze squarely. 'You're no more a lackey than I am, so maybe you'll understand what I'm about to say...and do.'

Something inside him froze. He didn't know why but he wanted to beg her to stop. He wanted it to start snowing and for her face to light up as she dashed out into it. 'What do you mean to do?' he said instead. He'd have winced at the sheer hard brilliance of his voice, but he couldn't. It was as if an invisible barrier stood between him and the rest of the world.

She twisted her hands together. 'I'm not going to sell you Lorna Lee's, Flynn. I'm going to take advantage of the cooling-off period stated in our contract and renege on our deal.'

Her words knocked the breath out of him. It took all of his strength not to stagger. The dream of a home of his own, a place where he could belong and be himself, slipped out of reach, evaporated into a poof of nothingness.

They'd just spent two amazing days in the Alps and all that time she'd been planning to pull out of their deal?

'You were right. I'm not lackey material.' Her hands continued to twist. 'The more I consider having to take orders from anyone in relation to Lorna Lee's, the more everything inside me rebels. It's my home.' She slapped a hand to her chest. 'I want to be the one who shapes it, to determine which direction it should take…and to decide who can and can't live there.'

Apparently she didn't want *him* living there.

He folded his arms, something inside him hardening. 'You're doing this because you don't approve of my business dealings with Mueller. If you think this will turn me back from that course of action, you're sadly mistaken.'

'To hell with Herr Mueller,' she shot back rudely. 'And to hell with you too, Flynn. I'm doing this for me!' Her hands clenched. 'Did you really not see this coming? As far as I can tell you've been one step ahead of me when it comes to my true feelings.' She moved in closer to peer up into his face. 'I want to be the one to call the shots. I don't want to be told to get rid of a beloved bull or that I can't have Frank and Jeannie live with me. I don't want to be your lackey, Flynn, and I don't want to be Robbie's either. I just…I just want to be my own person.'

'Pretty speech,' he taunted, 'but what about your neighbours? They need this sale.'

'The bank will lend me the money to buy them out.'

He could feel his face twist. 'You've checked already?'

'Oh, for heaven's sake, are you really that intent on seeing conspiracies all around you? I checked with the bank before you ever made on offer on the place in case it became the only option.'

'I could fight you on this.'

'What?' It was her turn to taunt. 'Are you going to turn me into your next vendetta? Are you going to do everything in your power to destroy me?'

Of course not, but…

'The funny thing is it's you who's responsible for my change of heart. You dared me to discover what it was I really wanted. And Lorna Lee's is what I really want.' She threw her arms up and wheeled away. 'Yes, I also want to travel and see the world, but I want a home base. I want to live in the world where I grew up, where Robbie grew up and where all of my friends are. I want to work at something I'm good at and I want to canter over green fields at the end of a day's honest work and to know I'm where I should be.' She bit her lip and glanced up at him. 'Maybe that's the way you feel about your property in Channel country.'

He didn't feel that way about anywhere. He'd thought he might find it at Lorna Lee's but… He cut off that thought. He had no intention of sharing it with her.

'There'll be no cash injection for expansion.'

Something in her eyes told him he'd disappointed her. 'I'm well aware of that. Expansion is something I can work towards.'

So that was that, then, was it?

She swiped her hands down the front of her skirt. 'I

want to thank you, Flynn. I suspect it's no comfort, but you've helped me—'

'Spare me!'

She flinched.

'I should've known you were trouble the moment I heard you bawling to that darn bull.'

Her intake of breath told him he'd hit the mark. Finally. She brushed a hand across her eyes. 'You heard that?'

He kinked an eyebrow because a ball of stone had lodged in his chest, making it impossible to speak.

Her eyes shimmered. She swallowed hard. 'You offered me Munich because you felt sorry for me?' She stared at him as if she'd never seen him before. 'I don't get you at all.'

He forced a harsh laugh. 'But you did, didn't you? You've taken me for a complete ride. You weaselled a free trip to Munich out of me, sabotaged my business dealings while we were here and then reneged on a contract I'd signed in good faith. You must be laughing up your sleeve.'

She paled. 'That's not true.'

He shrugged and turned away as if he didn't care, as if none of it mattered to him. 'I think it'd be best all round if you just caught the first available flight back to Australia, don't you?'

'I know you're angry with me at the moment and disappointed about Lorna Lee's, but we're friends! I'm sorry, truly sorry, that things have turned out this way. If there's anything I can do to make amends...I mean, I'm still your PA for as long as you need me to and—'

'Don't bother. I'll hire someone competent.'

That was hardly fair, but he didn't care. He wanted Addie and all of her false promises gone. He didn't need reminding how bad his judgment was when it came to women. 'Like I said, it's time you were out of my hair.'

Silence and then, 'If that's what you want.'

He kept his back to her even though something in her

voice chafed at him. 'That's exactly what I want.' His heart
bellowed a protest, but he ignored it.

The click of the door told him that she was gone.

For good.

He limped over to the armchair and sank into it, closing his eyes and trying to shut his mind to the pain that
flooded him.

Addie stumbled back into her room. She glanced from
side to side, turned on the spot and then kicked herself
forward to perch on the sofa. She clutched a cushion to
her stomach.

Oh, that hadn't gone well.

It was never going to go well.

Perhaps not, but she hadn't realised it would leave her
feeling so depleted. So guilty. So hurt.

She dropped to her knees on the floor and pressed
her face into the soft leather of the sofa. There had to be
something she could do to make things right between
them. It was such poor form to back out of the Lorna
Lee sale. He'd made his offer fair and square, he'd gone
to the expense of bringing a foreman in, he'd brought her
to Munich, but...

Lorna Lee's was her home. It was where she belonged.
Surely Flynn could understand that. Surely—

Everything inside her froze. She uncurled herself from
the floor to stand. He didn't, though, did he? She moved
to the window, but the view outside didn't register. Flynn
bought things—he owned them, developed them and once
he'd done that he sold them off at a profit—but he had no
roots. There wasn't a single place he called home. Lorna
Lee's wouldn't have been any different—just another in a
long line of enterprises. Flynn shunned those kind of roots
while she, she'd discovered, craved them.

'So, why so heartbroken?' she whispered into the silence.

Because none of it stops you from loving him.

For a moment she was too tired even for tears. She just stood there and stared out at a grey sky.

Flynn sat in his room. He sat and did nothing. He tried to feel nothing. Addie's news had shattered something inside him.

Not her revelation of Herr Mueller's spurious allegations. He hadn't expected any less from the other man. That had angered him, true, but it occurred to him now that much of his anger was directed at himself—for creating a situation where Addie had been forced to play go-between, that he'd involved her in dealings that turned her stomach.

Revenge might be satisfying, but it wasn't noble. He should've kept her well away from it. He glanced at the packet of letters and photographs. *Not your business.* He seized them, stalked into the bedroom and threw them into the bottom of his suitcase, threw the suitcase to the top of the wardrobe and stalked back into the living area. He threw himself back into his chair.

It wasn't Mueller's machinations that maddened him— he'd been expecting those. It was Addie's news that she wasn't going to sell him Lorna Lee's.

He leapt up and paced from one side of the room to the other. He flung out an arm. Contract-wise she was well within her rights to pull out. Besides, it wasn't as if he wouldn't be able to purchase another cattle property just like Lorna Lee's. So why did he feel so betrayed?

Because he'd thought them friends?

He dragged a hand down his face. This was business. It wasn't personal. It had nothing to do with friendship. She hadn't pulled out with the intention of hurting him.

He bent to rest his hands on his knees and dragged in a breath. He could buy another farm, but he wouldn't have Addie working for him. It wouldn't be a place that eased his soul when he entered its gates. It wouldn't feel like home.

He stumbled back to his chair.

Addie pulling out of their deal had shattered a dream he'd hardly realised had been growing within him. He would now never get the chance to work with her—to experience and observe her expertise, to witness her excitement when he gave her the opportunity to expand her programme. He would never get the chance to laugh with her, discuss moral issues, travel with her and...and experience the world through her eyes. A more attractive world than the one in which he lived.

That's your choice.

He shot upright. What the hell? He'd started to do what he'd sworn he'd never do again—become involved with a woman. His hands clenched. In walking away, Addie had done them both a favour. His realisation at the near miss had him resting his hands on the back of a chair and breathing deeply. He wasn't giving another woman the opportunity to stomp all over his heart. Not even Addie.

He didn't doubt she'd do her best to treat his heart with care and kindness, but eventually he'd make some mistake, do something wrong, and she'd turn away.

He swallowed, fighting the vice-like pain gripping his chest. When he could move again he pulled on a tracksuit and running shoes and headed outside. He ran by the Isar, drawing the scent of the river and winter into his lungs. His world might never become as congenial and gratifying as Addie's, but he wouldn't forget to appreciate the little things again.

Your world will never be like hers for as long as you continue with your vendetta.

He shook that thought off. Herr Mueller deserved everything that was coming to him.

He ran and ran until he was sick of sliding on the ice-slicked paths, and then he walked. He walked for miles and miles. He walked until he was exhausted and then he turned and headed back to the hotel—miles away.

Flynn had just passed beneath the Isartor in all of its

medieval grandness when Addie emerged from the hotel doors with Bruno at her side carrying her bags. The concierge had obviously chosen to wait on Addie himself rather than leave it to a porter. They moved towards a waiting taxi. Flynn's heart started to pound. He stepped back beneath the tor, into the shadows where Addie wouldn't see him.

You could stop this.

All he'd have to do was call out...ask her to stay. Would she?

He recalled the way she'd looked at him earlier, the way her voice had trembled, and knew she would. He closed his eyes and rested his head back against aged stone. Addie might be willing to risk her heart, but he wasn't.

He remained in the shadows until the taxi had driven away. He leant against the wall and pretended to study the structure like the other sightseers until he had the strength to push forward. He didn't want to go back to the hotel, but...

There was nowhere else to go.

Bruno greeted him as he entered. 'Good afternoon, Herr Mather.' He didn't smile.

Was it afternoon already?

'Miss Addie got away safely for her flight home.'

He swallowed. 'Excellent.'

'She asked me to give you this.'

He handed Flynn the carved bull—Bruce Augustus—and a letter.

Dammit! He'd given her that bull as a gift.

At the last moment he remembered his manners—it was almost as if Addie had dug him in the ribs. 'Thank you, Bruno.'

He moved towards the elevator. He should wait until he was in his room, but... He tore the letter open.

Dear Flynn,
You gave me this as a promise, but as I broke mine to you I don't feel I have the right to keep it.

He clenched his hand so hard the carving dug into it.

*I'm sorry I disappointed you and let you down.
My life is better for knowing you, but I understand
that you can't say the same.*

A lump weighed in his chest. His eyes burned.

*I don't want you to think I took advantage of you
on purpose. Please send me the bill for my share of
the trip to Munich. Don't worry. I do have the funds
to cover it.*

Not a chance!

*From the bottom of my heart—thank you. For ev-
erything. If you ever find yourself in the neighbourhood drop in for a cuppa. You can always be assured
of a warm welcome at Lorna Lee's.*

He wanted to accept that invitation. Everything inside
him clamoured for him to.

Love, Addie.

He folded the letter. He wanted it too badly. It was why
he had to resist.

'Flynn, I'm glad I caught you.'

He stiffened. George Mueller.

A fist tightened about his chest and did all it could to
squeeze the air from his body. 'Herr Mueller, I'm afraid
I'm not in the mood at the moment.' He turned. 'And don't
bother pestering Adelaide again. She's no longer here.' He
pushed the button for the elevator.

George scanned his face and something inside him
seemed to sag. 'You sent her away.'

He didn't reply to that.

The older man shook his head. 'You still refuse to see the truth.'

'The one truth I do know is that whatever happened between my father and you, you turned away from him. You turned away from my mother and you turned away from me. You call that friendship? I don't think so. If nothing else, that defines you, indicates the kind of man you are.'

The elevator door slid open. Flynn stepped inside and pushed the button for the fourth floor.

Mueller reached out a hand to stop it closing. 'It is the greatest regret of my life, Flynn. I'm sorry. I should've tried harder, but when I contacted your mother she wanted nothing to do with me. I thought...'

Mueller had contacted his mother?

'I understand it's easier to hate me. Maybe I do deserve all of this, but I can't believe you sent that lovely girl away when anyone could see how much she cared for you.'

If Addie did care for him, she'd get over it. It was better this way.

Mueller straightened and met Flynn's gaze squarely. 'You can take away my business and my livelihood, you can ruin me financially, but you can never take from me my family. You will never be able to turn my loved ones against me because they love me as strongly as I love them. And for all your money and your power, Flynn, I can't help thinking that still makes me the richer man.'

Nausea churned in the pit of his stomach.

'Where is that love and connection in your life, I ask myself? You're so intent on the past that you have no future. Regardless of what you do, I would not trade places with you.'

Mueller shook his head, real disgust reflected in his eyes. 'You sent her away. You're a fool. Careful, Flynn, or you'll find yourself in danger of becoming the cruel, heartless man you think I am.'

And then he moved and the elevator door slid closed.

* * *

On the flight home, Addie fired up her laptop and opened her 'Till the Cows Come Home' diary.

> *Dear Daisy*
> *What I wouldn't give to see you right now. I need a smile and a shoulder.*

In her mind's eye she conjured that exact smile and the precise dimensions of Robbie's shoulders. How had she thought she'd ever forget?

> *I've fallen in love. I've fallen in love with a man who thinks I don't possess a faithful bone in my body—a man who thinks I used him.*

And then it all came tumbling out—the whole rush of falling in love with Flynn, of trying to resist him, of how his reasons for being in Munich had filled her with misgiving. She told Daisy how kind and thoughtful he was, how his zeal could capture hold of him and fire him to life and how that had always stolen her breath. She relayed how he dreamed impossible dreams and made them come true.

> *Daisy, I've fallen in love with a man I'm never going to see again and I don't know what to do.*

What would she like to have happen?

> *I'd like for him to turn up next week at Lorna Lee's and tell me he loves me too; that he's prepared to risk his heart one more time because he trusts me. That's what I want, but I know it's impossible.*

She moistened her lips. She'd never had a chance to tell Flynn how she felt about him. There'd be no point in trying to contact him now. He'd refuse to take her calls, would delete her emails. He would never seek out her company or speak to her again. She didn't hold any hope that he'd ever return her feelings. He'd warned her. He'd told her he didn't do relationships.

She closed the lid of her laptop. She should've listened.

CHAPTER ELEVEN

TWO DAYS LATER Flynn snapped his laptop closed. It was pointless. There wasn't a scrap of dirt or scandal to be found on George Mueller. How could that be?

He glanced at the contract. Finally... *finally* it was his. All it required was his signature and George Mueller would be a ruined man.

He strode to the window. Correction—Mueller would be financially ruined. He wouldn't fall into the same pit of despair Flynn's father had. He wouldn't kill himself.

He snapped away, heart pounding. He didn't want the other man to kill himself! He dragged a hand down his face. He just wanted justice.

Addie's face rose up in his mind and raised an eyebrow.

He swung back to the window. Today the sky in Munich was blue and he could see the frosty air on the breath of the passers-by below.

Are you sure he's guilty?

He glanced at his watch, drummed his fingers on the window ledge before straightening and stalking over to the telephone. He punched in a number.

'Hello, Mum, it's Flynn,' he said when she answered.

'What do you want?'

Hello, son, lovely to hear from you. He bit back his sarcasm, but dispensed with pleasantries. 'I want to know if George Mueller ever contacted you after Dad died.'

A pause followed.

'And I want the truth.'

'Things are really tight around here at the moment…'

He glared at the ceiling. 'How much do you want?'

She named a sum.

'I'll have it wired into your account by the close of business today.'

She didn't even thank him.

'George Mueller?' he prompted.

'He paid for your father's funeral.'

Flynn sat, swallowed. 'Why?'

'It was the least he could do! We'd been happy before him and your father became partners in that cursed pub. Why do you want to know about him after all this time?'

Her strident tone scratched through him. 'Because our paths have crossed again. I'm in Munich and…' He trailed off.

There was another pause and then a harsh laugh. 'You're there to take over his company, aren't you?'

Yes.

'Do it!' she ordered. 'Let him see what it feels like to lose what he's worked so hard for. Let him see what it's like when the shoe is on the other foot.'

Bile burned the back of his throat. 'I have to go.'

'The money…you won't forget?'

'No,' he ground out. 'I won't forget.'

He slammed down the phone. Her bitterness and her antipathy made his stomach churn and his temples pound. He had an insane urge to shower, to wash the dirt off, but he'd only showered a few short hours ago. *Let him see what it feels like to lose what he's worked so hard for.* His hands clenched. She'd never worked hard a day in her life! Unless you counted her incessant nagging of his father.

He rested his head in his hands before lifting it with a harsh laugh. 'The apple doesn't fall far from the tree, does it?' Was this the man he'd truly become? He'd been so busy putting his father on a pedestal that he hadn't realised that all of this time he'd been turning into his mother.

He suddenly wished Addie were here to tell him he was wrong and that he was nothing like his mother.

He swallowed the bile that rose in his throat. Addie was where she belonged. And he... He finally had Mueller exactly where he wanted him. So why was he hesitating?

Flynn took a leaf from Addie's book and went sightseeing. He strode up to the Residenz and lost himself in art and architecture. He absorbed himself in accounts of history utterly foreign to him. Four hours later he found himself in the coffee shop above Marienplatz where he and Addie had once shared coffee.

He ordered coffee and apple strudel. He stared at the town halls—old and new—and wondered what on earth he was doing there. Sitting here without Addie cracked something open in his chest, something he wasn't sure he'd ever be able to shut again. He threw money onto the table and strode back out having barely touched his refreshments.

He stalked the streets, round and round, coming to an abrupt halt when he almost collided with a statue of three stone oxen. They lorded it over a fountain that tripped down levels like a gentle waterfall.

Oxen...cattle...Bruce Augustus...Addie.

He collapsed on a nearby bench to stare at the statue, recalling the way Addie had cried against the giant bull's shoulder. He'd bet it was the first thing she'd done when she'd returned to Lorna Lee's—headed straight down to the bull's pen.

He rested his head in his hands. And she'd have cried. His abrupt dismissal would've made her cry. For a moment he wished he had a Bruce Augustus too.

For heaven's sake. He lifted his head. He didn't want coffee and cake. He didn't want Bruce Augustus. He wanted Addie. What was the point in hiding from it?

Yeah, well, you can't have her.

His mouth filled with acid and his future with darkness. Who said? Maybe he—

You said.

He pulled in a breath and nodded. He'd said. And it was for the best. It'd be for the best all round if he just stopped thinking about her.

Ha! As if that were possible.

Do what you came here to do and then go home and put it all behind you.

He slumped back against the bench, staring at the oxen. Why was he hesitating?

Because once it was done it would put him out of Addie's reach forever.

He shot to his feet. She was out of reach already!

Flynn strode back to the hotel. He made sure to enquire after Bruno's mother's health—the older woman was ailing—and sped straight up to his room. He strode over to the contract, pulled the pen Addie had given him from its case and scrawled his signature along the bottom.

Done.

His stomach churned. The blood in his veins turned alternately hot and cold. If he'd been expecting peace he'd have been seriously disappointed.

If he went through with this, there would never be a chance for him and Addie. He dragged a hand down his face. If he didn't go through with it there were no guarantees that there'd ever be a chance for him and Addie either.

If he went through with this it'd prove he was exactly like his mother.

His mouth dried. His heart pounded. What would his father choose in the same situation?

Love. The answer came to him from some secret place filled with truth. His father would've chosen love. His father would've chosen Addie.

He fell into a seat, frozen. He'd sent Addie away. She hadn't wanted to go. A lump stretched his throat in a painful ache. He blinked against the burning in his eyes.

If only he dared, could she be his?

Did he dare?

The blood pounded so hard in his ears it deafened him. He stood, but he didn't know what to do so he sat again. *Think!* Make no mistake, Addie would want it all—marriage, kids, commitment. Did he dare risk it? Could he make a marriage with Addie work?

If it went wrong he wasn't sure he'd have the strength to dust himself off again.

He stared across the room and the longer he stared, the darker it seemed to get. A choice lay before him that would affect the rest of his life. It would define the very man he'd become.

He could choose his mother's way—bitterness and revenge.

Or he could choose Addie and love; but with no guarantees.

He strode over to the contract, seized it in his hands. He'd spent a lifetime working towards this. Addie would never have to know if...

But you'd know.

'Relax, Bruce Augustus.' Addie petted the giant bull's shoulder as she settled on the fence. 'I haven't come down here to cry all over you.'

She'd been home for ten whole days and she'd spent more of that time bawling all over her poor old pal than she had in deciding Lorna Lee's future. The secret crying had helped her keep up a semi-cheerful façade for everyone else, but it hadn't made the ache in her heart go away.

She forced herself to smile. Wasn't that supposed to make you feel better? She grimaced. If so, it was a lie.

No, no. She forced another smile. 'Today we have good

news, Bruce Augustus. Today the bank agreed to lend me the money to buy out Frank and Jeannie and the Seymours.'

Jeannie and Frank were going to pay her a nominal rent on their house. She'd told them they could stay for as long as they wanted. Without the worry of having to work the land they'd developed a new lease of life. Addie was glad. She'd rent out the Seymour house too and it'd give her enough money to hire an additional hand. She'd had interest from several local farmers who wanted to agist their stock here if she were amenable. It'd all help pay the mortgage.

She turned to gaze out at the land that rolled away in front of her. Dams twinkled silver in the sunlight, grass rustled and bent in the breeze and the enormous and ancient gums stood as brooding and eternal as ever. She pressed a hand to her chest when she realised how closely she'd come to giving it all away.

'My home,' she whispered. She belonged here. It was where she wanted to be. But that didn't make the ache in her heart go away either.

She turned back to Bruce Augustus. 'I know you're sick of me talking about Flynn, but I worked something out. It's like emotionally I've been through a flood or a drought or a bushfire. Anyway—' she shook her head '—it doesn't matter what it is specifically, just that it's some kind of natural disaster. And it takes time to rebuild after something like that.'

Bruce Augustus remained silent.

'I know, I know.' She sighed. 'I have no idea how long it'll take either.'

She kicked the ground, picked a splinter of wood from the railing. She heard a car purr up the driveway. 'Sounds like we have company.' She peeked around the side of the pen when the car pulled to a halt outside the homestead. 'A black Mercedes Benz,' she told her bull, moving back into the privacy provided by the pen. 'There were lots of those in Munich. Funny thing I've noticed recently, but in the movies and on cop shows the villains always seem to drive a black Mercedes.'

She glanced back to see who would emerge from the car and then slammed back, flattening herself against the railing. Her heart hammered. Flynn! 'What's he doing here?' Had he come with his big guns to enforce the contract they'd signed?

She forced air into cramped lungs. 'Don't you worry, Bruce Augustus. I got legal advice about that.' He'd have a fight on his hands if he tried anything.

She pushed her shoulders back and moved towards the house, and slammed right into Flynn as he rounded the corner. 'Oh!'

He reached out to steady her. 'I thought I'd find you down here.'

She wanted to hurl herself into his arms. She forced herself to step back. His arms dropped back to his sides. She made herself smile brightly. 'So, you were in the area and decided to pop in for a cuppa?'

Gently he shook his head. 'No.' And her heart sank.

'I see.'

He frowned. 'You do?'

She pushed her chin up. 'Flynn, you ought to know that I did get legal advice. I was well within my rights to pull out of the sale when I did.'

His frown deepened.

'You can drag me through the courts if you want to and it may take years to settle, but no court in the country will rule against me and in the end you'll be forced to pay all of the court costs and I won't be any the worse off. I know you're angry with me, but do you really think that's the best use of your time and money?'

He turned grey. 'Of course that's what you'd think of me.'

Her heart burned. She ached to pull his head down to her shoulder.

'I haven't come here to try and take your home from you, Addie.'

The breeze ruffled his hair. She stared at it, wanting— 'Addie?'

She started. 'You haven't?'

He shook his head.

Okay, that was good to know, but... 'How was Herr Mueller when you left Munich?'

'I don't know.' He wore a business suit and she wanted to tear it off him and force him into jeans and a T-shirt. 'I didn't see him, but I expect he's relieved. I burned the contract and left Munich.'

She gripped a post to stop from falling over. 'You did what?' It didn't make sense. 'You...you read the letters, saw the photos and...'

'No, I burned those too. Bruno and I had quite the blaze. He sends his best, by the way.'

She rubbed her forehead. 'What does Bruno have to do with it?'

'There weren't fireplaces in our rooms, see, but he let me light one in the guest lounge.'

She pressed a hand to her forehead and breathed in deeply. 'Let me get this straight. You burned the contract?'

'Yes.'

She straightened. 'You found out some other way that Herr Mueller wasn't a cheat and a thief?'

He shook his head, but his eyes burned into hers. 'I'm never going to know the truth of what happened back then. I very much doubt, though, that George Mueller is the monster I made him out to be. The thing is, you were right about those letters. They weren't any of my business. They were written by two people who'd have been mortified to discover I'd ever read them. And once I understood that I realised the whole affair between Mueller and my father was none of my business either.'

She stared at him. 'Wow.'

'You were right on another head. Slaying that dragon wouldn't bring my father back. It wouldn't right wrongs and it wouldn't turn back time. It'd just start a whole new cycle of hate. I chose to turn my back and walk away.'

She couldn't get out a second wow. Her lungs had cramped too much.

As if he found it hard to meet her gaze, he turned to the bull. 'Hey, Bruce Augustus, how're you doing?'

The bull eyeballed him. Addie took his arm and edged him away. 'Old Bruce Augustus here can take a while to warm to strangers.'

She led them to a large boulder beneath an enormous spreading gum, and then gestured to his suit. 'You might get dirty. Would you like to go up to the house for a cold drink or...?'

His answer was to settle on the rock. After a moment's hesitation she settled down beside him.

'I wanted to come by and tell you that I harbour no hard feelings about you pulling out of the sale.'

She stared from her feet and up into the cool blue of his eyes. 'You mean that?'

'This is your home, Addie. You belong here. I'm glad you realised that. The cooling-off clause in a contract is there for a reason.'

A weight lifted from her. 'Thank you.'

'I also wanted to return this.' He pulled the carved bull from his pocket. 'I gave this to you last time to seal a verbal contract. I'm giving it to you this time as a token of gratitude.'

She took the miniature Bruce Augustus with a smile. 'I missed this. But, Flynn, I don't see what I could have possibly done to inspire gratitude.' That belonged solely to her, surely?

His eyes dimmed. 'You pulled me back from the brink. You stopped me from making a mistake and doing a very bad thing.'

He glanced at her with such a look in his eyes her heart started to hammer.

'You once warned me about karma. I don't want it to come calling on me to kick my butt.'

That made her grin. She forced her gaze away. In the sky, miles away, a wedge-tail eagle circled on lazy drifts of warm air. She kept her gaze trained on it rather than the man beside her. She'd spent the last ten days crying over him and she was glad he'd taken the time to tell her all he had, but she needed him to go now. It was too hard seeing him and not being able to...

'Could we go for a gallop?'

She closed her eyes. 'Why?'

'Because I want to see that look of absolute contentment and relish on your face again. I missed it when you left Munich.'

'When you sent me away,' she corrected, turning to finally meet the gaze that burned through her.

'Guilty as charged.'

What did he want? 'I appreciate you taking time out of your busy schedule, Flynn, but you could've sent the carving through the mail. You could've explained everything else in an email. Why are you here?'

'I wanted to see you.'

'Why?'

She swallowed when she recognised the flare of hunger that crossed his face. Wow! She folded her arms to keep from reaching for him. 'I'm no longer an employee. That means...'

He folded his arms too and raised an eyebrow. 'What does it mean?'

Her heart sank. 'That I now tick your box as temporary girlfriend material.'

'There's nothing temporary about you, Addie.'

She let out a breath. 'I'm glad you realise that.' She knew

in her bones that if she had an affair with Flynn her heart would never fully recover.

'Which is why I was going to ask you to marry me.'

She leapt off the rock as if scalded. 'I beg your pardon?'

His expression didn't change. 'You heard. You might have trouble taking orders, but there's nothing wrong with your hearing.'

'I…' *Say yes, you fool!* She thrust out her jaw. 'Why would I take a risk on someone with such a poor matrimonial record?'

One side of his mouth hooked up. 'Because you love me, perhaps?'

Her heart thumped. How did he know that? Was she so transparent?

'And because I love you.'

She stared at him. Her knees trembled. 'Why would you go and change your mind so completely about matrimony?'

He didn't answer. She glared. 'You must really want Lorna Lee's.'

He turned so grey and haggard she almost threw her arms around him. 'When you left Munich, Addie…when I so stupidly sent you away, your absence left such a hole inside me that I couldn't fill it up.'

She swallowed. She had to plant her feet to stop from swaying towards him.

'All I wanted was you, but I didn't believe I could have you. And then I spoke to my mother.'

What did his mother have to do with it? 'Your mother?' she prompted when he didn't continue.

He shook himself. 'She's so bitter. When she found out I was in Munich she ordered me to destroy Mueller.'

She tried to swallow the bad taste that rose in her mouth.

'That's when I realised I'd become just like her.'

Oh, no, he wasn't, he—

'And I don't want to be like her, Addie. I want to be like

my father.' He swallowed, vulnerability stretching through his eyes. 'I want to be like you.'

He did?

'To be worthy of you, I knew I'd have to give up my vendetta and initially that was a struggle.' The lines framing his eyes and bracketing his mouth deepened for a moment. 'In the end, though, I wanted to choose the future instead of the past. I wanted to be a man who built a life he could be proud of. And, Addie…' his gaze speared hers '…I want that life with you. I love you.'

Golden light pierced her from the inside out. She tossed her head, her smile growing. 'Why haven't you kissed me yet?'

He closed the gap between them in an instant and pulled her into his arms. 'Because I'm afraid that once I start I won't be able to stop,' he growled.

'I wouldn't mind,' she whispered against his lips the moment before they claimed hers.

Her head rocked back from the force of the kiss, but his hand moved to her nape to steady her. 'Sorry.' He lifted his head. 'I—'

She dragged his head back down to hers and kissed him back with the same ferocity. Her arms wrapped around him. His arms wrapped around her and they kissed and kissed. His kisses told her of his struggles and how much he'd missed her, of his frustration, fear and shame, of his loneliness. She poured all the love she had in her soul into her kisses to fill him instead with happiness and pride, joy and satisfaction.

Finally he lifted his head, dragging a breath into his lungs. She did too, leaning against him with her whole weight, relishing the strength in his powerful frame. 'I love you, Addie.' The words came out raw and ragged. 'Everything I have is yours. Please put me out of my misery. Your kisses say you'll marry me, but…' His eyes blazed down into hers. 'I need to hear it.'

'You've come home, Flynn,' she promised. 'I love you. You're mine and I'm yours. Yes, I'll marry you.'

She watched as the shadows faded from his eyes. 'Home?' he said.

Arm in arm they turned to survey the rolling fields. 'Home,' she repeated, 'because everything I have is yours too, Flynn, and I mean you to have the very best of it.'

'The very best of it is here in my arms.'

'Right answer.' She stretched up on tiptoe to kiss him. His arms snaked about her waist. 'Would you like to go for that gallop now or would you prefer to come up to the house for that, uh…cuppa?'

He grinned. 'The cuppa.'

Taking his hand, she led him back towards the homestead. She led him into the future he'd chosen. She took him home.

* * * * *

LET'S TALK
Romance

For exclusive extracts, competitions
and special offers, find us online:

f facebook.com/millsandboon

⊙ @millsandboonuk

🐦 @millsandboon

Or get in touch on 0844 844 1351*

For all the latest titles coming soon, visit
millsandboon.co.uk/nextmonth